Emmanuelle II

Emmanuelle II

EMMANUELLE ARSAN

Translated by

Anselm Hollo

Grove Press
New York

Published simultaneously in Canada
Printed in the United States of America

ISBN: 978-0-8021-2236-0
eBook ISBN: 978-0-8021-9270-7

Grove Press
an imprint of Grove/Atlantic, Inc
154 West 14th Street
New York, NY 10011

Distributed by Publishers Group West

www.groveatlantic.com

To Ph. and D.B.

The world is real only after I have rearranged it.
Alain Bosquet,
The Second Testament

Contents

Emmanuelle II

1

It Is the Love of Loving
That Makes You
the World's Betrothed

We who must, perhaps, die one day, shall declare
man immortal on the very threshold of that instant.
—Saint-John Perse, *Amers*

"Anna Maria Serguine."

In sounding the *i* in the young woman's first name, Mario had held it, for the longest time, on a high, isolate note, thus giving the remainder of the syllables an air of abrupt and tender confidentiality.

She remained seated behind the steering wheel of her car. Mario took her hand and presented the long, ringless fingers to Emmanuelle, holding them on his own palm.

"Anna Maria," says the echo within Emmanuelle, as she tries to recapture the caressing thrill of the sound that had followed upon the Florentine roll of the *r*. Fragments of plainchant come to her mind, and with them, the scents of

1

incense and melting wax. *Panis angelicus.* Young girls' knees under the decent cover of skirts. Delicious daydreams. *O res mirabilis!* And throats, prolonging the *i*-sounds, tongues, moistening them with their saliva, lips, opening, offering up their teeth. . . . *O salutaris hostia.* . . . With the light shining through a stained-glass window, from the other end of the world, Emmanuelle gilds this unfamiliar face, reproaching herself for her inability to transcend a schoolgirl's vocabulary in her response to its beauty:

"She's marvelous!" Emmanuelle whispers to herself. "And of a purity so sure of herself, so jubilant, so happy." It is almost breaking her heart. Such grace can only be a dream!

"It's up to you to make it real," says Mario, and she asks herself whether she hasn't, after all, been thinking out loud.

Anna Maria laughed, a peal of amusement so unembarrassed that Emmanuelle regained her composure. She decided to take the visitor's hand into her own.

"But not right now," Anna Maria said with a smile. "I mustn't be late for this ladies' tea party I'm going to."

Then she turned toward Mario, looking him over as if he had grown since she had last seen him. Her car was a very low-slung affair.

"I'm sure you'll find some good soul to take you back?"

"*Via, cara, via!*"

The wheels spun in the gravel, skidded off. No windshield, no mudguards, no top! Emmanuelle thought, anxiously looking up at the dark sky. Instantly unhappy, she watched the dream fading into the distance.

"And I had thought I knew the most beautiful creatures on this earth! Where did you ever find that archangel?"

"Oh, she's related to my family," Mario said. "Sometimes I have her drive me around."

Then, sounding curious:

"You find her interesting?"

Emmanuelle looked inscrutable.

"She'll be back tomorrow," he said.

After a moment's silence, he went on:

"I have to tell you this: you would have to get her more than just a little excited. But I'm sure that you'll be able to make her listen to reason."

"Me?" protested Emmanuelle. "But how do you think I could do such a thing? I'm just a beginner."

A twinge of spite entered her feelings. Was it perhaps that he, as far as he was concerned, regarded their affair as finished, after one single lesson?

They had walked across Emmanuelle's garden and terrace, and were now standing in the living room, in front of the large mobile sculpture constructed out of black metal. Mario breathed on its leaves and made them turn.

Emmanuelle said:

"But I'm sure you must have taken care of her education, yourself. What would I be able to add to that?"

"It isn't Anna Maria we're talking about. It's you."

He stopped to wait for a reply from her, but she only rearranged her features in an expression meant to look skeptical. So he went on, explaining:

"You see, the act that makes you new, is the one that you have to accomplish. There is no form that is *yours* to such a degree as the one that turns you into another being. But perhaps you are satisfied with what you are?"

Emmanuelle shook her great black mane.

"No, I'm not," she said, resolutely.

"Well, then. Do it." Mario sounded weary.

Nevertheless, he went on:

"As a woman, your love for yourself quite certainly is a fitting preoccupation. But you are a goddess, as well: therefore the well-being of others has to be an equal concern of yours."

She smiled, remembering the boardwalk, the temple, the night. He looked at her, with a questioning mien:

"And have you started enlightening your husband?"

She shook her head, looking half defiant, half ashamed.

"But wasn't he surprised by how long you were gone?"

"He was."

"What did you tell him?"

"I told him that you had taken me to an opium den."

"And he didn't give you a lecture?"

"He made love to me."

She read the question in her father confessor's eyes.

"Yes," she said, "I was thinking about it, all the time."

4

"And you liked it that way?"

Emmanuelle's face was eloquent: in her mind, she was reliving the tremendous new thrill she had experienced when her husband's semen had spurted forth to mingle with the *sam-lo*'s.

"You'd like to do it again, right now," Mario observed.

"But I told you, I believe in your law."

And it was true. At this moment, she found herself unable even to remember what could have raised any doubts in her mind. In order to convince Mario, she repeated the maxim that he had caused her to formulate, the day before:

"All time spent in other pursuits but that of making love, embraced by an ever-increasing number of arms, is time lost."

Then she wanted to know:

"And what does Anna Maria believe she ought to spend her time on?"

"On the preparation for other times; on self-mortification in this world, in order to achieve endless ecstasy in the other."

Emmanuelle's voice sounded impartial:

"Well, that means that there are other values in her life, besides those of eroticism. She, too, has her gods and her laws."

Mario looked at her quizzically:

'What I'm waiting to see," he said, "is whether the dream of heaven is going to lead a daughter of man to damnation, or if the love of the real is going to win a soul, here on earth."

Emmanuelle puts her hand on his arm.

"But I'm such a miserable hostess. I haven't even offered you a drink, not even a cigarette."

She wants to guide him over to the bar, but he holds her back.

"I hope, to say the very least, that you're not wearing anything under those shorts?" he asks, looking roguish.

"Look again."

The shorts are so minimal that they're hardly visible beneath the coral-red sweater. Emmanuelle's black, curly pubic hair is peeking out both sides of the crotch.

Mario looks, but has still further comment to make:

"I don't like this kind of clothing. A skirt may be raised: it is a gate permitting entry. Those shorts are like a wall. I'll get bored with your legs, as long as I see them emerging from that little bag."

"I'll take them off," Emmanuelle says, good-humoredly. "But first you have to tell me what you would like to drink?"

He has another bee in his bonnet:

"Why stay in here? I like the trees in your garden."

"But it's going to rain!"

"It isn't raining yet."

He takes Emmanuelle where he wants to go: out to the wide ledge of flat rocks bordering the terrace. A lightning-bolt turns the spaces between the motionless, flamboyant flowers a vivid hue of green.

"Oh, Mario, look at that beautiful boy walking by in the street!"

"Yes, he's handsome all right."

"Why don't you call him over here and make love to him?"

"There is a time for everything under heaven, saith the Preacher: a time to run after the boys, and a time to let them run."

"I'm positive he never said anything like it. Listen, Mario, I'm thirsty!"

He crosses his arms, in a display of patience. She knows what he is waiting for. She shrugs, looking obstinate, and examines her naked thighs: naked up to the groin, where the edge of her shorts draws a red line across the skin. To expose oneself beyond that line is incompatible with dignity.

"Well, then?"

"Please, Mario, not out here! They can see us from the house across the street. Look!"

She points at a pair of curtains moving in one of the windows.

"You know these Siamese. There's always someone skulking around."

"But that's perfect!" Mario exclaims. "Didn't you tell me that you like people admiring your body?"

Emmanuelle's shamefaced look makes him smile. Then he gets going, once again.

"Remember: nothing that's discreet can be erotic. The erotic heroine is not unlike the chosen of God: she is the one who brings about strife and scandal. A masterpiece always scandalizes the world. What nakedness is it that hides itself in order to be naked? Your lechery makes little sense, if you draw the curtains of your bedroom on it: it won't liberate your neighbor from his ignorance, his shame, his fear. The important thing is not that you get naked, but that you are *seen* naked; not that you cry out with pleasure, but that you can be heard; not that you count your lovers, but that *he* can count them; not that your own eyes have been opened to the truth of loving love, but that that other one, who is still groping about amongst his own chimeras, and in his own night, may discover, by seeing you, that there *is* no other light, and see your gestures testify to the fact that *there is no other beauty.*"

His voice assumes a more urgent tone:

"Every relapse into false shame will demoralize a multitude. Each time you start worrying about causing a scandal, think of those who secretly yearn for you to show them the way. Do not betray them. Don't make light of the hope they put in you, whether they know it or not! If out of timidity or doubt you should ever—yes, even just once—prevent the accomplishment of an erotic act, no future audacity or merit would ever make up for such backsliding."

He pauses to draw breath, and then, with an almost imperceptible note of disdain in his voice:

"Or is it propriety you're thinking about? Is it that you only want to do as others do—or that you want all others to act like you? Is it Emmanuelle you want to be . . . or just anybody?"

"But surely I can respect the beliefs of my neighbors," she defends herself. "That doesn't mean that I share them, does it?

And if they do not like my kinds of pleasure, why should I enjoy shocking them, or creating a scandal? It's no skin off my back to let them conduct their lives according to their own lights. Is it possible to live at all, without a little discretion, tolerance, politeness? What is wrong with letting those people persuade themselves that I really do think and act like them—society is made out of such conventions, compromises."

"If one behaves like the people across the street, one *is* the people across the street. Instead of changing the world, one merely becomes the reflection of what one would like to destroy."

Emmanuelle looks impressed. Mario hastens to add:

"Well, that's not by me, that's Jean Genet."

He continues in a gentler vein:

"As another playwright puts it: in the matter of love, too much isn't even enough. If you already have done well, it is necessary to do even better. You must constantly surpass yourself, as well as all others. You can not afford to have anyone match your achievement, much less allow him to transcend it. It is not enough to be exemplary, you have to be exemplary *before* anyone else."

Emmanuelle stares into the distance. She has nothing to say. She sits down on the low wall, folding her arms round her crossed legs and resting her chin on the double pommel of her knees. After a while, she asks, sounding tense, almost hostile:

"And why is it that I have to do all that? Why me?"

"Why you? Because you're capable of doing it. As others are able to solve equations, to write symphonies, your genius lies in physical love and beauty. Or let's put it this way: you become what you can do. Surely you don't want to live out your life without making some mark on the world?"

"But I'm only nineteen years old! I'm not about to end my life. . . ."

"Do you have to wait any longer to even *begin* to live? Are you just a little kid? It's true, I'm telling you to be heroic. But the world needs that. Your species demands it from you."

"My species?"

"Yes, indeed: that ancient amino acid, that ancient amoeba, that ancient tarsier, that *unbelievable that has to be believed*—always destined to turn into something else. Animal? Vertebrate? Mammal? Primate? Hominid? *Homo? Homo sapiens?* Outdated labels, all of them! The forerunner of those to come: man of space-time, man of boundless thought-power, man of multiple bodies and a single spirit, man, the creator and modifier of men, always threatened by his own creatures, and bleeding, stigmatized, by his errors and his mysteries. Don't you want to help him?"

"So if I take my shorts off, that's helping him?"

"What use is it to perpetuate illusion, swindles, phobias? To perpetuate modesty?"

"Listen, do you really believe that it's important, for past and future mankind, whether one bares one's pubis or keeps it covered?"

"The future depends on your powers of imagination, on your courage. Not on your fidelity to old customs. What once was the wisdom of the caves may have become our idiocy. Let's take modesty: is that an innate virtue, a positive or negative value for all time? As a matter of fact, it is nothing of the sort. Originally, a sound notion, a smart idea, fitting and salutary: but today, a mere pretense, a sophism, senseless, a false jewel of absurdity, a refuge of iniquity, a vessel of perversion. . . ."

"You know very well that I'm no prude. And I find your litanies quite ravishing. But is it necessary to take all that so seriously?"

"Man came down into the underbrush, still holding on to the saving lianas hanging from the branches. He was scared of the claws and teeth of the competition, and spent more time in climbing, jumping, hopping about on the ground among the thorns and flints than in caressing his females in the saline humidity of his caves. And the first one who got the idea to protect those organs on which the creation and number of his progeny depended, true, he rendered the species a service. If he hadn't managed to turn this simple precaution into an ethical law, a ritual, a matter of elegance, a *charm*, who knows if he would have been able to impose his supremacy on the rest of creation? What was to become bigotry initially was a kind of biological clairvoyance: it was an initiative in the direction of evolution, a good thing, in the most moral sense."

Mario sits down, facing Emmanuelle:

"Then, later, the invention of clothing saved the species from perishing in the great freeze."

With an irritated gesture, he pinches the material of his shirt, now lightly stained with perspiration:

"But now, look! The reindeer have retreated, the great glaciers have melted away. Nevertheless we go on disguising ourselves, just because it would be *bad* to go naked!"

A dramatic sigh. Then:

"Our resting places are covered with velvet, our gardens are lovely lawns. Our domestic animals have no armor, no fangs. But we are still afraid something might hurt our genitals. Its function accomplished, its true meaning forgotten, the pair of panties has become sacred. And you're asking me why it is necessary to rid oneself of it, as urgently as if it were Deianira's tunic? Clinging to a myth that has outlived its purpose is bound to stultify mankind. The energy wasted in the service of a mere superstition saps our creative powers."

Mario's face brightens, as he shifts gears:

"In fact, the task the ancient Greeks felt to be the most urgent one, once they'd gotten it into their heads to civilize us, was: to take their clothes off! In the beginning, still harking back to the Stone Age, they went on concealing their phalloi—but once the age of reason and high culture began, their statuary became nude. If those great warriors and philosophers hadn't realized, in time, how ridiculous their jockstraps were, we might still be barbarians, to this day."

There is a sly gleam in the Italian's eyes.

"And don't you believe that the Dorian ephebes chose to compete in their pentathlons with nothing on *only* because it granted them maximal freedom of movement! Surely their *prime* intention was to show off their beauty to their admirers, who then went on to immortalize them. In the gymnasium, the statue of Eros stood next to that of Pallas Athena, and it was at *his* feet that man achieved his first insights into philosophy."

For a moment, Mario seems lost in reverie about an epoch which Emmanuelle knows he would have liked to live in. Then he goes on, emphasizing his words with sweeping gestures:

"What I've just said about the history of modesty goes just as well for the other sexual taboos. Your peers would heap such immense opprobrium on you if you were to admit, openly, that you just love to feel a male member entering your mouth and taking its pleasure there, right to the very end! That you delight in the caresses your own fingers provide you, every day! And that you take pleasure in sharing your bed with other bodies besides your husband's! Once upon a time, all those taboos made sense. When it was man's task to populate the planet, wasting sperm didn't make much sense, and it seemed an excellent idea to proclaim masturbation a sin. Now that the proliferation of human beings has become a menace, men should be forbidden the practice of coming inside the female vagina: it ought to be regarded a virtue to spill one's semen *only* in those places where there is no risk of fertilizing an ovum. Once that is recognized, the husband's archaic fear that his wife might bear another man's child loses its raison d'être—even more so since we can now rely on our arts of contraception, in addition to those of our lips and tongues and fingers. It's surely ridiculous, in this century, and offensive to the intelligence, to regard the search for sensual pleasure outside of the reproductory mechanism as in any sense blameworthy—and it's time, too, for us men to recognize our wives' taste for new penises as both inoffensive and legitimate."

Mario seems to expect a reply from Emmanuelle, but she does not say anything, and so he continues:

"If we wish our children to have greater mental capabilities than our own, we must bequeath to them an earth delivered, by our courage, from absurd prohibitions and useless anguish. A prudish, a devout scholar is a shackled one: what might Pascal or Pasteur not have discovered, more, and greater things, had they not been such trapped spirits? And what is there to say about the artist if he allows himself to be blinkered and tethered? None are worthy of the name of man, that glory of tomorrow, if they believe or pretend to believe that the body showing itself must be damned! These stamens, these pistils, the gift to our eyes of these naked graces, for which we praise nature who adorns its flowers with them—surely some perverse god did not give them to his best-loved creature merely to constrain him and to cause his downfall? But, of course, *you* have nothing to worry about! That strange little pretense that your shorts are will amply suffice to guarantee the favors of Eternity. . . . Oh! please forgive me my anger, my dearest, but does it bear thinking about? That the entire, great nation of human beings, capable of so much intelligence and skepticism, tempered by so many millennia of bravery and risk, so strong in its laughter, so beautiful in its poetry—that it should now be such a frightened Achilles, looking for his salvation in the frippery, the false modesty, the simpering of virgins? The task of eroticism is this: to rid the living from the hair shirts that constrain them, and from the virtue-mongers who make them look ridiculous."

Emmanuelle is serenely contemplating her thin sweater, her nipples pointing out through it. Mario, however, pays no attention, but continues to remind her of her duty:

"I don't even care for eroticism as an end in itself. All I know is that it gives one a distaste for stupidity and hypocrisy, a desire to be free, and the strength to achieve this. When the world turns into a prison, eroticism is the file that can cut through the bars, it is the ladder, it is the password! I don't know of any secret that could, better than this *lucidity*, free man from his most sterile terrors, give him the chance to tear himself away from the Paleozoic burden and to penetrate outer space, without any assistance from the stars. And, as it is repugnant to me that in our age, the age of great wings, such prehistoric self-immolations, pruderies, and artifices continue to determine your actions, I do beseech you to parade your naked beauty and your senses openly, so that they may cause your beholders to found a new lineage—one that will be less ugly, more potent, less credulous and servile, and not so obsessed by simulacra as they themselves have been."

Mario stretches himself out on his back, his head at Emmanuelle's feet.

"For humans who are running the risk of becoming dehumanized by the laws of nature, which are too young, and by the laws of the city, which are too old, the challenge of your bare cunt, on this slab of stone, may provide an upsurge of their spirits, of the love of danger."

He gets up again.

"If it is the task of intelligence to *know* the truth, our moral sense provides us with the means of *recognizing* it—by a very simple method, that of opening one's eyes, and one equally simple rule, that of telling no lies. An easy task altogether, or so it would seem. And yet, and yet!"

A dramatic shrug.

"But, patience. You know the saying of one of your countrymen, a mathematician: Truth never triumphs, but its adversaries end up dying."

Some sudden vision seems to cheer him up:

"Who knows," he says, with a smile, "perhaps it wouldn't be all that wise to await its arrival too long? In an era that likes to admire robots more than human beings, we ought to hurry to put our bodies to the test, to glorify their powers, if we want to remain in charge. We already know that our clearest distinction from the other fauna of this world lies in our ability to drink even when we aren't thirsty—and to make love at any time. I wouldn't be surprised if—not too long from now—the only way to distinguish a human being from a machine would be based on the former's insistence on defying the sexual order through the disorder of eroticism. No doubt about it, the transistorized androids who will pilot our rocket ships will also, one day, acquire the knack of reproduction through sexual intercourse— and have a whale of a good time doing it, too! But as long as they won't question the laws of nature and common sense by preferring to masturbate, as long as their females have not acquired a taste for the juices of orgasm on their lovers' cocks, we'll still be ahead in the game."

Emmanuelle appears quite enchanted. Mario relaxes for a moment, looking at her, but not for long. His subject has a most urgent grasp on him.

"Humanity doesn't need only transfinite numbers, synchrotrons, cortisone, and heart transplants. Of course, it is wonderful that it is now able to disarm the attackers of metabolism, to turn mesons and molecules into its servants. But in a world where man knows his rhesus factor, and is capable of measuring, with the aid of some solenoid of his own invention, the wavelengths of his desires, he does run the danger of remaining forever ignorant of the true value of his own life."

Mario's voice grows more impassioned:

"As long as that form of barbarism that prides itself on eating meat tenderized under the saddle can coexist, no matter how indecent the spectacle, with the embryo whose chromosomes have been changed, with the atom whose structure has been altered, we have to watch out not to let that precious Ariadne's thread slip from between our fingers which alone saves us from beating our heads against the wall and losing heart, in the midst of such confusion, such madness: our passion for beauty. Our love of loving, as well: because love is not only our means of entering the workings of the entire universe while still in our bodies, it is also the most beautiful of all works of beauty: it is an art, created by man, the art of creating man, and it is *man become art*! Let art be exactly that, the love of our own flesh, a prodigious eternalizer! Thus we shall become perennial as the stones, or as those alluvial deposits of the infinite the great quanta-rivers are forever hurling across the great plains of space. . . . I'm telling you, there is no greater future for the perishable and solitary spirits we are, stricken with the angelic plague of our pulsating cells, in all their fragility, than this one chance we have to bequeath to the indestructible void of matter those figures with outstretched arms and eyes like stars, which we shall have sculpted for our pleasure, finding them to be our greatest glory. Ah, yes, the only true survival of man, his acknowledged progeny, his defiant victory over death, his *oeuvre*! You have reason to fear death, if you are not going to leave anything that is not greater than yourself. But to what heights won't you rise, above all secular pieties and agonies, when the chisel of your life immortalizes this body, constantly threatened by hair shirts and winding sheets, carving the lineaments of gratified desire into the marble of beauty."

Mario spreads out his arms, raises his face toward the sky. His voice sounds choked with emotion.

"Before the Sun goes dark,
And there is an end to its light, to the Moon, the Stars. . . ."
Emmanuelle relinquishes her grip on her imprisoned knees. She looks at Mario as she had been looking at him when he was holding forth earlier by the *khlong*. And he continues:
"Yes, it's true—it all works, in its given moment. Even Christianity. One day there came a man to those mortals, haggard with their sacrifices and superstitions, tribes beaten down by their own disdain and ignorance, a man who said to them: 'Love one another: You are a unique and fraternal species. There are no chosen people; there are no slaves; there are no damned. I call upon you to rise from your fantasies, your carnage. I deliver you from your false gods, from the chimerical burden of your original sins. Your preachers, your temples, and the books in them no longer hold the answers to everything: it is to yourselves that you now have to address your questions, not forgetting that there will never be an answer. It is this quest, aimless and ceaseless, upon which your existence and your freedom rests. Your judgment will depend only upon what you yourselves have accomplished. . . .' That day the world took a step forward. Later, the meaning of the message was lost, and the doctrine of progress became a great system of constraint, condemning all manifestations of the life force as sinful. The Messiah had served evolution: his church became an obstacle to it. My darling, it is now up to you, this very day, to bear the good tidings. A love that is no offense, a love that frees from shame: sacrilege only to the pharisees who

will, once again, refuse to let their eyes feast on it. A love that demystifies, yet is like a proud sail of true magic, swelled by the mystery of great beginnings. A love that will be a victory over all weakness and fear: a victory for life. 'Rejoice in life with the woman you love,' crieth the Preacher: 'All that your hand can do, let it do with all your might, because there shall be no more doing or knowing, no science or wisdom, in the realm of the dead where you must go.' It is the *body* that matters when one weeps for love: 'No, not Heaven!' cries the dying woman. 'I do not want Heaven, I want my Lover!' Only the lunatic proclaims a love of death—reason replies that it desires to believe only in the goodness of life, in the carnal feast of the living: 'Better a live dog than a dead lion. . . .' Only a disdain for the body makes the body perishable, and who finds the body's laws vile, renders them vile. If there is anything sacred in this world, surely it is the body's incarnation, its sexual organs. Happy the one who when it is time for him to die can say: 'I placed my bet on this body, and I did not lose my life!' Emmanuelle, I am not afraid, nor am I ashamed, to wager all the tomorrows of the world on your body!"

Mario pauses, collects his thoughts, calms down:

"No preacher would ever dare advance that far, to the Erosphere, which seems far more distant than the Noösphere. Eroticism, the secret name of evolution, is nothing but the increasing spiritualization of matter. The brain alone does not suffice to let us perceive its nature: we need a booster rocket, the organ able to create visions beyond nature, capable of

projecting us beyond the earth—and that is our sex. Without it, we remain nailed to the ground. If the human brain is
so superior to that of the angels, and likewise superior to any
cybernetic contraption, that is due to the fact that it is acti-
vated by rivers of sperm. The phallus is our only chance: without it, we would be mere machines, cold as ice."

For a moment, Mario's ruminations take a loftier turn:

"I hope, however, that when you hear me talking about
the sexual organs and about the brain, you'll bear in mind that
both factors have to be rendered their dues, and that the art of
eroticism must not be confused with a simple appetite of the
senses. For the great majority of humans, the powers of the
senses are pearls cast before swine: the use they make of them
is no better than what a slightly-brighter-than-average monkey might be capable of. Eroticism requires a reorganization of
thought that alone can dignify the senses on the human level.
Make no mistake: the true face of eroticism is not a lascivious
one: it is the face of love."

There is a sudden note of hurt in Mario's voice:

"Surely you haven't been regarding me as a heartless
maniac? It is the suffering of mankind that makes me so vocif-
erous! I believe that happiness is our reason for being, and
I believe that it can be achieved, provided that your curiosity and your courage do not weaken in its pursuit! I believe
that we can learn to live by learning how to change, in a universe that is governed by change. Men must liberate themselves from their obsession with the past; from time to time

they must renew their patterns of thought and their laws. Of those, the most backward, the most blinkered, the most unjust are the ones imposed by the arithmetic of present sexual mores—with its units and binomials, ridiculous in an epoch during which the study of isolated entities has given way to the study of *groups*, as you well know, being something of a mathematician yourself. But, alas! it does need heroism, to rid oneself of habits that are good for nothing but suffering. We call ourselves moral creatures, and yet we haven't even managed to convince ourselves that it is our duty to lead happy lives! It is not true that 'there is no such thing as happiness in love.' The love I am teaching you is one that gives happiness a chance. It does not arise from boredom or decadence, but is a sign of health in those whose youth still lies before them. It is their experience of a world which has not yet been created. So do not weep, Emmanuelle: the joys of tomorrow are greeting your carnal reality with outstretched arms! Solitude can never be humanity's eternal vocation: it is, no doubt, an elementary stage in man's consciousness, a measles of the spirit, cured by adulthood. I believe that the future of the species lies in union rather than in isolation: first of all, the union of one with one, then with two, then three, in groups that constitute true units, combinations with complex variables, spirits with a multiplicity of bodies. And perhaps we shall thus surmount, in a billion years, that condition that today allows us to begin our lives only on 'the other side of despair.' The prime virtue I attribute to eroticism is simply this: it breaks down the walls of solitude.

At long last, it gives humans a taste for other humans. And I am convinced that it can succeed, and succeed far better than any other discipline, better than all modes of asceticism, all sacraments, and all drugs. You have to understand that, to me, the exclusive, the jealous are marks of absolute criminality: attempts to assassinate evolution itself, born from the hypocritic malice of suicidal sects who hate the prodigious innate powers of the species. To make love to more than one other body in no way injures the idea of love, nor does it betray that idea: it is the gateway to an abundant life, in which love multiplies the lover and at the same time prevents him from amputating the beloved. This love that we shall one day be capable of will be the end of our befuddlement and ignorance, the end of childhood, and the time of the truly humane will begin. A time, one hopes, of unfeigned joy. The self-love of our sexual organs and golden breasts, the circle of our dancing arms, our crazy wings, the spreading of our legs and their high jumps, free of shame—these will make the lugubrious tangos of our little side trips look terribly outmoded. . . . It will be possible to be young again, even in the midst of graves. But, hell! I don't need to convince myself of that. It is my one and only belief!"

The look in Mario's eyes moves Emmanuelle. She allows him one final spurt:

"The world will become what the genius of invention and the temerity of your body will make it. My mission is merely to make you aware of that possibility. It will be up to those who come after me to see that you won't be turned into yet another false deity. When eroticism itself has become a religion with its own cults, churches, bishops, and devils, with its own Latin and tabernacles, excommunications, indulgences, curiae, wars of religion—when it, too, finally pretends to have the answer to everything, thus turning the world into a miserable place with its own laws and butchers: *then* man will know it well enough to be able to go on to further revolutions. But now, this instant, it is up to you to topple the false gods, their desolate temples, their rites devoid of faith. Emmanuelle, deliver us from our evil!"

She looks at him for a while, as if waiting. Her eyelids move, once or twice; then she closes her eyes and sits there, motionless. After a couple of minutes that seem too long to Mario she sits up straight, and, with slow-motion gestures, lifts the hem of her sweater, unzips her shorts and slides them down to her knees, then to her ankles. She shakes them off her feet, letting them fall into the grass below the terrace wall. At the touch of the stone, neither hot nor cold, merely sleek and hard, she feels her buttocks contracting.

She has no objections when Mario asks her to stretch herself out on her back, exposing everything below the navel. To offer herself up even more completely, she lets her legs hang down both sides of the parapet; her thighs open, her pubic mound jutting up in a delightful display of rippling muscles under the flawless skin, amber and shadowy by turns under the ever-changing monsoon sky.

2
The Invitation

*She would enter that small society of the damned
and the blessed that is the only aristocracy one
may still regard with a certain degree of respect.
Contrary to belief, it is not as easy to join as it
is to become a member of "café society."*
—André Pieyre de Mandiargues, *Le Belvédère,*
"The Irons, the Fire, the Night of the Soul"

She can not really be seen from the street, as there are trees obscuring the view. But she has no doubts whatsoever that her neighbors are ogling her behind their windows opening onto her garden across the hedge. Who are they? She has no idea. She has never seen them. Will they resent the sight? Perhaps they are masturbating? She imagines their frenzied hands— and her clitoris rises and hardens, sending urgent messages all the way up to her throbbing temples. . . .

Mario's voice gives her a start.

"Do you ever stroke yourself in front of your servants?" he wants to know.

"Oh, sure."

But in actual fact only Ea is her mute confidante when Emmanuelle makes love to herself in the mornings, in her bed or in the shower, or, after lunch, on the chaise-longue, while reading or listening to records. Her other domestics—as far as she knows, at least—are lacking in such curiosity.

"Well then," her visitor goes on, "be generous, call your houseboy. Yes, right now. He's so handsome!"

Emmanuelle feels her heart sink. No, that really goes too far! Mario must understand. . . . It would seem, she remarks, that he is making up for time lost! Then, for a moment, she thinks she can hear the "beeps" of fate, measuring her guilt. That's one, and there goes another: how many minutes of eternity have already been entered on her debit side? Then she realizes she will, sooner or later, act according to his predictions (because he is not giving her any orders, but simply reading her own wishes, only half a step ahead of her own consciousness); so what is the use procrastinating? Without even a sigh, she calls out the boy's name, not very audibly at first, then loudly.

The servant appears, his eyes and gait like those of a jungle cat. Mario motions him closer and makes him kneel right in front of her.

"Do you want him to make you come?" Mario asks.

Emmanuelie bites her lip; she wants to warn Mario that the young man understands French. But Mario has already started talking to him, in a language she has never heard before. The boy replies, muttering under his breath, his eyes downcast, and as ill-at-ease, it seems, as Emmanuelle herself. Mario sounds like a lecturer—the tone is familiar! How nice it sounds, she thinks, a little lesson in erotology, in demotic Thai. . . . She finds it amusing, despite the awkwardness of the situation. Nevertheless she is startled to the point of bounding off the wall when Mario—without warning—guides the boy's hand to her vulva, showing him what needs to be done, preventing him from undoing his own clothes, and correcting his initial fumbling. But it doesn't take the boy's fingers more than a moment or two to acquire the right strokes, and Mario lets them pursue their task without his assistance.

"He confessed to me that he has the hots for you," says Mario. "Surely it is cruel to let him suffer?"

Emmanuelle does not reply, and he goes on to inquire:

"Or do you feel that would be stooping too low?"

"Certainly not!" Emmanuelle says, indignantly, suddenly furious in the midst of all the titillation and confusion, forcing herself to add: "A man is a man!"

"Well, this one hungers and thirsts for your breasts and belly, your mouth, your cunt—he's yearning to touch your body and to enter it. From the day you arrived he's been dreaming of the moment when he would finally dare to seduce you. But isn't it up to you, in this case as in all others, to glory in your own initiative, your own forwardness? What would you have thought if this youngster had proven himself to be more of a conqueror than yourself?"

And then, in what sounds like a *non sequitur,* he suggests:

"Think about Anna Maria!"

She tries to do so, closing her eyes, but is instantly taken unawares by the memory of Bee. Perhaps that is due to the pervasive fragrance of roses.

She remembers the letter she had been writing to her lost friend, the day before. Bits and pieces of it come back to her—words she knows to be useless, Bee will never get to see them:

"What I want to tell you is simply that the sun over Siam has risen once again, only for you, and for me. The sun, whose rays caress you the very moment after they have roused me from sleep: the sun, like a bell ringer, happy in his passion for punctuality. And there we are, close enough to be shared by him, the god of the sky.

"I am reaching out to you, opening, unfolding there, behind so many walls—you, a dream, teeming with your very absence. I press myself against you, sweet sleeping beauty quite frosted over with sleep, and my breath makes your lips glisten.

"With my fingers, I give you eyes to see with, I smooth your hair and return their springy liveliness to your silken legs; I uncover your face, removing its enameled mask. I have made you yourself again.

"I arrange the motions of my life according to the flickerings of your image on the screen of memory, more faithful than the seasons. I turn around you from the first light of dawn, from the ends of space, moving with the hours on the sundial; and yet, I am a planet lacking its sun.

"And from tree to tree I advance toward you, who are my fountain in that clearing where I know I shall arrive to rest. Stretching out beside you I'll bend down to see my own face, to refresh it with your live water, dear spring, after my long march! I'll quench my thirst with you, yet you will remain on my lips forever. In the mornings you'll wash me clean of my nights; in the evenings, you'll provide the sweetest oblivion from the events of the day.

"I extend to you the promise of a dark bridge, separating, yet uniting us every night, across the waters of oblivion. . . ."

In her mind there is a great parade of desires, of voluptuousness, with cheers and ovations. . . . And now, never mind whose hand it is, caressing her clit as she lies there, spread-eagled, on the granite parapet—never mind whose eyes are contemplating her, whose ears are eavesdropping on her, from behind the shelter of their Venetian blinds: all she feels is sheer pride.

Then Emmanuelle and Mario are back in the living room.

"How would you like your tea?" she asks, "with eight lumps of sugar, or with fourteen? Or would you like a yard of it?"*

"If you don't mind," he says, "I know of no sweeter drink than *this*."

He looks at her, calmly.

---

* See *Emmanuelle I*, "The Lesson of Man."

"Come and sit next to me," he says.

She sits down, wants to fondle him. He doesn't let her, but she stays there, right next to him, happy to watch him and eager to learn more. Who, better than Mario, knows what must be done in order to exalt oneself? The glorious pleasure that she feels in her own body at this very moment . . . is it any different, she wonders, from the pleasure known by men? Why would it be? An imagined cock swells and throbs at the base of her belly, hardens, blooms between her fingers. She almost swoons in following in her mind's eye the semen which, under the stimulation of a virile hand, climbs the entire length of the shaft and prepares to explode within and over her. Pressed against this other body, in whom she loves at this instant her own sex most, she comes at the same time as he, emptying herself of nights and nights of unspent semen.

Their lips half open. What liqueur, his or hers, will be able to slake their thirst?

Mario hands her a long-stemmed crystal glass into which he has shot. Emmanuelle takes long, sweet, greedy gulps, followed by Mario, both enamored of a body more than by itself alone consumed. Oh, enjoyable communion! The discovery of self in the substance come out of another. . . !

"Now, be woman!" Mario commands.

She protests. She wishes to be a man for him, exactly as she is a woman to women. She tells him this, and asks him if he would like to make love to her the way he makes love to boys.

"What boy could ever caress himself in front of me the way a woman can—no matter how eager to please he'd be?" Mario says. "Don't offer me anything I can have elsewhere."

Emmanuelle does not argue with him, but takes off her sweater, smiling at her own superb nudity. Her hands slide all over this naked body that she loves, moving up to her breasts, cupping and bouncing them, twiddling their nipples, sensitizing them until they stand out like twin clits; then she lets them go, moves her hands along her flanks as if to calm herself down, slides them over her buttocks, back up into the armpits, where they brush against her breasts again, and she resumes her fondling of them, as if to say, "Thank you for being so patient". . . .

Her lips move, searching for other lips, or nipples, or genitals. But now her hand arrives at her own crotch, and her fingers chance to touch a minute opening, a tiny little pinprick in a cushion of rosy flesh. The fingertips start turning around this tiny center, titillating it, squeezing it without respite, inflaming it with little slaps and tremors and almost imperceptible grazings of her fingernails.

With her eyes closed now, her buttocks taut, her legs describing a great letter V, planted firmly on her bare feet, she looks the picture of an amazing crucifixion, painted in the black, ocher, and pink of the falling dusk.

Her own caresses overwhelm her, drawing forth tears of joy, little moans: she is weeping at her own pleasure and gathering new strength from this delicious mortification. In vain she tries to prolong this state of suspension, to allow a period of grace to that part of herself in which she feels herself totally immersed: but she can't do it, she has to go on, right to the end, right to that limit she feels to be the ultimate one, every time, not to be surpassed, not even attained again. . . .

Her hand curves like a mussel shell around her vulva, as if to protect it, to contain its violence, as the torrents of pleasure sweep through Emmanuelle, as heaven and earth are rent asunder, and she herself is flung, like a great naked bird, against the chest of her watcher.

Mario takes her hands in his own, and she no longer knows, now, whether she owes this incredible sense of happiness to herself or to him. . . .

But then he disengages himself and places her flat stomach on the silk-covered seat, her face rubbing against the slightly rough surface of the cover. Her pitch-black mane tumbles over her shoulders, tresses reaching down past the small of her back. Her buttocks still twitch in little spasms.

"Actually, I came as a royal messenger," Mario says. "So it's time now for me to accomplish my mission."

Then he emotes, in a tone of voice suited to the formality of the occasion:

"His Most Serene Highness, the Prince Orme Séna Orméaséna, requests the honor of your presence at a soirée he is giving the day after tomorrow at his palace of Maligâth. If you accept the invitation, I shall be glad to escort you there."

"Do I know this Prince?" Emmanuelle asks, trying to sound interested. She is still in the drowsy throes of aftermath.

"He has not yet been introduced to you, and that is exactly the reason why he has not taken the liberty of delivering this invitation in person. In any case, I told him I thought I would be able to persuade you to accept."

"What about Jean?"

"Your husband? He is not expected to come with you."

"But, well . . ."

Mario does not let her go on:

"Darling, I mustn't let you remain ignorant of what kind of occasion it is that you have been invited to attend. There will be much to eat, much to drink. Music and dancing. But, first and foremost, it will be an opportunity for you to offer your body to all those present whom you find worthy of receiving this honor. And your accomplishments there will help you in gaining further insight into your powers—provided that your pursuit of these studies, as I have no doubt it will, matches your native talent for them."

"To put it more plainly, it's an orgy you want to drag me to?"

"That word 'orgy' displeases me, with its mundane connotations of free-for-all and slobber: I would rather think of it as a celebration of bodily joys. You should also know that unless you yourself feel an urge to experience it, no one will commit any violence against you whatsoever. At the risk of offending certain schools of thought, our host prefers his female guests to act purely out of their own free will in their erotic pursuits."

Emmanuelle thinks it over for a couple of seconds.

"And after such a night, I guess I'd be closer to your ideal, wouldn't I?"

Before Mario can answer she goes on:

"Well, I'm ready to give it a try."

Nevertheless, there are certain misgivings.

"What am I going to tell Jean?"

"I would imagine you'd rather not tell him anything."

"But he isn't going to let me run around every night without worrying about where I'm going and what I'm doing. . . .'"

"Well, he'll find out, sooner or later."

"And what then?"

"Well, then you'll know whether you were deceiving yourself or not."

"Me? Deceiving myself? About what?"

"About his love for you."

"But I've never doubted it!"

"But as I've had occasion to tell you, love is . . .'"

Emmanuelle remembered the theses delivered by Mario in his house surrounded by dark waters. She did not feel unintermittently certain about their absolute validity.

"Well, put it to the test!" Mario proposed.

"And what if I then find out that Jean does not love me in the way you have in mind?"

"Why, then you'll be a two-time loser in matters of intelligence as well as in those of love."

"I *do* love him," she thought, out loud. "I don't want to lose Jean, nor do I want him to lose me."

"So you'd prefer to call a halt to everything, right now?"

"No, I'm not sure I could even do that," she admitted. "It's not just Jean and myself that I want—I want more."

"You aren't, and you'll never be, a mere chattel, a fenced-in piece of territory. You have no choice: you have to be a real *person* to your husband."

"And for the other men that get to make love to me, what will I be to them?"

"First of all you should think about what they'll be to you: then you'll know what you'll be to them. Surely, you don't believe they're all that different from you?"

"I wish they weren't."

"When you give yourself to them, is your own private pleasure all you have in mind?"

"No, I really love it when I can make others come."

"How could men's desire for you in any way restrict your freedom? Does it offend you?"

"I'm happy when they want me."

"Does your happiness cease when they ask you to fulfill that desire?"

"You ought to know the answer to that."

"It's exactly to those men who put that demand on you that you have to give yourself! Because they won't know that you are there, that you are there for them—until the very moment they can stop being afraid of you. Only then will your wish be granted; and you and your lovers be as one, indistinguishable from one another. That is what they themselves are hoping for, without even knowing it, and what they have been hoping for since the beginning of time!"

"And so, I shouldn't deceive anyone?"

"Not anyone. No man will make any sense to you unless he's inside you."

She smiles. He goes on:

"And as your own consciousness depends on that of all humans . . ."

For a moment, Emmanuelle remains lost in thought. Then, she asks a final question:

"And what if I should become . . . pregnant? I wouldn't even know who sired the child!"

Mario reassures her:

"You certainly wouldn't. Again, you'll have to comprehend the true import of that."

Emmanuelle wasn't about to tell Mario, but she didn't really find that perspective so difficult to integrate. Until the time when Jean had left her alone in Paris, he and she had been in agreement that they did not want any offspring. However, from the day of her arrival in Bangkok she had taken no precautions whatsoever. Nor had she taken any in the plane over, for that matter, nor when she was being fucked by the *sam-lo.* It was a strange thing: she couldn't feel any grave apprehension at the thought that one day she might have to tell Jean that she was about to give birth to another man's child. Without being able to explain it to herself, she felt certain that he would receive such news with understanding, as an event in its own right.

* * *

"Well, Christopher, how do you like it here?" she says, later that same day. "Jean, how is it you're not introducing your friend to some pretty Siamese girls? Why don't you take him out on the town to have some fun?"

"Good idea," says Jean. "Let's go to see one of those Chinese striptease shows."

"Oh, no! What a revolting notion!" Christopher exclaims.

This manifestation of human concern, in the young man, delights Emmanuelle:

"How come Christopher is such a virtuous young man?" she asks.

"Listen, he isn't! He's just being a hypocrite."

The young Englishman merely groans. His friend insists:

"You should see him when he gets close to little girls."

"Little girls!" Emmanuelle gasps. "How little?"

"Well, like that."

Jean's palm indicates about three feet from the floor. His wife pouts:

"Too small, I should say."

Christopher decides to join in their hearty laughter.

After dinner they start out through the labyrinth of the native quarter, and finally arrive at a theater that looks like a giant supermarket. Hundreds of spectators, shining with sweat and excitement, milling about, most of them on their feet, facing a catwalk paraded by lines of naked female teenagers. Well, not quite naked, as the newcomers find out as soon as they install themselves in the metal folding chairs (empty because they are so expensive) which they are offered, right in the front row: a length of braid running across and around the girls' buttocks ends in a playing-card-sized piece of some black, pliable material, dangling before that strategic opening. With two fingers at a time, the performers are flicking this important accessory up and down, in time to the music, to uncover momentarily their downy abdomens—such fugitive revelations being greeted with yells of delight from the audience. This goes on for at least a half-hour, without any variation, without any slackening of the aficionados' enthusiasm. The three European visitors distract themselves by discussing the young ladies' respective charms.

Emmanuelle declares her preference for "the big one with no tits." No one seconds her in that opinion. Finally Jean and Emmanuelle find a great deal of common ground in their taste for the long and deep crack, framed by such sweet and succulent-looking lips, the girl right in front of them keeps flashing.

"Well, I say, until now I never heard a married couple chatting away about such matters," says Christopher, not too seriously, yet quite obviously amazed.

To scandalize him further, Emmanuelle says, with a sigh: "Oh boy, could I dig making love to her . . . !"

She's trying to test my modesty, he thinks. I'll show her! Emmanuelle's legs, their skin naked against his, excite him a good deal more than the Oriental charms up there.

"As for me," he says, "I'd rather do that with you."

Hope she realizes I'm kidding, he says to himself: hope she doesn't think I've gone *too* far. . . .

"Christopher's learning fast," says Jean.

The Britisher is breathing quite heavily now. He hadn't been aware of the possibility of his voice carrying through all the brouhaha of the nightclub to Jean's ears. He feels stupid, contrite, miserable.

All of a sudden, Emmanuelle experiences a crazy urge to give herself to him. "I'll do it, and I'll do it tonight," she vows silently. And before she can arrest the impulse, she leans toward her husband and whispers into his ear, caressingly:

"Darling, listen! Can I make it with Christopher?"

"Yes," says Jean.

She squeeezes his arm, passionately, and leans over to kiss him, feeling happier than she's ever felt since she first fell in love with him.

3

The Battle of Eve

O my soul, do not aspire to immortality,
but exhaust the realm of the possible.

—Pindar

Our Father who art in heaven
Stay there
And we'll stay here on earth
At times so beautiful
With its seasons
With its years
Its beautiful girls . . .

—Jacques Prévert, *Paroles*

The following day, Ariane calls Emmanuelle, asking her to come over to her house. Easy to guess at the objective of such a visit! Emmanuelle begs off, pretending to be busy with errands for Jean. As soon as she hangs up, she asks herself the reason for her evasiveness: is it true that she doesn't find Ariane tempting at all? Remembering the time the young Countess made a pass at her, Emmanuelle immediately feels her body responding.

No doubt about it, she would enjoy Ariane's caresses. Well, then, is she just being faithful to Bee? That does not seem so certain, either. . . . Her grief over the loss of Bee is already moving into a mythical dimension: it's not her heart hurting so much, it's her pride. Thus Emmanuelle arrives, a trifle superficially perhaps, at the conclusion that her indifference toward Ariane, at this moment, is merely a reflection of the curiosity and the attraction she has been feeling since the day before for that young girl she met by the garden gate: a mystery Mario had made no particular effort to clarify.

"Anna Maria Serguine," that's what he'd said. But who was she? Different, to be sure. . . . He had promised that she would come and visit Emmanuelle this very afternoon. And arrive she did, around three o'clock, in her distinctive automobile.

An annoyed frown appears on Emmanuelle's face: it's impossible to see the legs of this "archangel," as she's wearing slacks. . . . Can't see her breasts either, so well covered are they by a shirtwaist, which is far from being as generously unbuttoned as Emmanuelle's own. Yet it strikes her quite forcibly that a thoroughly clothed human form can be just as seductive as a naked one.

She stood there, staring at her visitor, not attempting to disguise her interest in the least. Anna Maria found it impossible to restrain an urge to laugh. Emmanuelle, confused, lowered her head.

"Am I being rude?" she asked.

"No, you're just being honest."

What did this Anna Maria know about her? Well, why not ask her:

"Why do you say that? Did Mario tell you that I like girls?"

And yet, at that moment, she felt no desire in that direction. She was suddenly timid, surprisingly enough, considering her customary ease and enterprise in making it with other beauties. Happily, the visitor responded with a total lack of embarrassment. It made Emmanuelle smile again.

"But of course. And the rest of it, too. That you're quite insatiable!"

"Such a remark really makes me wonder what Mario's been telling you!"

"But there's no shortage of gossip, is there? Lots of wild escapades in native hovels, bouts of exhibitionism, frolicking in threesomes, God knows what else! I've probably forgotten at least three-quarters of it all."

It didn't bother Emmanuelle that Mario could be so indiscreet. In fact, she wanted him to make such publicity.

"And what do you think of it all?" she asked, with a matter-of-fact expression.

"Oh, it's been a long time since I took anything my handsome cousin says at face value."

Emmanuelle made a mental note: her visitor had quite tactfully circumnavigated the necessity to pass judgment on her conduct. But, out of some slight masochistic impulse perhaps, she had no intention of allowing herself to benefit from such delicate manners.

"What about me, then? Do you think it's proper of me to . . . for instance, to cuckold my husband?"

"Not proper at all."

Anna Maria's relaxed tone and affectionate smile took the edge off the negative judgment.

"I hope you made Mario feel ashamed of it," Emmanuelle said flippantly.

"No, I didn't. There's no reason to be angry with him."

"There isn't? With whom should I be angry, then?"

"With yourself, to be sure. Because it's you who really enjoys those things."

Emmanuelle registered that as a direct hit. She insisted, nevertheless, on the principle of the thing:

"But Mario and his theories aren't one hundred percent altruistic, either."

Anna Maria laughed again, a clear, pleasing peal. They had seated themselves, both straddling a little wooden bench under a gigantic tamarind, well protected from the scorching August sun by its fresh shade. They sat facing each other, both leaning forward, bracing themselves on their outstretched arms. Anna Maria wore a blue pants-and-shirtwaist outfit, whereas Emmanuelle was clad only in a minuscule bikini (you could see it whenever she moved one of her legs) under a thin lemon-colored sweater that set her breasts and nipples off to full advantage. The thick tresses of her hair fell over her cheeks and forehead: she shook them off, tossing her neck like a filly, or caught a few between her teeth and sucked on their ends for a couple of pensive seconds, moist-lipped, with a little frown. She gave Anna Maria the once-over again, without bothering to conceal her lust any more than the previous time. She found her incredibly beautiful: more beautiful than Ariane and her entourage of half-naked, pretty girls engaged in athletic pursuits, more so than Marie-Anne with her feline nipples and elfin eyes. More so than Bee. . . . Emmanuelle's conscience gave her a little twinge. She tried to justify herself to herself: after all, those others, even Bee, were mere terrestrials—but Anna Maria wasn't. It was obvious that she wasn't! A secret arrival from another planet. . . . For a moment or two, Emmanuelle's fancy roamed through the galaxies: just thinking about what the universe might not offer in terms of unknown beauty, way beyond somewhere, beyond the black abysses between the nebulae, filled her heart with painful longing. But Anna Maria's amused voice brought her back to earth—and, after all, she told herself, there appeared to be plenty of fine occasions down here, too!

"Oh, Mario's theories," said the young girl, in reply to Emmanuelle's last spoken words, "I know them, all right. What's more, I approve of them."

She relished Emmanuelle's obvious surprise and continued, with gusto:

"I believe, just as he does, that the human race has to 'denaturize' itself: it has to go against nature, and go beyond it, detach itself from it. The voice of nature is merely the voice of sin."

"That's a term I've never yet caught Mario using," Emmanuelle said, giggling.

Anna Maria smiled tolerantly.

"Haven't you noticed how scared that poor boy is, of *words*? He's quite bashful in relation to quite a number of things. Well, he's an aristocrat, you know."

They both laughed, this time in complete harmony.

"But you yourself, surely, are of noble birth?" Emmanuelle asked.

"Art school has made far nobler young ladies than I come down off their high horses."

"Oh, I see! Where did you go? Rome?"

"No, not at all. Paris."

"And here Mario was trying to convince me that you were a prude!"

"A prude? Well, that, too—which is not to say I ever was a prude—they'd have knocked that out of me, too, in the ateliers of that dear old Beaux-Arts."

"And I imagined you as being capable of even worse atrocities: like virginity, chastity, morality, religion!"

"Really?" Anna Maria seemed delighted. "Not a bad guess: as a matter of fact, I *am* a virgin, I *am* continent, I take great care in all moral matters and in all those spectacular aspects of my condition—of being a child of God, a daughter of His Holy Church."

She reveled in Emmanuelle's disgusted mien.

"As I told you, your wild capers don't bother me at all: but I didn't say I was on your side," she went on to explain. "On the contrary, I find it quite sad that you like to live this way. It's similar to my reaction to nature: it doesn't *shock* me, but I'm against it."

"What kind of a girl are you?" asked Emmanuelle, rather harshly. "What really hurts most, is that you're so damn beautiful!"

Anna Maria smiled gently.

"Thank you," she said. "You're no frump yourself."

Emmanuelle sighed. She felt far removed now from the kind of situation she had become so used to, where reciprocal admiration quite logically led to an intertwining of limbs, to lips against lips, nipples against nipples. Anna Maria seemed to make an effort to be sympathetic:

"It doesn't seem right to you that a girl believes in God?" she inquired.

"Not merely that, it seems downright obscene. Unnatural."

"But that's just what I'm saying!" Anna Maria cheered. "It *is* fabulously unnatural! That's what's so great about it. Although it can be a bore sometimes. Because I, too, like anybody else, am capable of enjoying a little natural recreation. I wasn't *born* pure in spirit."

"So you're telling me that you're really quite sensual?"

"Do I *look* frigid?"

Emmanuelle refused to let outward appearances influence her.

"I don't know."

She hesitated, then said:

"But what do you do when you feel that way?"

"I just tell myself not to give in to the impulse."

Emmanuelle grimaced with distaste.

"You don't even make love to yourself, ever?"

Anna Maria didn't look the least embarrassed.

"That happens, sometimes. But I always feel so bad afterward."

"Why?"

Emmanuelle was truly indignant

"Because it's sinful. Every time I give in to temptation, I regret it with all my being. Compared to the intensity of my remorse, the pleasure I've had isn't worth mentioning. That's just what's so hateful, in nature: she likes to trap you, to take you in with her shams. A dazzle, an illusion, a sigh: how can you rejoice in what you must lose, so soon? Could one really become attached to that? And is it worth sacrificing all the rest, only to have that?"

"What rest?"

"What makes a human being a different thing from any other animal. Call it what you will: the spirit, the soul, hope."

"But that isn't the same thing at all!" Emmanuelle protested. "I have no intention of sacrificing my spirit, nor my soul, for that matter! As for hope, I have plenty of hope."

"But what hope deserves that name, apart from the hope to see God one day? If you don't believe in eternal life, you are in a state of despair."

"I just believe in life, period. That's more than enough. And I'm not desperate in the least. I'm the very contrary of that: I am happy. As for me, no remorse can ever ruin a day. I love having a good time, but that doesn't prevent me from thinking about my soul. I enjoy my life, because it is all I am."

"But why do you insist on confusing life itself with the sensations of your body? I marvel at happiness, at beauty, just like you: but true pleasure is not the pleasure of the body! It's an entirely different thing from the accelerated heartbeat of an animal. Our life isn't the same thing at all as the life of those pretty flowers. It is so much more beautiful. Our life has already left nature behind, it has detached itself from it, it soars far above earth. It is this life that saves us from the universe, ruled by death, by entropy. Mankind has evolved from the sweetness of the body to the sweetness of the soul."

"I think that's just fine," said Emmanuelle, "but surely it's enough to call that conscience, reason, poetry? And it isn't opposed to the body at all. When I have an orgasm, it's my spirit having an orgasm in my body: it's not my body returning to some earlier, bestial state! You want the spirit to take pleasure only in itself. Why? Life is wonderful throughout, in the flesh as well as in spirit. *Are* those really two separate entities? You don't want anyone to experience pleasure in this world: where should they then? And will it be so much better there? It doesn't make sense, to go on looking for another world to accommodate a 'soul'—which, after all, is exactly what makes us masters of this one."

"It isn't another world," said Anna Maria.

Emmanuelle was dumbfounded. She didn't believe her ears.

"Eternal life, though," her guest continued, "doesn't that notion tempt you in the least?"

"Of course it does! I would love life to be eternal! But not the way you're driving at. Not in your paradise. I would not like to lead a life that has escaped away from earth. The only life everlasting I would like to experience would simply consist of going on with it in my present state! Not to grow old. Not to grow ugly. Not to die. Living is so great: and it's the only miracle there is. The earth who has given us our life, the earth who one day will turn us cold as stones—it is hateful even to think of leaving her. The only way I can face the thought is to think, well, it is in spite of ourselves! It is not our fault! But why, why are you dreaming of a flight away from this world?"

"I'm not at all sure the world is such a wonderful place as you describe it. It is full of deception, killing, cold, hunger, disease. . . . There's certainly a whole lot more suffering and ugliness than there is beauty and joy in it."

"I'm not that stupid. I know that too. But that is exactly why I want all human beings to put their shoulders, all their powers, all their knowledge, all their dreams to the wheel, to *help* the earth, rather than sit around resigned to their misery and telling themselves that they'll be rewarded in some hereafter! The pains they take to invent God, and the love and courage they need to then observe His laws—if they directed those toward loving the earth, toward making it so beautiful and so happy that no one would ever want to lose it again—then, perhaps, life could be good for all of us."

It seemed to her that that was the longest speech she had ever made. Anna Maria's eyes were scorching.

"Emmanuelle," the young girl said, "you know so well what you want to make out of your life: have you ever thought what you'll do about your death?"

For a moment, Emmanuelle remained silent, as if stunned. But then she almost shouted:

"Nothing at all! But why does that worry you? Oh, I know. Christians dream of nothing else but dying."

"No, they don't. They only want to turn death into a meaningful experience."

Emmanuelle shrugged. Death was the supreme absurdity, the incomprehensible injustice, the irreparable accident. There was no meaning in death. She detested Anna Maria for taking such an interest in what would, one day, be the absolute abolition of Emmanuelle, the negation of Emmanuelle—even worse: anti-Emmanuelle is what it would be, the opposite of all that existed. And so she said, in a hoarse voice that sounded strange even to herself as it rose through her constricted throat and passed her lips, her eyes suddenly shining with tears:

"You should worry more about my life. When it comes, that thing, to put an end to everything: when I won't, ever again, be able to see this world brimming with colors and stars, when I won't ever know what others will discover in it, when all that will be beautiful, after I'm gone, won't be there for me any more—*that's* when it will be too late for you to take an interest in me, to love me, to want to get to know me. I, I, when I won't be alive any more, I won't know it if someone loves me, I won't be able to see anything, hear anything, feel anything. I beseech you, don't wait until I'm dead! I don't want to be someone of whom they'll discover, after he's gone, that he—or she—was born to live, I don't want to be turned into a legend! I feel enough pain already when I consider that there will be, later, equally, perhaps more beautiful days than the ones we have: that centuries and centuries will pass and that human beings will be awakened by other suns. . . . Perhaps I'll die before growing old, grieving with all my heart, because I'll be forced to leave this world that I'm now hoping for, anticipating before it has arrived. . . . I am sure it will! And I want so very much to share that world, this one, where all miracles are possible. But it's true: I have to die. I'll never know what I have been waiting for. I'll be deprived of the only thing that counts. Things will continue their existence without me. Nothing will serve as consolation: even if there were a God, and another world, I wouldn't want them! I do not want to trade in my world, my life, for anything: thus I know that I'll have to lose everything. But at least I won't have vegetated toward some pension, I won't have sold my birthright for some spurious ecstasy and celestial asylum! I don't want any security, any snug retreat. When my life will be stolen from me, leaving nothing, yes, I'll weep and cry, I'll wail in my sorrow, I'll want all the world to hear! I'll howl, because I won't be able to go on living—not because of any regrets about the life I've had! No remorse, either, at having lived for nothing else but for my earth, which I'll have to cease looking at, at the very moment of my most intense love for it. . . . My earth, whom I would love to touch one more time. I want to stay here. Nowhere else. With human beings. Not with God!"

Emmanuelle was not looking at Anna Maria any more, she was gazing at some remote point, through the tamarind branches. Then she suddenly turned back to her guest, letting her stare burrow right into her eyes, and her voice had an edge to it that was quite surprising:

"Death! Your God can't *know* what death is, being immortal himself. Nor do the dead know anything about it, being in a state where they cannot know anything at all. There's only us, only the living; no one else but us, to know what it is, that death."

"I find your cousin quite annoying," Emmanuelle complains to Mario that evening, speaking to him on the telephone. "I don't particularly care to pass my time in theological discussions."

"You have, indeed, better things to do."

"She has no passion except for the great beyond."

"Remember what Goethe said: that the true ideal is merely the spirit of reality."

"You ought to tell that to her yourself. Yes, why don't you unload a few of your precious nuggets of wisdom on her, too, instead of showering me with them?"

"Have you perchance already forgotten that the redemption of Anna Maria happens to be *your* task?"

"How do you expect me to accomplish that? I've never seduced any convent girls."

"Well, doesn't it sound exciting?"

"Not to me it doesn't. I'm a simple girl. I love what comes naturally."

"But you're also in love with Anna Maria."

Emmanuelle didn't reply to that. As a matter of fact, she felt confused on that point. She sighed, loudly enough for the sound to be transmitted down the line.

"You'll be rewarded for your persistence," prophesied Mario, trying to sound reassuring.

"Her last name . . ."

"Didn't I tell you?"

"Yes, you did. It intrigues me. It sounds like a Slavic version of your own. Isn't she Italian?"

"She is. But my ancestors liked to fuck around, without paying too much attention to national frontiers. The sweet little bud Anna Maria flowered in Tuscany on a White Russian branch grafted onto an Alexandrian tree grown from a Cretan shoot transplanted to Byzantium."

"All right, all right. I get the picture."

"History knows only the fair lady gardener, never the male planter."

"Listen, I don't want to fall in love still one more time."

"Well, then, do something about it. Have some fun. How about some little escapade?"

"I tried one, last night."

"Tell me about it."

Emmanuelle related their outing to the display of Siamese vulvas.

"Well, the next treat was this rather unattractive creature running through her clever repertoire. She pushed a hard-boiled egg into her cunt and brought it out from there a few seconds later in neat slices. Then she cut a banana the same way. After that, she stuck a lighted cigarette between her labia and walked around with it, blowing smoke rings. Finally, she stuck a Chinese paintbrush in there and inscribed, vertically, a whole poem on a silk ribbon—in artistic and extremely well-formed characters, I might add."

"Banal," said Mario. "You can see stuff like that even in Rome."

"Then a Hindu appeared, wearing a turban, with an enormous erection protruding from his *dhoti*. He proceeded to hang all kinds of heavy objects on it, without it bending an inch."

"Any well-endowed male could do as well. What rewards did he treat his inflexible member to?"

"I don't know. He walked offstage with it still in the same state."

"That sounds suspicious. In fact, it probably was an artificial prick. And then?"

"A young girl came on, clothed only in transparent veils. We were quite stunned to see how beautiful she was. From a basket, she produced a snake, at least six feet long, with ivory-colored scales, truly almost as gorgeous as herself. It seems they only come across one like it once every century, back in India. She danced with it, twining it around her arms, her neck, her waist. Then she stripped, veil by veil. The snake snuggled up between her breasts, coiled around them, tickled her nipples with its flickering tongue. It kissed her on the mouth, on the eyelids, and she seemed so excited that I was getting jealous. She let the snake put its head into her mouth, gently, and then she sucked it and kept it there for a long moment, her eyes closed. It seemed as if she was drinking. Then she unbuckled the golden belt that held up her last veil, round her hips, and stood there quite naked. As soon as that happened, the python slithered down to her belly, passed between her legs and up between her buttocks, coiled round her waist and proceeded toward her cunt. Its forked tongue started licking her clitoris with such quick strokes you could only see the surrounding air flicker a bit, the way you do when you watch an airplane propeller turning. The snake's mistress moaned with pleasure, as assistants brought her some cushions and she lay down on them, upon her back, her legs spread wide apart in front of us: I could see her lower lips, quite dewy and rosy like a sea shell."

"And the snake?"

"It went right into her: she used its head like a cock, made it disappear altogether: I was wondering how it could go on breathing."

"She only put its head in?"

"Oh no, a good portion of its body went in, too. You could see its scales moving, see it vibrating, throughout its entire length. Maybe it was licking her inside, with that vibrant tongue."

"Was it thick?"

"Thicker than any man's cock. Almost as thick as my wrist. Its head was pointed, though: she had no trouble getting it in."

"Then what happened?"

"The girl took hold of the snake's body and pulled until its head reappeared, then she plunged it back in. She went on doing that I don't know how many times. She was coming, too, by now, twisting and turning on those cushions as if she were a snake herself. She was gasping and screaming."

"You too?"

"Oh! I wish I had a snake to make love to me like that!"

"I'll give you one."

"When it finally came out, she held it tight in her arms."

"And then she left?"

"Yes. Jean told me that a lot of men go and visit her in her dressing room, every night."

"You should have tried your luck with her."

"I'd certainly have liked to. But the idea of standing in line with all those over-excited men put me off."

"Well, that might've been an experience in itself."

"Instead, I escaped into daydreaming."

"What did you tell yourself?"

"Well, the usual: I made love to her, in making love to myself. But all I had were my fingers, instead of a snake."

"And now you have no further desire for her?"

"Quite the contrary! I want her more than ever."

"Because of her big reptilian friend?"

"No. It's something else, it's a new kind of itch. . . ."

"For what?"

"To make love with a woman and pay her for it."

Mario let a couple of seconds pass in silence.

"Who would you like to do it with more: with Anna Maria, or with the python girl?"

"The python girl!"

She thought it over, then:

"I'm sure Anna Maria wouldn't know what to do with a snake."

Mario's end of the line was silent; perhaps he was meditating. Emmanuelle took the initiative again.

"You say you'll get me one?"

"Well, yes, I promised."

"A white one?"

"His scales will be as soft as lips."

"And he'll know how to make love to me?"

"I'll make myself personally responsible for his education."

Emmanuelle giggled like a little girl.

"Tell me the rest of it," urged Mario.

"The long line of teenage dancers came back, and then we took off."

"You gave up so soon?"

"There wasn't anything else to see," Emmanuelle said, with a disenchanted little sigh.

"Well, it was up to you, then, to put on a little exhibition of your own."

"Yes, but that didn't work out."

"How come?"

Emmanuelle told Mario about her sudden desire for Christopher, how she had asked her husband for permission, how he had granted it.

"I hope you're pleased to hear all this?"

Mario was, and told her so. The event, he hastened to point out, was of an equal importance to the spiritual development of Emmanuelle as, in its time, the adoption of an erect posture had been to the previously quadruped human race. Well then, had the night of love with the houseguest proved satisfactory?

"There was no night of love with the houseguest," Emmanuelle confessed, sounding neither contrite nor regretful.

"What?"

"When we got back to the house, I didn't feel like it any more. I was sleepy. So, in front of his bedroom door, I kissed Christopher on both cheeks, then on the nose, and then just a little peck on his lips. And after that I just left him standing there—and pretty excited he looked, too!"

"*Che peccato!*" Mario lamented.

"But not all was lost. As soon as I was in bed, I did not feel sleepy any longer. So I made love to Jean! And it was quite a bit better than usual. Every time I had to yell a little, I thought of Christopher. I'll wager that noise kept him awake for a long while, on the other side of the wall! But we didn't mention him at all, Jean and I. We only talked about what a good time we were having. I don't think I ever told my husband such obscene stuff as I did last night. Jean got into me in every possible way! He ended up falling asleep, but I still couldn't, not even after all that fun. Once again I was getting hot thinking about Christopher, I felt like going into the next room and offering myself to him, still soaked and sweaty as I was with Jean's love-making. But then I didn't dare. I was too afraid I'd shock him. So I went on fondling myself, to the point where I can't remember falling asleep, finally. The first thing I noticed again was hearing the two of them talking over breakfast! I myself didn't get out of bed until noon. I didn't put any clothes on, but had lunch with both of them quite naked on the terrace, to atone a little for leaving Christopher so high and dry earlier."

"*Ottimo,*" Mario said approvingly. "Tonight you should just get into his bed and let him find you there when he comes in."

"Can't do it. He's left."

"Left?"

"For a couple of days, with Jean. You see, Jean told me over lunch that he'd received a telegram from the construction site, and that he would have to catch a plane to get there. And of course his young friend decided to go with him."

"What a pity. Well, did you have time to mention that invitation to Jean, the one to Prince Orméaséna's party?"

"No."

"You didn't dare to?"

"It wasn't that. After last night, I wouldn't be afraid to ask him for this further permission. But . . . I don't know how to say it. . . ."

"His acquiescence would have taken away a bit of the pleasure you'll have in giving yourself to others?"

"I'd like to go on deceiving him while I still can. Later, when he'll allow me everything, I won't have the opportunity."

"You'll do better than that. . . ."

He went on:

"Are you preparing yourself for the great moment, in a fitting manner?"

"What great moment?"

"The night of Maligâth."

"Oh. Is it really so remarkable?"

"There you go again, acting high and mighty!"

"No, honestly! But it seems I've been doing such a lot of things already! What else is there to discover?"

"The joys of *number*. There's a *lot* of them, you know, burning to explode inside you! The word's out that you'll be there. The very thought that the one whom they had thought the most inaccessible among women will make herself available to all comers seems to have gripped the males of this country like a fever!"

"Now, really! Is that your doing?"

"Well, surely it would be remiss to deprive those who most desire you of the torture and the delight of two days of fantasizing and despairing, by turns? The expectation of possessing you, isn't it a form of happiness that's almost equal to the fulfillment of that expectation? You yourself, aren't you trembling and dreaming, too?"

"After what you've just told me, my dominant emotion is fear! I have no desire to see a veritable horde of rutting males fighting over my body. The very idea that those men, at this very moment, may be repeating my name to themselves. . . . And the things they must be saying . . . !"

Emmanuelle heard Mario laughing. She grew angry, to the point of tears:

"You think that is amusing, don't you, to poke fun at me among your friends? I help you to be the success of the party, as you announce to them: 'That little cunt, you know, the one that's just arrived from France? God, I've really worked her over: what a silly little goose she was! Now that I've had my way with her, I'm passing her on to all of you. She's still pretty fresh. And in return I hope you guys keep me in mind when you get into your next one!'"

"So I've had my way with you, have I?" Mario said gently.

As no reply was forthcoming, he went on:

"Except for that point, and your tone, which doesn't catch my conversational style at all, plus the fact that I haven't asked for any compensation, you certainly do get the picture. I've taken great pains to describe the freshness of your flesh, experienced by so few men as yet. One day you'll be covered with another kind of glory, more desirable exactly for having had a hundred lovers: but at this moment it is your innocence that rouses the spirits! But it is necessary for you to savor, in advance, the masterpiece which you'll make possible. Your as-yet-adolescent body, known only by your spouse and a few others in some insignificant apprentice tricks, will, tomorrow night, and for the first time, be pierced and exhausted by a great number of men, to whom it has been promised as a very special and most precious treat."

Mario's tone underwent a sudden change:

"You're still a virgin, Emmanuelle! But after tomorrow night you won't be one any longer, not in my opinion. It'll be such an initiation for you, tomorrow night will! You'll get to know something far more exciting than any Holy Grail! And you want me to remain quiet about it? You don't want those who are in charge of this sacred experience to prepare themselves for it? Oh! but you're gravely mistaken if you think that we sit around laughing at you, or that we talk about your body in a gross manner. There are few great things in this world that ever get freely offered to men: make no mistake, they know how to recognize them. You ought to understand, from what I've been telling you, that it's no cabal of indignity and derision I've dedicated myself to subject you to, but that it is a great honor. I'm not delivering you up to anybody! It's to *you* that I am offering a sacred rite, with its assembly, its procession, its etiquette, its solemnities, and its libations. Is it possible that you don't comprehend this? Have I been spending all those days with you to no avail?"

Emmanuelle feels repentant. Let Mario rest assured: she would doubt no longer! She is in no danger of backsliding into ignorance. She'll prove it to him the next night, at Maligâth. Let him tell his friends anything he wants to tell them about her, to help them enjoy her even more. She gives him her consent. Her body is ready for their bodies. She desires them all. She wants them all.

Having thus completed the long conversation, Emmanuelle goes to bed. The big bed seems very empty to her. The visions Mario has evoked keep passing and passing again on the screen behind her closed eyelids. Despite what she has told him, the anxiety's still there. Her nerves are still on edge. She tries to fall asleep: time to think about those tribulations tomorrow. Right now she just wants some rest and oblivion. But it's all in vain. The sense of apprehension keeps her awake.

Well, she knows what'll work. She starts caressing herself. But, to her surprise, the orgasm eludes her. As far as she can remember, this has never happened before. Her fingers grow impatient, but her mind is elsewhere: a new temptation, of a previously unknown taste, both sweet and bitter, rises within her, feels hot in her throat. She tries to negate it. She resists. Quite a while. Until the struggle starts boring her and tires her: and with an aching feeling of abandon, a voluptuous softening of all parts, the heart beating with joy at accepted desire, she switches off the light, and slowly slides over to the edge of bed. She lets her left leg dangle over the side. Her cunt is pointing toward the door. Her hand moves toward the service bell on the bedside table. Then her fingers let go of it again, and her body spreads out, her breasts rise with a great deep breath of abandon, as she hears the houseboy opening the lattice door.

4
The Night of Maligâth

The body is a great intellectual system,
it is a complex structure with but one meaning,
it is a war, and it is peace,
it is the flock, and it is the shepherd.
                              —Friedrich Nietzsche,
                              Thus Spake Zarathustra

The long Ionian tunic, finely pleated, Emmanuelle is wearing is a very pale jade-green, so light that it looks almost white. One of her shoulders is bare: on the other, a golden brooch in the shape of an owl holds the material together. Under her breasts, a chain with large, flat links holds up the tunic, unadorned by any embroidery or decoration: but between the breasts, holding down the material, there is a heavy pendant of old gold, with a square hole in the middle, engraved with animal designs. It looks like a coin of some long since vanished realm. A little below the elbow a wide "slave" bracelet, studded with emeralds, encircles her right arm.

"Well, I'm going to my own holocaust—I thought Iphigenia's getup would be most appropriate."

"You look stunning," Mario says. "But, a little too proper. . . ."

Without a word, Emmanuelle moves in front of a low floor lamp: weak as its light is, it is sufficient to make her legs show as clearly as if the tunic were glass. Mario still looks dissatisfied. Emmanuelle smiles, raises one knee: the robe opens of its own accord, gaping wide from belt to ground. Thus, on the dance floor, her legs will flash forth in all their naked beauty, and anyone can feel her up with the greatest of ease! The amber-skinned flesh of her belly, and farther down, that most luscious aperture of her body, are accessible to one and all, any given moment.

"And look!"

Her black pubic triangle is glorious with a multitude of tiny pearls. It has taken dear patient Ea four hours to attach them, one by one, to the rebellious wool.

"Well, that's the finest jewelry setting I've ever seen," says Mario, with approval.

"Yes? And what do you think of the top half?"

Emmanuelle lifts both arms high. From armpit to hip, the upper part of her dress is wide open. Looking at Emmanuelle from one side, whenever she raises an arm or bends forward, Mario realizes that one will see the full profile of her bare breasts. It should be easy for dance partners to please their palms by slipping their hands through these lateral vents.

Mario is amazed that Emmanuelle's clothes closet provides her with such a phenomenal outfit. Or is it a new acquisition, made during the last couple of days? The dressmaker must have had a very exciting time. . . . But his fair pupil chides him: surely he ought to know enough about female wiles to realize that this chiffon is normally worn over some opaque "foundation"? Thus, all Emmanuelle needed to do, was to leave the other half in her closet. . . . "You should burn it!" growls Mario. "All garments are an outrage, if they aren't designed to extol the glory of nudity."

"You'll have to go through my wardrobe one day. I'll let you burn every item that displeases you."

"I'll be glad to do that," Mario promises, looking somber.

Maligâth is a conglomeration of marble edifices, separated by gardens with fountains and archways, lit up by parchment-covered lanterns and the moon, a cool, magical radiance. The grounds are terraced, and one ascends stairways bordered with hibiscus hedges and white columns, and, beyond them, wide, greenhouse-dotted lawns, the expanse of which makes the sounds of the city quite remote. The falling of the fountains' water jets, faraway notes of a slow dance, and the almost imperceptible counterpoint of human voices—these fill the ear, in the grounds of Maligâth.

A strong perfume, emanating from big, fleshy-looking flowers—giant gardenias planted in great Chinese vases—envelops the newcomers, guided by a mere garland of rush lights burning with a purple flame to the corridors and halls, where they seem to find themselves the first arrivals.

There is no host there to receive them. Or is the reception room somewhere else, have Mario and Emmanuelle taken a wrong turn, back there in the realm of water and shadow? Or are they, perhaps, really early?

"Who has been invited?" Emmanuelle says, in a half-whisper.

"All that Bangkok has to offer in the way of beauty and intelligence," says Mario. "Only the elect—those truly intelligent, truly beautiful."

"Are you sure *we* are that?"

Mario grins.

I wonder what the master of this realm is like? Emmanuelle asks herself. He must be powerful, and certainly demanding. Perhaps even perverse, some kind of maniac? Isn't it sheer madness to take such risks, in such a strange place? Does she really know what to expect? Perhaps the Prince and his henchmen will never let her go back to Jean?

Well, there is still time to turn around. No one has seen her, the great park is empty, there are no guards to be seen. But there's Mario. . . . What would he think—and what wouldn't he have to say!—about her timidity?

So she keeps on following him, as in a nightmare. She feels certain that she is doing the wrong thing: she ought to have the courage to run away. . . .

Now she sees windows, lit with a dim, rosy light. And were those peals of laughter she just thought she heard, or were they screams? All doors are closed, there is no one outside at all, for instance, on this terrace that they are crossing this very moment—which would seem such an attractive spot: the night is just a trifle humid.

"Mario," she murmurs, but so quietly that he (no doubt) does not hear.

They enter a small room. Three men and a woman are sitting on a couch, side by side. Emmanuelle is relieved not to encounter the Laocoon-like group of bodies engaged in plural activities that she has half expected to see, right there in the entrance hall. The woman is quite young. Her jet-black eyes are extraordinarily long and slanted toward her temples, in a serene face. Her hair is done up in a casque, with a thick fringe over the forhead, evocative of ancient Egypt. A black fur coat accentuates her petiteness. There is not the slightest hint of immodesty about her appearance, and Emmanuelle becomes painfully aware of her own blatancy. Maybe it has all been a big practical joke of Mario's? Mario says something, in Siamese. The young girl replies, without so much as a smile: it seems she has given him the information he requires, for he propels Emmanuelle out of the room with utmost determination.

"Where are we going?" she says plaintively. "Who was that? Isn't she a bit young to be here?"

"The soirée is in her honor. She's the Prince's only daughter. It's her fifteenth birthday."

Before she has time to consider this interesting fact, they enter a much larger hall. It is dimly lit, and there are a few couples dancing. They don't even turn their heads to look at the newcomers. A maid comes up, gives them their drinks. A fruity-tasting concoction, smooth and very strong.

"I suppose this is some kind of love-philter?" Emmanuelle jokes, to reassure herself.

(The Siamese girl is naked but for a coarse linen loincloth, hugging her hips, leaving her navel and the tops of her thighs bare; Emmanuelle lets her eyes roam approvingly over the antelope-like legs, the apple-shaped breasts.)

"I'm sure it is," Mario answers. "But then, practically everything one eats and drinks, in these parts, is some kind of aphrodisiac."

It was really dark. . . . God, I hope he doesn't leave me alone here! Emmanuelle sighed. At that moment, a man walked up to them: he seemed to know Mario, and Mario introduced him to her. She forgot his name instantly. He bowed, impersonally, courteously, and asked her to dance with him. Reluctantly, Emmanuelle followed him to the floor, holding the folds of her dress together, one hand on thigh.

He was tall, had to bend down a little, to keep his face level with Emmanuelle's. He wanted to know how old she was, where she had passed her childhood; he wanted her to tell him about her tastes, her preferences. Did she like to read?

Did she enjoy going to the theater? Did she have any favorite authors? At first, her replies were none too friendly. She felt rather put upon, by all those questions. But then she started enjoying the way her partner was leading her in the dance. She didn't want to chat about literature, she wanted to give in to the rhythm. The mere act of dancing was reassuring, a link back to the known world. She felt a little calmer already, held by those steady arms.

Soon she realized that she, herself, was pressing her body against his, provoking him. It wasn't that she felt particularly attracted to him: she simply responded to a conditioned reflex—dancing, her partner's erection, and even his coming had always appeared to her as interconnected and inseparable events. Her Parisian admirers (who hadn't had the balls to take her to their beds, whenever the absence of her husband would have made this possible) had, however, been marvelously eager to engage in such pastimes. It wasn't only that she dedicated herself to them with ideal docility, her body reacted almost in spite of herself, as soon as it found itself in the required circumstance. It did not have to be coaxed or convinced by the partner's desire or even by her own consciousness: it knew, automatically, what to do in order to bring the dance to its proper conclusion, which was to make them come.

Until now, Emmanuelle had always found this kind of libertinage quite satisfying in all respects. It allowed her to appear as a woman of the world without obliging her to commit formal adultery. Her own senses were sufficiently keen to permit her to find in such vertical activity a pleasure equal to that accorded to the partner; it was obviously tainted with furtiveness, factitiousness, but that very taint made it that much more spicy. . . .

That evening, resuming familiar gestures, she rubbed up against the guest of Maligâth, felt his cock harden and press up against her belly. She felt much more at ease doing it than she thought she would have felt confronting what she imagined to be the mysterious caprices of an Oriental sovereign, and she wasn't far from regarding her proximity to this unknown companion as some kind of refuge and defense.

He, on his part, seemed to enjoy the talents of his partner. He let her take him right up to the point of spasm, but withdrew just as she was about to give the finishing touch. It annoyed her. She couldn't understand how a man could reject a chance like that, even if his intention was to save his spunk for some better occasion. Why should he be so mean?

Appearing absolutely certain of the rightness of his action, the recalcitrant fellow held up Emmanuelle's ring-finger, adorned with a fine cluster of diamonds, and asked her if she was married.

"Of course I am," she answered sullenly, as if he had cast some aspersion on her femininity.

Oh, yes? Very good. And had she had any lovers?

"I've only been married for a year!"

But seriously, she asked herself, did she have any lovers? Her first thought was, well yes, at least *one*: Mario. But then the notion seemed quite amusing to her: did such a thing exist, a lover who has never made love to you? But if it was making love that conferred this title upon a man, then her true lovers were those strangers in the plane, the *sam-lo*. Did the young boy in the votive temple count as well? Then why not those young men she had jerked off while dancing with them? If ejaculation is the event that turns a man into your lover, then there really wasn't any reason not to include all the men who had engaged in quiet masturbation while contemplating her!

Visualizing them at it, she had to laugh out loud, all her worries gone:

"Tell me, dear sir, what exactly is a 'lover'?"

He smiled politely, thinking she just wished to be cute, and not crediting her with too much wit. But then Emmanuelle went on to explain her train of thought, not omitting any of the intimate details, quite amazed at her own sudden ability to confide, so meticulously and with such a supreme absence of embarrassment, to someone who really was a total stranger, secrets she had not revealed before—not to Jean, nor to Marie-Anne (and that *was* even more surprising), nor even to Mario.

Now her partner seemed genuinely interested. He started pressing her for further details, and she related them with great frankness. And he himself replied most obligingly to the questions she asked him, despite their quite intentional scabrousness.

"I wonder if you aren't attaching excessive importance to a mere question of vocabulary," he remarked, finally (they had been talking and dancing quite a while now). "Is it so important to know whether to call a man a lover or not, depending on whether he has made love to you in this particular fashion or that? If you ask me, I think that that little Siamese fellow was your lover, all right, and so were the passengers on the plane, and the rickshaw-runner, too." (Was it a mere omission, or was he being discreet? he did not mention Mario at all.) "But, well, whom would *you* call your lovers?"

"I guess you're right," Emmanuelle said, looking thoughtful. "And my dance partners in Paris?"

"That, I think, is a little different. The pleasure you provided them was, in a way, a rather twisted form of refusal! It may well be that it is some such *intention* that counts. When you were lubricating them, weren't you thinking something along those lines—that you were really being faithful to your husband? Whereas that was not the case, I assume, while you were caressing that young Siamese?'

"But then I don't feel I'm being an adulteress when I'm making love to girls, either: how do you explain that difference?"

He didn't care to explain. He had obviously reached the point at which theory ceased to be interesting: instead of providing Emmanuelle with brilliantly reasoned clarifications, he just squeezed her, so vehemently that she, too, was soon distracted from her ratiocinations. She kissed him, returned his embrace, and thought of nothing but fucking. She stretched out her naked leg, and he squeezed it between his own. He started groping for her breasts, for her cunt. They were hardly dancing any more, but sometimes jostling other couples. Were these all engaged in similar fondlings?

Quickly, Emmanuelle recovers her awareness of the surrounding world, momentarily obscured by her memories. Strange thing, the other women dancing nearby (there are perhaps five, six) resemble her a lot: for a moment, Emmanuelle gains the hallucinatory impression that she is looking into a many-faceted mirror. They are all beautiful, clad in transparent veils, with long, black hair, and shoulders as bare as her own. Their thighs glide between their partners' legs, to the measure of a slow music, emanating from who knows where, that moves them in analogous circles. They are looking at Emmanuelle with gentle curiosity, turning their eyes away as soon as their gaze encounters hers.

Emmanuelle thinks it would be a pleasure to watch one of them in the act of making love, but her partner has decided that it is, in fact, she who is going to provide that spectacle. He leads her, without disengaging himself, toward a roofed-over terrace that runs all along the outside of the hall. There are other guests standing around. He sits down on a low stool, upholstered in green silk, and pulls Emmanuelle toward himself until she stands facing him, her legs pressed against his knees. He parts her Greek robe, uncovers the long legs, parts them with his hands and makes her stand astraddle his thighs. Then he makes her bend her knees, to move toward him: when the moist cunt touches his prick, he inserts it, using his fingers, then takes hold of her buttocks and makes her envelop it completely.

He says:

"Now ask me to make you come."

"Yes," Emmanuelle says, in a hoarse whisper. "I want to come."

"Louder! So everybody can hear."

She bends backward, shouts: "Make me come!"

He insists:

"Again! Go on!"

She obeys, attracting an increasing number of spectators, who stand watching her bounce up and down, then hear her cry out, groaning with pleasure:

"Oh, oh, I'm coming! I'm coming! Oh, it's so *good*. . . ."

When she finally stops, he holds on to her, limp and soft in his arms, until she has returned to her senses. He stays right inside her, makes her move again, making her breasts bobble up and down, thrusting into her, twice, thrice, twenty times. A groan arises from Emmanuelle's throat. The man bites her shoulder, explodes inside her. She feels him spurting into her, and once again she soars like an eagle.

One of the spectators asks Emmanuelle's partner to let him have her now. She gets up. She has neither time nor sense enough to ask herself if she'll miss her lover of a moment ago, to whom she has told so many things: she finds herself giving her hand to the newcomer, following him into an antechamber opening up to their right. A houseboy appears, hands them refreshments.

"*Voilà*," she says to herself, munching on a *gâteau*, "I've made it with a total stranger. And now I'm going to do it again, with another one. I really don't know what's so terribly evolutionary about that."

Her new master stops, under a ceiling light, and inspects his prize with satisfied mien.

"I've been looking for you for over an hour!" he sighs.

"For me, you mean, me in particular?" Emmanuelle asks, genuinely surprised. "I wouldn't have thought there was any shortage of talent on these premises."

"No, I guess there's plenty. But I came here for you."

"Oh, I see now. Mario's little publicity campaign."

"You're not just like any woman."

"What's so different about me?"

"I still can't believe that you are here. That I can see you, stark naked, through your dress. . . ."

Suddenly Emmanuelle feels fed up with this crooner. She remarks:

"You can see me more naked than this any morning, at the beach."

Her eyes are already roaming, searching for less tedious company. Where's Mario? How boorish of him to leave her here, at the mercy of imbeciles!

She makes a getaway, walks straight ahead. She passes groups of people who seem to have nothing better to do than to wander aimlessly through the corridors, not talking, not paying any attention to her. It seemed as if there were two quite distinct brotherhoods conducting their reunions within these walls, each one according to its own rules, totally ignoring the other. Emmanuelle remembers having experienced a similar impression at a visit to a castle on the Loire, in the company of other tourists: they walked along from hall to hall, admiring, in docile concord with their guide's predilections, the great tapestries, the ancestral portraits, while quite close by, not paying any attention to them, there moved a bespectacled group from some congress of learned individuals. Then Emmanuelle had suddenly chanced upon the proprietors of the domain, sitting out on the lawn, drinking tea, not casting a single glance in her direction. This time, though, she was a member of the elite gathering. . . . It was easy to tell who looked as if they had come here as tourists; but where were the hosts?

If the truth be known, she felt so little yearning to meet her host that she even thought she might be able to avoid being introduced to him altogether: and wouldn't it, perhaps, really be better to just fade away quietly, without any fuss? The evening had none of the festive air Mario had promised her. . . .

A group of strangers—two men in dinner jackets, a young woman in an evening gown—stopped and tried to communicate with her in several languages at once: finally, one of them managed to explain, in rather good French, that they were looking for a pretty girl to take along, out of the palace, to make up a "foursome" with them. Emmanuelle felt tempted. But curiously, at the very moment that an opportunity to leave presented itself, she began to feel reluctant. It seemed to her that she would be committing a faux pas if she went away with these young people, pleasing as they appeared.

While she was still hesitating, another trio arrived from the opposite direction and, without a word, dragged her along at a brisk pace through several rooms in a row. She had no time to protest. From a half-open door in front of them came peals of laughter and the sound of music. They entered, and the tableau before them forced an exclamation of surprise from Emmanuelle's lips.

On a fur-covered divan, as wide as it was long, reclines Ariane de Saynes, a big grin on her face as always, between two males as stark naked as herself.

When she hears Emmanuelle's little cry, Ariane raises herself on one elbow, not seeming in the least surprised to find her here, and proceeds to hail her exuberantly.

"O my dear immaculate virgin, come and join us! My God, what a lovely outfit that is! But hurry up, take it off."

In her right hand, Ariane is holding, with perfect grace, the erect member of one of her neighbors on the divan. Her left breast serves as a cushion for the other fellow's penis. All three are smiling amiably at Emmanuelle.

"Do have some of the mango cake," Ariane urges her. "I'll bet you're absolutely famished. And take some champagne, too. It's one of Daddy's finest vintages."

Emmanuelle's eyes are smarting from the sudden brightness: ever since her arrival she has been moving around in dimly lit halls and passages. Once and for all, Maligâth has become a realm of shadows in her mind. But now she finds herself quite suddenly in a room so brilliantly illuminated that she asks herself if it isn't really a theatrical stage or a movie set she has stumbled into, glaring with arc lights and spots. The impression is so compelling that Emmanuelle can't help looking up to make sure the place has a real ceiling: the walls are high enough to excuse her doubts. The decor of the place is as weird as can be imagined: a Klee canvas above a Buddhist temple portal from Sukhothai; a blind wall, entirely shrouded in white; in the middle of another one, an Etruscan frieze; yet a third one, covered from top to bottom and over all its width with precious tapestries, overlapping and crowding each other, entirely concealing any doors there may be in that wall. A bundle of long poles, inlaid or covered with gold, which Emmanuelle takes to be halberd shafts but which really are oars from the royal galley, hangs in precarious equilibrium above the monumental couch on which Ariane and her swains are reclining. There are no other pieces of furniture in the room, except for a profusion of chests of dark wood, some leather-covered and others fashioned out of bronze: these serve as seats and tables, and the guests who brought Emmanuelle here have already arranged themselves on them, poured drinks, and now sit there looking at her.

"Welcome to my humble abode," says a voice behind her, in an accent she has never heard before.

Well, this is it, she says to herself, feeling more dead than alive: it's the Prince himself! She doesn't dare turn around; he walks around her, stands in front of her, scrutinizes her, with a little frown: her face, her breasts, her abdomen, her legs, all the way down to her feet. Again, she feels like a contestant of sorts. Then the thought strikes her—what if he is merely wondering who I am, and what I'm doing here? She explains, in a voice reflecting stage fright:

"I came here with the Marchese Serghini. He told me—"

"I know," the Prince interrupts her. "I thank you for having accepted my invitation. Are you having a good time?"

She smiles politely, mute once again. He goes on piercing her with his critical regard. She casts around for something to say, to avoid the pronouncing of the sentence. But her host gestures her to direct her attention to the great couch, and she obeys, without so much as a peep.

One of the men is now penetrating Ariane, while the other one goes on rubbing his prick against her breasts. The young Countess undulates, contracts, vibrates, and stretches: every muscle in her body seems to be in perpetual motion.

"Aren't you tempted to go and join them?" the Prince wants to know.

Not in the least, but she does not dare to say that.

"I'm sure you'll feel more at your ease if you take that dress off."

Without having to be told twice, she unbuckles her belt, looks around for a place to put it. Her host holds out his hand. . . . Then the brooch holding up her dress. In one long wave motion the *chitón* slides off her body, surrounding her ankles in glaucous foam. . . . She retains her other jewelry and stands there, waiting, very upright, tense, and touching.

The Prince compliments her. What is he going to do to me? she asks herself, her mouth dry.

The non-penetrating partner of Ariane's gets up and takes Emmanuelle by the hand. She follows him, lets him stretch her out on her back, arrange her legs so that they hang over the edge of the divan and her black pubis with its constellations of pearls juts out over the edge of the white fur cover. Then he gets down on his knees and starts licking her. She closes her eyes, abandoning herself to the best of her ability, telling herself to concentrate on the caress, and soon she is nothing but a voluptuous body that has forgotten all its fears and alarms and once again sings its familiar paean:

"Oh, oh! I'm coming!"

He goes on licking until she has spent all her breath, given up all struggle. But then it is she who pulls him up and on top of herself: she feels the weight of his cock against her thighs: she works with her hands to make him enter into her. He accepts and takes her, most attentively, holding back his own pleasure until she has again reached the point where she is uttering her long, ecstatic yells; and then the fragrance of sperm seems to rise within her to delight her tastebuds. . . .

But a number of others are upon her now, dragging the man off her, grabbing her buttocks, playing with her breasts, pulling her off the cushions. She hears a couple of brief commands in a foreign language. Someone translates, tells her to raise her legs toward the ceiling: she complies, then folds the top of her thighs against her breasts. A dry, brutal phallus is trying to force its way in between her buttocks: the pain makes her cry out. She turns her head to the right, to the left, calls for help. Ariane comes close to her. Emmanuelle takes her hand:

"Oh, no! Get them off me! I don't want to . . ."

At the same moment, a wave of bodies carries her assailant away: she hastens to stretch out her legs and to embrace her girlfriend.

Ariane whispers in her ear:

"This gentleman" (she points at the one Emmanuelle had seen, only a little while ago, pumping Ariane herself) "would like to put it in your mouth; but he's too timid to ask you. You don't mind, do you?"

Emmanuelle shakes her head, affirmatively.

Ariane's body leaves her and is replaced by a male body stretching out on top of hers, with all its weight. Lips take possession of her own, crushing them, the tongue penetrating between her teeth, running its tip over her palate, over her own tongue, insistent, hard, bringing tears of pleasure to her eyes. She feels herself going, thinks she is ready to come once again, just by kissing, then refuses such sensual extravagance, fights against her abandon, her own submissiveness and weakness. She gives in to it after all, lets herself be overwhelmed by the sweetness of consent, of being passive, given over, abandoned to liberating joy.

The man looks pleased with her. He holds her by the shoulders, his hands like talons.

"Now then," he murmurs. "You feel my belly on your belly? And now, how it's moving upward? I'll move up all the way to your breasts: and then, later, up to your face. First I'll shove my prick into your tits. Not *between* them, you see: *into* them, into that lovely thick tissue, one after the other—I'll stick it right through them, I'll make the milk flow from your glands. Will you let me do that?"

Emmanuelle does not reply. He goes on:

"And after I've taken your tits, I'll stick it into your throat, going in through your mouth. With all the muscles at my disposal I'll shove it into your mouth and force you to unclench your teeth, to open your lips, I'll make you choke on it, so fast you won't even have time to cry out for help. I'll hold your flanks between my knees, I'll go up and down, I'll screw it into you, I'll make it bruise your tongue, your uvula—and I'll push it even beyond that, all the way down back into your cunt, but from *above*! I'll fuck you in the mouth, exactly as if I was fucking your cunt! I'll feel your tears splashing onto my belly, laving my prick! But I can already see them coming, I had better hurry up."

She has to open her mouth so wide it starts hurting even before he is able to insert his truly enormous rod. Quite obviously, he is running out of time: before he can proceed to any of those phenomenal tortures, his spunk flies, thick and copious, pints of it, accompanied by great groans of gratification.

"Go on, gulp it down," he urges her, in a croaking voice. "Use your mouth. Don't move. I'm going to stay in you awhile, I haven't finished yet, I'll just go on coming. . . ."

Emmanuelle, her face squeezed flat by the heavy abdomen, becomes aware that they are spreading her legs again. She tries to resist, but in vain: someone she can't even see rips into her all the way, possesses her without further ado. Throat and vulva occupied thus, she starts going into panic: she is lost now, nothing can save her any more: she really *is* going to die. . . . The very next minute she is chiding herself for such prissy apprehensions: if she could, she would cry out, but in exultation and triumph!

What do you know, she congratulates herself. Here I am, being fucked by two men at once! What a memorable experience. It's like a second defloration. The rite of initiation that Mario was talking about . . . I'm being cleansed, and publicly, of the last little stains of innocence. She had to chuckle, in the midst of her voluptuous enjoyment. She was celebrating her true glory: it is over, it's over once and for all—I'm not a virgin any more!

Joyfully, she wanted to hug and kiss those who had brought about such promotion; like a friend, on both cheeks. In her enthusiasm she had completely forgotten that her mouth was still captive: once again, she forgot to breathe, choked, and started to sputter, loudly, so that the man took pity on her and withdrew. She didn't even notice her other lover coming into her. She found herself again, confused, totally exhausted, in their arms.

A little while later, after hands that weren't always easy to identify had lifted her up and carried her to another place, chancing, in the process, to come to rest on one or another portion of her anatomy, kneading it or poking into it, Emmanuelle was able to recognize the one who had made love to her mouth.

She had never seen a man as hairy as this one: he was furry all over, with a real fur so thick it completely obscured the skin on his legs, his belly, his chest, his shoulders; where the fur was a little less dense, the flesh appeared tanned, but lusterless.

The knotty muscles are those of a prizefighter or a butcher. Thick eyebrows, grown together between his eyes, extend upward almost to the equally black hairline.

He's quite something, Emmanuelle thinks, then asks him: "Where are you from?"

"From Georgia. I'll take you there."

Emmanuelle estimates his age to be about forty, give or take a couple of years. She tells him this. He laughs, he's used to it:

"You're far off the mark, my dear. I'm sixty-four."

Emmanuelle is amazed. How horrible! No, it's impossible. . . . He *can't* be that old! Surely it can't be *her*, either, so young, lying there this very moment, naked, stretched out on the naked body of a man older than her own grandfather! Her granddad, a Commander of the Legion of Honor, with the silvery head of hair to match such dignity. Has she ever imagined, even in her most extravagant reveries, that she would one day be making love to him? Well, but that's what's happening!

This man who is, among all those she has had the pleasure to meet recently, the one whom she finds the most exciting. . . . She doesn't know whether she ought to feel ashamed of her inclinations, or simply doubt the evidence of her own senses. On the other hand, why should she go on worrying about it, to the point of an *idée fixe*? He's made good love to her, she feels at ease on top of his hairy chest; what better ways are there of telling the good from the bad? He has made me happy, and that's enough reason for having given myself to him, she reassures herself. Then, a little sigh: I'd sure like to have a grandfather who looks like this one, I'd love to be his mistress. She sees herself at the theater, or dining out, in a low-cut evening dress, showing off her legs, on the arm of her decorated escort in his cape of pure silk, his white—no, black—hair. . . . Her actual lover's voice brings her back from the phantasmagoric reverie of sexagenarian incest.

"Let me suck your tits."

She gets up on elbows and knees and moves her breasts up to where her left nipple hovers above his bushy mustache, then bends down a little to let the little round point, swollen with blood, descend to those red lips whose kisses she has enjoyed so much.

Ariane's face reappears under Emmanuelle's right arm, addresses the hairy man:

"Would you like to share her with me?"

"With pleasure."

"I know she loves being shared."

That's true, Emmanuelle admits to herself: I do think that is true!

The nipple of one breast in the Georgian's mouth, the other in Ariane's, she gives in to her body, lapped by waves that are offering her up to the wind: a thousand heads of spume, a thousand tongues of seaweed, a thousand sweet reefs caress her hull, freighted to the brim with a treasure cargo of precious stones and spices, loaded into her by men with golden skins, on unknown shores. . . .

There were some new arrivals, and Emmanuelle took a short break from love-making in order to chitchat. She had regained all her composure, did not even remember her demoralized state, fleeting as it had been, an hour before this time. She found it perfectly normal to be stark naked in this salon, frequented by what seemed to be a fine class of people, after all: the majority had remained in full evening regalia, buttoned up to their chins and quite remote, it seemed, from any ribald intentions. And why not leave it that way, she asked herself, philosophically. Let those who liked to be dressed up, dress up, and those who'd rather go naked, go naked! It was as simple as that.

Yet, perspectives kept shifting in this palace, in a manner that frequently made Emmanuelle doubt if she really knew not only where she was but what time sphere all these events were taking place in. The mysteries she was being initiated into were perhaps contemporaneous with some Orphic or Dionysiac antiquity, while seeming to take place in the future. Now and again she caught glimpses of non-terrestrial cities where naked women walked upon streets of metal, among men in spacesuits and others clothed in black.

Two of the guests dressed in white tie and tails, without losing any of their proper composure, implored her to lie down on her back, very straight, and then persuaded Ariane to get down on all fours above her, with her pubis right above Emmanuelle's mouth. The latter told herself that they were then going to ask her and her friend to perform a classical position (which annoyed her a little, after all the games she had been playing with Ariane the last couple of days), but that was not the case at all. One of the men produced, out of his immaculately pressed trousers, a long and sturdy cock, which he proceeded to introduce into Ariane's slit, fucking her right in front of Emmanuelle's eyes: from where she was lying, she couldn't possibly miss the least detail.

For a duration that seemed to approach infinity, Emmanuelle lay watching the shaft sink in right up to the testicles, then saw it reappear, plunge back in, and so on and on, with a deliberateness that excited her enormously. Never in her life had she experienced any spectacle as powerfully aphrodisiac as this one, performed right in front of her face. She could hear the slurping noises in the vagina, well lubricated by the prick's steady and magisterial in-and-out, and she waited for the great spray to rain upon her face. She could have gone on watching forever: the excitement of her senses was so superb that she cried out, shaken by tremors of voluptuousness, while no one even touched her: she didn't need the assistance of her own caresses to be the first one of the three to obtain orgasm.

However, after her initial spasm, the second visitor (who had not intervened until now) took hold of her right hand and firmly directed it to her clitoris, to make her masturbate. Then he opened a little case, took out his camera, and filmed the scene. Emmanuelle was totally incapable of paying attention to that: she had eyes only for the fascinating motions of copulation.

When the moment arrived, the rod withdrew, brusquely, and hastened to dip down into Emmanuelle's waiting mouth, discharging its sperm into it, aromatic with the flavors of Ariane.

Emmanuelle was still swallowing, when a hand brushed her own aside and took a firm hold on her genitals, as if to reserve them to itself. At first, she thought it was Ariane: but no, the grip was too virile. Well then, it had to be the other man in full evening dress. She raised her head and peered down, between her breasts: it was neither one nor the other, but it was some-one she had met before. He had then been wearing a naval officer's uniform, at a reception given by the Ambassador. He had been one of those guests who had been deeply excited by the extent of her décolletage when she had made her entrance. She remembered the stammers that betrayed the conflict created between their desires and their good manners, and that memory pleased her a great deal. Here I am now, she thought, exposed to one and all, without the slightest covering—and here's one of them, looking much less embarrassed than back there!

Ariane seemed worn out, reclining on her side. Emmanuelle sat up, gracefully.

"Sailors never have a tan: I wonder why?" she thought out loud.

"Next to you, I really should feel ashamed of the pallor of my skin," the man admitted. "But then we men don't have to provide that kind of beauty."

"What *do* you have to provide?"

"The law."

Emmanuelle looked for traces of the timidity and deference the same protagonist had shown only four days before this encounter. There were none to be seen: nothing but smiling strength, and a manner indicating that he was used to having his orders obeyed. She found it most stimulating.

"Well, what do I have to do, to live up to my role?" she asked.

"Nothing out of the ordinary. Just submit, that's all." His tone was matter-of-fact. No answer was required.

Nevertheless, Emmanuelle felt impelled to say:

"That's all I could ask for."

Yet, suddenly, she wanted more than that: to render her submission complete, she wanted it to be public, proclaimed. She wanted him to dispose not only of her flesh, but of her reputation as well. Thus, his possessing her would not remain a secret of this alcove, but would become, for her masters, a subject of glorification in their forum.

She asked him:

"Will you tell everybody that you've fucked me?"

"But, of course . . . not!" the officer said, defensively, and obviously surprised.

"But why not? Isn't it nice, for a man, to be able to talk about the girls he's fucked?"

"Not about women like you."

"You mean I wouldn't be sufficient cause for pride?"

He merely laughed, uncertain as he was as to what kind of quarrel she was picking. He dimly suspected that she wanted to subject him to some kind of test, try his reliability in some very special way, not of this jaded world—nor of its times. They were now sitting on the immense couch, facing each other, Emmanuelle hugging her knees, he with his legs to one side. No parts of their bodies were touching.

"Well then?" she insisted. "If you're not ashamed of me, why make a secret of it! As for me, I'll be flattered if you go around telling your mates that you've fucked me."

"Are you really serious?" He stared at Emmanuelle, seemed to conclude that she wasn't joking. This only increased his perplexity.

"You are . . . indeed strange!" he mumbled. "I would have expected just the opposite. . . . Is it some form of exhibitionism?"

Emmanuelle made an involuntary sound which could, in a pinch, be taken as an affirmative response. She didn't think that the term really covered what she had in mind; but, after all, this wasn't the place for embarking on subtle analytical conversation. On the other hand, the passive eroticism implied by the word "exhibitionism" did not please her.

"All right," said the young officer, "if that's what you like, I'll do it."

He realized that he found the prospect exciting. The pleasure he would experience in fucking Emmanuelle would return to his mind every time he'd relate it to others, while making it perfectly clear that it was she, herself, who had asked him to be that indiscreet. His desire for her waxed so violent that he felt like getting on top of her then and there: but, no! there was something even better. To make quite sure, he asked, not yet entirely over the hump of his amazement:

'You're saying that I should tell them your real name?"

"Yes, please."

There was no doubting it: the idea that her new-found lubricity would become the talk of the town obviously made this lady's juices flow: a kind of perverse refinement, evidently.

"You're a weird one," he said, rather rudely. "Ever since you came to Bangkok you've remained faithful to your husband— perhaps even a little *too* faithful, for the taste of some! And tonight, romping about in the buff, you hurl yourself from one extreme to the other. What's the reason for such a dramatic transformation?"

'You're quite mistaken," Emmanuelle said, calmly. "I have always been this way."

She really didn't believe that any transformation had taken place. She certainly did not feel she had "mutated" in a single night. True, Mario had been helping her, not so much to change as to grow up, to become conscious of her right to be herself: perhaps even of her *duty* to be herself—but Emmanuelle much perferred not to think of love as a duty: on that point, her preceptor had not convinced her at all. . . .

The man of the sea went on looking at her, saying nothing; but as soon as she seemed to want to make some further statement, he jumped to his feet.

"We're wasting time with all this small talk," he said, quite the man-of-action now. "Come on!"

He took her arm, holding it in a strong grip above the elbow.

"Where are you taking her?" Ariane called out. "Don't take her away from us! She's ours."

"For the time being, she's mine," the young naval officer corrected her.

"You'll be back?" Ariane shouted after them.

Emmanuelle turned, made a reassuring sign.

5

The Hetairion

*What would our spirits be, O Lord, if they did not have
the bread of terrestrial things to nourish them, the wine
of creation's beauties to intoxicate them? . . . The road
that we are climbing to rise higher is built out of matter.*
—R. P. Pierre Teilhard de Chardin

At one o'clock in the morning, the following dishes were served
at Maligâth: a consommé of red and green peppers seasoned
with citronella, basil, and mint; a chowder of calamary squid
with lotus-hearts and cubeb fruit; shark fins in crab milk; sea
urchins, finely sliced, so that no visible trace remained of their
obscene shape and quite unappetizing aspect while alive;
lobster claws stuffed with cardamom seeds; barracuda meat,
tenderized with coconut milk and steamed with a mixture of
twenty-seven kinds of spices smuggled in from China, Indo-
nesia, and Vietnam; tiny grilled birds, to be eaten entire, not
excluding the long tender beak, the crackly claws, and the
creamy brain; the crests of guinea cocks as well as those of the
more ordinary barnyard variety, seasoned with arrack and sage,

scorching to the palate; and, finally, some translucent, irides-
cent, gelatinous filaments that looked like vermicelli, but were,
in actuality, the venomous tentacles of the so-called develop-
mental medusa jellyfish, who is male in its youth, hermaphroditic in middle age, and female in its dotage—consumed raw,
of course, in order to get the full benefit of its high protein
and equally high phosphoric acid content, despite which it
remains completely tasteless.

Young men, flaunting their bare buttocks and in fact
wearing nothing but a low-slung belt with a minimal apron
in front, this consisting of strips of pink material and silver
chain-links, thus allowing visual appreciation of their equipment, and young girls with budding breasts, their pubes
adorned with jasmine, hibiscus, or frangipani blossoms,
and wearing round their necks, suspended from a silk cord,
ivory amulets inlaid with gold and shaped like phalloi of a
size quite sufficient to permit certain guests to use them in
the course of the evening in order to deflower their wearers
(hand-picked virgins, expressly destined to be so no longer
by the end of the party), circulated in all the rooms, on all
the terraces, offering those delicacies—and more, colocynths
cut in half, containing a marvelous broth of nightingales'
nests and turtle eggs; tidbits of crocodile curry, squirrel pâté,
cobra fritters; mushrooms cooked in their own spores and
in powdered stag's antlers; bamboo shoots in oyster sauce;
and small covered niello enamel dishes concealing mounds
of fresh monkey brains.

Emmanuelle has a little bit of everything; and, for dessert, some candied giant moths, scarab beetles, and mandrake roots, plus a few drinks of fiery Khouang-Tong liqueur; beer brewed from the white rice grain of Khôrât; and even some *eau de soleil* ("sun water") from the southern provinces, a real stinger that, not unlike being whacked in the guts with a mulewhip. After the meal is over, she finds it quite hard to tell whether she has been at it for a day, an hour, a year, or all her life.

Nor does she have the faintest idea as to which part of the palace she is in. She is sitting with a group of people she has never seen before, lounging about, talking, laughing, and generally having a good time. A big brown-skinned man, stretched out on the thick blue wool carpet, is resting his head on her thighs, while another one is stroking her feet. Her heart is intoning barcarolles of praise: sweet night! wonderful night!

A little later, the Prince comes to fetch her to his table, in another room. He presents her to his other guests. They gather round, men and women, admiring her, touching her hair, kissing her on the lips, fondling her body. She has a hard time distinguishing one from the other, she feels too hot, she voices a complaint to her host. He takes her hand, disengages her from the revelers, and accompanies her outside onto a patio.

The fresh air revives her. May she put her robe back on? The Prince grants permission, calls a servant, gives an order. They stand, waiting, and Emmanuelle hopes that the young man will be able to retrieve her nice jade tunic. She would be sorry to lose it. But here he is again, carrying the garment desired and the golden brooch and belt, it's all there. Using sign language, he tells her where she can find a mirror to use while dressing, as well as assorted perfumes to refresh her skin and a brush to tease her hair with. She thanks him. He salutes, palms together in front of his bowed head.

"Come with me," the Prince says "You haven't seen my gardens yet. A little walk will do us good."

Is he going to make love to me, too? she wonders. She still has not entirely recovered from the treatment the intrepid mariner submitted her to.

She follows the master of the realm, past fountains, basins, flower-beds, trying to guess if he'll possess her here, on one of these lawns moistened by water jets, or there, on that little stone seat under the great aerial roots of a banyan tree. And will he first take off his strange damask costume that makes him look like some fairy tale personage? Well, if he does, he'll look a little less majestic. Perhaps.

Two young girls, flushed out of an arbor by their approach, jump to their feet and disappear from sight in two great bounds, leaving their sarongs behind. Emmanuelle regrets the brevity of this glimpse of their chamois bodies.

"I know you've a taste for girls. Did you meet any here tonight that you could have a good time with?"

She expresses astonishment:

"It seems everybody knows everything about me! And I've only been here for three weeks. . . . Don't people have anybody else to talk about?"

"The people in this city, maybe, but not the ones in this city within the city. Of course they would be passionately interested in you. They have been waiting for you."

"Why? It seems to me that this secret city is populated by ladies a whole lot like me."

"'One can only love one's own sister, twin, or Siamese twin,' so said a man of quality. So it's quite natural that we love you."

"What about Anna Maria Serguine: she isn't your sister?" Emmanuelle asks, sounding slightly mollified.

But the Prince isn't easily daunted.

"Well, who can say?" he asks, softly. "Sometimes it may take an entire lifetime to really get to know one's brother. And at other times, it can take several lifetimes."

"So you believe in the transmigration of souls?"

"I don't know anything about it. I don't even know if we are mortal."

"Well, I certainly don't want to die."

"Then you won't have to."

He makes her sit down on some marble steps leading up to a swimming pool.

"Listen, this is a poem written by a young Chinese engineer, a man of our time:

"'The mountain is my pillow,
The sky is my ceiling:
Tomorrow I'll crack the mountain,
But the sky won't fall.'"

Emmanuelle still has a lump in her throat.

"I know what to do with my life," she says, "but what will I do with my death?"

The Prince looks at her with sympathy.

"'Don't know life: how can we know death?' A saying of Confucius's. Why torment yourself?"

"I never used to think about it—but then Anna Maria came by and reminded me of my ultimate end. Ever since, I've been thinking about it."

"You are always free to think about anything you wish," says the Prince. "But you mustn't be afraid. As soon as you start hiding your head in your hands, because existence and the end of existence seem impenetrably mysterious, you'll just end up by getting religion again. After that you can live in fear of God. Not much of an improvement!"

Emmanuelle can't help giggling. Still, her heart is heavy. The Prince continues his cheering talk:

"A writer, a countryman of yours, Georges Bataille, has made a very perceptive statement: 'I don't want to appear boastful,' he says, 'but to me, death seems like the most ridiculous thing in the world.'"

"I don't find it so," says Emmanuelle.

The Prince smiles. Emmanuelle sighs.

"I really don't know what's happening. Seems it has all led up to this, these last two or three days. I've never made love—nor talked about death—so much! It doesn't seem to fit, somehow."

"Oh, but it does. There's nothing more logical than that: the very thing that makes life worth living makes you want to hang on to life!"

"Yes, that's just it. We have to lose it all."

"Who knows, though? Mario Serghini once told me that you like mathematics. Perhaps they can help you understand it all better. The calculations of your scientists, so it seems, prove that when matter attains the speed of light, it contracts to the point of disappearing. Well, it does disappear, certainly, to our eyes, our instruments: but who would be so audacious as to say that it really ceases to exist? We, ourselves, on this planet, have long since passed out of existence for those who observe us from the other side of the universe. We have faded away into the *néant* of velocity, the selfsame one that to us appeared to engulf their galaxies, ten billion light-years away! Nor will anything ever again make us and them visible to each other. But, separated by a mind-boggling constant of nature, by a mystery of numbers, perhaps we do go on living, and they as well, in our discrete systems, non-communicating spaces, each according to his fashion. No reason to become glum because our senses, for the time being, make us feel lonesome like Hadaly who sat weighing the light rays of dead stars. . . ."

"Well, that's all true," says Emmanuelle. "I know about that."

"Then you ought to know that time does not end in hell, either. The future is not identical with the death of the present: it is merely another facet. Formerly, we knew only one side of the moon: didn't the other side still seem real to us? Certainly we didn't think it was death. When we die, perhaps we still remain ourselves, still seen by others, visible in another way. . . ."

Emmanuelle was feeling happy and yet on the verge of tears. No doubt happiness consisted of that, too, this imminence of tears on the radiant face of life? Her head thrown back, her black tresses almost touching the marble steps, she contemplated, her heart filled with hope and despair, those most distant stars that were, each second of her life, going out, back there at the frontiers of space, taking with them in their sibylline fall those little parcels of love she was attaching to them, as well as her crazy dream, one that would always remain with her, of getting to know them one day, of being able to live long enough to travel far enough to wrap her arms around their flaming waists and shoulders.

A man walked up and sat down. His Titian-red, close-cropped hair enhanced his youth. Emmanuelle found him interesting, not too much of an intrusion. . . .

"Michael," said the Prince, "I think this young lady needs your company more than she can use mine. Please entertain her."

Emmanuelle raised her voice in protest. She was quite content with the company of the Prince, she did not feel like being "entertained." But her host took her hand and put it in the young man's palm:

"Go on," he said. "You two take a swim with my swans."

The water in the pool looked inviting, gently lit by the white lotus flowers and the reflected moonlight. Emmanuelle tried it with her foot, found it lukewarm. She turned her head toward the newcomer, a question in her eyes. The answer was an encouraging smile. She disengaged her hand, stretched, took a couple of steps, and raised her arms to her shoulder to undo the golden owl brooch.

Although she had been stark naked most of the night, it seemed to her that undressing this way, standing up in a park, in transparent obscurity, would be an even greater act of abandon, of abandoning herself, than nudity itself had been. An atavistic sense of shame caused her fingers to fumble. Then she realized that her companions were waiting: that she would be giving them this gift of magical transformation—what a lovely incentive! It made undressing a most sensible act, an erotic one, with its own protocol, its solemn preliminaries. She was pleased she wasn't naked yet, it enabled her to create beauty in becoming it, thus giving form to something greater than an immobile and already achieved beauty: it would be a beauty in the process of being born, the moment when clay turns into breast, belly, legs, figure.

She took off her belt, and the light breeze inflated her tunic before it slid down to her waist, baring her curved back, with its long groove down the middle that distinguished it from its shadow. For a moment, the material bunched around her hips, creating folds around the thighs and legs similar to those sculptors had so liked to adorn their statues of Venus with. She did look like something out of a dream of antiquity; so close to the image preserved for centuries in men's hearts that she was an apparition.

It did not last very long: it was enough for her to shake her long hair and to flash the profile of a breast, the most contemporary narrowness of her bare waist, to make the statue lose its otherworldliness. Yet the living body had gained a kind of grace and shimmering prestige of not merely fleshly powers. All of a sudden, it was no longer the human beauty of Emmanuelle, more perfect than the goddess's curves, that men's hands were reaching out for, but for the delusion of stone that the magic of her immortal irreality had enveloped her in for the duration of a mirage. The stone breasts of Praxiteles' Aphrodite of Cnidus, were it possible to make them come alive, who would even look at them when Emmanuelle's counterparts were within easy reach? And yet, as inimitable, beyond the powers of even a sculptor of deities, as her breasts of female tissue were: nothing would ever give Emmanuelle in her flesh such love as is that unspeakable and chimerical love that scorches those who, in the temples and caves where they are holding her prisoner, violate the goddess of stone whose broken torso mere men still puzzle over, without comprehending it!

Without a word, the Prince and Michael watched the apparition enter the water. The waves in the pool fragmented it, dispersed her, made her disappear except for the dark cloud of her hair that kept floating on, not unlike the dark spot that

reminds the ocean's surface for a long time of the sunken tri-
reme, its amphorae decorated with images of young girls, their
sacred dances, their dreams of islands. . . .

Michael took off his clothes and joined Emmanuelle
among the antigones and fallen jasmine blossoms that made
the basin fragrant. They let themselves drift, caught sometimes on the tendrils of long aquatic plant stems or playing at
diving under the gigantic water-lily leaves that looked capable of supporting the weight of a man. The Prince had gone.
Their bodies moved close to each other. Emmanuelle's senses
encouraged her to finger the boy's long, stiff rod like a flute,
ready to voice a man's desire. He tried to make love to her in
the water, awkwardly: their bodies were slippery, and he was
too impatient and too strong. He managed to enter into her
and make her cry out, with both pleasure and pain. She asked
him to take mercy on her, and he allowed her to swim back
to the pool's edge. There she started caressing him with her
tongue and her fingers, with belly and thighs, and between
her breasts which she squeezed up against each other so that
he could insert his prick between them, tight as in a virgin
cunt. She kept pulling him off, and was finally rewarded with
long spurts of thick sperm, enough to almost fill the double
cup of her hands to the brim: she raised it to her lips, then
offered it to her lover:

"Like some?"

He shook his head, smiling, but put his cheek against hers
to watch her drink, and Emmanuelle's damp tresses fell over

both their shoulders, fashioning a single head for their twin bodies.

Then, as she felt chilly, he stretched out on top of her, and they exchanged endearments. Orion was above them, with his sword adorned with nebulae and those gems in his belt, whose names Emmanuelle repeated in a cabbalistic formula: *Anilam, Alnitak, Mintaka.* . . . Her thoughts dissolved in a dream.

She emerged from it in a doleful mood and unable to understand what she was doing there, in this park, lying naked and inert under a male body that she had never seen, that was, perhaps, dead. . . . Her panic dispersed as her memory started functioning again, but she did not feel like remaining there. She asked her companion to take her home. She was worn out. She was sleepy, she wanted to sleep in her bed, and for days and days, like a log. . . .

He countered by saying it was still too early, that she had to stay until daybreak. Emmanuelle felt annoyed. She decided to track down Mario. She put her robe back on again; her skin had dried, and the touch and protection of the folds of silk made her feel calmer. She would have liked to have been able to comb her tangled hair, but had to content herself with picking damp petals and dead leaves out of it. Back at the palace, she remembered the bathrooms with their gold and silver accessories, where one was attended by adolescents, simply round-eyed with admiration and desire. She started looking for one of these, found one, and left her escort at the door, telling him not to wait for her.

She took a bath in near-scalding water, let herself be dried, powdered, perfumed, massaged, caressed, had her hair done, and would have spent the rest of the night there; but the Prince (no doubt alerted by Michael) arrived to meet her.

"So many are complaining that you have been monopolized by someone: won't you come and put an end to such rumors?"

"When I just walked through the house it seemed to me that the party was slackening: there didn't even seem to be so many men around any more! I think they've all gone to sleep."

"Well, over-indulgence catches up with one, on these occasions," her host said indulgently. "But it's mind over matter, in these fleshly matters. I've assembled, in propitious surroundings, a little hetairion whose members feel the evening games thus far have been nothing but a prelude. I mean, you haven't really been doing much more than dabbling about a bit yourself up to now, have you?"

"That reminds me," said Emmanuelle, "who was that beautiful boy you presented me to, back there in the park?"

"Michael? I think you know him. He's the United States Naval Attaché."

Emmanuelle didn't bat an eyelid, although she felt as if she had been slapped. Bee's brother! And she had made love to him without suspecting anything! How could she have been so blind? Those eyes, those lips, the same smile, that coppery hair, the imperious manner! Even his way of talking . . . That wasn't only her brother, it was her double. And she hadn't recognized him!

So she let the Prince take her along, without paying attention to the route, to a door made out of ancient wood, almost wine-colored, worn like a ship's deck and encrusted with iron bands that crossed in lozenge-shapes or else were joined together to form massive hinges, armor-plated locks, with sliding bolts, and possibly even some symbolic ornaments; but at that moment Emmanuelle was in no mood to study any of it.

Her guide pushed it open, made her enter the room first. She shivered: the air conditioners made it seem cool compared to the night air outside. A reddish smoke rendered everything hazy. A heavy, sharp odor, a Chinese odor, distinctive yet complex, something like ginger and saffron, in any case more herbal than flowery—unless it was a wood smell, after all, a smell of the open air rather than a man or woman smell—seemed to emanate from the layers of penumbra in the room: she felt it wrap itself around her, tasting her skin. . . .

At first all she could discern were some oblong lamps with hexagonal bases and thick glass chimneys, standing on the floor behind dwarf silver-plated screens, casting vague foursquare patterns on the pile rugs, like some giant checkerboard or hopscotch design. Flat-surfaced cushions, of various dimensions and thicknesses, yet always rectangular or square, never oval or round, covered in lemon yellow felt, deep blue velvet, short-haired fur, fishnet dyed black with cuttlefish ink, or else covered in masses of feathers such as Maori chiefs sported, were strewn about on the white carpet.

Although her eyes quickly adjusted to this strange, wavering half-light, half-dark—colorful, and almost palpable, but changing density from one moment to the next, which was perhaps due to the inrush of air upon their opening the door—Emmanuelle did not seem able to see farther than a body's length. All she could be certain of discerning were three women lounging on those motley cushions. They were even younger than herself. They lay stretched out on their backs, not touching each other, their legs spread wide apart. One of them was the Prince's daughter. Around them, in the outer reaches of the lamps, changing shape with the swirling vapors, stood some presumably male forms, observing them.

Emmanuelle turned toward her host. She wanted to hear his voice. She said the first name that came into her head, in order to feel less strange in the midst of such a multitude of dangers.

"Ariane . . . Is she here?"

"Would you like her to be?" the Prince replied, eagerly. "I'll send for her."

"Oh no, please don't," Emmanuelle said hurriedly, as if she had committed a blunder.

Then, wanting to appear casual:

"Did she have a good time?"

She noticed she was using the past tense, as if the party was over.

"Well, if you ask me," her host said with a smile, "I think she's had more success than anyone else tonight."

How come? Emmanuelle asked herself. She realized she didn't like the assumption at all.

"More than me, even?" she heard herself wonder.

There were notes of pride and a new kind of emotion in her voice. She tried her best to keep them down, to retain a tone of banter:

"Is that because she's more beautiful than I?"

"No, she isn't," Orméaséna admitted.

"Well then? If I'm more beautiful, I have a right to have more lovers. More than I don't care who!"

Her voice rang out in triumph, filling the red room. A man emerged from the shadows, walked up to her, and grabbed her wrists.

"That is for us to decide," he said.

She recognized him, with a shiver. It was the intrepid mariner.

He started pulling her along, and the reddish fog receded in front of them, revealing other bodies, mostly male. Some were mere boys, still almost pubescent, with white Anglo-Saxon bomber pilot faces topped by light and close-cropped hair; others were more mature, tanned, with craggy Siberian features, ironical and determined wrinkles round their eyes. Then there were others—of all kinds. . . .

Hands pressed down on her shoulders, and she found herself seated on some cool and slippery material. They were touching her. Spreading her legs and instantly proceeding to finger her genitals, without even giving her time to undress, without kissing her or saying a word to her. She did not dare to stretch herself out, although she expected to be taken by several of them at once, through every available aperture. The hands groping around between her legs were hurting her, but she did not complain, even when they insisted on opening her up without much ado and pushing themselves into her. She expected to submit to them from now on, and was determined to like it. A sudden gust of pride and pleasure swelled her chest when she realized that she was not afraid any longer: she could sense no physical fright, no timidity of spirit.

Obeying an order given by the naval officer all the hands suddenly withdrew and let her go. She was free, perhaps even alone: the gropers only had to retreat beyond an arm's length to be completely lost in the chiaroscuro, practically dissolved in it. The incense-scented opacity traced a circle of emptiness around her, it seemed, by the stroke of a magic wand. . . .

"Send for Ariane," said one of the invisible coryphées, and one could hear someone leaving the room.

A gust of warm air entered, and Emmanuelle noted that it was still possible for her, this very moment, probably the last such chance, to escape from the place. She knew no one would try to stop her. She was permitted the choice. That was the meaning of the open door.

She stayed. Not out of any human consideration, nor out of apathy or fatalism, but because she wanted to stay. She felt her desire in her throat, on all sides of her larynx, like a hand, gently squeezing. Her tongue unfroze, her pulse beat quickened, she felt a rosy glow on her temples. It was a kind of desire she had never experienced before. Why don't they hurry up! she sighed, to herself. I'm sure they can see I'm ready for anything. To let them use my body any way they think will please them.

"What do you want to be done to you?" asked the games master's voice, and Emmanuelle appreciated the incipient irony of the formulation.

She didn't know whether the Navy man had misread the meaning of her smile or if it was a further concession to usage when he pursued his questioning:

"Would you prefer a male or a female?"

Yet before she had time to say anything, he himself provided the answer:

"As a matter of fact, that's of no importance. At a certain level of eroticism, there are no sex distinctions any more."

He resumed his tone of command.

"Show yourself!"

Emmanuelle leaned back, supporting her weight on her left elbow. She threw the edges of the tunic aside, baring her pubis; most of the pearls had parted company with the curly hair. She raised her right knee, spread out sideways. Slowly, gracefully, using two fingers, she parted the lips of her vulva.

"Go to it!" said the officer, no doubt addressing himself to the men gathered around her.

How many of them were there? She didn't even know the dimensions of the room for sure. What if there were a hundred? So what! After such a night, surely only a certain proportion of them were still capable of enjoying her.

What she was really hoping, without daring to be frank enough to admit it to herself, was that there still was a sufficient number of stiff cocks left to turn the experience into something more than a travesty. She felt somewhat reassured when a big fellow, thick-lipped and crinkly-haired, a black no doubt, appeared and kneeled down between her legs, pushed aside the hand she had kept on her vulva, balanced himself on one arm and with his other hand introduced a penis as hot and hard as Emmanuelle could have wished for. She would, in fact, have been quite content with something of slightly less imposing dimensions, at least for the first assault.

She made it a point of honor not to complain, but the tears started flowing, as if she were still a mere virgin. The super-prick kept on going into her: Emmanuelle was amazed at the depth of her own vagina. When the man finally reached his goal, not giving an inch, so to speak, he was gracious enough not to start the old in-out at the moment of maximal painful distension; he remained where he was, but began flexing his muscles, stomach and thighs, turning his member gently inside her, taking advantage of its thickness and rigidity to soften up and laterally distend Emmanuelle's interior tissues, until she became wet, hot, and glad to throw her arms around him, uttering the first throaty sounds of pleasure.

Then he unleashed a sudden fury, pulling it out and shoving it back in with positively savage speed, making her howl at each stroke. It was apparent that these cries excited him even more, and he started adding his own accompaniment, hoarse and near-bestial grunts and groans that peaked when a wad of sperm, thick and heavy by the feel of it, charged out of his balls and penetrated her so thoroughly that she almost immediately felt its salty taste upon her tongue. Long after he had come, he went on fucking her, lying down now on his fair victim's breasts, his face buried in her hair, his rump bobbing up and down in spasms that seemed to engender each other and gave Emmanuelle a new sensation, exceedingly intense and savory. She cooed against his rough cheek, bit it hard, kissed it, punctuating this entertainment of her senses with little squalls of tears.

The man went on laboring inside her, keeping up the same degree of penetration, the same frenetic rhythm, for a longer time than she had ever known any man capable, and she came more often and with a greater intensity than ever before. She thought (in a lucid moment between two bouts of ecstasy) that there always seemed to be something new around the corner, in these matters of love. If she hadn't made it with this stranger, she might have remained ignorant all her life long of the possibility of such pleasure.

I have to surpass myself, she thought, *and may this be the night when I do it.* But after one final orgasm, more shattering than all the preceding ones, had struck her like a lightning-bolt, she suddenly felt she had had enough. The fire storm within her subsided into sovereign calm, into unparalleled lucidity and serenity. If what she had just experienced was pleasure, well then, this new state had to be happiness itself.

With a great groan the man discharged his semen for a second time. Then he remained motionless, like one struck in the back with a dagger. Others pulled him off her and took his place. She, for her part, did not know anything any more.

When she came back to her senses, she asked herself how many of these totally unfelt lovers she could have had.

"I must keep counting them," she admonished herself. "Otherwise it isn't worthwhile."

And as they kept on coming, she discovered a new form of enjoyment: no sensual paroxysms this time, but a cerebral kind of pleasure, even more fascinating than the other. She said to herself that she had graduated from the carnal orgasm, the orgasm of the body, to the erotic one, the orgasm of the spirit. To give oneself out of unthinking desire is nothing at all: true eroticism is served only when one gives oneself consciously, voluntarily! Eroticism begins where lust ends: perhaps it cannot even start unfolding all its majestic significance until pleasure is over. . . . Beauty occurs only on the off-beat.

She was, however, a little disturbed to notice that there were some who seemed to take their time with her a little too leisurely: she wanted all of them to have a piece of her. How disappointing it would be if some others would grow impatient and look for something else, or even give her up entirely!

She stopped worrying about this only at those moments when she felt one of them shoot off into her, because that meant he was ready to make place for the next one. And she found it quite ravishing to watch them pull out, crawl over her legs, and disappear into the swirling penumbra without even getting to their feet; in this room, everything seemed to be occurring at floor level, the vertical was to be avoided; and she felt an upsurge of emotion that tasted of love for the one who in his turn knelt down between her legs, or stretched out on top of her, depending upon taste, then penetrated her with a single stroke of his member, if he could manage, or gave himself a helping hand, which was most often the case.

Some glued their lips to hers while their bodies got into the rhythm that would provide the most suitable enjoyment to their submerged members. Others kept their distance, leaning on outstretched arms to be able to stare down at her while fucking. For all of them, she put into practice the skills she had acquired in tutorials with Jean, to heighten their pleasure. Each time her actions made her partners yell out loud in ecstasy she addressed a grateful and loving thought to her husband, thanking him for having made her such an expert mistress—she certainly hadn't been one when she first made him the gift of her erotic Lesbian virginity.

It was a tacit understanding—or perhaps the naval officer had given an order to that effect—that none of the men should caress her. This no-nonsense approach, much as it would have offended her at other, more humdrum times, seemed extremely compatible with her present state of mind. All she wanted was that they should come: she wanted to conceive of herself, to see herself, as an instrument of pleasure for many men. She wanted them to find her cunt pleasing, to enjoy the sensations experienced by their organs; to satisfy their own egotistical lust, and never mind her. What she had was better: the self-delight of the artist. She used her amorous talents, her inventiveness, and her willpower to procure the most perfect satisfaction for them, so that they could go and make it the talk of the town that she was a great fuck, as obliging and accommodating as the finest prostitute; and, in fact, full of more surprises.

There came a moment when she felt bad. Then the one where she did not feel anything at all and even gave up thinking. And finally, the moment of cessation. No one was using her any more. That was when she realized that it had been quite all right to forget to keep count.

Much later, she was awakened by a voice. The room seemed to have grown even chillier: perhaps some of its occupants had left?

It took Emmanuelle a moment to distinguish who was talking to her, although the light was better than it had been before. Her eyes were still fogged by sleep. At last, she recognized the creature standing above her, legs akimbo: and such legs they were! And up there, at their meeting point, such a superb bush, so young, so sensuous, so lascivious, and of such a

fiery color! It grew on a pubis of such ample and bulging proportions that it looked almost abnormal. She remembered having had previous occasion to admire this cunt—at that time,
it was perfunctorily covered, but not in the least concealed
by a tiny bikini. She had desired this girl, precisely because of
that little piece of white material, designed to accentuate not
only the bush, but the entire vulva: it was so tight and formfit-
ting that it made her labia stand out in relief, attracting more
admiring stares than if she had been naked. Now Emmanuelle almost regretted the absence of that perverse bikini. But it
was wonderful to see that aggressive mound, to wait for those
soaring nipples above it to descend toward her lips. But, no! It
would be even better if it were the cunt itself, not the breasts,
that descended onto her mouth, planting itself there like a
salty sea-fruit, refreshing her with its juices.

A sudden, humid shiver ran through all her senses again,
but the enigmatic being just stood there.

"I know you," Emmanuelle said at last, as if to reassure
herself that the apparition wasn't just a dream. "I've seen you
down by the pool. But I don't know your name."

She added:

"The Lion Cub, that's who you are."

"My name is Mervée," the young girl said. "The Romans
prefer to call me Fiamma, because I burn them, or Renata,
because I rise again out of their ashes. My lover calls me Mara,
after the Indian demon. But I am Mâyâ, too. And Lilith."

"How nice to have so many names," Emmanuelle said approvingly. Nevertheless the girl's little speech quite amazed her.

"I've got other names, too, but I can't remember them tonight. The ones I've told you just now are the names I go by when I am naked."

She added, squinting a little, without a smile:

"Then, of course, I've also got some boys' names, for those days when I am a boy."

Emmanuelle raised her eyebrows. She decided to make the best of the situation. After all, everything must be possible for such a strange animal. She only had one formal objection:

"I hope you don't lose your hair when you change yourself into a man?"

Because that would be a shame, she thought: to lose that incredible jungle, thicker and longer even than mine, and of such a golden color. Reddish, like Chinese gold.

Boy or girl, what did it matter, she concluded. I'd like to make love to it. Her eyes roamed over the burning bush.

The creature was also scrutinizing her. Then it pronounced:

"A pity you didn't come to Siam sooner. I could have sold you dearly!"

It pursed its lips as if to indicate that that wasn't to be taken so seriously, after all.

"But it doesn't matter. There'll be a time."

Emmanuelle wanted to know:

"You sell women?"

The Lion Cub, she was thinking at the same time, not even expecting an answer, obviously belonged to a species that did not know virtue or vice, guilt or innocence. Nor age, for that matter: it was hard to tell if it was ten years old, like its face, or twenty, like its breasts, or eternal like that cunt which had to be that of an angel—or a devil.

"Where is Ariane?" Emmanuelle asked.

Mervée looked at her lips, with a weird fixity.

"Come with me to the baths," she said, nonchalantly, as if it didn't really matter or wasn't even to be taken too seriously as a proposition.

Why? Emmanuelle wondered. She was certain that it was no invitation to make love, or at least not to make love in any quotidian sense. She had a vague inkling that one could expect anything from this lion-woman. She felt like accepting, but, she would have to get up. . . .

Before Emmanuelle had time to become conscious of it, to do anything about it, the sound of approaching footsteps made Mervée go away. The rhythm that seemed to alternate, at regular intervals, the meals and the love bouts here at Maligâth, now produced great platters of victuals and refreshments. About time, too, as it turned out: Emmanuelle realized she was hungry.

She could not recall meeting any of her companions at table (or, more precisely, on the motley cushions), but they all looked handsome to her. Were they the very same who had made love to her a little while ago? She could always ask: but wasn't it, after all, more titillating to remain in a state of uncertainty?

Pipes filled with opium were passed around. The haze gained a blue tint, and a new olfactory ingredient. Emmanuelle was not tempted. She had tried it once, that was enough for her. She heard someone declaim:

"'The air so sweet, it keeps you from dying. . . .'"

Where had she read that? She couldn't recall. But she wasn't sleepy any longer. Yet she was dreaming, awake.

"What are you going to do about your husband?" asked a young man who had appeared beside her.

She contented herself with an evasive smile; that was a complex subject.

"Here's Ariane," a voice announced.

But the door had not opened, nor did Emmanuelle perceive any change in personnel.

She was thirsty.

"Here," said the young man, holding a glass to her lips, supporting her back. Then he sighed:

"I would love to make love to you again. But to tell the truth, I'm no longer able!"

Me neither, thought Emmanuelle. So what. Can't go on doing the same thing all the time. She looked at herself: really weird, baroque even, to find herself with all these people, stark naked. So they had taken her clothes off, after all? She hadn't even noticed. Her legs were spread apart: she closed them. A cunt that no one's touching is a ridiculous thing, she told herself. Nor did she feel like touching it herself, at this time. What time was it, really? And where was her lovely tunic? I bet I've really lost it this time, she thought. How would she be able to get back home?

"What am I going to tell Jean?"

The man shook his head, indicating sympathy. Then he had an idea:

"Why don't you offer Mara to him?" he suggested.

So he's her lover, Emmanuelle registered.

"You three should live together," he went on, with sudden conviction. "You'd really get along famously. No doubt about it—that's what you must do."

Why Mara—or Renata, or Fiamma, whatever her name is? Emmanuelle thought. Why her, why not Ariane, or, even better, Marie-Anne? Or some other girl? Anna Maria, for instance, she wouldn't be bad at all. But she doesn't want to hurt this young man's feelings: quite obviously there's no other woman in the world as worthy of love as his mistress.

"Oh yes," she said, "that would suit me just fine."

"There's no time to lose," he said with impatient enthusiasm. "It's ridiculous, the way you and Jean let all the opportunities pass by."

Which ones? Emmanuelle asks herself, but without any real curiosity. And what is the best combination: two women and one man, or one woman and two men? The latter formula looks pretty tempting to her. The other man could be Christopher, for instance. Or Mario. No, not Mario. Nor Christopher, either.

"What are you thinking about?" she asked, after five somnolent minutes.

"Two women seems to make more sense to me, seeing that you're Lesbian. But in any case, the main thing is to get started. This way or that, it doesn't make that much difference. I'll send you my book."

"Is it about living in a *ménage à trois*?"

"Among other things, yes."

"Well, I must read it, because I can't really see how it works. It can't be all that easy, you know? It must be a little like three people dancing together."

"Just about."

Emmanuelle showed her surprise at her companion's quick agreement. But he went on:

"It's even a little harder, maybe. Thank God! If it was just child's play, that'd be a bad sign, wouldn't it? There'd be no incentive. Easy things aren't our game at all."

We're not here in order to amuse ourselves, Emmanuelle reminded herself: we are here to give the species of tomorrow its chance. Not to defy morality, nor to surpass it, but to create another! The scruples of Galahad will be outdated when we become star-travelers. To grow cider apples in the good old days, the good old morality may have been good enough: but if we want to become worthy explorers of Betelgeuse we have to do better than that.

Just look at that: I'm playing at being Mario.

"Well, I don't think we ourselves can really change that much," she went on thinking, this time out loud. "But if we want to have children who'll be more advanced than ourselves, we surely have to go about it that way."

The young man nodded gravely:

"You're just a sentimental woman."

"Me?" Emmanuelle cried out, insulted.

"All of us, all of us. We're intelligent, all right, but our feelings are way behind our recognitions. We think like Einstein: yet we conduct our love affairs like Bernardin de Saint-Pierre's *Paul et Virginie*."

She shrugged.

"The laws of Einstein did not concern, nor will they ever concern, human love. Love is not a natural phenomenon."

"Quite right!" her companion agreed. "Quite right! it's exactly there that the trouble starts. Mankind knows only its present stupid kind of loving. It's the tragedy of the species. We owe our intelligence to an organization of matter that, at this moment in time, surpasses our own competence, but we've been able to construct love quite by ourselves. No wonder the construct is rather a shambles!"

"The universe," said Emmanuelle, "is just a cold, smooth piece of percale: we've put in a few pleats to make it more pleasing. Or, at least, that's what we tell ourselves, in order to leave our own mark upon it."

"The great flatiron of time will take care of that. Come back in a couple of hundred millennia and tell me if you'll see any trace left of your dressmaker's art!"

"Well, perhaps love won't be there any more," said Emmanuelle, "but its traces will remain, all right."

The young man gulped down the contents of a large glass and decided to change his approach, perhaps even the subject.

"Spending an orgiastic night with a whole bunch of men isn't all that metaphysical, it's just an acting-out of a fantasy. You're just having a nice vacation here. It is an exception from your normal way of life: you're merely evading its morality, you're not constructing a new one."

"You're mistaken. I'm here tonight and doing what I'm doing because I know it to be right!"

"'All is pure to the pure, there is nothing that is impure in itself,' said Saint Paul, but he added: 'All is permitted, but not all of it is edifying'! If you want to change the world, don't think you can get out of that obligation by going to a party. You have to start by implementing your new morality at home, weekdays as well as holidays. Your conduct will acquire a message, and the validity of proof, as soon as the way of life pursued here at Maligâth becomes a daily routine for you. As long as you pass your days conforming to convention, what do I care if you change into a perfect succubus once the sun has set?

I'll only start being impressed when they tell me, for instance, that you have introduced Jean into Mara. Or that you've told your husband to offer your body to his friends, after dinner. Not in secret, but in plain view of everybody. Not just on midsummer's night, but every night."

He concluded, with a fatigued gesture intended to indicate that this would be his final effort:

"Shamelessness, adultery, libertinage—those things don't interest me in the least as long as they're mere escapades, indulgences, secretive games, little furtive sins. If you want me to believe you, you have to show one and all, in public acts and with insolent pride, that you insist on the beauty of being naked and on the liberty to physically enjoy others, and have them enjoy your body, as your birthright! Bear the witness of virtue; that is, of sincerity and courage. Don't content yourself with being the fickle wife of a foolish husband: proclaim and manifest that your being married to one man does not prevent you from loving and making love to several others at the same time. Do it in the streets! In doorways! Let the stupefaction of those who daren't be your lovers enhance your reputation—without ever compromising their own chances. Maybe one day you'll get the opportunity to touch, with your enchanted fingers, their numbed genitals—to transform them into real men, at last. Of course, they could simply call you a witch, and make that a further reason for not taking you seriously. So you ought to resist the temptation to perform miracles. Rather prove your theories by the employ of reason and method. Don't ask your contemporaries anything but that they should observe your life and reflect upon it. The success of your experiments, known by all, verifiable to all, as all scientific data have to be, will prove to your followers that the simultaneity of amorous associations and carnal intimacies, the multiplicity of passions, each one of which is irreducibly itself, is no disorder of the mind, caused by some flaw in the soul, but the very vocation of adulthood—and that we cannot afford to remain children any longer: infancy bores us, we don't want to play fidelity hopscotch any more, we're tired of all those old games of jealousy and injured pride. We have had enough of promises kept only for a day, of tears lasting for all eternity; we've outgrown murderous loves and broken hearts. We want to live like human beings extended to our full capability: the time of spankings and curfews is over!"

He falls silent. Emmanuelle gets up, taking care not to arouse him. She wonders if she'll be able to find Mervée again. Suddenly she bumps against the metal ornaments on the door. She's had no idea of leaving, but as the door is there, she opens it and steps out of the room. She crosses a deserted gallery. It is a hot night. She sees another room, people moving around in it. And look, there's Mario, among them! She shouts for joy. He does not hear her, hasn't seen her yet: one might say that he is busy, worshiping some young ganymede. . . .

He presents a three-quarter profile image of his back to Emmanuelle. She tiptoes up, suppressing a giggle, and peeps over his shoulder at the naked body thrashing about beneath him. It is Bee.

Emmanuelle's heart seems to drop out of her. Her chaste little Bee! Mario, who does not care for women, engaged in most vigorous copulation with the mistress she, Emmanuelle, had not been able to attach to herself! She wants to look, but tears obscure her vision. She bites her lip, turns, runs back across the room, flees, she does not know where, runs, sobs, pants through hallways and alleys, until she has no idea where she is.

But all of a sudden Ariane is there, sitting with a group of others. Emmanuelle falls on her knees before her, rests her head on her thighs:

"Take me away from here!" she pleads. "I don't want to stay here any longer. Let's go!"

"But what is it, my darling?" Ariane says, gentle and mocking. "Has someone hurt you?"

"No. No, not at all. But I want to go home."

"Home? But there's no one there. What will you do there?"

"All right, take me to your house."

"Do you really want me to?"

"Yes."

"You'll stay with me?"

"Yes, yes!"

"You'll make love to me?"

"Yes, I promise I will."

"You're not deceiving me?"

"But don't you see, I have no one but you!"

Ariane bends down, kisses her.

"Come then."

Emmanuelle grabs Ariane's tousled hair.

"I'll do everything you want me to!"

Her friend takes her by the hand, on the moonlit marble, and guides her across the lawns.

"But I'm stark naked," Emmanuelle complains, sounding like a little girl.

"What difference does that make?"

Driving, in Ariane's car, they are silent. Emmanuelle's head rests on Ariane's shoulder. It is dawn, the streetlights are going out, one by one. Buses go honking past, the fruit vendors start hawking their wares. At the intersections, when the roadster has to wait for the light to change, startled boys with widening eyes and bulging crotches utter squeals of amazement at the sight of the naked girl stretched out on the black leather seat. . . .

The doorman opens the wrought-iron gates of the Embassy. The river in front of the old façade is bustling with boats and the sound of whistles. The two women go upstairs and into Ariane's room. It is pervaded by a fresh odor of fern. Emmanuelle throws herself on the bed, crosses her arms and legs. Ariane's voice reaches her only in a dream.

The Countess gets out of the kimono she donned upon leaving Maligâth. Quietly she opens a door, slips into a neighboring room:

"Come and see," she says, forefinger pressed against lips. Her husband rises, walks with her to the side of her bed.

"Just look at her," Ariane whispers delightedly. "She's mine, but I'll let you borrow her."

She makes a sign, he retires, and she stretches out next to Emmanuelle, putting both arms around her. Then she, too, falls asleep.

6

To Ariane's Happiness

A sensible woman is what I like to have in the house . . .
—Guillaume Apollinaire, *The Bestiary,*
or Orpheus's Wagon Train

The sacrament of marriage can only be verified
by sacrilege.

—Pierre Klossowski, *The Prompter,*
or Society's Theater

Living with Ariane abolishes both nights and days. How long
has Emmanuelle been there? Has her husband come back yet?
She has lost all count.

"Every time I catch you idle, that is, not diddling yourself,
I'll give you a whacking." Thus Ariane has warned her. She has
kept her word, too, keeping strict tally of the hours Emmanuelle spends enjoying her own body. If Emmanuelle sleeps too
much, or spends too much time making up and dressing or taking her meals, she gets punished. She grows used to spending

most of her time in bed, undergoing an apprenticeship of an intensity and rhythmicity hitherto unknown.

"Be insatiable!" her instructress exhorts her. And to her own amazement, Emmanuelle perceives that she is indeed becoming so.

The praises of what she calls *autorasty* constitute one of Ariane's favorite topics of conversation.

"Neither nature nor city need it," she says, "no more than they need a good darts player or bowler. . . . Making love is indispensable, you can't avoid it, any more than you can help eating or breathing: but masturbation is time lost, as is thinking, or painting improbable creatures on squares of canvas, or composing flute concertos. . . . If you ask me, sheer poetry is what it is, to enjoy yourself in that fashion!"

Furthermore:

"I suppose I could take it if you said you were tired of making love—but I'd rather see you dead than have you stop having fun with yourself!"

And:

"When you meet a new girl, first of all ask her how many times a day she diddles herself. If she doesn't do it as often as you do, what use is she to you?"

Or:

"Do you realize that some men get married without even knowing if their partners ever masturbate? What kind of love can there be between them?"

She footnotes that:

"It's true, of course, that there are men who like to marry women who don't like their own sex. . . . I guess there's no end to perversity!"

Ariane forces her prisoner to caress herself until she comes. Then she lies down on her inert body and rubs herself against her legs, her belly, her breasts, or her face—until *she* comes.

Or, when fancy takes her, she stretches out on her back, her head resting on arms crossed behind her neck, and Emmanuelle gets to lick her. Ariane's clitoris is prominent and hard, standing up to be sucked like a little penis. Emmanuelle keeps it in her mouth for hours.

When Ariane grows tired, she calls Gilbert and says: "She's yours."

He keeps pumping sperm into her, twice, thrice, four times a day. He makes love only to her now. When he ejaculates into Emmanuelle's cunt, Ariane bends over and sips the hermaphroditic liqueur from it.

"Don't you think," she asks him one day, "that Emmanuelle would make an ideal spouse for you? She'd be very handy for your friends, too—they could have her whenever they felt like it."

When they're alone again, she goes on indoctrinating Emmanuelle.

"A single husband can never be enough for you," she tells her.

"But . . . what about you?"

"I like to give my husbands away."

"Your *husbands*? You've had several already?"

The handsome Countess laughed.

"I'm talking about the future ones!"

Emmanuelle becomes suspicious:

"You don't like Gilbert any more?"

"What makes you think that?"

"Because you're giving him to me."

"If I didn't like him, I wouldn't give him to you."

"You just want to share him with others?"

"Well, not really. As a matter of fact, I don't really *want* anything. I have a horror of plans and projects. I'm all for what's happening. What's happening is always good."

"So if you keep your husband, that's good? But if you lose him, you'll find that just as good?"

"That's right."

"Well, that's just because you don't love him."

"Really?" Ariane says, with a look that makes Emmanuelle blush. She asks:

"Ariane, isn't it just that you're trying everything simply for the pleasure of trying it?"

"Certainly, yes. That's what intelligence means, isn't it?"

"Nothing ever seems bad to you?"

"Oh yes, some things do: those that deprive, or exclude. And all those are evil who refuse to learn. All the people who live like slugs in their milksoppy virtue, satisfied with their own surroundings, priding themselves on not wanting to know anything else, claiming that the only reason they don't care to do this or that is *because they don't like it. . . .* Then you ask them what they found so repulsive about it, to cause such an aversion—and surprise!—they haven't even tried it once! They're like people who claim to have a prejudice against Martians. The very spirit of evil consists of this delectation of one's own ignorance and mediocrity—and of the renunciation of curiosity, of experience, of discovery."

"But it is possible to try something and *not* like it?"

"Barring congenital handicaps, there's a good chance that one will find everything pleasurable."

"But you can also get tired of what has pleased you before."

"Not if one knows how to renew oneself. Now we say: oh, the other day, there was this guy, and oh, did he know how to make love! But the truth is that making love is *always* good, whenever you make it with *someone new*."

"In that case, why get married?"

"Because one has to know that, too. Do you think marriage is some kind of dungeon? One has to get married in order to be more free. A smart girl knows that she'll have more lovers after her marriage than she had before: isn't that a fine reason in itself?"

"That'll be fine as long as the husbands agree: but it seems women get married, then, in order to sleep with many men, while men marry them so that they'll sleep only with them!"

"Well, the women just have to educate them, instead of whining."

"Even at the risk of losing them?"

"If that's necessary, yes. Anything is better than turning back."

"You now have a husband who thinks exactly like you. Why do you want to separate from him?"

"But whoever says that I want to do such a thing?"

"You told him he should marry me."

"Does that mean he has to divorce me?"

"Well, if he isn't your husband any more . . . Didn't you say that anything that entails deprivation is evil?"

"And so? Is it a question of depriving ourselves of each other? Gilbert can have another woman, he can be on the other side of the globe, but I'll always be there for him."

"Even if you remarry?"

"Do I stop being Ariane? I'll simply love one more man."

"But, but . . . "

"Each love has its own place. No one can ever replace anyone else. No one can prevent another from happening."

"If Gilbert has a woman who isn't you, and you have another man, and you never see each other again—what will you have in common, then, at all?"

"Our love, of course."

Emmanuelle still looks perplexed. Ariane amplifies:

"He and I, we love each other the same way. It's not the kind of love that stares deeply into each other's eyes and likes holding hands. The greatest joy for each one of us is to see that the other one doesn't miss a chance."

"But it's surely good to live with the one you love, too?"

"Of course it is. Have I said it isn't?"

"Sort of."

"I don't think so, my sweet. All I know is that life consists of changes, and that that is good. It doesn't bother me that it also involves uncertainties, impermanence: so we don't know what the reward of life is? So it's best to throw oneself into it, simply to live. But, of course, once you think you know your end, once you have found your form, and your ruling passion is to preserve that form, then you do have a right, it's true, to the stability that befits your age: a place among the skulls and bones, so certain of their future, in the ossuary of all apprehensions calmed forever."

Ariane de Saynes smiled at the portraits of her moralistic ancestors.

"Of course I'll be happy to keep Gilbert as my husband. But I'll be just as happy whenever both of us, or either of us, decides to start over, to embark on another adventure. To change is not the same as to lose: but what resists change *is* frightening! What we have going with each other, there's only one thing that can take it away from us."

Ariane looked at her guest, thoughtfully.

"If Gilbert dies, I'll kill myself. You have no idea what it really means: love."

"Maybe I don't," Emmanuelle agreed. "Maybe it's true that I don't know it yet. But I'm learning."

*　*　*

Another time. Emmanuelle is reminiscing about the mysteries of Maligâth:

"That girl with the crazy lion's mane, who is she?"

"She is a Commandress of our Order."

"She must have joined it at a very tender age?"

"Her merits were most distinguished, right from the start."

"I'd love to get to know her."

"If you like, I can introduce you."

"Oh no, don't bother. We have been introduced, all right. But that's as far as we got."

"What do you think you'll gain from her acquaintance?"

"What a silly question!"

"Take care not to scorch your wings in her flame."

'Listen to you, all caution, all of a sudden—you, who always encourages me to try everything once!"

"But you see, I don't know how far you want to go."

"Why don't you tell me what dangers I'd expose myself to?"

"There are certain pleasures that entail death."

"What on earth are they? What are you talking about? Forbidden drugs?"

"Well, not the ones you're thinking of. But, please, don't ask me any more questions."

"But . . . Have you had any experiences like that?"

"I told you I won't give you any more answers."

"I'd still like to be done by Mervée, some time."

"And what makes you think she's that interested in you?"

"Isn't it enough if I want it?"

Ariane looks at her with satisfied mien.

"TelL me," she asks, "do you really love women more than men?"

Emmanuelle thinks it over, frowning a little. She can't make up her mind.

"Really and truly, I don't know. I love to look at girls. I love to touch their breasts, to slip my tongue into their mouths, to rub my clit against them and have them do the same to me. I love their thighs between my own. I love the taste of their genitals on my tongue. . . ."

She daydreams a minute, then goes on to admit:

"But it's true that I love sperm, too. And I like it when someone sticks something inside me."

'Well, as far as the latter service goes, I can render it."

"It's not the same thing."

"It can be even better."

"That would seem to depend on what it is you insert!"

"Make up your mind: would you like me to call in a male, or do you entrust yourself to my care?"

"You do it!"

Ariane leans over, kisses her:

"And as a reward, I'll let you suck off Gilbert."

She gets up to fetch a round coffer, made out of tooled Florentine leather with old gold-leaf decorations, about the size of a hatbox. It looks heavy. She puts it down on the bed.

"Try to open it!"

Emmanuelle starts looking for a lock, a zipper. Nothing.
"It's a secret box," she says.

Triumphantly, Ariane slides a fingernail under a groove,
and the lid pops up. Emmanuelle claps her hands:

"Oh, what a collection!" she laughs, bouncing on her
knees, making the bedsprings jounce.

Irregularly arranged, of various lengths, in a capricious
assortment of colors and shapes—phalloi, an entire little plan-
tation of them!

Some look like snakes, others like fat mushrooms. There
are rectilinear ones with a chubby glans, the apertures pointing heavenward; curved ones, Oriental-looking things, of a
coppery hue; long ones, short ones, slender ones, stocky ones,
smooth ones, rough ones. . . . The bottoms of their shafts are
invisible, embedded as they are in velvet vulvas, narrow ones,
wide ones, as the case may be.

Proudly, their owner takes them out, one after the other.
Those made out of foam rubber feel as soft and elastic as flesh
and skin, and they range from gigantic knobkerries to mere rat-
pricks; some of them have a pear-shaped extension, fashioned
out of rubber: when you squeeze it, the thing inflates to twice
its volume. There are others made out of china, out of decorated porcelain, that are designed to ejaculate water or cream.
The wooden ones, painted or polished, remind Emmanuelle
of the temple Mario had taken her to one night, and of her
embarrassment and exaltation at that first courageous venture.
Well, she's certainly come a long way!

She picks up an ebony creation, hefts it in her hand. It has black, knotty veins, carved in relief, not unlike the roots of a banyan tree. Others, their heads or shafts bristling with tufts of stiff hair, or wart-shaped excrescences and little nylon rasps, don't interest her as much. She actually prefers those fashioned out of rare materials. Here's one, an *olisbos* of slightly yellowed ivory, gently curved, well used, silky to the touch— she could easily fall in love with it! And what a sense of luxury it would give one to own any of these fine specimens of the goldsmith's art whose testicles have been closely modeled on nature. . . . They feel cold, exciting to her fingertips. She'd certainly like to put them to the test.

But Ariane has other things in mind.

"Oh, don't bother with those still lifes," she says. "Tell me rather what you think of inventions like this one?"

She holds out an ivory object that is whiter, thus obviously newer, than the one Emmanuelle has been admiring. Its shape is quite extraordinary. Not even attempting verisimilitude, the artist has been free to improvise quite shamelessly and has produced a short, bulging banana, rounded identically at both ends. Emmanuelle asks herself how it would be possible to hold on to it, once it has been inserted: it looks like it would slip away from one's fingers and simply vanish completely into the vagina!

"That's exactly the usage it's been designed for," Ariane explains. "You don't use it like a lover, on the push-pull principle. You just insert it and leave it there, and then it's a good idea to go for a walk or to sit down in a rocking chair."

"A rocking chair?"

"You see, it's hollow, and filled with mercury: it keeps moving about in there, dividing, expanding, congealing again, swelling out the sides, never stopping for a moment. You have no idea how that can bring out the best in you. . . ."

"I want to try it right now!"

"Be patient. Take a look at this one first."

At first sight, the new specimen does not appear remarkable at all. It has been manufactured out of some shiny metal and does not look very engaging; it's of average size, traditional shape. Still, there is something intriguing about it: its weight. Noticing that, Emmanuelle also notices the cord extending out of its base and ending in an electrical plug.

"So what's this, an electric lover?" she wants to know.

"It's a vibro-massager prick! It produces—but right in the center of things—those sensations that impressed you so much, peripheral as they were, in that bathing establishment I took you to, the other day."

"Well, that should be educational."

"Not bad, but there are better ones. Here."

From a smaller case, Ariane produces quite a different engine. This one looks so lifelike, Emmanuelle's heart misses a beat: it couldn't be severed from a man . . . ? Not only the suppleness, the mobility, the lines and folds of its skin impress one that way, but also the apparently living warmth of its very substance. Emmanuelle pulls herself together and grabs it: it immediately swells and stiffens, as if it were attached to a man.

Emmanuelle screams. She drops it and thinks: thank God it fell on the bed, that can't hurt. . . .

"Oh, but that's awful!" she protests. "The Devil himself must have given you that one!"

Ariane laughs, a little disdainfully.

"I didn't know you were such a Manichean."

She picks up the fruit of her supposed pact with the Lord of Darkness and strokes it, absent-mindedly. Instantly it becomes congested, grows purple, pulsates in her hand. The glans is so tumescent, the skin so distended, it looks ready to explode. Its dimensions have become positively amazing. The dark purple balls are trembling.

"You see, it'll do all that while it's inside you, without your having to do anything about it. You can just lie there stock-still, it'll take care of business: it'll go in and out, get a little shorter, a little thinner, then dilate again, get longer, get stiff as, well, stiff as a prick! Its temperature changes, it takes little rests, it buzzes away like crazy, and if all that isn't enough to drive you wild, it also emits certain waves that'll make you shake and shiver up and down your spine. After you've used this, the most well-endowed gallant doesn't seem such a hot stud any more!"

Emmanuelle does not look totally impressed, but stares defiantly at the eulogized homunculus.

"And finally," Ariane continues, "when it assumes that you've come often enough, it ejaculates."

"Listen, do you take me for an idiot?"

"Go ahead, try it, if you don't believe me."

Emmanuelle isn't tempted at all. To tell the truth, the thing scares her.

"What has it got inside of it?"

"A complete electronic system, batteries, printed circuits, transistors, everything. It's really quite easy to construct, if you know about such things."

"That's possible, but it's a little too cybernetic for my taste," Emmanuelle says. "I don't need anything as complicated as that."

"Don't I know that! But sometimes it's good to try something a bit out of the ordinary."

Ariane meditates a moment, then:

"In matters of eroticism, I'd advise you to be more extravagant."

She laughs at Emmanuelle's offended look.

"I'd certainly like to see you in the house of one of my acquaintances, where you can play with far more elaborate mechanical aids than this little toy. But I can see you're really opposed to progress."

Her boarder, aware of an attempt to provoke her, does not respond.

So it's up to Ariane to go on:

"You find it boring, the stuff I'm talking about?"

Emmanuelle's curiosity gets the better of her rational mind. Her hostess realizes she can now set conditions:

"What will you give me, in exchange for my story?"

"I'll rid myself of the last vestiges of shame!"

"All right then: tonight, for tennis, you'll put on that little pleated miniskirt of yours—with nothing on underneath. You won't mind in the least when the wind lifts it right up—in fact, you'll bound about like a mountain goat!"

"Fine, but for whose benefit?"

"For Caminade's. He hasn't met you yet. It'll really impress him."

"You've never told me about him."

"I've nothing to tell. As far as I'm concerned, he's a complete question mark."

"Is he young, or old?"

"Your age."

"Well, he'll be lucky."

"How is it you didn't marry an adolescent? You seem to like the innocent ones."

"I need my elders to instruct me. But don't you think I'm advanced enough, in my studies, to do a little teaching of my own now?"

"With little boys standing in line to peer at your cunt and die of happiness?"

"Well, I certainly hope you'll help me give them a better taste for life than that. We can teach the courses together."

"Why not start by putting my friend Caminade to the test?"

"What area is he weakest in?"

"Satisfaction. When you get up there in front of your class, what will you do to prevent your pupils from becoming sick with their own frustrated desires, like the men we see now every day?"

"I'll make them dream. And I'll turn myself into the reality of those dreams."

"If only you could teach them to stop refusing anything! What a new world that would be."

"You've told me that you've already been initiated into the secrets of that coming world's outposts."

"Just because robots are superhuman, you mustn't think that they'll ever be able to replace men."

"Well, if not, what use are they?"

"They help us wait."

"For what? The time when men have attained the proficiency of their inventions?"

"No, no, that would be too much to ask! Simply the time when men decide to join the world."

Ariane makes herself comfortable, rests her head on Emmanuelle's groin, caressing the breast of her friend with one hand, gently turning the nipple between her fingers, and holding one of her own breasts with the other.

"First of all, imagine a steel wall, cold like a cliff, covered with dials and levers, microphones and circuit-breakers. The other three walls have been covered in silk, sometimes lilac-colored, sometimes maroon or some other pastel shade, because there are several of these cabins: considering the great number of clients, one certainly wouldn't be enough. These cells are not very large: six feet long, less than five feet wide, and yet tall enough to permit one to stand upright. There are no windows—no, of course not. . . . The light is provided by hidden sources, three-quarters up the cubicle wall: it is evenly distributed, and quite bright. The cubicles are air-conditioned. An almost imperceptible, rather strange music provides an aural backdrop that causes more anxiety than relaxation. The general impression is that of a laboratory or a clinic, very modern, anonymous, impeccable—nothing at all of the boudoir about it. It's not a very reassuring impression. You stand there and don't have the faintest idea how to go about it. There's no bed, no chair."

Ariane pauses for a couple of seconds to enjoy her tactile impressions of the two mammary glands, gives a little sigh, then continues:

"But then you realize that all you have to do is lie down on the floor: as soon as you examine its covering, this becomes evident. It's silk, too, but richer and softer than the walls, and quilted in lozenge-shapes, like an old-fashioned comforter. Under it there is, in fact, a big feathery eiderdown and a thick foam rubber pad, equaling the luxury of the finest mattress. Well, whether you're an old hand at it or not, the door then closes behind you, padded and silk-covered like the rest of the room but for that great console wall, and there you are, all alone, or with an assistant, male or female, or one of each, just as you wish, who have come in with you to initiate you into the workings of the machinery. They explain to you the various employ of buttons and levers and dials, and of course you don't understand a thing, and you all have a good laugh over that! If it's you, Emmanuelle, I'm afraid you'll just forget the entire machine trip, and start making out with the assistants. . . . In which case, you won't get what you paid for. But, let's suppose it is someone less impulsive, perhaps more discerning. . . ."

"Like you, for instance!"

"All right, like me. I let the technician explain it all to me, but find myself unable to retain any but the most elementary points. Still, I send him away and start acting according to instructions. I lie down on my back, feet facing the metal wall, spreading them wide, of course. Now I see that the ceiling which I thought was the only bare surface comes to life—all kinds of shapes and silhouettes and colors start appearing, and the most erotic scenes imaginable start unfolding! Anything goes, regardless of sex, age, or number: old bearded fellows doing it to little girls; pre-pubescent boys doing it with each other; five savages having fun with one fair prisoner, all at the same time, using every possible part of her, all nine orifices of her, and then serving her up, surrounded by other tempting victuals, on a festive dining table; wood nymphs coupling with centaurs and swans; and modern young things going wild sucking off and being fucked by burros and big dogs! These licentious movies alone are enough to animate the flesh: but now the soles of my feet encounter two huge pedals, covered in padding: I push against them, gently; and out of the wall extend, one after the other or simultaneously (this depends upon how well I've remembered my instructions), in any case, very slowly, a number of metal arms, looking like nothing so much as flexible metal shower hoses, writhing chromium serpents. . . . As I'm watching, I see that at the end of each hose protrudes a magnificent male organ, no one like any of the others. There are some as soft as a baby's skin, sweet like the sound of oboes, spicy and fresh-smelling as a meadow . . . and others that look positively corrupt, distended, mottled, triumphant . . ."

"Mmm . . . mmm . . ."

". . . and all of them ready to metamorphose into something even richer and stranger. Just imagine how that makes a woman feel! But she has to make a choice. She has to start somewhere. And that's where the genius of the inventor of the cubicle becomes evident. No matter how experienced you are, no matter how subtle the impulses you try to convey through those pedals, never, or only by sheer accident, will you manage to guide your favorite toward yourself! As soon as you've made up your mind as to which one of these magical rods (that never stop weaving about for a second while you're reflecting) you want, they all go into an even wilder, occult dance, like charmed cobras, undulating, hovering, twining round each other, coiling and uncoiling ever so nonchalantly, striking the air with the languor and capriciousness of reeds in the wind, yet always retreating at the very last moment before they touch you, making you feel quite hot and dizzy—and you almost despair and decide to start masturbating, when suddenly one of those desirable yet hateful reptiles strikes, dead on target, never missing the hole! The contact is so perfectly delectable that you forget your frustration immediately and cry out: oh yes! right there! give it to me! You're overwhelmed, you surrender yourself entirely. And why not, to such powers of art and science? Where you have been expecting disdainful metal, it now feels petal-soft and gentle as a lover's breath. You expected a savage piercing and possible mutilation, and now the foreplay and the penetration are so sweet that you weep for joy. It goes faster and slower, in and out, it swells and it twists: it doesn't stop; suddenly you're afraid it won't know when to stop, you resign yourself to being fucked to death by it. But, miraculously, it knows better than you what your limits are, and it explores them as no one, no thing has ever done before. Your body lies there, wide open, exposed to a kind of invisible anatomy lesson. But then, quite soon, you aren't thinking any more, you're laughing, you're twitching, you're weeping, you're coming, you're dying, you're living like never before, you're flying off into outer space.

"You think it's all over, but those marvelous pedals set the nest of tender vipers into motion again. Another writhing head takes the place of the one you've just extruded, in your great spasm. You find yourself submerged in new sensations. This time it's like a powerful and regular piston working away, growing ever more determined and irresistible with each stroke, and you howl with pleasure. As you lie there, panting, the things take another turn, and again, there's a new frequency, new kinds of pressure: you're dilated by gigantic apparatuses, you find yourself squeezing long, thin, supple rods trembling inside you. . . ."

"And that just goes on forever?"

"No. Strong as the robots are, they're males, nevertheless. There comes a time when all those artificial pricks give in to their own pleasure and pump you full of their juices, if they happen to be inside you, or ejaculate all over your belly, your tits, your face, if they happen to be dancing around in the air above you. Their sperm is wonderfully rich and musky. If you want, you can take them in your mouth and drink your fill for once—for, unlike ordinary flesh-and-blood lovers, their supply is abundant. They'll satisfy you to the very limits of your thirst. One after the other, the huge rods slide into your mouth, more succulent and voluptuous to the touch of your tongue than any human tissue, and disgorge, in long sweet spurts, their sexual juices, none of which tastes the same as any other. Their exquisite flavors are sweet and intoxicating. Then, after a signal from the machine, the assistants will come and carry you from the cubicle to another room where waiting clients—who have paid a fortune for this privilege—will have their way with you before you're even aware of their presence. Thus, the clever managers of this establishment gain a multiple profit: the large sum you yourself are paying for using the automaton, plus the price of your body, which they merchandise without your even knowing it."

From the leather case, Ariane takes two very long foam rubber phalloi, identical, both of them ending in abnormally large heads. She joins them together, base against base, to form a double dildo, with a leather belt round its middle. Using all her strength, she then bends it: it appears to be reinforced with a steel spring—for as soon as she has brought the two glans together and lets go, the apparatus snaps back into its original arched shape.

Ariane shoves the *ithyphallos* into Emmanuelle's vagina, as far as it will go. Then, straddling her girlfriend and lowering her own cunt toward hers, she impales herself on the other rod, sinking down on it until their pubic hairs mesh. After that, she stretches herself out on top of Emmanuelle, like a male lover, and starts fucking her gently. At each thrust, she herself feels the latex member with its steel spring inside it, and it feels good, she starts moaning, she bends down and crushes Emmanuelle's lips in a passionate kiss, stifling her little exclamations of delight. The nipples of her breasts swell and rub against Emmanuelle's. To increase the pleasures of abandon, Ariane extricates herself from Emmanuelle's embrace and has her partner stretch out her arms on both sides. Ariane's firm buttocks are bobbing up and down, accelerating, and when she comes, her spasm is so similar to a man's that she imagines she feels herself ejaculating—with the difference, however, that she isn't losing any of her impetus, and thus does not have to stop fucking Emmanuelle. Who, in her turn, flickering from one orgasm to the next, practically deaf and dumb and blinded by tears of joy, runs her long fingernails across the statuesque back of her indefatigable mistress, drawing blood. And so they go on, forgetting all other projects, men and such, until nightfall. They remain linked together even in sleep. Nor does Gilbert, after having stood there and gloated over them with a lecherous grin, attempt to separate them: he tiptoes out of the room again, without disturbing them.

"Gilbert, tell me, how many lovers has Ariane had?"

"Lots and lots of them."

"How did she get started?"

"Before she got to know me, she had been content with simply having a good time. I taught her to like giving a good time to others."

"So she owes her good fortune to you, is that it?"

"Well, that applies to everybody, doesn't it? No one can educate oneself entirely."

"But how many virgins, gifted girls at that, have died virgins, for lack of instructors!"

"Well, you don't cease being a virgin until after the seventh time with the seventh lover."

"Ariane, tell me about how you lost it."

"I was engaged to Gilbert, madly in love with him. All his friends liked me, they were proud to show me off. Gilbert entrusted me to their attentions quite often, and in a way that I found quite disconcerting at times. Thus, after some dinner party, quite late at night, he would simply decide to say goodnight to me and ask his friends to take me home. At first, I was hurt: was I boring him? did he have enough of me? had

I become a drag for him? But then I realized that he didn't part from me in order to put some distance between us, but exactly in order to leave me with the others, so that he could then fantasize about me and them! Even before that, when we were all together, he was pleased to see how I made their crotches bulge, and that was why he continued to invite them, in fact. But his pleasure grew even keener when he could sit there by himself and visualize me at the mercy of all those men! I learned, quite soon, to share that sensation; it made me feel tense, vibrant as a piano-string. At first, it was painful, but quite soon a new strange appetite seized my imagination, as I started rubbing my thighs together beneath my gown on the seat of that limousine that was carrying me through the night, sandwiched between two young men who were my fiancé's closest and most trusted friends. He never said anything about it, and I never asked him. Then, it just happened one day, a new, unknown sense of freedom filled my senses and provided them with quite an unexpected voluptuousness. Sitting in that car, I was thinking only of Gilbert, growing hot between my thighs over him, but at the same time, quite furtively, I was trying to aggravate the temptation I knew I was to my two escorts. My breasts brushed their arms, my shoulders abandoned themselves against theirs, with a perfidious trustingness. . . . If we had a long way to go, I would always fall asleep with my head under their chin, my hair tickling their lips. I would keep my legs uncrossed, and if one of their hands, quite by chance, of course, happened to come to rest against my crotch, I would gladly retain it there, to keep it warm. I was ready to go to bed with every one of them, but they didn't dare. . . . When we arrived in front of my house, and stood before the iron gate, no lights anywhere, no sounds, I let them kiss me on the cheek and hold me by the waist, pressing up against them so languidly that they must have been well aware of my desire for them. The next day I told Gilbert how much I liked them and how I was wetting my pants, squeezing against them in the front seat: he made love to me with increased fervor, and I felt all kinds of delightful ideas germinating in my head. . . . We kept on going out together. Each time they took me home I lowered the guard a little more, as my own desire grew greater. Finally, one night, one of them ran his palm over my breasts. I let him go on, with a kind of point-of-no-return feeling that was more wonderful than any pleasure I had known until then. When he started to open my dress and was fumbling around with the hooks, I helped him, with a gesture I was hardly even conscious of. Now he had his hand on my bare skin, inside the dress, and slowly, gently, he caressed my breast until he reached the nipple and took it between his fingers, knowing that that was exactly what I wanted him to do. It was all over, I was ready for him. I don't know how long this state lasted, in the car that was slowing down now, with the driver looking unperturbed and keeping his eyes upon a road that had tall poplars growing on both sides of it. But I felt the throbbing within his solid body against my own, and I was delirious! The car suddenly stopped. Great, I thought: I hadn't said a word, yet they knew that they could have me now. If they hadn't decided to do it, I would have hated them. I was thinking about what it would be like to see Gilbert again after this, but then I decided that that was looking ahead too far. They were in no great hurry, and that was good, too. The first one was still playing with my nipples, and the other one, the driver, sat there and watched us. I wanted to give myself to them stark naked, because I knew that the idea of my nude body obsessed them. For quite a while, I had been feeding that obsession, leaving my legs uncovered when I was sitting between them, wearing unbelievably low-cut evening gowns. And now I would have them all over me, not only on my breasts, but upon my ass and crotch as well, everywhere, their hands, their hot hands, not Gilbert's hands, not his hands to whom I 'belonged,' and whom I was deceiving even before I became his wife! Well, you adulterous spouse, you, you'll know what it felt like! Only, can you really? To give myself to the friends of my fiancé, to whom he had pretended to entrust me, as only a bride can be entrusted: surely it was unheard-of that such upright escorts, such a woman could abolish all myths with a few joyous strokes—no, you can't really have an idea what a dream it was! I looked down at my legs. The driver was staring at them, too. How sensuous and available they looked! Undulating under the other one's caresses, I had slid my gown up above my waist. I wanted them both to see my tuft, still encased in a black lace brief. I thrust my pelvis forward, and one rough hand immediately let go of a tit and slid down to grab my cunt. I can't quite recall what my physical sensations were, but I do think that the one who was caressing me wasn't solely concerned with his own pleasure. Then they opened the car door and led me over into the shade of the trees, made me a pallet out of their own clothes, and took turns fucking me, running through their entire repertoire of sex fantasies, never once daring to speak to each other, let alone to me. I couldn't even begin to enumerate all the things we did, going at it until dawn. We were cold, covered in dirt and sweat and sperm, quite wasted, really, and my back was hurting. But how we laughed—finally! I looked at myself with the greatest admiration: there I was, in the buff, the imprint of twigs and leaves all over my body, a one-night-stand-become-miracle, a good little girl who had opened her legs to two men on the moist aromatic surface of the earth, drunk with happiness and daring."

Emmanuelle takes care not to interrupt Ariane. She listens to her, lying on her belly, leaning on her elbows, a sphinx in love:

"After that, Gilbert and I were ready for marriage. I didn't tell him anything, nor did his friends, for sure. It wasn't necessary. If love does not provide us with such intuitions, what use is it? To be his wife, oh, how I wished for it, and it proved a feast! At first, we just did what all young-marrieds do—stared at each other for days on end, our hearts pounding. But then we remembered the rest of mankind, and started considering who among those around us, friends and strangers, were worthy of our love, as well. And such research has been the story of our marriage. It's true; we've really taken that first impression of our Creator seriously, whose creatures we all are: that verse in *Genesis* that says, quite simply, 'It is not good that man should be alone.' Well, now you know. For that's our only secret, if it is one, my sweet little marvel—and that is what I owe to my husband. He taught me . . . friendship."

The lineaments of gratified desire, thinks Emmanuelle, looking up at Ariane's face.

"And I found out that the friends who did not really feel any desire for us weren't our true friends at all. And that those who longed for our bodies but wouldn't admit it, still had a long way to go, to earn our friendship."

"And what do we have to do, to prove ours, for them?"

"Simply what I do when I give myself to them. What do I want friends for? To cause them suffering? Have I sought them out merely to deprive them of my charms? It's they who make this earth habitable for me: they have a right to everything I've got. They deserve, at least, that I make them a gift of my most precious possession: and what is more precious to me than my own body?"

The bells of the cathedral across the street are calling the faithful to evening vespers, curiously enough using a profane dance tune.

"You see, I didn't always know there is only one way of loving," says Ariane. "The morality of my childhood insisted on different kinds of love for bodies and for souls, and also for those who possessed such things as souls. One had to be very subtle and precise so as not to confuse the sacred with the profane. Yet one made mistakes all the time—but so did all the Saints, as any reading of their lives will demonstrate. In spite of my innate talents and energy, it would have taken me a very long time to arrive at the truth had I been left to a merely theoretical study of the matter! Fortunately, I married quite young, and I've been able to learn from practical experience. Then, too, I've had a fine instructor."

Ariane's bantering tone glosses over her very real emotion, as she finishes her confession:

"Gilbert was my first friend. Even the best among all those who came after him, I owe truly to him. And their nakedness in my arms has resolved those problems caused by the duplicity of my early education: it's not so easy to distinguish a naked friend from a naked lover. Tell me, Emmanuelle, would you give me the cold shoulder tonight if I told you that, for me, you're one and the same woman—whether I call you my mistress or my friend?"

7

The Age of Reason

*LOVE.—Passion of one sex for the other. Conjugal,
legitimate love. See: Marriage, nuptials. Illegitimate,
free love. See: Concubine, debauch, gallantry, liaison,
libertine, lecher, union (free w.) Venal love.
See: Prostitution. Ancillary loves. Impure, culpable,
criminal love. See: Adultery, incest.*
—Paul Robert, *Alphabetical and Analogical
Dictionary of the French Language,*
"Words and Ideational Associations"

*. . . but this one thing I do, forgetting those things which
are behind, and reaching forth unto those things which
are before, I press toward the mark.*
—Saint Paul, *Epistle to the Philippians,* 3:13–14

"Well, we all thought you were lost," said Anna Maria, getting out of her car and removing from it an easel, a paint box, and a bunch of paintbrushes.

"Maybe I was," Emmanuelle replied, lackadaisically.

"Where shall we go?"

Emmanuelle raised an arm, pointed.

"Over there. On the terrace."

That was, as Emmanuelle well remembered, the place where she had discovered Marie-Anne's charms. Anna Maria held no such surprises in store.

In passing, she picked up some chocolates and cookies and told Ea to prepare some fresh orange juice.

"As long as I can keep my eyes on you," said Anna Maria, putting her hands on Emmanuelle's shoulders and seating her on the pile of cushions, "at least I know you aren't up to any of your little tricks."

Emmanuelle chuckled a bit, contentedly, smugly.

"Look at me," her visitor said, putting a firm finger under her chin and raising it.

Then she stared straight into her model's eyes. Emmanuelle noticed how her heartbeat picked up speed. Anna Maria sat down on the bare terrace tiles, crossing her legs, in front of the divan she had arranged Emmanuelle on. The low easel was next to her, and she put a moderately sized canvas on it.

"You're going to fit all of me into that little space?" the model inquired, with mock indignation.

Anna Maria just laughed.

"Don't you think it would be better if I took my clothes off?"

"That doesn't bother me either way. All I really want to paint is your eyes."

Emmanuelle looked frankly perplexed.

"But I don't like posing!"

"Don't pose. Just start telling me about all the horrible things you've done, hiding out with Ariane."

"So you are interested in stuff like that?"

"Well . . . why shouldn't I be? Perhaps it'll help me understand you better."

"In order to paint my eyes?"

"Yes, who knows?"

Emmanuelle sighed, obviously anything but mollified. She tried to think of something to say that would really shake Anna Maria's composure. Right!:

"It's such a wretched time in my life, anyway. I might as well spend it having my picture painted. . . ."

Without flinching, Anna Maria looked at Emmanuelle, as if to ask: "Why is it such a wretched time?" Her hostess didn't wait for any further expressions of interest, but hurried to furnish an explanation:

"You see, I found out yesterday that I wasn't pregnant after all."

Thinking that she had discerned a fleeting expression of disapproval, Emmanuelle hastened to continue:

"For four days I thought that I would become a mother. But I guess it was just a change of climate or something. . . ."

"You've been luckier than you deserve."

"Luckier! How so? I would really enjoy being pregnant, now."

"Without knowing who the child's father was?"

"Well precisely, that's what would've made it so amusing!"

She heaved a great sigh, and Anna Maria thought: she really means it, too. What a hopeless case.

"Still, I would have tried to figure out who it could have been," Emmanuelle said dreamily.

She seemed to get lost in some complicated mental calculations, aiding them with her fingers, licking their tips, one after the other. . . .

Anna Maria preferred not to follow her onto what seemed to her a road paved with infernal intentions. Without a word, she became absorbed in her work, marking the center of her canvas with gray and black lines that soon cohered into a kind of anguished landscape. Emmanuelle, disappointed to see that her subject was found so lacking in interest, came back from dreamland and asked her:

"Can I take a look?"

"No, it's nothing yet. And it's no use talking about what it is I'm doing, at least not until I've finished it."

"When will it be finished?"

"There's no hurry, is there? You yourself said you didn't think there was anything better for you to do, these four or five days."

"There's still all kinds of great things one can *do,* you know," Emmanuelle corrected her.

Anna Maria knew without the shadow of the doubt that those things consisted of various more or less unorthodox ways of making love. She didn't ask for any details.

"Well, despite everything, it's brought you back to your husband, hasn't it?" she said. "Ariane doesn't love you when you've got the curse?"

Emmanuelle shrugged, impatiently.

"You don't understand. I just wanted to see Jean again, that's all. I was missing him."

"Well, you could have invited him to tea, with your new playmates."

"That's exactly what I did."

"And how did he react?"

"With great good humor. We were all sitting there laughing our heads off, stuffing ourselves on little *gâteaux*."

"That was all?"

"Well, then Jean and I left together, like two little turtledoves."

"Poor Ariane!"

"Why poor? I'll see her again."

"And the Count de Saynes?"

"Oh, he can have me any time he feels like it."

This time Anna Maria's silence was fairly thunderous. Then:

"So Jean didn't really have anything to say about your escapade? Hadn't he been missing you?"

"He was happy to know that I was happy. That's what he told me."

"And you? Knowing that he was all alone didn't spoil the fun for you?"

"He wasn't all alone. I was thinking of him."

Emmanuelle flared up a little:

"There's no use exaggerating things, you know. I didn't 'abandon' him for such a very long time, you know! He's been back from Yarn Hee less than four days, and only spent two nights without me."

"What would you have said if he had passed those in the company of one of your girlfriends?"

Emmanuelle looked at her wide-eyed, sincerely astonished by the absurdity of the question.

"But I would have been delighted! Nothing could have been better. If only I'd known Mervée better. . . ."

"Mervée!"

"Don't you think she's awfully pretty?"

"Pretty, I don't know. But her . . . and Jean!"

"Why do you say that? Wouldn't they get along?"

"My dear Emmanuelle, it's quite obvious that you're a bit deranged—or, perhaps, more innocent than I would have believed. Are you saying that you'd like to provide that girl with an opportunity to take Jean away from you?"

"To *take* him *away*? Why even think of that? Surely a woman can sleep with my husband without *taking* him *away* from me!"

Anna Maria shook her head. She looked genuinely alarmed. Emmanuelle burst out laughing.

"Oh, Anna Maria, listen! I've made love with men who have given me greater physical pleasure than my husband ever did. And yet, not only do I not feel like leaving him in order to go and live with them, but I love him, *him,* even more than I did before meeting those others! How would you explain that?"

"I'm not even trying to explain."

"But it's so simple! It only proves two things—first, that I love Jean, and secondly, that the more I make love, the better I know how to love!"

The other girl frowned. Emmanuelle went on:

"If the love one feels for a man can't survive a bout of making love to another, just because that other makes one come better—then that love wouldn't be much to brag about it, would it?"

"That, surely, is one of the reasons why we prefer a woman to remain faithful to her husband," Anna Maria explained, trying to sound cool and objective about it.

"Who 'prefers' that?" Emmanuelle said, with some emotion. "Only people who are frightened! It's just plain old blue funk, that's all your virtue is based on!"

"But what if Jean does suffer from your debauches, without admitting it to you?"

"He doesn't have any hangups like that. Men who guard their lives with utmost jealousy are very unsure of themselves, the kind who secretly suspect themselves of being inferior lovers. Jean isn't afraid of that, ever—not one way or the other. That's why I love him."

"Did he himself *encourage* you to take on other men?"

169

Emmanuelle blinked. That was her one regret.

"No, he didn't. He just gives me permission."

Then she added, with characteristic frankness:

"But it's true, it would have been even greater if Jean had done what Gilbert does. That would be the one thing in the world that could make me even happier!"

"Gilbert? What is it he does?"

"He lends Ariane to his friends. What a lucky woman she is!"

"But that's terrible!"

"There you go again. You're one of the frightened!"

"But Emmanuelle, have you totally lost your sense of what's good and what's evil? How can you approve of a husband who traffics in his own wife's body, as if it were just another consumer commodity?"

"Traffics? That isn't the right word. He doesn't ask for anything in return. And it isn't all that terrible to be just a commodity, as you say: I love being consumed!"

She scrutinized the effect of that shot and found it satisfactory.

"Surely, such lending and borrowing just enhances one's sense of possession? A jealous husband can have no idea what he's losing, in keeping his woman to himself alone, like a miser fingering his coins."

"If that's the case, why don't you tell Jean to start pimping for you?"

Emmanuelle raised her eyebrows, looking as if she had just received a pretty good idea. For a moment, both of them were silent. Anna Maria seemed completely engrossed in her painting. And yet, when she straightened her back with a tired little sigh, put the brushes away, and rested her elbow on the divan to take a short rest, Emmanuelle was delighted to hear her portraitist return to the same old subject:

"So Ariane gives herself only to those men her husband offers her to?"

"Oh, no."

"Well, then she doesn't act right, according to your theories, even! She deprives Gilbert of his right to lend her only to those he chooses—she ignores his rights as a husband, even there. She acts like a free woman, not like a wife."

Anna Maria appeared enchanted by her own reasoning, and ventured further:

"And you, you're worse than her—giving yourself only to men Jean doesn't know anything about!"

"There's more than one way of being a good spouse," Emmanuelle said, reflectively. "The main thing, surely, is to harness one's erotic life and energies in the service of marriage. After all, that's what we want, isn't it—to establish a happy love relationship?"

"I have strong doubts about your methods."

"But you're wrong. I told you, making love has taught me how to love!"

"So happiness is merely a question of amorous techniques?"

"The progress I've been making hasn't been only on the physical, but on the mental level as well! I have learned not to suffer from things which in themselves do not cause any suffering. Lovers tend to torment themselves and each other, more than they tend to simply love each other. I've cured myself of such morbid tastes! I don't want love to be a cause for worry, to myself and Jean, but a true solace. Not exam week, so to speak, but continuous vacations! It's high time I realized that, too. Before settling down to being married, one has to earn the right to simply *be*."

"But virginity is the inalienable right of one's future husband, even before one has ever seen him."

"That's what they're still saying, yes. But it ought to be the other way around. Instead of her ignorance and awkwardness, her crown of inhibitions and her bouquet of prejudices, a bride's dowry should consist of a taste for love, for the art and science of it! Or, at least, if she hasn't had the guts to gather some experience before her wedding night, she should hurry to make up for lost time immediately after! The girls who start running around and coming back from their side trips like fresh flowers give their husbands more cause for pride and delight than those who wilt in the candlelight of the spiky altars of conjugal fidelity."

"Such poetic eloquence, trying to doom every honest couple to dullness and etiolation!"

"No, it's just a simple fact of life, that's all. A marriage can only renew itself through the stimulation of eccentric affairs, numerous escapades—these are the salt of its long, long dinner *à deux*."

"But what if instead of spicing up things, they poison your relations? What if the marriage dies from them? Or would you deny that that isn't the most probable outcome of such conduct, in the majority of cases?"

"If it dies, it has been a bad marriage! No use crying over that kind of spilt milk. The breakup of such a union doesn't harm anyone."

"So you're saying that only the disciples of Eros will survive."

"The others aren't even alive. What use are such zombies, anyway?"

"What about the jealousy other women must feel—say, the ones whose husbands you're appropriating with such light fingers. Don't they have any right to it either?"

"Am I supposed to be a guardian of stupidities? A champion of outdated savagery? Among some primitive tribes I gather it's customary to amputate girls' clits, to make sure they won't have too good a time, ever. In our culture, one doesn't even need a medicine man's services for such an operation: the young women themselves consent to similar self-immolation. I have no patience for those whose world view is more retarded than that of any Pgymy tribe!"

"You don't seem to have much patience for anything, you eccentric and prodigal spouses, you. . . . I guess your husbands will have to get used to the idea that any day, whenever fancy grabs you, you'll present them with children fathered by other men?"

"Those children aren't 'by other men': they are human beings. With human beings one doesn't fuss over their provenance the way one does with wines or cheeses! When I'll have a baby, I won't worry so much about its lineage, but I'll certainly worry about the world it'll have to live in. If it isn't a world suffused with intelligence and freedom, the poor kid'll be just a poor bastard in any case."

Anna Maria was silent for a moment, staring at her palette. Then she raised her head, asked:

"Tell me, Emmanuelle: will you give your children complete freedom?"

"No. I'll forbid them to regress to the year 1000."

"What will you teach them in matters of love?"

"Love is one, and indivisible."

"But will the love you feel for them be the same you feel for Jean?"

"I've told you, there is only one kind of love."

"But you go to bed with Jean—even if you don't regard it as his exclusive right."

"And so?"

"Will you make love to your children as well?"

"I can't tell you. I'll let you know when I've made their acquaintance."

"And you'll allow them to love each other?"

"Allow them? But of course! It would be monstrous if I didn't."

"I see that the worst is yet to come."

"So that's it! You're really terrified! Those are the 'true taboos' to you, aren't they?"

"Leaving the laws of God aside, don't you even recognize some elementary laws of nature?"

"I accept them all—I have no other choice! My electrons spin round their cores, just as they please; gravity pulls me down, and one day, I'll have to die. As long as science cannot help me overwhelm those laws—and it never will be able to reverse all of them—I can do nothing but conform to them. But I don't see anything in them that would forbid a brother to make love to his sister. To tell the truth, it seems to me that nature even favors such liaisons in our time."

"It isn't permissible to love someone without touching them?"

"It's *you* who are setting up all these restrictions! All I'm saying is that I think everything is permissible."

Emmanuelle stretches on the divan like a big cat, yawns, making no effort whatsoever to conceal the fact the conversation is beginning to bore her. But then, an outburst:

"To love without touching, to touch without loving: for two thousand years Christians have been milling around those problems of passion, like moths swarming round a lantern. Nothing wrong with that, if such an obsession had only made *them* a little crazy in the head—but they've gone on to derange the entire earth! They've put fig-leaves on statues, calico dresses on Tahitian beauties. They've managed to make us be afraid of our own bodies. Isn't there anything better to do in this world, on this planet, than to wear a hair shirt and chastise oneself?"

"There are other values, beyond the carnal ones."

"Come now, who says 'carnal'? The soul I feel growing within myself is certainly worth as much as one that's perpetually drugged by prayers!"

"And that soul, it doesn't see any other purpose in life but to indulge in erotic pastimes?"

"What I'm saying is that those who are blind to eroticism are equally blind to all of life's other purposes. And those for whom the flesh is worthless find the values of the spirit equally incomprehensible."

"Oh, Emmanuelle . . . Such a prophetic voice, intent on casting me into the shadows! If only you could make me see your truth more clearly, perhaps that would increase my desire to follow in your footsteps."

"Well then, please look at me. Do I look like someone who is an incarnation of evil? Is my face like that of one of your demons? And look at my body: does it exhibit the signs of damnation?"

She whips off her sweater, cups her breasts in her hands, and holds them out to Anna Maria. Anna Maria is smiling.

"They say the Devil is beautiful," she half-whispers. "But I don't believe that. Beauty comes from God."

"Wrong again," says Emmanuelle. "Beauty is the work of human beings."

Anna Maria contemplates her for a moment, without a word. Then she jumps up, with a slight twinge of regret, and gathers up her paintbrushes, re-caps the tubes.

"It's done?" the model asks, expectantly.

"We're done for today. Tomorow we'll see how much further we can get."

Emmanuelle bounds off the divan, leans over the canvas, makes a face:

"That doesn't look like anything," she opines. "That's not the Oval Portrait. . . ."

This Sunday afternoon, Jean takes his wife and friend Christopher to the races. Emmanuelle scrutinizes the faces in the crowd, does not recognize anyone. Admiring looks, as always, but none of them with any hints or leers that would indicate knowledge of scandal. She concludes that the hippodrome is not too popular with the elite of this city.

So much greater her surprise when she suddenly runs into Ariane, escorted by two strangers who are neither young nor handsome.

"Two diplomats I'm chaperoning round town," the Countess informs her. "What are you doing here?"

"Jean's teaching me how to bet and win."

"And are you winning?"

"Oh, all the time."

"Well, you are a natural."

They laugh. A loudspeaker bleats some incomprehensible message. Emmanuelle pivots gracefully on her heels, to see where the sound comes from: her skirt rises like a wheel round her thighs, and for a moment she's flashing the pretty curves of her bare buttocks to the world. Then the skirt gently settles over them again.

"Not bad," Ariane says appreciatively. "Will you look at Christopher! His eyes are falling out of his head."

"He's in love with me."

"And you?"

"I think he's a dear."

"Is he good in bed?"

"I'll tell you later."

She changes the subject.

"I got a letter from Marie-Anne."

"That one! What does she have to say?"

"She talks about the sea, the wind, the sand, the traces of wind on the waves, the traces of the sea on the sands. . . . It's an outpouring of poetry."

"So she must be hiding something."

"Yet she's signing herself: The Reverend Mother Virgin Mary of Saint Orgasm, Prioress to Our Lady of Masturbation."

"That sounds better."

"She also tells me Bee has been to see her."

"Oh? Just that?"

"Listen, you must know her real name?"

"Who are you talking about?"

"About Bee. Stop pretending."

"Oh, her? It's Abigail. Abigail Arnault."

"Arnault! You must be joking. How is that spelled?"

"Same as in French spelling: *a-r-n-a-u-l-t*."

"But listen! That's impossible. . . ."

Emmanuelle looks confused. Ariane is surprised:

"What's the matter with you?"

"Because that's *my name*! My maiden name. The name of my family. . . ."

"And so what's so extraordinary about that? I'm sure you must have some uncle who emigrated to America."

"Don't be silly."

"All right. Listen, I'll tell you something: Bee doesn't exist. You just dreamed her up."

Emmanuelle rubs her forehead.

"Sometimes I ask myself if it hasn't been just a dream for quite some time now."

After a little pause, she says:

"What about her brother? He's a figment of my imagination, too?"

"Not for me, he isn't," Ariane says emphatically. "At least not since Maligâth. Before that he was just part of the decor."

"That night, he made love to you?"

"Oh, divinely."

"To me, too."

"Truly? Bravo, my sweet! We were *both* lucky then."

"How's that?"

"What I meant to say is that he's got eyes only for his sister, normally."

"For his sister?"

"Yes, you remember her: your dearest friend?"

"But . . . why? Does he love her so much?"

"To the point of madness."

Emmanuelle hesitates:

"Is . . . I mean . . . do you think she's his mistress?

"What an absurd question! You didn't know that? They make no secret of it. Michael and Abigail, Abigail and Michael. . . . it's Daphnis and Chloë, or Cleopatra and her brothers. She didn't tell you that?"

Emmanuelle avoids the answer, damaging as it would be to her self-esteem. She just says, dreamily:

"They're lovers."

"You feel your moral indignation rising?"

"No, oh no. . . ."

"Remember what one expert said: Incest strengthens family ties, and thus it furthers the citizens' devotion to their fatherland." Ariane winked. "The family that lays together stays together."

Emmanuelle grinned, suddenly very gay.

"They'll stay here for at least another couple of hours, staring at their four-legged friends," Ariane remarks a little later. "Do you find them interesting, these galloping creatures?"

"No, not really."

"You're right. Why don't you size up the men, instead? Who knows? You might even come up with a thoroughbred!"

"Terrific idea. See you later!"

She rejoins her husband:

"Is it all right if I go for a little walk? I'll be back before the last race."

"Fine. If you don't find us here when you get back, we'll be in the bar."

She walks through the building which separates the race track from the tennis and squash courts and swimming pools. Perhaps her adventuresome mood is reflected in her face: male attentions grow more insistent. Or is it due to the fact that the daylight behind her in the corridor shows her to be perfectly nude under her shantung dress rendered transparent by the slanting rays of the September sun?

Emmanuelle finds her own costume rather on the modest side. The dress is buttoned all the way down the front. But, as always, Emmanuelle has left the top buttons open, so that her breasts can be seen: and now, without breaking stride, quite casually, she raises the front of her skirt with one hand. The onlookers and passers-by stumble and stop to reassure them-selves that they're not hallucinating—that they've really seen that black triangle of an uncovered cunt, all of a sudden, right in front of their eyes. . . . Calmly, Emmanuelle unbuttons the dress from her hem to groin: now every step uncovers her bare legs, and she watches them flash forth, golden-skinned, from the swirling raw silk material. My legs are beautiful, she congratulates herself. My breasts are beautiful. My entire body is beautiful. I want to make love.

She'd cast inviting glances at all the males she passed. By the time they recovered, she had already gone by, and they turned around, but were unable to muster the courage for pursuit. Emmanuelle felt like singing. She sang. A large group of people stopped, smiled admiringly. Her bare legs were carrying her along, jouncy like a dancer's; she started running; her dress flared out behind her. *I am happy: I won't allow myself to suffer ever again. The age of ignorance is over. Over, all the sorrows of my childhood! Now I know how to love.*

She had reached the huge parking lot, not an inch of space of which wasn't taken up by some automobile, all colors, shapes, and sizes. Should she pick one? Slowly she sauntered past pink and blue giants of American make, a muscular red Italian, a white dwarf (*a nostalgic memory came to mind: the last book she had been reading before quitting the science faculty had been titled* A Contribution to the Study of the Spectrum of White Dwarfs; *she had wanted to become a great astronomer; but Mario had said it was necessary to leave the equations and their unknown factors to others: her role, her very own, was to create a great work of physical love and beauty. . . .*); with a sigh, she caressed the low, short snout of the little white auto: it was English, she was sure of that, with its huge eyes bulging out of its fenders.

"You like Gussie?" said a lighthearted voice, in English.

She gave a start, then saw its source: a young man with a good-humored face, sitting behind the car's steering wheel. He had close-cropped hair and eyes so light and clear that it took her a moment to ascertain that they were, in fact, blue. Emmanuelle gave him an encouraging sidelong glance.

"How about a ride?" the young man said, still speaking English.

He slapped with the flat of his palm the aluminum flank of his dear steed, from which a pleasant smell of leather was emanating. Emmanuelle drew closer. He certainly is handsome, she thought, but he must know it's I who's doing the picking up.

She raised one knee, propped her foot against the weather stripping that protected the bottom edge of the car door: her dress slid off her thigh. The young man took his time examining her. Then he clicked his tongue with approval and said:

"You sure are one lovely doll!"

He pointed to the empty seat beside him:

"Come along, baby!"

Emmanuelle raised both legs and climbed onto the back trunk. Suddenly she pivoted on her buttocks, and let herself slide down onto the seat, her skirt hiking up to her waist, revealing her total nudity below. She turned her face to the man questioningly. He kissed her cheeks, grazed her lips, spoke to her. She pushed herself against him. She couldn't understand why he didn't touch her cunt immediately.

Finally he started up the car, drove out of the sunny parking lot and across the city, out past the rice fields that were inundated and muddy. The water buffalo raised their slow heads to watch them zoom by. Chattering away, ducks and geese scattered before them. Emmanuelle was resting her head on his shoulder, pressing both knees against him, and with his free hand, while they were traveling at a steady speed, he began fondling them, his fingers still not daring to proceed to the luxuriant black bush or to the breasts, now uncovered by the wind.

Several times, Emmanuelle thought she saw an oasis of shade under some tamarind or kapok tree, standing in the midst of a field, and she pointed and shouted:

"There!"

But they were already far past it, and they burst out laughing at their own silliness. Then, however, the sky started clouding over, and the young man looked worried. At an intersection, and almost without slowing down, he made a U-turn that threw Emmanuelle close up against him, and they were headed back toward the city again. Emmanuelle decided that she had already seen this scenery on the way out, and so she shifted her position, now resting her head upon the driver's thighs. The steering wheel, fashioned out of steel and wood, looked threatening above her, and she pushed back harder against the young man's belly. Before long, she felt that swelling against the back of her head she had been waiting for. With subtle movements of her neck she encouraged it and succeeded so well that she couldn't contain herself any longer, but inserted her hand between her own bare thighs, and time exploded in one continuous *frisson* of pleasure.

The big, heavy, warm raindrops that started falling on them were unable to disrupt her ecstasy. The car came to a stop in a gravel drive, and the young man gathered her up in his arms and carried her into a little cottage. Emmanuelle's hair was streaming down to the ground, the ocher yellow silk of her dress clung to her skin. He put her down on a raffia divan and sipped the rain water from her eyelids. He took off her dress, let his own trousers fall to the floor, and without further ado inserted his cock into her. Instantly he started ejaculating, coming in lengthy spurts, grinding his teeth, his eyes closed, while she was holding him tightly, not even wanting to come again herself, nor in any way to change the egotistical perfection of male pleasure, the solitary and hermetic world of the remorseless spasm.

He pulled out, got up. How amazingly handsome he is, Emmanuelle thought, with delight. We're a well-matched couple.

"I'd like to take a shower," she announced, out loud.

He showed her the shower stall, and she enjoyed it to the full. The water jets made the strands of her hair stretch over her back, and down between her breasts, like fierce black rays. The young man grabbed hold of her again, rubbing himself against her cool body, and bit her on the shoulder, hard enough to make her utter a little cry.

"My husband doesn't like tooth marks," she reprimanded him, but with a mocking glint in her eye.

He seemed overcome by remorse and started massaging out the traces of his impetuosity. Emmanuelle disengaged herself, knelt down in front of him, took, before he could utter a word of protest, his prick into her mouth and treated it so tenderly that it came to attention again. Emmanuelle's cheeks inflated and deflated, her tongue curled and swirled around the tip of the cock. She continued until the massive, erect member seemed about ready to explode: she then took it out of her mouth and leaned back to admire her handiwork, vibrating in the void as it was now and looking positively apoplectic. . . . Undaunted by such mute supplication, Emmanuelle proceeded to rub her host all over his body, using a huge cake of perfumed soap, quickly covering him with a layer of opaque foam.

"Come on, let me do it!" she insisted, smiling beatifically.

With the palms of her hands she drew circles on the chest and belly of her hour-old lover, massaging his muscles, whipping up the lather, giggling, blowing into the soap bubbles. She went on to rub his back, his legs, while he just stood there and let her have her way, then his buttocks, and finally, his cock, with such persuasive hands that it quickly returned to the state it had been in a moment before. Using both palms and fingertips she worked on it, long strokes, quick jerks, never stopping, and the white-frothed penis began to shudder. Its owner stood there, waves of heat rising up to dim his vision. His will seemed to have disappeared entirely, there was nothing for it, he thought, but to submit to this beauty's administrations, even if they should kill him. His thighs were knotted and tense, his knees hurt, he was whimpering. Emmanuelle, still glistening with the shower water that kept falling on her as if she had been the central figure of a fountain, kept her eyes steadily on the thick glans, and she could see it turning purple, even through the white lather. Now and again she applied herself to his balls as well, stroking them, tickling them with her fingernails, extending these caresses beyond them a little ways, up to and around his asshole. Then, suddenly, she squeezed the prick hard and pulled the foreskin back as far as it would go without tearing, and repeated this motion until a violent spurt surged out of the prick's eye and into hers. She had still time to plunge the phallus into her mouth before the spasms were quite over, and to get enough of a taste of his spunk to make the taste of soap seem less bitter.

She regretted losing part of the royal fluid, and she thought of how nice it would have been had the shower stall contained yet another lover, so that she could have sucked both of them off at once. Next year, for her twentieth birthday, she would make sure to have twenty males coming into her mouth, one after the other. What a phenomenal birthday party that would be! The idea seemed so exhilarating that she jumped to her feet and jumped up and down a couple of times, totally in love with both the present and the future.

"Let me rinse you off," she told her partner, who was just standing there, still anesthetized.

She scrubbed him, dried him, gave him a big kiss, then dried herself and declared:

"Time for me to take off: it's getting late. Thankfully, it isn't raining any more."

She came out of the bathroom, bent down to the rush-mat-covered floor, and picked up her dress, scrutinizing it. It looked as if it had come straight out of the tub.

"Well, I can't put *that* on again," she said, matter-of-factly.

Most probably this boy wouldn't have any women's clothes to lend her. She looked at him, indicating perplexity, drank half of the drink he offered her, sighed.

"I suppose I'll have to stay here until it dries out."

Her host considered the problem, without appearing too competent:

"What if I gave it to my maid, she could iron it dry?" he suggested, in grammatically perfect French.

Emmanuelle laughed at his naïveté. A better idea:

"She could probably lend me a sarong?"

"Well, I've got some shirts and slacks here. . . ."

Emmanuelle made an impatient gesture.

"Slacks, no thanks. But I could probably use a pair of shorts. I'll fix them somehow."

She pinched in the too-ample waistband and then rolled the short legs midway up her thighs. The young man's expression seemed to indicate that he couldn't quite see her point in covering everything up again. But the shirt really looked sexy, the way she tied it in a knot below her breasts, not using the buttons at all. . . .

"All right, take me back, and fast."

Once again the white sports car made its way across Bangkok.

"Where do you live?"

"Take me to the Sports Club. My husband is waiting for me there."

He decided to forget about trying to figure her out, and simply obeyed her orders. The parking lot was empty of all but two cars, one of them Emmanuelle's. And there stood her chauffeur, waiting as usual. He said, in that peculiar drone Vietnamese affect whenever speaking French:

"Monsieur has gone home. Monsieur sent the car back for Madame."

"You see, I must hurry," said Emmanuelle to her young conquest and bounded out of the roadster, holding her drenched gown in one hand.

"But . . . but when can I see you again?"

"I don't know. I have to rush off now!" With her fingertips against her lips, she blew a cloud of kisses at him. He just sat there, looking resigned.

As they were passing the swimming pool, separated from the road by a tall cactus hedge, Emmanuelle thought she heard someone calling her name. Or was it really her they were calling? She signaled to the chauffeur to stop and leaned out of the window. On the mosaic pathway leading to the pool stood a shadowy figure making large, beckoning gestures in her direction. Who was that? It didn't look like any one of Emmanuelle's recent acquaintances. Then the shadowy form started running and arrived by the car in a couple of bounds. It was a woman, not "young" in Emmanuelle's eyes, since she appeared to be in her late twenties. She was extremely slender and finely built, all the way from her elegant neck to her shoulders, waist, and thighs; her belly was muscular and so flat it seemed almost concave, and her legs were long, svelte, and firm as well. Her trimness was all the more astounding because, atop a thorax and rib cage that revealed itself at every breath the woman took, she sported a pair of perfectly round breasts not unlike those found in the erotic statuary of Indian temples. They were firm, their skin of a satiny amber color, almost demanding to be touched. They seemed so firm, so full, so juicy, that their weight did not appear to weigh on them at all. While she was staring at them with stupefied admiration, Emmanuelle thought that they were so bursting with life, that they seemed, actually, to be *rearing* . . . ! And it was plain to see that their wonderful shape owed nothing to the bikini bra which didn't even pretend to support or conceal them.

Those breasts fascinated Emmanuelle so powerfully that it took her a moment or two to scrutinize the woman's face. Deep, wide, dark eyes, with an almost feverish brilliance in them. A narrow and straight nose, high cheekbones, a fleshy mouth, smeared with white lipstick. Half the forehead was concealed by a slate-covered bathing cap, a big mop of curly rubber-strands that looked like a slightly inhuman head of hair.

"Come and take a swim," the woman said invitingly, in a deep voice that Emmanuelle found beautiful and strange.

"I'm late already," she tried to argue, but gave up almost immediately. But then another objection came to mind.

"I don't have a bathing suit."

"That doesn't matter, there's no one here but us."

That "us" was fraught with mystery. Emmanuelle hesitated. The other woman opened the car door, held out her hand. Her voice was caressing:

"Please!"

Emmanuelle found her exciting. She made a quick decision, got out of the car, and told the chauffeur:

"Wait for me in the parking lot. I won't be a minute."

She took the stranger's hand and followed her at a brisk trot. In a matter of seconds they were on the other side of the tall hedge. Emmanuelle bumped into her guide: she had suddenly stopped, turned around, and proceeded to divest Emmanuelle of her shirt and shorts. She found herself stripped naked before she had time to say a word. It was a very special and extreme nudity, seeing that it took place, for the first time, in such public surroundings. Although it was dusk already, the night did not provide her with the slightest cover, because tall flood lamps were beaming down onto the marble sides and the rosy water of the pool, with a light even starker than day.

Two men were standing in the pool, over by the shallow end, the water rising only to their chests. The woman guided Emmanuelle over to them, made her descend the steps. She introduced the bigger man as her husband. He, too, was dark and bony, with a deeply lined face, a sharp nose, very dark eyes: their stare was so intense that Emmanuelle thought the man was attempting to read her thoughts. Perhaps he was some kind of fakir? The other fellow appeared rather ordinary, but Emmanuelle liked his looks more. He seemed to be her own age.

And now, she was asking herself, what happens now? It was obvious these three had congregated here for some amorous fun and games: it would have been positively perverse to assume anything else. So she decided to wait until they assigned her part to her.

"Who is she?" the older man asked.

His wife shrugged, indicating that she didn't know.

"You don't know who I am?" Emmanuelle exclaimed. "But why on earth were you calling me, then?"

"I saw you this afternoon at the race track," the woman said. "You were naked, under your dress."

"You could see that?"

"Well, you were taking great care to make it quite obvious."

Emmanuelle smiled, acknowledged the appropriateness of that reply. The woman addressed her again:

"You are a nymphomaniac, aren't you?"

Her captive regarded her with flabbergasted mien. Why not "schizophrenic"? Or epileptic, ataxic, aphasic, while we're at it? She had to laugh out loud.

"You've got some pretty strange ideas."

To her surprise, the dark-skinned man took her up on that.

"But it is *good* to be a nymphomaniac! If you aren't one, you had better become one."

Emmanuelle didn't know what to think. Perhaps, after all, her concept of what nymphomania meant was a false one? She had to admit to herself that she wasn't quite sure what exactly the nature of that illness really was. . . . Was it an illness, at all? Or merely a state . . . ? The younger man burst out talking, startling her:

"Hell yes, I know who she is! It's the little Lesbian who's married to the director of the dam project."

That description amused Emmanuelle.

"Not a bad introduction," she confirmed.

The young man made an annoyed face.

"She doesn't care for men in the least," he claimed.

The older man looked at him with equanimity.

"Well, so much the better," he said.

Emmanuelle felt an almost irresistible urge to burst into giggles. She pretended to be indifferent while the dark-skinned one fondled her breasts, her buttocks, her vulva. So successful was her simulated frigidity that the man decided to appeal to his wife.

"Come on, *you* get her ready," he said.

Faithful to her assumed role, Emmanuelle almost swooned in the arms of her female partner, who was diddling her with agile fingertips. The touch of those superb breasts against her own was, moreover, quite sufficiently exciting to turn pretense into reality. . . .

"Why don't you take off your bra," Emmanuelle moaned.

The woman gave no reply but continued to masturbate her, staring straight into her eyes all the while. Emmanuelle didn't take long to come, gasping, seeing the floodlights revolving above her in the blackness. Her hair was floating on the water's surface.

"Now, hurry up," said the woman, offering the trembling body to her husband.

He pulled down his bathing trunks, but only midway to his knees, took his thick cock in his hand, spread Emmanuelle's legs, while his wife was still supporting her. After a couple of tries, he was all the way in. His companions assisted by supporting Emmanuelle with their four hands and moving her back and forth on his member, like a big masturbation doll. As that notion occurred to Emmanuelle, she felt great delight: how wonderful! she thought, I'm nothing but a vagina, an anonymous vagina, a utensil in the service of the god. . . .

The two acolytes had eyes only for the leader of the group, observing the progression of pleasure upon his face, speeding up the rhythm, slowing it down until he seemed to be on the verge of coming, then speeding it up again, to see him draw a great breath and get his nerves under control once more. Emmanuelle was light and easy to move, in the cool water. The cock circulated freely within her, without interruption. She felt a pressure mounting inside her that she wouldn't be able to contain for very long, thinking that it was bound to explode her, carry her away in a vertiginous conflagration of pleasure.

To allow the man to plunder her even more fully, she raised her knees and squeezed the man's hips between her thighs. She also wound her arms around his neck. Now the supporting hands let go of her, permitting her to continue her motions on her own. No longer did she pretend to be cold: she would come any minute now, and it would be a perfect orgasm. After that, her vanquisher could do with her whatever he wanted, even auction her off to the highest bidder, if that was his pleasure. . . ! But first of all, he would probably hand her over to his young friend, provided that cherubic fellow liked women.

She glanced around to catch a glimpse of the young man's supposedly minuscule member, but when she saw it, she had to gasp: he was standing there holding it in both his hands and pumping it with unbelievable brutality, his eyes steadily on the spectacle of coupling genitals right in front of him. However, it wasn't this violence that frightened her, but the positively monstrous dimensions of the glans and the shaft he was working so hard. There was nothing human about them. If that one tries to get into me, she thought, he'll just tear me to pieces, he'll shred me, render me useless forever! And such a prospect drained away all sensuality. Pleadingly she looked at the other two: but there was no response.

A stifled groan made her turn back to look at the young man, and she was most relieved by what she saw: the voluptuous spectacle of clouds of sperm, long, convoluted strands and little puffs of it, bubbling around the cherub with the minotaur's phallus, finally floating toward and sticking to her own skin. Well, now she could let herself go! She came brusquely, a rattle and a loud cry rising from her throat. The man who was fucking her looked at her closely, reflecting her own expressions of passion and intensifying them until she thought she would lose consciousness altogether.

He pulled out of her without ejaculating. They lifted her out of the water and stretched her along the poolside. For a moment, they just stood there, contemplating her in silence.

"Do you want to do it right now?" the woman asked.

Her husband appeared undecided. Finally he said, shrugging his shoulders:

"Well, she's your prize, after all. You had better decide."

"Tomorow we'd have more time," the woman remarked, in the same neutral voice that all three seemed to use, and that corresponded with the obsessive fixedness of their looks.

When Emmanuelle came to, her newest lover told her, politely but firmly:

"Tomorrow, at three o'clock in the afternoon, I expect you at my house. I trust that you'll be punctual."

196

Emmanuelle found nothing odd in being addressed in this manner. After all, a man had a right to tell a girl to do this or that, after he had given her such a good time.

But she wanted to know:

"How will I find your place?"

"Oh, it's very easy. You know the skyscraper building? I live right on top. My name's on the door: Doctor Marais."

She picked her shorts and skirt off the mosaic tiles, considering for a moment whether she should put them on again, or whether she should go home nude. She decided to compromise by walking over to the parking lot as she was, to put her things on in the car. The chauffeur's face did not betray any of his thoughts.

Her husband was sitting on the terrace, reading.

"Oh, darling, it's terrible, I'm so late!"

He took her arm, studied her costume, burst out laughing.

"You've been cuckolding me a whole lot?" he wanted to know.

She nodded emphatically, making a cooing, affirmative sound. He took her face between his hands and kissed her lightly on the mouth.

"But you're soaked through," he noted.

"My dress is in the car," she said, as if that would explain everything. Then:

"What time is it, anyhow?"

He checked his wrist watch:

"Twenty-five after nine. Have you had dinner?"

"No. But I hope you haven't waited for me all this time?"

"Christopher's got a slight fever, he didn't want anything. So I dined in splendid solitude."

"But that's awful! I'm sorry, I should have come home sooner."

Then, as if she'd only now understood his earlier remark: "Christopher's sick? What happened?"

"Oh, nothing to worry about. He just stayed out in the sun a little too long, that's all. You know what he's like: trying to get acquainted with all the little fillies at the track. He never does anything by half-measures."

Emmanuelle sighed with relief. She felt happy to be home again. She said:

"Don't I look like an idiot, in these shorts," took them off, threw them behind the sofa, unknotted the ends of the shirt and let them fall over her belly. The shirt was barely long enough to cover her pubis and her buttocks. She buttoned it, one single button, at the waist.

"That looks nice," Jean said approvingly. "And now, have something to eat."

He sat down at the table, facing her. The boy placed a steaming bowl of soup in front of her, and she started sipping it, daintily, smiling angelically all the while.

"Did you fall into the water somewhere?"

She looked radiant:

"Yes, I did, and I got the worst of a thunderstorm as well!"

He went on looking at her, in silence, with evident pleasure. In less than five minutes she had finished her meal. She jumped up, embraced him:

"I must look in on Christopher."

"Yes, hurry. And here, take this with you, to revive him a bit."

He handed her a bottle of gin.

"Good for sunstrokes, you know."

"You think so? One of those ancient Egyptian remedies . . . ?"

She put the bottle under her arm, hiking up her shirt-tails, exposing her thighs.

She ran up the stairs and burst into the guest room without knocking. Christopher suddenly seemed to be engaged in a frantic struggle with his bedsheet, trying to make it cover his nakedness. Emmanuelle had to grin: poor fellow, always so concerned with propriety!

"My sweet little Cristobal, so you aren't going to die after all?"

"But of course not, I feel better already."

He was glistening with sweat. She looked around, left, returned with a towel, sat down on the bed, and wiped his face dry. He tried to protest:

"But please, don't bother. . . . Thank you very much."

"Just lie there and take it easy."

She went on to rub his chest, then tried to pull down the sheet to get at his belly, but he clutched the top with such pathetic energy that she had to burst out laughing.

"I'll get you some broth, and perhaps a little porridge. . . ."

"Please don't! I'm not hungry at all. But what I could do with, for sure, is a small gin-and-tonic and some ice. . . ."

"So Jean really does know your tastes, I can see that."

She got up to ring the bell for the houseboy. When she sat down again, her skirt didn't only uncover her thighs, it was open wide enough to expose her belly and its little fleece. Christopher found it a positively hypnotic sight. His temples were throbbing. What a silly fool I am! he told himself. I've seen her in the nude God knows how many times, I can't start acting like an idiot now, just because she's sitting on my bed. . . . Brusquely, he turned his back to her. Emmanuelle looked worried, put her hand on his forehead, tried to feel his pulse.

"Don't get excited now, Christopher. I think that ice would be better employed in a little bag to cool your head. Are you sure we shouldn't call a doctor?"

"No, no. I assure you, by tomorrow morning I'll be perfectly all right again."

But right now, he thought, with some bitterness, I'm not all right at all. I'm a pathetic bastard! Far from calming down, he felt an irresistible urge to feast his eyes some more on the spectacle of Emmanuelle's thighs, her black triangle. . . . Still, so long as he kept his back turned to her, she would not be able to discern the state *he* was in. If she did, that would certainly put an end to his friendship with Jean and with her. . . .

She thinks of me as a brother. That is why she is not in the least embarrassed, why she doesn't want to hide anything from me.

"But you're quite red in the face, Chris! I'm sure your temperature is rising." She wiped his face once more, throwing him into a panic at the idea that she might discover the sign of his criminal feelings. He tried to snub her:

"Oh, why don't you just leave me alone!"

But that didn't do the trick. Emmanuelle had decided that Christopher was definitely getting worse. She ought to go and tell Jean about it.

But perhaps, he thought, perhaps she'll think the erection's just a fever symptom? If only I could grab hold of it for a moment, to ease the pain a bit. . . .

His desire was so strong now that he whimpered a little, thus increasing the solicitude of his nurse. She asked him a question, but he didn't hear it. The only thing he wanted, now, was for her to take his suffering cock into her hands and console it. He was almost ready to risk everything, even if it meant that he would have to leave the house immediately afterward and be blackballed forever from the world of gentlemen. Well, then, he'd suffer! He envisaged, he yearned for an entire life of opprobrium, if it had to be the price of a single moment of such felicity. . . .

He sighed and turned over on his back, looking at Emmanuelle with despairing eyes. She instantly noticed the bulge under the bedsheet, and it made her feel quite tender.

Poor Christopher! she said to herself. So that's why he is so unhappy. But if I make love to him now, that may just make him even more miserable. I really don't know. Still, I don't really want to leave him in this uncomfortable condition. Oh dear, what should I do?

She couldn't possibly leave the room: he'd certainly think that he had shocked her with the sight of his erection, bizarre fellow that he was! Well, why not be frank, why not say: "Would you like me to stroke it?" But he'd simply blush all the way up to his scalp, hoping that the earth would swallow him up. How about being a little more circumspect about it: "Is there anything I can do for you?" No. Then he'd just ask for another shot of gin! The easiest way would be to just slide one's hand gently under that sheet and . . . but, the poor dear, he might start yelling! If only he would extend himself a little more, himself! Emmanuelle had to smile, once again, and Christopher, who took it to be a mocking smile, felt more miserable than ever.

Never mind, come what may, he'd fight a duel with Jean, he'd let himself be killed, but he *wanted* Emmanuelle, he'd take her by force, he'd violate her, by heaven! He'd stifle her protests with the pillow, and then he would make such savage love to her that he'd die in the process, exhausted by his exertions and his fever. That way there would be no need to worry about consequences. But what about her? She would be dishonored, she might even commit suicide! And it would all be his fault, he, the friend, their chosen brother, the author of all those horrors. He felt a wave of nausea rising in his throat. What a beast he was, what a depraved creature! He would have cried over his own misery, but he was even more ashamed of that tearful impulse than of his concupiscence.

She is the very incarnation of fidelity! For her, her husband is the only man in the world. In her eyes, I'm nothing; she doesn't even see me, really. But oh, if only she would just squeeze it in her palm a bit, wrap her fingers round it, down there, give me a little ease! I'll wriggle a little closer to her: as long as she stays put, perhaps I can manage to rub it against her buttocks a little, without her noticing. . . .

Emmanuelle looks at him, doesn't know what to think. What a strange fellow! Three weeks he has been staying with them—why hasn't he tried to make it with her yet? Having her there, at arm's length, but missing every opportunity. Surely he has to realize that everything that belongs to Jean is his to use as well. Wouldn't it be too absurd to have his friend lend him his house, his car, his books, his pipes—but not his wife? What use is a pretty wife, if one keeps her all to oneself?

She feels hot, so she takes her shirt off. Christopher stares, admiringly, almost sadly, at her breasts. She is so perfect, so pure, he thinks. Capable of these gestures that in any other woman should be plainly provocative . . . I should get down on my knees. . . .

Emmanuelle stands up, tiptoes out of the room, returns back to Jean.

"He looks like he's asleep, but he keeps on babbling. Do you think he is delirious?"

"He tends to ramble a bit, doesn't he, even in the rudest of health: haven't you noticed?"

He puts his arm round her.

"Would you like to make love?"

"I'm always ready for that."

She starts taking his clothes off:

"Tonight," she says, "I'll get on top of you first."

And later, murmuring, between two outcries:

"You don't mind having an adulterous wife?"

If I manage to get across the street in this getup without being arrested by a cop, Emmanuelle says to herself in the car that is taking her to her appointment, and if the doorman doesn't throw me out, I'll be lucky if I don't get raped in the elevator.

But then, she reflects, could anyone rape me any more, now that I give myself to everybody who wants me? That would be difficult. I've become inviolable.

And yet, she goes on, I suppose there will always be ways one may feel violated. It's a question of atmosphere. Or person. Or intention. In any case, a turbulent experience. If I were just any woman, she says to herself, I'd like to be violated all the time. . . .

The chasuble of red jute material, her only item of clothing, is quite an unconventional garment. It consists of a rectangular piece of cloth, without any trimmings or buttonholes or hooks, nothing but an opening for the head to pass through. The two halves of it cover her body in front and in back, and they are held together at the waist by a thin leather strap. But they are wide open on both sides, giving an excellent profile view of her breasts and thighs, and, in the lightest breeze, of her buttocks and belly, too.

She has decided that a true philosophy of clothing does not allow any compromises, and she has made up these guidelines: if she is wearing a skirt, it has to be either transparent or vented in some manner, and always at least a hand's breadth shorter than the prevailing fashion; if it is full or pleated, she must raise it whenever she sits down; if it is tight, the material has to be such as to slide up along her thighs of its own accord. For daytime wear, she prefers translucent jersey skirts and onion-skin-thin tops that give her breasts a little color and accentu-ate their nipples. Or else tailored shirts, which she leaves open down to the waist. For the evening, square or round décolletés, revealing the darker-skinned areolae surrounding the nipples; and, whenever she leans forward, exhibiting her bosom to the fullest. She does not like strapless dresses, because these fit too tightly over the breasts: loose, low-cut capable of yawning is much more appealing. As for undergarments, she has decided never to wear any.

She does not have to affront public propriety on the street, because the chauffeur, despite the "no stopping" sign, takes the car right up to the front entrance of the skyscraper. The major-domo does not bat an eye, nor does the elevator boy, nor the other people going in or out of the various floors of the building. Emmanuelle feels proud: audacity has won another battle.

The terrace, overlooking the city, resembles a large garden, with the doctor's apartment standing like a villa in its midst. The façade is overgrown with roses. The name is on the door all right.

Doctor Marais was busy trimming his rosebushes. . . . No, she decided, that would be a poor beginning: better to have the story start with the unknown. No one about; a wall; a door; everything lies behind it. But what? Would anything happen? Or nothing? Did she have the faintest idea of what was waiting for her?

The wolf's jaws, she thought, staring at that door. If I don't come out again, no one will even know where to look for me. She inspected the expensive-looking stone: what was it? Not marble. Flint? None of her familiar witnesses would be there. Would it not be better to turn around and get them? Or, simply to stick to the games at the Club, where the terrain was familiar. . . .

She roused herself: this was no time to beat a retreat! She rang the doorbell.

The very young girl who came to open it was obviously a maid, to go by her costume, and yet this was the most surprising element: instead of the traditional sarong worn by Siamese servants, it consisted of a very tight-fitting dress, as short as Emmanuelle's, if not even shorter, but woven out of—in this climate!—a black woolen material, with long sleeves, and with a high, round, white collar. Her coiffure, ringlets and fringe, was held together by a pert triangle of lace, in the classical stage-chambermaid fashion. Even more unexpected were the fine black stockings covering legs that Emmanuelle found breathtakingly beautiful: they were very long and uncommonly delicate at the ankles and round the knees.

"Please come in, Madame."

The voice was suave, the accent so good that Emmanuelle wondered if this ravishing creature wasn't French, after all: but that was certainly contradicted by her tawny complexion, her almond-shaped eyes, and high cheekbones. She was looking at the visitor with an intensity that could well have been mere innocence. She added:

"My master and mistress are waiting for you."

Emmanuelle followed her through air-conditioned halls, her feet sinking into the carpeting, her eyes admiring the old paintings hung on the walls. Bangkok seemed a long way off. . . .

The room she was introduced into was large, cool, dimly lit: at least, it took her eyes a moment to get accustomed to the twilight, tempered by lamps shaded with natural silk. No light whatsoever entered from the outside: all around there were only screens and tapestries, no windows or doors except for the one she had just come through. Icons, precious woods, embossed leather, books, rare old arms, ancient gold coins came slowly into focus. A sweet silence, a silence that was positively furry, enveloped her, caressing her like a gentle breeze.

And the people she had met the evening before were there, watching her come in.

The woman who had "discovered" her was now wearing a pale green leotard, looking like a ballerina or a hotel thief; it was all of one piece from head to toe, covering even her hands. Even now, Emmanuelle could not really tell whether her hostess was blonde or brunette. But her breasts, happily (and that was the most important thing), remained just as preeminent under the tight-fitting nylon as they had been in the bikini top.

The conductor of the séance watched Emmanuelle from his armchair with studied indifference. He was clad in tight corduroy pants, a finely knit sweater, a silk foulard round his neck. Emmanuelle remarked to herself that these two were obviously a couple suffering from chilliness. There was another person standing beyond him, this one in full evening dress; but what was most remarkable about him, in Emmanuelle's eyes, was his perfectly polished cranium, an object carved out of ivory, it seemed, with not the least trace of hair. The next moment she realized that the man had no eyebrows or eyelashes, either. . . . Yet he seemed neither repulsive nor frightening.

She noticed, finally, that the adolescent from the swimming pool was also present, lounging on his back on a black leather couch, pretty as a picture, eyes closed, stark naked.

As far as Emmanuelle could make out there was no one else. The chambermaid had probably retired. . . . But no, there she was, a dim figure in a dark corner. Her pointed breasts rose and fell in a tranquil rhythm.

The doctor got to his feet, bowed, kissed Emmanuelle's hand, offering her the armchair he had just vacated. She found herself next to the hairless fellow. Her host introduced him:

"My illustrious friend, Georg von Hohe."

Illustrious, thought Emmanuelle: I wonder who he is?

"Little Eric seems to be taking a nap," her host added, in an affectionate tone.

Well, he's got a right to do whatever he wishes, Emmanuelle said to herself. With that cannon he has down there between his legs. . . .

The German held out a glass to her. And that seemed to be all the conversation for the time being. For a moment Emmanuelle had the impression that everybody else had fallen asleep, too.

Trying to appear unconcerned, she sipped the beverage that she had been offered. She did not realize how treacherous it was before she had swallowed it: her head was turning! She felt annoyed.

"You're trying to drug me, is that it?" she said, angrily.

The physician came to life again, but only to shrug his shoulders.

"Nothing but alcohol in your glass," he said.

"Well, then you must be trying to get me drunk, at least."

"It's up to you to exercise moderation."

Emmanuelle was in no mood for such comments. She laughed, defiantly.

"So that's what you got me here for! To have me exercise moderation!"

It is quite possible that my train of thought isn't all that radiantly logical, she admitted to herself, but, to be quite frank about it, I'm beginning to wonder what on earth I am doing here! No one seemed particularly impatient to benefit from her presence. Perhaps, after all, the only objective of this get-together was to sit around and do some quiet drinking? The brusqueness of the reply she called forth took her unawares:

"As you seem so intent on knowing your role in advance, I'll tell you what it is going to be. You are here because we intend to make the *fullest* use of you."

He spun around on his chair and slapped it, with an affectation of hauteur that impressed Emmanuelle less than the words that followed:

"The kind of fun and games we provided you with yesterday doesn't interest us at all, I'd like you to know. But if that's enough for you, so much the better. It takes more to provide a really exciting time for us. We don't much care about your own orgasms, now: today you'll permit us to use the means that provide *us* with the most satisfaction. You've had your pleasure: now it's our turn to take ours."

The temptation of fear raised its ugly head within Emmanuelle. No need to dramatize things, though, she said to herself: the most urgent thing was to try to find out the particular tastes of this bunch. Thus, she continued the dialogue:

"The cocktail I've just swallowed is not one of the means to that end?"

"I haven't said that it was given to you without any motive."

"So you think you'll find me more satisfactory when I'm drunk?"

"More complaisant, in any case."

"I should think I can do better with my wits about me."

For the first time, the doctor smiled, with some condescension:

"It seemed easier to me if we could skip the preliminaries."

"But why deprive me of the pleasure of giving myself?" Emmanuelle said, bravely, in her own defense.

"You don't know what we have in mind," the woman suddenly spoke, as if emerging from a dream.

But Emmanuelle had already formed certain notions, to do with chains and whips and so forth. . . .

"You're going to torture me?"

The master of the house seemed to find the idea amusing.

"You've been reading trashy books," he said magisterially. "We've got more imagination that that."

"We want to *denature* you," said the hostess.

Her husband amplified:

"Modify your senses and your consciousness. Replace your will by another faculty. After that, perhaps, your physical attributes might seem more interesting to us, again."

Emmanuelle said to herself that she had been wrong, most probably, in resisting the impulse to turn back at the door.

"And what are you going to have me do, when you have transformed me according to your ideas?"

"Those things that you would never do in your normal state."

"Will it change my looks?" She was alarmed.

"Yes, but for the better."

"I find myself pretty enough the way I am now."

"You could look a little more animalistic. But, in any case, it's your *mind* that will be altered, primarily."

"Will I become a monster?"

"Going by society's criteria, one can admit that that word describes, fairly enough, the nature of your future actions and your future mentality."

"I'll commit crimes?"

"Certainly, but aren't you committing them already?"

"But mine do not harm anything except stupidity!"

"Well, we all have our pet hates. Our only antipathy is directed against your liberty."

Well, I've done it, I've delivered myself into the hands of madmen, Emmanuelle said to herself. And now she would have to pay for her imprudence. But not without putting up a fight first!

"Slavery has never really frightened women," she said, finding her own voice sounding like a croak. "Bondage, and so forth . . . It's just another way of having an interesting time."

"We'll turn you into something beyond a slave."

The impossibility of finding out the exact nature of the danger—that was the most frightening thing!

"I know now," she said, "you're going to hypnotize me."

"Please, kindly forget all those dime-novel hypotheses. It would be better for you to remain calm."

"So you think I'm scared?"

"I don't give a damn. The only thing that's important to me is the state that you'll find yourself in quite soon."

"But why not describe it to me? Perhaps I can enjoy the anticipation of it as well as you."

The doctor looked at her with what seemed to be a glimmer of curiosity.

"It doesn't matter one way or the other," he said, as if talking to himself, "whether you find it enjoyable or not. . . . Surely you must understand that you have no other choice, now, but to go through with what we want you to do?"

"But you didn't bring me here by force, did you? I came here in all good faith: and surely that shows that I was interested in the experience, whatever it may be?"

This time, the doctor looked obviously intrigued.

"But . . . You didn't have the faintest idea what it would consist of?"

"That's just it. I'll know it when I've done it."

He was lost in thought for a moment, then seemed to make a sudden decision.

"Well, here's what it is all about," he said. "To begin with, you'll enter into a state of super-orgasm. This will happen

213

without anyone so much as touching you—not even you your-self. The quality and intensity of what you'll sense cannot in any way be compared to the pleasures you may have previously experienced, as brilliant as the resources of your temperament appear to be. You'll be literally *crazed* with pleasure. And this condition will last, without any interruption, for several hours."

"How many?" Emmanuelle wanted to know.

"This time, only a couple, I think."

She made a grimace, indicating that this did not seem all that special to her.

"And then?"

"Psychologically, you'll be seized by a veritable passion for acquiescence. Your whole desire will be for others to use you like an object, like a soulless commodity, not for your own pleasure, but for the pleasure of those who are holding you. With frenetic intensity you'll offer yourself up to the sating of all their fantasies. You'll become obsessed by the idea of mak-ing them come."

Emmanuelle burst into laughter.

"But really, I can't see anything in that worth making a fuss about!" she exclaimed. "I've already been through all that I don't know how many times! If *that's* what you're trying to discover, I can tell you right now: it's very pleasant."

The physician turned toward his accomplices, as if to have them witness this impudence.

"You really won't be outdone, will you now?" he then said to Emmanuelle, with a sarcasm that did not seem to be altogether devoid of indulgence. "But there's still something else you ought to know: our sensations, while we are using you for our own purposes, will be of a degree of perfection you can't even imagine. Compared to such refinements, the satisfactions provided by nature can only give rise to sheer boredom."

"How marvelous!" Emmanuelle applauded. "And what does one have to do to get there? Because I assume there has to be some kind of conveyance?"

"Precisely. It is a certain drug."

"That stuff you gave me to drink?"

"No. This has to be injected."

Emmanuelle turned pale.

"Oh! I hate needles."

"Don't worry, this won't cause you any pain at all."

Her heart was pounding, but for other reasons than the fear of a passing twinge of pain. She tried a diversionary tactic:

"And yet, you are going to hurt me, at least my feelings," she said, turning on her most engaging smile. "Because, you know, I don't need any aphrodisiacs whatsoever, to put myself into any state I'm capable of! I'm quite naturally crazy about my own body! Maybe your stimulant only works for girls who are a wee bit short on hormones?"

"This is no aphrodisiac: those things merely inflame desire. My drug *satisfies*. It satisfies all desires beyond measure."

"Like opium, or hashish?"

"Not at all. The effect I've described to you does not come from anything outside, but from within yourself."

"Like LSD, then?"

"No, not that either. It is a different kind of action, much more radical in nature."

"Please explain that."

"I can't go into details."

"Too bad," Emmanuelle said, and sighed.

She meditated for a moment. Then:

"It's dangerous, though, isn't it? It's possible that I might die?"

He smiled, once again.

"No. Certainly not."

She seemed skeptical.

"That's what doctors always say," she remarked, without any apparent animosity. "But in any case, surely, there's a serious possibility that I might remain permanently deranged?"

"No, not the least chance of that."

"After that kind of . . . trance, one comes back to one's senses?"

"The only regret one has is that it's over! And one wants to start all over again."

"One can't do without it any more?"

"No, you can't do without it any more."

Emmanuelle did not blanch. Her expression did not betray her fears in the least. Marais went on, in his particular, dispassionate vein:

"After a couple of experiences, you'll need a daily dose. But that won't interfere with your life at all: on the contrary. . . ."

He looked at his wife. Emmanuelle wondered, feeling a sense of excitement that she was ashamed of, if that handsome creature pursued her own existence in such a world of permanent, crazed pleasure. . . . To come every day, to the point of losing one's mind, and to make one's lovers experience ever madder sensations. . . . The thought was not unlike a temptation.

"After a couple of experiences?" she said, astonished, repeating her host's words. "Are you saying that one does not become addicted straightaway?"

"It is necessary to take a number of doses," the physician affirmed, in an almost apologetic tone. "You don't acquire the habit before the tenth or twelfth time."

"But then," Emmanuelle said, appearing amused, "then what you're going to do to me today won't be any use at all. . . ."

"It'll do for this afternoon," the doctor replied, a trifle mordantly. "It's true, you won't have any permanent benefit until you have undergone the entire treatment: that won't take more than ten days or so."

"And where would I be treated?"

"Right here. You'll have to come back—we'll arrange your appointments."

Emmanuelle could hardly believe her own good fortune: so they weren't going to keep her prisoner, after all!

"I won't come back," she announced, throwing all prudence to the wind.

And suddenly she didn't feel any fear at all. She amplified her statement:

217

"Paradise really isn't my style, you know."

Then, before any of the others were able to say anything, she continued, smiling radiantly:

"But don't you worry: you'll have your little party after all. I don't like wasting my time, either. And as one time is just a one-shot affair . . ."

She looked at every one of them in turn, quite regally.

". . . I'll try your potion. I want to know what it's like."

Marais was staring at her, looking incredulous. His wife retained her customary impenetrable expression. As for the Junker, Emmanuelle did not bother to turn her head to see his reaction. All these people, she thought, they're much too solemn! Not the least little touch of her own good sense of humor. They really needed to be shaken up a little.

"All right, then, doctor, what are we waiting for? As you can see, I've made up my mind. Let's go! Don't be afraid now. Let's have that needle!"

8

Deus Escreve
Direito Por Linhas Tortas

God writes straight on crooked lines.
>   —Old Portuguese Proverb

*I have caused great calamities, I have depopulated
entire provinces and kingdoms. But I did this for the
love of Christ and His Holy Mother.*
>   —Isabella the Catholic,
>   Queen of Castile and Leon

*Let us seek, as those seek who will find, and let us find
like those who find, and have to go on seeking.*
>   —Saint Augustine

Marie-Anne surged out of the landscape one early afternoon,
the air blue with the damp sighs of the earth exhausted by
the rain. Emmanuelle was sitting on the threshold, resting
her chin on one knee, the other leg stretched out straight in
front of her, gazing into the rain-washed frangipani trees,
waiting for Anna Maria. A week had passed since her last
session with her.

"It's you! You!" she shouted, scrambling to greet her little friend. "Where did you come from? How come you're here?"

With both hands she took hold of Marie-Anne's golden-blonde plaits, laughing out loud with the pleasure of rubbing her lips against the girl's sea-and-suntanned cheeks.

"I'm here with Daddy: he needed Mom to be here, because there are people coming from Paris. We'll be here all week."

"Only a week!" exclaimed Emmanuelle, sounding disappointed.

"Why haven't you come to visit with us by the seaside?" Marie-Anne said. "I told you to."

Then she extricated herself:

"Please stop pulling my hair. It hurts."

With lightning speed, Emmanuelle tied the two plaits in a knot and twisted them around Marie-Anne's neck, as if to strangle her.

"Oh, I've missed you. You're so pretty!"

"So you had forgotten?"

"You've grown even more beautiful."

"Well, that's just normal."

Emmanuelle had a twinge of anxiety:

"What about me, do you still like me?"

"Well, I have to find out. What have you been doing while I haven't been around to keep an eye on you?"

"Terrible things, just terrible!"

"You better prove that."

"Why don't you start by confessing *your* misdeeds. This time you'll talk and I'll listen. The roles have been reversed."

"Come on, how do you justify that?"

"Because this time around I'm the less virginal one."

There was a glimmer of skepticism in Marie-Anne's smoldering green eyes.

"Seems like you're cold-shouldering Mario these days," the fey creature said, with studied nonchalance. "You're not seeing him any more?"

"That's because I've been such a great success: he just has to wait in line, like everyone else."

It was necessary to show who was boss:

"But don't you try to sidetrack me! Tell me, now. Have you had any adventures?"

"Oh, thousands."

"Well, let's hear about *one,* for starters."

The open-throttle roar of a sports car made them spin around to look down to the road.

"What kind of a machine is that?" Marie-Anne wondered. "And who's the driver?"

"That's Anna Maria Serguine. Do you know her?"

"Oh, her. She's painting your portrait. I'll watch you."

"But you know everything! How come you're so well-informed?"

Marie-Anne half closed her eyes, and, with a sleepy glance at her friend, passed on to another question, in her very own manner:

"I hope it'll come out nice, that portrait."

"I'm sure of that. But it's only my face. Pity."

"You should have a male artist do the rest."

"Have you been making love?" twittered Anna Maria, gaily.

Emmanuelle stared at her in amazement.

"No . . . Why do you ask?"

"Well, if you won't make love to this marvelous creature," Anna Maria stated matter-of-factly, "then, who'll you ever make it with?"

"I see, you're just trying to poke fun at me!"

"Not at all. I'm just trying to think the way you do."

Marie-Anne adopted a haughty tone:

"Don't ever believe Emmanuelle when she tells you she's a Lesbian. That's what she tells all the men."

"Have you any idea what you're talking about?" Emmanuelle said, suddenly bristling. "Anna Maria is right, it's time for me to have a go at you."

Her voice sounded a note of command:

"First of all, what are you doing here with all those clothes on? Come on, get naked."

"But surely that would shock your visitor. . . ."

"Not in the least," the Italian girl said, totally baffling Emmanuelle. "On the contrary!"

"Well, then." Marie-Anne curtseyed lightly, affecting complaisance.

She stripped, in a second or two, and strutted to and fro in front of her elders.

"You find me satisfactory?"

"Oh, yes," said Anna Maria. "I'll put you on my list. As soon as I've finished Emmanuelle, I want to do a sculpture of you."

"In what material?"

"Can't say that yet. In something that feels soft to the touch."

"And thus, Anna Maria will discover Sapphic love," Emmanuelle intoned, "through the medium of marble!"

"I'd like that," said Marie-Anne. "I'd like people to fondle my statue. . . ."

"Come over here," said Emmanuelle. "Let me feel your tits."

Marie-Anne obeyed immediately, and her friend reached out and started rubbing her breasts with both hands, surreptitiously glancing at Anna Maria. The Italian girl didn't bat an eye.

"You don't think I'm being disgusting?" Emmanuelle said.

Anna Maria feigned innocence:

"Do you think I'd be able to sculpt her figure if I didn't do what you're just doing?"

Enunanuelle was vexed.

"It all depends on one's intentions," she remarked.

Anna Maria laughed.

"What a world this would be, if it were a crime to touch the breasts of such a living Tanagra!"

"Why do you never touch mine, then?"

Anna Maria did not reply. Emmanuelle decided to pursue the matter:

"What about this, then?"

She slipped a finger between Marie-Anne's thighs, under the ravishing pubic fur, sun-bleached to the color of an arctic lynx. Anna Maria remained unperturbed, but Marie-Anne protested:

"You're tickling me. Stop it! You don't know how to do it!"

A gust of grief, almost distress, swept through Emmanuelle's heart. With all her might, she tried to suppress that feeble emotion: I'm stupid, she told herself, it's just my vanity that's hurt. . . . But, no: it felt bitter, the way her longing for Bee had felt. Why, why? she asked herself, almost furiously. And then, all of a sudden, the feeling was gone, and replaced by a sweeter one. Nothing wrong with that, she said to herself, nothing wrong with falling in love! And Marie-Anne isn't really refusing herself to me. Her brusqueness is of the same order as mine, it is simply a way of insisting that we have hearts. That doesn't matter: those are just the vestiges of virginity. As soon as she and I manage to really escape from this miserable age, we won't feel ashamed to admit that we are creatures of tenderness. . . .

She smiled at her friend as if she had just received an embrace.

"You're right—we'll make love when we feel like it! Not just now. The atmosphere isn't right."

She turned round and caught a glimpse of an expression on Anna Maria's face that was so fugitive she asked herself if she hadn't just imagined it. It did look, however, as if the young artist felt disappointed: it seemed she would rather have enjoyed things taking another turn. Emmanuelle felt thoroughly cheered.

Marie-Anne made as if to put on her clothes again.

"No, stay the way you are," Emmanuelle insisted.

If she agrees, Emmanuelle thought, it's a sign that she loves me. . . . And Marie-Anne threw her dress aside again. Oh, life was wonderful!

"Let's go out to the terrace," Anna Maria said.

"Listen, would you be a dear and tell them to bring us some tea?" Emmanuelle asked Marie-Anne.

Perfectly composed. Marie-Anne smiled and started off for the kitchen.

"There's nothing wrong with having Marie-Anne naked in our company," admonished Anna Maria. "But to send her on an errand like that—that's where perversion begins!"

"You're not too good a judge of that," Emmanuelle retorted. "A naked girl in a bathroom, that's just humdrum, there's no value in that. But a naked girl in a kitchen is different."

"Erotic value, you mean? But eroticism is not the criterion for good and evil. Marie-Anne's body has its human value, in the fact of her being an adorable thirteen-year-old girl. And an esthetic value as well, independent of the sexual arousal it may provoke."

"But that's just it, that's where the artists are acting in bad faith! When they paint or sculpt nudes, rather than apples, it's not because art is sexless. It is because they, themselves, and those who later contemplate their works, like being aroused that way! Their intentions are quite, quite obvious. When they calm down again, they paint a few apples: what more proof do you want?"

Emmanuelle gave her dialectical adversary no time to interpolate:

"Don't you try to throw up any smoke screens, you darling little hypocrite! I know that you find Marie-Anne's body exciting, no matter what you pretend."

"But that's absurd! Marie-Anne doesn't arouse me in the least. Whereas . . ."

Anna Maria stopped, looked discontented. It was too late: Emmanuelle jumped up, threw her arms around her neck, and said, with a mocking smile on her lips, quite close to her friend's:

"Whereas with *me,* you don't want to paint me in the nude, because you are afraid the sight would make you stray from your principles. Isn't that so?"

"No, it isn't like that at all, I assure you! Rather the contrary."

"The contrary? What on earth does that mean? Please explain."

Anna Maria was so visibly at her wit's end that Emmanuelle asked herself if she shouldn't kiss those beautiful, contrite lips, to console them. But Marie-Anne returned just a moment too soon.

"You don't *want* to understand, Emmanuelle!" Anna Maria said plaintively, gathering her convictions round her again. "It isn't simply a question of vice or virtue. Just because you like women, you think everybody feels as you do. You're quite mistaken. Most of us aren't born that way."

"Well, then they should acquire the taste!" exclaimed Emmanuelle, with aplomb. "You can learn these things, you can learn them without any ceremonial: no need to be furtive about it! Ever since I can remember I've seen girls all around me having a good time with each other."

"Was that because you converted them to it?" asked Marie-Anne, already installed on the big cushions, totally at ease in her nudity, browsing through a stack of illustrated magazines.

"No, the simple *occasion* taught them! No matter how restricted the circumstances are, once in a while any woman feels tempted, some day, to make love to another woman. Out of sheer curiosity, if for no other reason."

"Or out of laziness," pontificated Marie-Anne. "Merely because they don't have any cocksmen at hand and don't feel like going to the trouble of picking them up. Or because they get bored with doing it to themselves: why not masturbate with four hands instead of two?"

Emmanuelle burst out laughing.

"That's just convent school philosophy," she quipped. "The truth is that a woman's body is desirable, in itself, to all human beings, not only to males! Any healthy individual knows that, instinctively. Those women who pretend indifference toward the attractions of other women are either irremediably frigid or simply refuse to admit that they are victims of this society, that they've become conditioned and crippled by conformism and taboos, sensibility has been amputated."

"An entire sex has been amputated," Marie-Anne added. "One way or the other, they *are* cripples."

"Right, they'll never know what love really is: if you don't love your own, your very own kind, who *can* you love?"

The arrival of the tea tray interrupted the conversation for a moment, but the subject was bound to reappear. Some remark of Marie-Anne's, to do with the concept of "taste," provided Emmanuelle with the awaited pretext:

"That's the way it is with Sapphic love. It's a matter of esthetics, first of all. If you don't love beautiful women, you're obviously lacking in taste. Anna Maria ought to have realized that by the time she left the Beaux-Arts—unless, of course, she flunked the course!"

"I do appreciate beautiful girls! But in a normal way. Why don't you stop pretending that homosexuality is a normal thing?"

"Less abnormal, it would seem to me, than loving the Holy Virgin."

Anna Maria looked offended, but Emmanuelle forged ahead.

"Are you telling me then that your ambition as an artist is to stay right inside the confines of the 'normal'? I always thought the function of art is to open up vistas beyond mere nature."

"I try to make a distinction in the realm of the supernatural, between what is divine and what is diabolical."

"Oh, don't tell me that you really believe in the Devil: *God,* that's bad enough! In any case, why don't you make up your mind and believe in one or the other: not in both at the same time. Me, I don't really have a preference."

Anna Maria was running out of arguments. Emmanuelle had a way of switching back and forth from Lesbos to the realms of theology that wasn't too easy to cope with.

"As for God, I guess, I prefer Him," Emmanuelle conceded, regally. "I'll be right back." She left and returned a couple of minutes later carrying a huge book with a sumptuous geometrical design in red, blue, yellow, and black on its cover.

"This is by someone whom I think you admire. . . ."

"Mondrian?"

"Himself. Here it is: '*Pure beauty is the very same thing that was referred to as divine in the past.*'"

Anna Maria made a face, remained mute. Emmanuelle handed her the book. Marie-Anne piped up again:

"Tell me, it's not just because she's so beautiful that you love Emmanuelle?"

* * *

Another day, and Emmanuelle came across a maxim from Che Tao:

"People think that painting and writing consist of the reproduction of forms and resemblances. That is not so: the brush is designed to make things emerge from the Chaos."

And the next day, another:

"Nature is full of dangers. The human being feels unsafe until it has constructed a refuge, a universe of non-natural forms." That one was by Marcel Brion.

"The truth is," she said to Anna Maria, "that we're still ashamed of our animal ancestry. We're all the time trying to invent ways that will enable us to forget it. The soul, handed down by God, is one of those ideas: but it doesn't go very far, really. An artificial space that God hasn't had anything to do with, that's better: you aren't even sure of it: but that is what you are trying to create for yourself when you're painting. But that's still just a form of 'do-it-yourself.'"

She had more to say on the subject:

"Art, finally, is a manner of creation, invented by a species that is not yet able to create nature. The day we acquire the skill to create life, to rearrange the stars, we won't waste our time daubing canvases any longer."

And more:

"Mario said that the finished work of art is just a life-less tracing. Those poor millionaires spending all that money on paintings, they really are suckers! They're just buying the dead husk of art: art itself has left the canvas, the very moment the painter put his brushes down. What remains is always merely a shell. The work of art is born and dies the very same instant. There are no immortal works, there are only these creative moments that are so beautiful, that wane away before they have time to grow old. Art resides within human beings, not in things. That is what I create when I make love the way I do."

"A rather primitive approach, wouldn't you say?'

"Art can never be primitive or naïve. It's true that love can be both, but that's exactly our goal, to improve its quality."

"What's so wrong with naïveté?"

"It is wrong, because it means that you are arrested at an infantile stage. Eroticism is the very opposite of naïve love."

"Well then, leave me in infantile health! Your adult adulteries, your complicated sex feasts, your women with male genitals, your exhibitions and daisy-chains are just symptoms of diseased love, that's all; there's no art in them whatsoever."

"If I had any doubt that what I'm doing is not good, I'd stop doing it! Pleasure is not as important as pride. I'm sure there are ways of making love that are bad, as there must be ways of praying that insult God. Eroticism does not obliterate all considerations of shame, or those things one has done while closing one's eyes to the possibility that they were really ugly. But, as for me, what do I have to be ashamed of? What? I have never done anybody harm. The grace of eroticism lies in rejoicing in one's own joy, and its virtue, in rejoicing in the joys of others."

"Well, it's clear that we live in very different and separate worlds. . . ."

"Are you so sure? If you really believe that love is a fault, then (it seems to me) you deviate from the teachings of Jesus, who certainly didn't think so: who had rather a weakness for women caught in adultery, for prostitutes, for sinners! Did he ever tell anyone not to make love: don't do it, it's bad, you won't go to heaven if you do it? I've studied the four Gospels, and I haven't found any apologies for chastity in them. So, you really make me laugh, with all your continence, all your virginity! I may well enter the kingdom before you. Matter of fact, I have entered it already: where else lies the kingdom of God if not in the place where we live, men and women who have eyes to see and ears to hear, who hunger and thirst for truth. . . ? It's the kingdom of this world we have to keep on rediscovering, and it is love, and making love, that helps *me* find it."

"You're just playing around with words: the love Jesus talked about has nothing to do with your kind of whoring!"

"And what, pray, do you know about my kind of whoring? It is the kind that distinguishes between eroticism and obsessive sexuality. One does not collect stale orgasms as one does silver figurines or still lifes: one tries to invent the art of love, over and over, and one surely is more ethical than the average modern physicist."

"Doctrinaire love versus endocrine love."

Emmanuelle smiled. Anna Maria weakened a bit:

"But whom do you think such propaganda will convince? You're just screwing around, every which way, because you think it's fun, and that's all there is to it. You just rid yourself of principles that you find embarrassing, and the ones you then invent to replace them don't, finally, add up to anything but the simple fact that you find it more exciting to have ten men assaulting you than just one."

"I could take the easy way out: I could remain content with my husband, or with my own fingers; but contentment isn't the main purpose of my life."

"Its purpose should be directed toward the next one."

"I'm here on earth in order to *learn*! I don't really need to practice love-making any more. I think I'm quite good at it already. And yet I have a long way to go before I know what love really means. It's not just that I become an ever more accomplished partner of pleasure in what you referred to as 'whoring,' Anna Maria: it's that I'm trying to become a better *lover*. And to achieve that goal I'll need all my life, and all the men and women in this universe."

"Your ideal is cerebral, rather than heartfelt. Are you so certain of what that abstract human passion is that you call 'true love'?"

"How can one give rein to one's heart, without a head? Love, the love that I want to become worthy of, is just another name for intelligence. It's our blessing to be able to love that which makes us capable of genius."

"You're just fighting myths! Yet I'm afraid that your 'eroticism' is even more chimerical than those."

"It is the school of the real. I believe only in the Archimedean kind of principle: the ones proposed by some Daddy in the Sky are too airy."

"Come now, there have always been girls who went to bed with everybody! But is it to them that we owe the progress of science?"

"Who knows? If those nymphets and courtesans hadn't prevented men from totally succumbing to the hypnotic haze of church religion, down the centuries, the church might well have succeeded in amputating their taste for knowledge, their taste for life! Without those worms they were, burrowing around inside the fruit of knowledge, who knows but this world would be by now completely castrated."

Emmanuelle grew more vehement:

"*Because* of those evil laws and commandments it is no longer permissible to be chaste and faithful. It has become a duty to have numerous lovers, as revolutionaries find it a duty to throw their bombs, despite their horror of bloodshed and violence. Those who cause violence in their attempt to overthrow tyrants are not to blame. The gentlemen of the Inquisition began it! The dark souls of God's servants are a judgment on God: their reign was one of the darkest nights in earth's history."

"The invectives you're heaping on God, they're just another way of recognizing Him! You do believe in Him, but you're against Him."

"That's doing me too much honor, my dear: I'm not all that brave! It's the past that is full of God, and the past is the era of error. The truth lies ahead: and it isn't my fault if I look in that direction and do not see any God there! Don't try to make me turn back. Let me go, and perhaps I'll be able to forget my grievances."

"The Creator is not that easily forgotten."

"Isn't He? Just you try to think of God while you're coming! Religion was invented for people who did not know how to make love."

"But why, why then *is* there something, instead of nothing?" Anna Maria said dramatically. "Why is nature chockfull of mysteries? Why do bats sleep with their heads hanging down? Why are you so beautiful, you who know how to love, who will have to die one day? Science does not answer any of these."

"Nor does religion. Let's work at finding out, instead of playing this portrait game."

"At Angkor, in the heyday of the Khmer," Jean explained over dinner (Emmanuelle had invited Anna Maria and Marie-Anne to stay), "the monks of the great temple were continually deflowering virgin girls brought to them as offerings by their parents. The girls were mostly under ten. Only the poor kept their daughters virgin beyond that age, because the ritual was expensive, and the usurers would not lend them the money without collateral. The monks used their fingers or their penis. They caught the blood and mixed it with wine, and the whole family daubed some of this mixture on their foreheads and lips. Each monk was allotted only one virgin per annum. Later, when the girls wanted to get married, they just went down to the lake to bathe there in the nude, and the men made their choice."

"Nothing has changed," said Marie-Anne to Emmanuelle the next morning, as they were lazing in the sun by the swimming pool. "The bonzes still have a taste for those little virgins."

"How do you know? Have you been hanging out behind their dark altars?"

"I can know something, can't I, without having done it myself?"

"All I'm saying is that I've been told Buddhist monks never touch women."

"A virgin isn't a woman."

"What an even stranger taste then!"

"Well, they're different from us."

"And where do they find these vestals?"

"It's difficult now. The Siamese parents are no longer as devout as the ancient Khmer."

"They don't throw their youngest daughters in with their temple contribution any more?"

"Alas, you know how religions wane. There is no Buddha any longer! Nowadays the bonzes have to pay for their pleasures."

"How can they pay for them, when their vows expressly forbid them to have any money?"

"They pay in gold."

"Come on, Marie-Anne, you're making all this up! You're just trying to impress me with your terrific imagination."

"If you don't believe me, ask Mervée."

Emmanuelle did not have to look for the Lion Cub. She had hardly registered her little friend's remark, and it had completely escaped her memory. But it so happened that she ran into the jungle-tressed girl one Sunday morning when shopping for orchids, accompanied by Ea, on the gigantic square in front of the Pagoda of the Emerald Buddha. The curls and twists and swirls of the coppery shock of hair seemed part of the display, like the great blossom of some strange, well-nigh monstrous plant grown in the Thai forests. Emmanuelle noticed how that chevelure's shapes matched the girl's pointed eyelashes, the graceful jawline, the very curve of her lips, so charmingly full and smiling in that light-skinned face. . . . Somehow, Mervée's face fitted in with the curvature of the Siamese roofs: its geometry paralleled the temples'.

"Buddhist architecture and you are homothetic," Emmanuelle said, grinning at the pleasure of using such an echo from her mathematical past.

"You are interested in Buddhism?"

"Oh, not really all that much."

She watched two monks passing, wrapped up in their saffron robes, one shoulder and both legs bare, their heads carefully shaven. A ten- or twelve-year-old boy, dressed in the same fashion, walked by their side: he was holding an embroidered silk fan, shaped like a leaf from the sacred fig tree, above their heads, protecting their persons from the ardor of the sun's rays. It was obvious that these monks didn't do anything but walk around, seemingly disinterested in everything.

"They don't look like they'd do a lot of meditating," Emmanuelle remarked.

"They still have time to do all that."

Two schoolgirls were crossing the monks' path, wearing little white blouses embroidered with the initials of their school, and red or blue pleated skirts, halfway up their buttocks. The men of religion did not appear to register them. It doesn't look as if they'd be interested in that, Emmanuelle thought. She continued the thought, out loud:

"Someone told me they're not beyond associating with nymphets. . . ."

"It's not their age that matters. What they need is virgins."

"So that is really true?"

Now Emmanuelle remembered Marie-Anne's remark.

"That's right, I was also told to ask you about it!"

With a half-skeptical smile she waited for Mervée's reply.

The Lion Cub took her time answering. She was scrutinizing the questioner so intensely that Emmanuelle felt as if she had had an X-ray taken.

"Why do you want to know those things: just for your own amusement? Or are you serious?" she asked, at long last.

Her voice had the same astonishing intensity as her gaze. For a brief moment, Emmanuelle felt removed from the place, even the time. . . .

"What these monks are afraid of, most of all," said Mervée, "is contamination. Sleeping with a virgin does not soil their purity."

"I guess they don't get to do it very often, do they?" Emmanuelle asked, in an attempt at raillery.

"It isn't necessary for the virgins to be 'real' ones: all that's essential is the appearance. The Perfect One has said: all is but an illusion. . . ."

"And his disciples are docile enough to believe that?"

"The Siamese never *believe*: they know that faith is the source of all manner of boredom. And boredom terrifies them."

Emmanuelle was beginning to find this conversation quite engrossing. Until that moment she had only thought of Mervée as made up of lustrous fur and teasing claws.

"Take you, for instance," the Lion Cub said. "They'd really appreciate you, a whole lot."

"Who? The monks? Now, really! And having to pretend to be a virgin, yet!"

Mervée didn't seem put off.

"I'll take care of all that," she declared, looking roguish. "You'll be perfectly suitable."

"But . . . I don't find that exciting at all. There's nothing tempting in the idea of making love to a monk, even if it's a Buddhist one! I guess I'm just lacking in a sense of the sacred. . . ."

"That's not the question. You told me, once, that you'd let me sell you: we did agree on that."

Emmanuelle remembered Mervée's proposal, but not that she had accepted it. The ruse made her laugh.

"So I have a right," the feline girl said and stared at her with her icy eyes.

I must be crazy, thought Emmanuelle, but I'd like to do it, to know what it feels like—to be sold by this girl, like an item of merchandise. . . .

"You're doing it for money?" she wanted to know.

"Yes. Can you do it tomorrow?"

"All right, yes. Where shall we meet?"

Will I be lucrative enough? she asked herself. Will they pay a lot for me? She had already forgotten that her supposed value was in her virginity.

Their boat was gliding noiselessly, poled along by a native, over the ocher and mauve reflections on the river's surface. The river was high, fed by the rains, and as they glided along, Emmanuelle poked her finger at the coconuts and bunches of vegetables, green ones, purple ones, bobbing alongside them. The water was thick as sperm, reaching right up to the edges of their narrow teakwood pirogue, whitened by time, yet indestructible. Emmanuelle thought that she'd surely fall into the water before they reached their destination, but what did that matter? The river was teeming with swimmers, she'd simply join their noisy frolics. And here were some boys, stark naked, hanging on to the prow of the pirogue, ignoring the boatman's curses: perhaps it would please them to overturn the boat? But their hands just kept sliding along the sides of the boat, and one of the boys came close to her: his mocking eyes shone like little suns, and she smiled at him. He raised himself half out of the water, shaking his black hair, and stretched out an arm. While she was still asking herself what he was reaching for, the answer came: with the agility of a sala-mander his hand slipped under her skirt, pushed up between her thighs, tickled her cunt . . . and the kid was gone again, with a yell of triumph.

Emmanuelle started scooping out some of the water in the boat.

"I bet we won't get there without a shipwreck or two," she predicted.

Mervée said she hoped not, as their luggage would suffer from that. That's right, remembered Emmanuelle: Mervée was bringing along a bag containing a costume that she would have to wear in order to perform the desired ritual, the prospect of which amused Emmanuelle more than it frightened her: for what else did those holy men have in mind but to have a good time with the body of a live young girl? All the masquerades and exorcisms did not add to nor detract from that simple and reassuring fact. If her outfit got wet, well then, she would present herself at the monastery in her birthday dress; that was nothing to worry about.

Before they had started out, she had done all that Mervée had asked her . . . After the night of Maligâth and the various reticent hints of Ariane, she had a good idea of what awaited her. And, having accepted to surrender herself up to the Lion Cub completely, Emmanuelle considered it only proper that she should follow through to the end, no matter how bitter, and that she bestow whatever pleasure was demanded of her. After all, it would be one thing more, in the end, that she would have known. . . .

The landing stage which they came up alongside was sculptured with stucco flowers, encrusted with pieces of bright glass, covered over with a roof in the shape of a dancer's tiara—exactly like the temple to which it led. The latter was composed of many edifices, all of them very ancient, separated from each other by large patches of luxuriant verdure. The most enormous edifice of all, engirdled by an ornate colonnade, probably contained within its dark depths a massive plaster Buddha, like those Emmanuelle had seen by the hundreds over the past six weeks. She felt no curiosity to find out if she was right.

The *stupa* set in the central portion of the monastery grounds seemed to her far worthier of attention. Its foundation, in the form of an inverted bowl, was remarkable for both its dimensions and the gracefulness of its curvature. Its spire, made out of concentric, ever-narrowing circles, plunged upward most purely, to a height of over three hundred feet. The ceramic tiles, flesh-colored, that it was clad in, looked so lovable in the afternoon light that Emmanuelle took off her shoes and ran barefoot across the grass to touch and caress, with both hands, the warm carapace of the great monument that seemed to be sleeping, shut in itself, incomprehensible and purposeless under the logical sky. . . .

A young monk, apparently just idling about, approached Mervée. Emmanuelle walked over to join them. He motioned them to follow him and conducted them to a rectangular pavilion with a moss-covered roof and white walls, in which the only opening was a thick, screechy-hinged door. Sweet-smelling candles, in pewter candle sticks, lighted the interior. The furniture consisted of some armoires, shaped like truncated pyramids, with gilded doors, a few rush mats, and a couple of low tables with tiny vessels on them.

In one corner there stood a bird, carved out of wood and painted red, its eyes precious stones, its legs like those of a heron, and with the breasts of a woman: it seemed to be admiring the feminine curves of its painted mouth in a ceramic-framed looking-glass, placed at an angle. Emmanuelle stopped to stare at the thing, quite awe-struck.

The monk sat down, fanning himself. A small boy entered, carrying a tea tray. He served it piping hot, in cups that were absurdly tiny: it was necessary to drink several of them, one after the other, before one could even taste it. And it was very hot. But as soon as that had been accomplished, a pleasant jasmine aroma spread over the taste buds. Emmanuelle relished it and wondered how such nectar could fit into a life of renunciation; perhaps there was something to be said for asceticism, after all. . . .

Then the young monk, daintily holding his cup, deigned to address himself to them, but so briefly and quietly that Emmanuelle could not really hear it. But Mervée answered, in Thai. She really knew that much of it? She was talking, going on much longer than the man. Emmanuelle ventured a guess: she's praising my accomplishments, jacking up the price! The monk appeared as disinterested as ever, not even glancing at the object for sale. But that, too, is just an old horse trader's trick, Emmanuelle told herself: let's not pay any attention to that. But what a pity she was unable to participate in all the haggling! It was really high time that she picked up more of the language: her ignorance of it was depriving her of pleasures that were rightfully hers.

As suddenly as he had started the conversation the monk got up and left. He closed the door behind him. The smoke of the big fat candles was making Emmanuelle a little dizzy. She, too, would have liked to leave this anteroom. But Mervée, who seemed to know the ropes, had something else in mind:

"I'll help you change," she said.

She unhooked her pupil's dress and pulled it over her head. Then she opened the bag and took out a long and wide length of white silk, embroidered with gold thread, and draped it around Emmanuelle with unexpected skill and speed. The latter was asking herself if this wasn't the kind of toga that would come unstuck and slip off her at the very first step she'd take; but perhaps that was exactly the intention, and it didn't bother her, anyway. The costume was positively elegant. She went over to the *kinari,* to see herself in its mirror; but the candles were so dim. . . .

"Come on now," Mervée said.

Emmanuelle sighed with relief as soon as she got out into the open air. But the daylight was making her eyes smart.

They entered a corridor. Mervée seemed to know where she was going: under her breath, she was counting the number of doors they passed. At the eleventh door, she stopped, in front of a carving with large eyes and a big beak.

"Go in there," she said, remaining outside herself.

In the room, Emmanuelle encountered the young monk again. He pointed to one of the mats with a prism-shaped cushion on it.

"Sit down and wait here," he said, pronouncing the French words with confidence.

Then he left again. Emmanuelle sat down, as she had been told, folding her legs a little to one side, as she had seen the Siamese women do, at royal receptions and in the temples.

The room had no window, and it was surprisingly cool. A faint, resinous odor was floating about: perhaps from the wooden walls? One could not see them: the sole source of light was a tiny oil lamp, more in the nature of a night light, in its own little circle of luminosity. Yet Emmanuelle felt certain that the cell was a small one. She couldn't see a single item of furniture in it. After a moment or two, she realized it wasn't entirely true that the walls were invisible: the one closest to the lamp could be discerned, and as she focused her eyes on it, she could even see a door in it, lower and narrower than the one through which she had entered. While she was staring at it, this door opened. Very slowly, without a noise. Emmanuelle's heart started beating wildly. She shifted about on her mat. When the door was open wide, on impenetrable darkness, something or somebody blew the lamp out. And it was pitch-dark.

A little moan escaped Emmanuelle's lips. She mustn't start crying! she told herself. But she was so afraid. . . .

She felt another presence in the cell. She was sure it was not the young monk. He wouldn't have gone to such lengths of mumbo jumbo. Oh, she would have liked him to come back! But this one, this phantom that wished to remain unseen, what would it do to her?

She was so tense, her muscles so knotted up, her nerves so on edge that she cried out when she felt the touch of a hand. This childish reaction (that was how she instantly classified it) made her feel both calmer and less claustrophobic. She recovered her customary coolness, even laughed at herself. The visitor had most probably been just as startled, because he had removed himself again. Oh, I'm pitiful, she reproached herself: what will it look like if he just leaves me here, convinced that they've brought him an utter lemon? I'll lose face in front of Mervée, that's for sure, and she'll have made this trip for nothing.

But then, come to think of it, her girlish fright had been quite in keeping with her role: no reason to regret it. Even less, considering that the darkness and air of mystification had not been designed merely to impress her, but to hide the monk's feelings of shame. It was he who was feeling sinful, feeling the need to hide himself. Emmanuelle's conscience was unperturbed by the situation, and thus she was on top of it, and would no doubt derive some benefit from it. Now that she was not afraid any longer she felt like having a good time! So the holy man thought she was innocent? Well, he was in for a surprise. Sacrilege! Sacrilege! Scandal! ran through Emmanuelle's head, like a refrain. She shook with noiseless laughter.

Then she stretched out her hands in front of her, groping about. It didn't take long for her fingers to make contact with something: a piece of flimsy, rather cheap cloth—saffron yellow, no doubt—and then, to the left of that, a bare shoulder. There, then. The flesh was hard, the skin felt like dry stone. This monk was surely thin and tough, but far from young.

An imperious hand reached out, seized the probing hand of Emmanuelle, opened the fingers, kept it prisoner, in order to prevent it from committing further offenses. She smiled. Of course . . . a woman must not touch the cock of one of the holy *Sangha*. But then, why was she here? She had no wish to play the hypocrite. Emmanuelle struggled to extricate her fingers from the rigid grip. And, in her movements to do so, she came closer to her host. She suddenly got a wild idea in her head: she would undress him!

He did not let that happen without resistance, and the white silk wrap unraveled and fell to the floor before she was able to unknot the yellow toga. Nevertheless, the Buddhist sage's efforts were no more expert and assured than her own, and she knew how to use fingernails and teeth to fight off the adversary, so that he, too, in his turn, uttered a few cries, and they were not cries of pleasure. But Emmanuelle did not call it quits yet.

When she finally found herself stretched out, full-length, panting, exhausted, on the man's naked body, she had reason to feel contented with her effort: the phallus, hard as an iron bar, palpitating against her belly, and the burning breath fanning her face, were sufficient proof of her victory. She deserved a moment's repose.

The monk's bony fingers parted her hair and took hold of her neck, hard enough to hurt, but it was pleasurable. Then they traveled down her back, explored her asshole, squeezed her buttocks. At the same time, the man's body arched and his cock grew even bigger: its tip penetrated the entrance to her cunt, and she started swaying her hips slightly, for their mutual pleasure. The invisible hands moved up again, so hard it felt like they were digging a furrow in her back, all the way to her shoulders, gripping them and applying pressure, to make her slide farther down: she submitted, and her face paused for a moment on a chest smelling of sandalwood, and then her mouth received the turgid organ.

She started sucking, dutifully, not bothering overmuch, not wanting to squander her talents; nor did she particularly want the old savant to come in her mouth.

It seemed the monk was disappointed. Brusquely, he pushed her head away, and before she had time to speculate what his next move might be, he had turned and pummeled her onto her side, forcing her chin down to her breastbone—I wonder why? Emmanuelle thought. Then he took hold of her legs and pushed her knees all the way up to her face: she was in the foetus position. And then the bone-hard prick set to work, forcing its way into her anus.

Emmanuelle's spittle still covering the cock provided a lubricant, yet she had to hold on to herself in order not to cry out. God, how tight I am, she murmured to herself, how that hurts!

When the man had managed to enter her, she realized, with further dismay, how long his member was: she hadn't paid any attention to that fact while it was still in her mouth. It pushed so far into her that she was afraid of a rupture. She had thought the most painful moment would be when the glans forced its way into her asshole, but now, as he was pounding away profoundly inside her, her eyes were brimming with tears.

She could not have pinpointed the exact moment pleasure began to mingle with the teardrops: it had taken her much longer to come than when being fucked in her vagina. Her tears had soaked into the mat, and it smelled of fresh herbs. After she came the first time, the monk went on sodomizing her, with such strength and endurance that quite rapidly she came several more times in a row. Then she screamed a good deal louder than in the painful beginning. She was unable to say whether all this had taken only minutes or hours, nor did she know when exactly her lover had ejaculated.

And now, alone again, she lay in the dark cell. A satisfied torpor suffused all her limbs. She waited, not knowing what to do, not daring to budge. Perhaps more was required of her: perhaps more monks? She wished she could see—the darkness was becoming oppressive. Or was it the density of the air in this little chamber? She felt exhausted. She stayed as she was, curled up into a ball, heaving a little sigh now and again.

At last someone opened the door leading outside. The sun had set: it was twilight. It was the young monk they had met when they arrived. He remained standing in the doorway, taking his time staring at Emmanuelle, who was taking her time, as well. She asked herself what the one she had made it with looked like: surely he was not as handsome as this one when deprived of the sheltering dark. . . . He had certainly been much older. Nevertheless, such ardor! Probably the Head Abbot himself. His Holiness the Supreme Patriarch of the Lesser Vehicle. . . . Impertinently, she grinned at her guide, whose face did not register any reaction. He simply said, in an even tone:

"Mademoiselle, you can go now."

That's right, she chuckled to herself, I'd quite forgotten that I'm a virgin!

The idea seemed so ridiculous that she laughed out loud.

Considering what the old cenobite had wanted to do to her, she would indeed have been a fool to have any qualms about her fraud being discovered. He had fucked her anally, leaving her cunt precisely as "virginal" as when she had arrived. In fact, she was welcome to return!

Or was it—a further subtlety struck her—another kind of virginity these monks were after? But, in that case, what means had they of ascertaining that they were making the first entry through that back door? They must be pretty credulous, Emmanuelle thought: or else, true sages.

She wrapped the white silk cloth around her (and that was another puzzling detail: what difference would it have made if she had come clothed in rags and tatters?), but with considerably less care than Mervée had expended earlier on it. Then she crossed the threshold; the young monk had turned his back on her and was walking down the cloister.

After a few steps, he entered another room, a much larger one, with light streaming in through a big window. He walked over to an almost cube-shaped chest standing on an encrusted pedestal, opened it, took something out, turned, and handed whatever it was to Emmanuelle.

"Our order wants to present you with this gift," he said.

She was surprised. Was she supposed to accept it? She had thought that Mervée would take care of that side of the affair. However, the atmosphere did not seem conducive to any queries, and she took the box without saying a word.

"Open it," the monk said.

Once again, she felt intimidated. The box was rectangular, carved out of black wood, fragrant. . . . Groping around for a lock, she somehow managed to slide the lid off, and as soon as she saw what it contained, she exclaimed with delight.

It was, opulently life-sized, a phallus made out of gold, so real-looking that it must have been cast from a mold: it had to be hollow, as it wasn't very heavy. It was long and thick and arched upward, with longitudinal veins that seemed to be swelling with sperm; the glans was powerful and so lovely to the touch that one was tempted to endow it with the qualities of a mucous membrane and throbbing life. Not even Ariane's collection sported such a marvel.

And this extraordinary joystick, it really was for her? She didn't want to pass it on to Mervée! She wanted to keep it, for some occasion that would be commensurate with its beauty. . . .

The monk had walked out of the room, and she hastened to follow him. In a few minutes they arrived at the landing stage. The Lion Cub was waiting.

The young man spun on his heels and headed back to the temple without even glancing at Emmanuelle by way of adieu. She restrained an impulse to run after him, to tell him. . . . But to tell him what? She shrugged, pressed the box against her heart.

"I don't understand," she murmured. "The reward seems much too grandiose."

She showed the gift to her friend, who did not say anything.

"Some little Buddha-statue would have been quite enough. . . ."

Night was descending on the river. The boat was there, with its bored-looking boatman.

"I won't go back to town in this getup," Emmanuelle said. (She had already rid herself of the white silk wrap.) How good it feels to be naked! she said to herself. The water looked tempting.

"How about a swim?"

But Mervée shook her head:

"It's too late. I have to see someone."

Regretfully, Emmanuelle put on her civilized dress.

"Me too. I feel like making love," she said, as the boat shoved off.

"With me?" Mervée wanted to know.

"No. With some handsome young fellow."

"I'll find one for you," Mervée said.

"I'd rather find him for myself. Or let myself be found."

Their boat was gliding with the current, past the illuminated banks of the river.

"That's right," admitted Mervée, "you achieve better results when you take the initiative."

"But it is wonderfully erotic to be picked up and fucked, too," said Emmanuelle. "We are women, after all."

"It's not a question of eroticism," Mervée said, impatiently. "It's a matter of conquest. Passivity is no use at all."

"Well, I can't complain," Emmanuelle stated, with great good humor.

"How *do* you go about it?"

"It's up to those who want me to take me! They've only to take a look at my legs, my tits, to know that I'm worth the trouble."

"But they won't believe their eyes."

"Nothing prevents them from touching."

"They're not brave enough to do that, though."

"Not even when I raise my skirts?"

"They'll just tell themselves they must be imagining things, or that it's all their own vanity. They're scared of their desires, they don't think they're real. Nothing intimidates men more than the thought of a snub."

"But I make eyes at them, too."

"That'll just confuse them even more."

"So I walk up to them and rub myself against them!"

"Only further proof of your innocence and purity; and if they abuse your naïve trust in any way, they think, you'll immediately call the cops. . . ."

"I'll squeeze a knee between their legs."

"Young girls are always making such unintentionally provocative gestures. A gentleman has to be aware of that."

"Oh well, I give up! And I always thought that they had nothing else on their mind but to fuck me!"

"Don't look so unhappy. That's what they have in mind. But they don't have the guts to do it."

"Does it take all that much, just to kiss me?"

"Only heroes dare assault citadels. And what fortress is more inaccessible than that monument to virtue: someone else's wife?"

"But what can I do, then?"

"Don't wait for them to swarm all over you."

"Just take to the streets in a bedsheet?"

"The only thing men want to know before they try anything, is some indication that it'll succeed. Or, even better, that it is the other person making the advances. A sign of recognition is not enough: the situation has to be made clear, explicit, unequivocal. Allusions, symbols, litotes, significant pauses just terrify them. They don't come alive until they meet a whore. It's not because prostitutes are particularly beautiful or talented, but because they accost them directly, and in quite unmistakable terms."

"So that's why you are into prostituting me!"

"I'm not selling you in order to render a service to males. I'm not on their side."

"Strange, the way you insist on dividing up the world between men and women. I see all those who are on the side of love in one camp: their sex doesn't make any difference! Isn't that the reason why we, for example, enjoy making love to women as well?"

"I'm no 'Warrior's Rest,' no five-minute vertical mattress! There have to be slaves and masters, conquerors and vanquished. I am of a lineage of queens. Men exist for *my* sake!"

Emmanuelle contented herself with a smile. The boat proceeded down the river. She felt good, in the balmy night air. Mervée spoke up again, sounding calmer:

"The age of the inverted world has begun. Long enough have men been running after girls: now it is our turn to give chase—our turn to pick them, to send them packing, to swap them, like coins of various worth—and of course, our tastes will change with the fashion, too! They have had their brothels, their *garconnières* where they could pick and choose and grow fat on our fresh meat: I think we must now have our own little clubs, too, our *fillières* where we can get us some loveboys! And that's where I'd shut all the men I have seduced, abusing their 'innocence' by sucking their spunk out of them."

Emmanuelle's laughter pealed across the water:

"You'll be quite rough with them, then?" she asked.

"As rough as I please. Males are easy to rape, because they believe that it is they who are raping us."

"They're not entirely wrong about that, either; or are they? And whether it's them taking us, or us taking them, they'll enjoy it anyhow."

"Less than us. Do you remember Tiresias?"

"No, I don't."

"For some obscure calumnious story that he had interfered with their love affairs, the gods decided to metamorphose him

256

into a woman. The switch didn't hurt him at all, though the deities, always rather misinformed about affairs on earth, did not realize that until too late. Once he had become a male again, Tiresias told Jupiter (to the god's great surprise) that the female's pleasure was nine times greater than the male's."

"Nine times!"

"No more, no less."

"How very lucky we are!" exclaimed Emmanuelle. "Those poor darlings! We must be very kind to them. Next time I'll try my best to pass on a little bit of my own pleasure to them."

Mervée giggled. Emmanuelle was surprised:

"Don't you think that queens should have their subjects' welfare on their minds and hearts?"

The Lion Cub countered:

"So you feel ashamed, doing it for money?"

"Of course I do. But it's a titillating kind of shame."

She thought it over for a moment, then added:

"All everybody asks me these days is whether I am a nymphomaniac, a prostitute, who knows what else! I don't feel like any of those. What is it, then, that distinguishes me from them?"

"Only your intentions."

Emmanuelle nodded her assent, for once. Mervée reached out, unbuttoned several buttons of her dress, announced:

"I won't keep my appointment. I'll take you home with me."

"How old are you?" asked Emmanuelle, as if her response would depend on that information.

"I was born on the same day as you, only a year later."

"Incredible!" Emmanuelle said, admiringly.

She fell silent for a couple of minutes. Then:

"Have you made love to as many men as Ariane has?"

"I haven't kept count of Ariane's. Me, I have a new one every day."

"You don't keep any lover longer than that? No, you've told me that you have a special friend."

"I don't make love to him. I never do it twice with the same man. I'd find it boring."

"Are you sure you enjoy it nine times more than they?" Emmanuelle asked, suddenly feeling doubtful.

Mervée pretended to be offended:

"Do you think I'm frigid or something?"

"No, not frigid . . . But it's true that we're really quite different. No man truly interests you—nor does, I'm afraid, any woman! With me, it's the other way around, they all excite me, and I get hot for all of them, I love them all. I could very well content myself with a single lover all my life. If I screw around, it's not out of need."

"For me, it's a game."

"For me, it's for beauty. I make love the way I'd carve a statue: and would I carve only one? I wasn't born to make one love relationship work, I was born to bring the world more beauty than I found in it when I entered it. I don't make love in order to rid myself of a sexual itch, I do it in order to extend the limits of possibility! I make love because I'm capable of happiness, and I do it unconditionally, because I am capable of liberty. If I were a poet, I'd express my tenderness in song. If I were a painter, I'd enrich reality with imaginary forms and colors. If I were a queen, I'd imprint my name on the stars. But I am Emmanuelle, and I'll engrave the trace of my body on this earth. I want it to remain warm and alive for thousands of years after I am gone; and in order to achieve that, I'll make my body acquainted with thousands and thousands of other live bodies: and they'll all be my love!"

She caught Mervée's strange look:

"It may well be that you'll end up making more love than I, Mara," she said, without even noticing that she had used another one of the Lion Cub's names. "But I'm not so sure that yours will be as intense. Because I know—and I know it better than anybody in this entire city, perhaps better than anyone in the whole world—*why* I'm doing it. And as you yourself just said, that makes all the difference."

9

The Birds Unmasked

Along the legs, as the captive lies there . . .
Advances the palate of that strange mouth
Rose-hued and pale, like an opened seashell.
　　　　—Stéphane Mallarmé, *Parnasse Satyrique*

Ah, let it smell, billow and grow, that hard
Yet most gentle witness, caught in my azure net . . .
Hard within me, yet gentle to the infinite mouth!
　　　　—Paul Valéry, *La Jeune Parque*

Good bearing: the fit regulation of bodily movements.
　　　　—Plato, *Definitions, 412, d.*

Marie-Anne returned to the seaside. Christopher went back to Malaysia without having found the courage to give in to his desire for his friend's wife, without having touched her. September was drawing to a close.

Anna Maria, having finally managed to paint Emmanuelle's eyes, now had her pose in the nude for a sculpture, as she had told Marie-Anne she would do with *her;* undoubtedly, that intention had slipped her mind. Emmanuelle did nothing to tempt her artistic friend. While she was posing, she avoided the topic of love, as well as the rubrics of "pleasure" or "the morals of our times."

The beautiful Italian girl had fallen in love with Emmanuelle, and Emmanuelle knew it. However, she did not want to give Anna Maria reason to reproach her for having seduced her. So she took her pleasures with Ariane, or with the Siamese, whose matte silk skin she found fascinating.

She realized that she missed Mario. She had not seen him since that night at the Prince's party. She had learned her lesson, and now he wasn't there any more! He was traveling all over the globe. She received this letter from him:

"How is it that I cannot let my eyes roam over Greece without thinking of you, wishing you well? This time, on the Peloponnesus, there is no snow. Its veined and swollen skin is the envelope of a heart. Just before it came into view, there was this total perfection of blue sea, in the vicinity of Cephalonia and Zante. But the capricious clouds did obscure the long Corinthian *yoni* from my view, coquettishly as it were, to prevent me from telling you yet another story. . . .

"I am flying. And the sky around me rests, with all the weight of its dome, on that horizon we learned about in school. It took thirty centuries for the anvils in these mountains to forge my iron wings. The air that supports them used to be the breath of the gods. My survival, my freedom are gifts given by their humanism to my disbelieving self. Oh gods with a great sense of humor, skeptical gods, gods of this earth, how well you would understand us now, us who never had to believe in you! From the start, you knew: you knew whose was this kingdom of earth, you who now envy us our women and our wars and our power to love.

"Emmanuelle, in this laconic (and Laconian) sky the certainty of our destiny becomes clear to me: there *is* happiness, and we, the Prometheans, the true fathers of Helen, are alone capable of it in this universe. Meanness, laziness, restlessness are not all there is to our lot. Listen to me: arise, and show yourself! You must make the world realize that it is master of its happiness. It does not yet know this. It is a child, and yet it is weary. Its hope it has transmuted into anguish. In its gloomy capitals, the air is thick with too much money, bacilli, ashes. And here I am, all this time, moving among those who no longer think of loving, who do not allow themselves any time for it; I certainly haven't forgotten my sense of honor, but it is true, their discouragement is catching. Perhaps, and after all, I am just a dreamer, and life is simply that: a lump in the throat, a scribbled sum, a shrug? Yet here, right now, at this great speed above the Dorian earth and perhaps already leaving it behind, the evidence of the azure high above the vapors of earth convinces me that man is god."

The weeks that followed were animated by preparations for festivities to mark Ariane's birthday. In Siam, where age is calculated in cycles that differ from the rest of the world's, the end of each one has particular and solemn significance. Ariane's friends and Ariane herself wanted to make their celebration worthy of these traditions. To begin with, they had decided to treat the neighborhood to the spectacle of a fancy dress ball.

The invited guests were to make their masks themselves, under the guidance of Mervée. Leonor Fini had transmitted the secrets of this delicate art to her.

This work was a feast in itself. The young women spent hours at Ariane's place, littering the floors with the plumes of swan and egret, the plumules of the canary, the quill feathers of turtledoves, parakeet tufts, merlin tail feathers, robin's down, the wisp of warblers, remiges of nightingales, barbules of blue-jays, the feather-spats of the screech owl, the pinfeathers of the seagull, storks' wings and lyrebirds' tails, throat feathers of the scarlet bee-eater, panaches of the bird of paradise. . . .

Their labors progressed slowly, with considerably more time off than at work. Plans were discussed, agreed upon, and then unraveled again, merely for the pleasure of doing so: finally the consensus was that the masks be tight-fitting, covering the entire face, hair, and neck: even their bearers' eyes were to disappear behind silken eyelids and eyelashes. No one would be permitted to remove them as long as the ball was in progress. Thus, no one would be recognizable, and everyone could go ahead and do everything they wouldn't dare do ordinarily, with their faces uncovered. . . .

As for the rest of the costume, it would merely consist of tight-fitting leotards. These, however, would be of an extremely fine knit wool, and absolutely transparent. Mervée (again!) knew where to obtain such garments: she brought back ten black and ten scarlet ones—the shade known as "executioner's red." This also determined the number of bird-women: there couldn't be more than twenty of them. Regardless of their vital statistics, these garments would fit them, being of an extremely elastic nature. Obviously, only breasts of certain dimensions would show advantageously under such constraint; a preliminary examination of their endowments thus obliged a certain number of candidates to accept, albeit reluctantly, that they would fare better reduced to a spectatorial role rather than renounce the festivities altogether.

The leotards had long sleeves, all the way down to the wrists; would it be right to extend them with gloves? The mistress of ceremonies, when consulted, was of the opinion that the caressing feel of very fine silk might indeed be more exciting than the touch of a simple bare hand, and thus it was decided that very thin and supple gloves be worn—red ones with the black leotards, black ones with the red. Here, too, the rule applied that they were not to be taken off under any circumstances.

At first, Ariane and Emmanuelle thought that the leotards Mervée had brought were like those worn by dancers, cut out of one piece from neck to ankles: as it turned out, they only covered the upper half of the body, barely extending to the waist. Mervée proposed to extend them by wide-meshed fishnet panty hose: if these were worn without a

G-string or such, it surely would look most titillating? But this time her co-conspirators did not follow her advice. Human impatience being what it is, they reasoned, and no matter how attractive they were—or rather, *because* of their very attractiveness!—such breeches wouldn't last the night. Either openings would be created in them, thus making for a rather slovenly appearance, or they would simply be pulled off, and this would be even worse, as such scenes of dishabille would violate the agreed-upon good taste of the proceedings: if the guests had to retain their masks and gloves all night long, by common edict, it surely didn't make any sense to permit them to take off their pants! And thus the Lion Cub's idea was voted down.

In order to remain correct in such a matter, Emmanuelle explained, all that was needed was for them to present themselves from the very beginning completely naked from the waist down. If Mara had some odds and ends of plumage left over, these could be used to adorn the pubic hair.

Such a costume, someone remarked, would not be all that difficult to don; the real difficulty, after all, was in deciding *who* would get to wear it! It wouldn't be difficult to find far more than twenty statuesque females; but the idea was not to arrange merely a pageant of such beauties. Not only was it necessary for the participants to be fairly intelligent, but they would also have to share common principles, in a spirit of mutual sympathy. It was Ariane's birthday, and they weren't preparing a mere spectacle, but a veritable love banquet.

The founding committee started drawing up lists, revising them from one day to the next—at first because of "second thoughts," then, after the invitations had been sent out, to fill gaps due to absences, indispositions, or mere cowardice on the part of the invited girls. Finally, around about the time the great feathered masks had been assembled, a sufficient number of the elect had been established to ensure the success of the soirée.

When the subject of male guests was tackled, there likewise was no shortage of arguments and controversies. Should they be in costume? Oh no: much better for the women alone to attract all attention to themselves. They would be the precious apparitions, an aviary swarming with weird bird-bodies, exposing their groins while hiding their faces: they would be superbly enigmatic. Why face any competition? The men, that night, would serve as votaries to their goddesses! Only the goddesses would be half-naked: the gentlemen would arrive in dinner jackets.

How many of them? Equal numbers? No, that would make it too easy for them: let them vie with each other for the favors of these incarnations, wooing them, waiting in line! To avoid any spontaneous rationing or calculation, it was decided to avoid any number being a multiple of that of the women: not twice as many, nor thrice as many; nor any number in any intelligible arithmetical relationship whatsoever.

Well, then. Which husbands? None, said Mervée. Ariane took the opposing view: all those among them, she said, who deserved it. Jean, first of all. Both were quite disconcerted when Emmanuelle intervened:

"No, not Jean," she snapped. "Not Jean. Anna Maria can't join us either, you see."

What was the logic of that? they wondered. Emmanuelle offered no explanation, and they did not ask her for any.

On the eve of the great day Ariane's friends assembled for one last time, in order to try on their costumes.

Superb in their heavy black velvet capes, sweeping the floor—these they would discard later, but only after having made their spectators languish long enough—they spent a long silent time contemplating each other's oneirological as well as ornithological masks, struggling to recall the mortal women they had previously been.

Emmanuelle's mask was that of a sweet Corinthian owl with rust-colored ear-tufts, looking lofty and solemn, with great trembling eyelashes adorned by pearly tears.

The large, thick ruff of amber feathers, the piercing eyes, and the blue beak of the common or garden amblyornis lent Ariane a positively mythical appearance. What feminine traits could have matched the magnificence of that?

Mervée was a long-necked bird, turquoise throat, jet-black crest: or was it, actually, the crown of some Inca emperor seen in a dream?

One African girl wore the head of a prehistoric avian: the feathers extending from her forehead like the horns of a great snail curved all the way down to the floor, emitting a nerve-jangling metallic sound as they vibrated, and one was tempted to wonder if not this material and this noise had arrived, by some terrifying intergalactic contraband route, from some planet of another sun.

The intriguing cortège of artists in love with their master-pieces dotted the floors of the empty halls in red and black, while the plumes and panaches described intricate balletic movements above those two primary colors. When they threw off their capes, their naked thighs and legs appeared quite curiously uniform, which was most likely due to their contrast with the exuberant originality of the masked heads. The female magicians' lower extremities hardly differed even in color: the blondes had tanned legs, the Siamese girls slightly duskier ones. In this archipelago of wonders, only the snail-bird's brilliantly black long legs stood out among the general swirl of lighter skin.

One lovely witch wore a head of plumes the color of mother-of-pearl, and the short hairs of her pubis matched that by a marine frothiness and density, though among them one could glimpse what looked like those half-animal, half-vegetable organisms the tide abandons on the cliffs—a hint at pretty formidable repertoires of love-making. So taken was she herself by her seaweed triangle that her gloved hands kept drifting down there, to caress the little nodules of coral. . . . It didn't take long before she reclined, in all her feathery splendor, on a bunch of velvet cushions, delighting the sweet lips of her cunt with the caresses her beaked mouth could not receive.

Emmanuelle watched her and considered that the ocean, in its fabulous powers of creation, could just as well have made the ingredients of this adventurous biped merely a bunch of amorous algae, adorning the submarine realm. Would she be equally happy, Emmanuelle wondered—leaving aside the possibility of alternative destinies—if she were at this moment the mistress of blue-green sirens, licking the salt of their exquisite sex organs, or relishing the spurts of iodine spunk that her caresses would draw from their scaly breasts?

The credulous eye and orange-red torso of a cock-of-the-rock with bulging forehead and breasts that were perfect hemispheres; the velvety cranium, the strangely furred ears, fringed with purple down, the splendiferous feather vestments of the coronet astrarchy; the almost vertical eyelids, the sharp beak and forked tail, cutting as a razor, of a blue cynanth—all these added up to more than a gathering in fancy dress: they were the partners the surrealism of life was about to offer men to distract them from the "enigma of woman"! And that was why, that night, and despite their fierce appearance, their beaks were more attractive than their luscious bodies.

The birds vowed to prolong this marvel as long as it would prove possible. They would not profane the experience by giggles or outbursts of emotion, but parade clothed in their airy thoughts, arcane and inviolate, close enough to excite the most crazy desires, remote enough to make one weep.

So thoroughgoing was the metamorphosis that even their erstwhile bedfellows would hesitate while trying to recognize the breasts of the red-tufted cockatoo, the soft shoulders of the hyacinth macaw, or, under the both grave and comical pointed head and quadricolored plumage of the exquisite Himalayan grouse, the unruly shock of hair of a sixteen-year-old Algerian girl who claimed, although meeting with incredulity, to have had a thousand lovers. They would have to, even in the case of women who were worshiped beyond measure, overcome any temptation to give in to a suspicion of sacrilege that might cause them to suddenly prostrate themselves at the feet of the Prince's daughter, whose naturally sphinx-like face was now obscured by the long, flexible neck, the indigo eyes, and the lascivious profile of the Sappho-hummingbird.

It was certainly to be expected that some of the men (one had to be prepared for that, and, what is more, the magical birds hoped for it) would take advantage of the possibilities of confusion. Not without ulterior motives they would pretend to assume that Laure was Mervée, call Djamila Malini, recognize Emmanuelle in Marayât (and thus, perhaps, discover some unsuspected predilections), see Daphne under Myriam's plumage, Maïté behind Ariane's beak, and take Nila for Inge. And, if they were haunted by even less advisable desires, they might even pretend that these faceless creatures they were holding in their arms were, in reality, some of those inaccessible jet set beauties who had not been invited to the feast, and who would later be surprised to hear that they had been seen at the ball and had, in fact, been balled by lovers they didn't even know. . . .

The young women spent all that day savoring the foretaste of these great games. They granted advance absolution to their sweet pretenders, for all their weaknesses. All except Emmanuelle, who claimed that their fantastic creations made possible such new emotions and experiences that the men would cut a pitiful figure indeed if they turned out to content themselves by fantasizing customary forms and traits behind those gorgeous masks. They were given the opportunity to make love to the nonterrestrial, the extrahuman, the unknown: surely they would find better things to think about than mere women, having such astonishing creatures at their fingertips?

It was quite late at night, during the actual festivities, that the supernatural birds announced that they were now going to remove their masks.

From the ceiling, a huge screen of fine white silk descended, dividing the immense salon in two. Up to that moment, no one had even noticed its existence, rolled up in a golden sheath. All the lights were turned off, except for a number of projectors located behind the screen.

The invited guests were installed in the darkened part of the hall, in positively hedonistic armchairs standing next to tables laden with every imaginable kind of beverage. There they sat, all the males, as well as all the females who had come to the ball unmasked, in curious, expectant, slightly perturbed silence. . . .

One by one, fantastic shapes make their appearance on the screen: phalluses of various shapes and sizes, held by outstretched fingers like delicate flower stems; two, four, eight, miming a stately pavane round the shadow of a young girl with wide open arms, whose real body lives in the forbidden space, between the projectors and the silk. Languidly, her shadow twists, turns, reclines: it almost vanishes from sight, only her breasts can still be seen thrusting upward: oh, why has she taken off that adorable structure of feathers and bones that was her bird-face! Metamorphosed back into a woman, she is completely indistinguishable.

A shadow arm descends, its hand touching the invisible belly of the girl. The wrist remains arched, and one can now see a finger, as yet dreamily, plunging in and out of what one hopefully assumes to be her cunt. Little by little the dance of the phallic specters accelerates, becomes a crazy jig! The loving hand adopts that rhythm, too. The prostrate body arches, touching the ground only with heels and neck, looking tense to the point of breaking in two. Then, suddenly, the finger disappears, the priapic shapes slow down and come to a halt, the female silhouette slumps back, the screen goes dark.

When the light returns, it reveals a profile view of a shape with pointed breasts, long supple legs, and a vaporous hairdo, tall as a deer's antlers. From the left side of the screen another silhouette appears, advances with a light dance step, keeping the rhythm of some faint accompaniment: in his blatant virility this shadow reminds the spectators of an Etruscan wall painting. . . .

The two forms meet, the one picking up the other as if it were completely weightless. Then, arching his back, and without any support but his straining legs, the shadow man thrusts his member into the ballerina, who is now moving her limbs in graceful arcs, curving her torso into the shape of a sickle moon. Night descends on the coupling shades.

The fictitious dawn rises on the view of a woman with indistinct features: is it still her, is it another one? (It was so much easier to tell those lost birds of paradise apart!) She is sitting down, one leg folded under her buttocks, the other stretched out, leaning on one hand. A man (the same faun, again?) appears, approaches, kneels down. The female silhouette extricates the leg she's been sitting on and places it on the man's shoulder, then leans back on her elbows, raises her body, and thrusts her belly toward his waiting mouth. The man's head vanishes in the shadow of her thighs. The woman shifts her weight onto her neck, on the floor, takes both her breasts into her hands and raises them toward the ceiling. The screen blacks out.

The fourth tableau presents a seated male. From nowhere, a shadow appears, with the breasts of a muse and a coiffure like a storm cloud. She dances up to him, sinks down at his feet. The hero's phallus rises slowly, and slowly it disappears into the nebulous outline of the divine face. It reappears only to plunge back in again, ceremoniously, hieratically, until the organ of incarnation, offered up as such sweet libation, shudders and spouts! The female figure disappears, the demigod remains alone.

Another form appears on the horizon, at first a mere black wisp. The man stretches out his arms, and as she comes within reach, pulls her toward himself, lifts her, and enters her the same way the faun pierced the earlier apparition: her gentle female curves flow over the knotted musculature of the lover's thighs. Arms twine round his neck, invisible lips lave his mouth. Then, slowly, the female body raises itself with an oceanic suppleness, stretching upward, toward some imaginary surface, and floats back down again. Each time, the member that anchors her to the man is hardly visible for a moment before it vanishes again, into her shadowy flesh.

The audience senses, in their arteries and nerves, the humid and marine pressure, the crushing weight of the depths, the suction, the muscles laboring, the sweat seeping through the pores of their palms, and the hallucinatory rise of the fluids—oh, joys of source!—along the entire length of that unseen prick. This scene is a long one. Finally the woman shudders, flails her arms and legs, nipples jutting, and what looks to be her hair comes undone, shadowy tresses falling, cascading down to the ground.

The man's belly is twitching as well, and the spectators think they can almost see the silvery sperm.

In the next tableau, the rigid shoulders of a woman squatting on a couch are covered by her abundant hair: even her face is indistinguishable in that shadowy mass. Her breasts hang down, full and heavy. Her buttocks are jutting up, motionless. Legs bent, knees resting on the couch right under her waist, she is balancing herself on her forearms like some savage beast of prey, ready to pounce.

A man charges onstage. Moving, then, with all deliberation, he grabs hold of the proffered posterior orbs, pulls them toward himself, plunges it in—all the way—until none of the shaft can be seen in silhouette. Then he remains immobile. The woman, too, appears to have turned to stone.

Quite soon, from the left side of the screen, another female shadow emerges. With a prowling tread she draws closer, hesitantly . . . her pubis arrives in front of the petrified woman's face. Suddenly, the latter raises her head, brusquely sweeps the tresses aside that have been obscuring her profile, and darts a greedy tongue toward the other girl's beckoning bush.

The male comes to life. With somnambulistic precision he takes hold of the woman's buttocks again, rapes her anus savagely. Startlingly, with a long animal cry that almost lifts the spectators out of their seats, the woman disengages herself and vanishes moaning into the rapidly falling darkness. . . .

After a long interval the screen lights up again, and there are two male silhouettes standing in its center, facing each other. Their members, impeccably stiff, stand parallel to each other, seeming to form one single phallus thick as an arm.

Behind each one of them, at some little distance, stands a table (or are those altars?).

At the far left and right, two ebony figures. Their exquisite breasts curve elegantly from their rib cages, above classically flat bellies. Then the long, tapering legs are set in motion, and slowly they approach the central group. The effigy on the right stops halfway, for a moment. The other one places herself between the two male profiles, merging her shadow with theirs. One has to be particularly attentive—perhaps even imaginative—to realize that she is bending down and kissing, or perhaps even taking into her mouth, the double *lingam*. Then she straightens herself again and slowly, rhythmically, proceeds over to one of the tables, stretching herself out on it, her breasts pointing heavenward. Her neck extends beyond the table's edge, her head hangs down, at a level with one of the men's backsides, which is, however, too far away for her lips to caress.

The other woman repeats that sequence, with meticulous exactitude, ending up in a position absolutely, symmetrical to the first one. Then the two central figures, abandoning their Uranian face-to-face, execute a half-turn and take a step forward: the mouths of the reclining figures open and receive the erect members.

Now two more silhouettes appear, carrying *lingam*-shaped amulets between their opulent breasts. Gracefully, unobtrusively, they detach these instruments and graft them onto the prostrated shapes. Then they kneel down between the thighs of the new hermaphrodites, bend over their groins, and start savoring the rods they have just endowed them with.

Two more men, from left and right. They step up to the kneeling women. For a moment, these turn from their preoccupation and have a taste of the penises jutting from the new arrivals. It seems, however, that they prefer the gustatory experience provided by the artificial erections: the men get to work, and in but a little while it is plain to see that they have penetrated the women from behind.

There still is an empty space between the two upright figures in the center, whose pricks are immersed in the (now androgynous) recliners' mouths. Enter two more masculine personages: they walk toward each other, right up to the middle of the screen, spin on their heels, swinging into the space provided, and take up the face-to-face, cock-to-cock position initially adopted by the first two men, whose buttocks now abut against theirs.

They have hardly taken up their position when two female forms rush from the screen's sides, followed by two more.

The first brace position themselves beside the tables, sucking the tits of the reclining women and caressing the region where the dildos have been affixed. The second couple hunker down facing the kneeling figures, still sucking the dildos, and reach out into the shadows of their bellies: presumably they find a place for their fingers there, in the openings not occupied by the lovers of these women. With their free hands, the newcomers fondle the breasts of their partners.

Six more shadows join the fray, three from each side: a man, two women. Each man takes one of the women by the waist, makes her lie down on her back, on the ground, in such a manner that her neck rests on the heels of the kneeling man who is sodomizing the fellatress of the fake prick. Then he arranges his second acolyte so that her cunt is on the first one's lips, her shoulders resting on those of the kneeling man, whose chest she embraces with arms stretched back—or perhaps they are long enough to reach all the way round to grab the prick that is three-quarters of its length inside its own sweet honey pot.

The identical scene occurs on the other side of the diptych. The men who brought in this last quartet of beauties finally stretch themselves out, thus completing the composition, on the bodies of those two of their mistresses whose vaginas are still unoccupied, and begin fucking them. At the same time, they squeeze the breasts of the one whose cunt their partner is licking, and join their tongues to her tongue in appeasing that figure.

Their motions harmonize with all those executed, at the same time and with equal gusto, by all the other participants: the women whom they are penetrating as well as those whose bodies they are caressing with hand and mouth, while they, in their turn, accord their various caresses to the others, both male and female; those who are on their knees, paying homage to the *lingams* they have fashioned out of thick young tree shoots, relishing the pleasure of the men penetrating their flanks and the sensuality of the companions who caress their body, dedicatedly titillating the androgynous recliners, who likewise, by their breasts and cunts, provide pleasure for their lovers, while their tongues and palates go on delighting the insatiable cocks of the vertical males backed up by their brothers-in-arms, standing there with crossed pricks. The artistry of the tableau lies in the harmonious conjunction of all these relationships.

In the meantime, the light seems to have grown dimmer, and the viewers have to make an effort to discern what it is that each participant is receiving or giving. The ever-growing shadow starts obscuring the individual shades, filling out the remaining blank spaces between them; but the spectacle is not over yet. The subtle interplay of the blacks and grays in motion prolongs the audience's concrete visions. The lights flickering over the fusion of bodies creates fantastic near-abstract patterns, preparing the hostesses of the ball for the fulfillment of their desires for unknown joys.

10

The Noblest
Talent

And this schooling he provided for me was not intended for his delectation, but for my own benefit: he did not merely give me erotic lessons, he was teaching me a unique lesson: if you say you love, be at least capable of acts of love, or else keep your mouth shut. Thus, it was a kind of sense of honor that obliged me to abandon myself more and more.

Honor: consisting of what, only yesterday, I would have called dishonorable . . .

—Christiane Rochefort, *Warrior's Rest*

Mario stretches his long legs, sighs, looking out at the pouring rain.

"It's going to go on for days and days," he prophesies, somberly.

"So what does that matter?" Emmanuelle says. "Why do you see even the weather in such tragic terms? What outdoor plans did you have in mind?"

"To be a prisoner of this rain or of anything else—always *is* to be a prisoner! Anything that infringes on my freedom is my enemy. I hate the rain!"

Emmanuelle laughs, without a care in the world. To her ears, the monotonous hammering sound of the water on the curved gables of the roof and on the terraces of her house has its own beauty. In any case, she is in a mood to perceive everything as beautiful.

"Let's pretend, then, that we *are* free," she proposes.

Her visitor makes a long face.

"Do you feel free, Emmanuelle?"

"Well, it must be possible to become more and more so, don't you think?"

He nods his assent:

"Yes, that is how we must conceive liberty: as a goal, forever beckoning."

"Before I came here to Bangkok, I thought of myself as so free that I was even a little worried about overdoing it. And yet I'm ten times as free now. From that I conclude that there must be further progress to be made."

"There is. There is always something more to be discovered."

"But I can't imagine, *what*? I'm probably short on imagination. Are you more gifted than I?"

"More gifted than you? Oh no. I'm just a man! But I can help you to be eternally dissatisfied."

"Oh, you have been sent to me, to instill in me the greatest thirst I've ever known!" Emmanuelle intones, over-dramatically, but the affection in her eyes contradicts her mocking words. Mario is fully aware of that.

"You've said it!"

She feels in a mood for confidences:

"Listen, Mario, I have some weird things to tell you about. I have been violated."

Mario is totally amused:

"'If you have heard them say that Parthenis has been violated,'" he declaims, "'know that these are vain boasts, for one does not take pleasure in our kind without our consent.'"

"I feel *so* good. God, I'm so happy. Why is that, I wonder."

"It's because we are here together. It's because you have such beautiful legs."

Already he is contemplating the rain with less jaundiced mien. She leans over toward him, pursuing her confessions.

"And I've been *sold,* too!"

Mario remains silent for a moment, then asks:

"Are you ready for the next step?"

"Certainly, if you tell me what it is."

"Play your part to the hilt: become a willing prostitute."

Emmanuelle protests:

"But I have done it already, I tell you!"

"What I mean is that you become a *real* prostitute: not just for a wager or for fun."

"And *that* is supposed to advance me toward freedom?" She is amazed. "I've always assumed that prostitution is a form of servitude, and one that no woman would choose,

283

unless compelled to. By someone, or by something: bad luck, thwarted love, sheer misery! And don't they all end up being captives of their condition?"

"The woman who prostitutes herself when there is no compelling reason for it whatsoever is the opposite of a slave."

"Granted. But what's the difference, then, between that and what I have already done?"

"It's not a difference in kind, but a matter of degree. Simply, *more* liberty. But perhaps that is not what you're after? The choice you're still exercising among the men to whom you give yourself constitutes a limitation of your freedom. You may imagine yourself as 'free in your freedom to choose,' but in reality you are enslaved by the necessity to choose! Only when you'll know that you're completely open to all comers, and that your lover of, say, the next hour is going to be a perfectly random sample—*then* you'll be completely free."

Emmanuelle smiles, still anything but convinced.

"As I think I've told you before," Mario went on, "all eroticism requires organization. It thrives on 'systems.' Your erotic life will be successful in direct proportion to your efforts to render it methodical. What I call prostituting yourself is merely a way of creating an intelligent framework within which you can make the gift of your body; of not leaving it up to trivial preference or caprice. And also, by systematizing the unknown factors, it is possible to achieve a satisfying esthetic effect! Why not regard it as one more victory of mind over matter? Who cares if your pleasure is increased or not—I can't keep insisting on it too often: more is at stake, in art, than mere pleasure."

"So it's prostitution considered as one of the arts, is it?"

"All art is *work,* first of all. Do you expect to live out your life without ever working?"

"Well, I don't have to have a job, you know. Jean is rich."

"And you find it quite normal to sell yourself to him. Perhaps it would be more honest to sell yourself *for* him?"

"I guess it might be. I'd be happy to do it, if ever he asks me. But why doesn't he?"

"Straight talk between man and wife—that's the most difficult thing in the world. And why should it be up to him to broach the subject, anyway? If you really want to be his wife, why not be of some use to him, the way he is to you. It's his job to build dams; let it be yours to make love. But not just dabbling in it. Be a professional."

"But I want love and love-making to remain a pleasure for me! I don't want it to turn into some humdrum routine."

"Isn't Jean's profession his pleasure as well? Does he construct those dikes *only* in order to make money? Does he not enjoy leaving his mark, a man's mark, on the body of the earth?"

"Why then is the world respecting architects and despising whores?"

"Maybe it's because those who *can* see the truth of these matters are too cowardly to shout it from the rooftops, and louder than the imbeciles spouting their mistaken notions!

But two thousand years of hypocrisy and stupidity won't determine destiny forever. Human beings are now old enough to understand that their moral pretenses—so young, yet so decrepit at the same time—are merely ridiculous. Never mind that they're ugly as well, that doesn't seem to bother them. Let's just try to demonstrate to them where these morals are entirely arbitrary, and what a confusion of values results from their obfuscations and involutions! They have nothing but praise for the woman who rents out her body to be a beast of burden or a machine slave—or even exposes it as a photographer's model: and no one finds their moral sense outraged by the fact that her employer remunerates her for such services, which are *physical* services, at that! But it is not legitimate, it is not decent, it is downright sinful, it is not meritorious, it is obscene, sordid, shocking, sacrilegious, if she decides to utilize the most delightful faculties of her body! Does that mean that it is less dignified to make love than to sit typing arrest warrants?"

"But if all women were such gallant ladies, who would answer the phone?"

"Are those two functions so incompatible? The only secretaries I have any respect for are those who whore."

"And who are physically well-endowed, I should think."

"That's absolutely right. Those whom nature has blessed with a much more generous talent for compiling card indexes than for the arts of the flesh we shall certainly be pleased to leave among their dear filing cabinets. But you, born beautiful as any man's dream, is it conceivable that your life could be dedicated to paper work?"

"In other words, all pretty girls ought to be pussy for sale?"

"Well, God willing, that's what they are! Matter of fact, I'm pleased to see that the heiresses of our nobility are much more tempted by such possibilities than by any convent, these days. What better proof that the light of the spirit has at long last begun to glimmer, even in our poor civilization?"

"If that's the case, Anna Maria, your dear cousin, must be quite behind the times."

"Well, would you like her to turn around and get ahead of you?"

"All right, I'll start working," Emmanuelle says.

"Come on, don't look so downcast," Mario says with a big grin. "It's a very sweet kind of labor, isn't it. . . ."

"Well, if it's just a matter of not being idle," she sighs, "I don't really mind at all. But I suppose that it's a problem of mine, to find words more shocking than acts. If only that job went by another name. . . ."

"But that's just it: I won't gild the lily! I'm simply reminding you of your calling as a woman, and telling you, eschewing euphemism, that the most satisfactory way of achieving it is by becoming a whore."

"You have to admit, though, that you've been depicting prostitution only in its rosiest aspects! I'm sure I won't find it all that wonderful to be pawed over by some obese old man. Not to mention the diseases he may have."

"My dear, whoever would refrain from eating oysters, just because now and again you come across a bad one? Why not think about the pleasant surprises. . . ."

"The men I find attractive don't have to pay me."

"Don't you ever suspect that they'd perhaps prefer to pay you in cash, instead of having to please you?'

"So I'm supposed to prostitute myself in order to make them feel at their ease? I've heard that one before. . . ."

"Well, that's good. Maybe you had occasion to think it over, then. If you did think about it, I'm sure you realized that a man who does not feel obliged to pretend mad passion and cut a dashing figure stands a better chance of concentrating on what it is he's really doing when he is fucking. You should be grateful to him for that."

"But don't men really enjoy it more when they get to execute a regular seduction? Aren't they prouder about it, later?"

"They do it more out of boredom than anything else. Your desirability, well, perhaps it does make you seem precious when there's nothing else to do. But we don't live in such leisurely times. Valmont in *Les Liaisons Dangeureuses* is pretty dated. Alpha Centauri is four light-years away, and we are being expected. I'm sure you don't really want us to waste more time traipsing down the garden path of romantic dalliance. *Bis dat qui cito dat!* 'He gives twice who gives promptly.' To me, any woman who doesn't give in after half an hour of small talk is about as interesting as the rain. And I don't even want to meet those again who didn't make love to me at our first rendezvous."

Mario lets a moment's silence slip by.

"And it has to be on her initiative, of course," he then adds.

"You've made me feel ashamed of my laziness, but now I see that you men want us women to relieve you of every effort, even that of making advances."

"It is merely a simple division of labor. Let the men take care of the work requiring all manner of exertion, and you take care of the loving. And there's a very good reason for it: the thing men cherish more than anything else these days, is to know exactly where they stand. They don't like the equivocal. Love's present-day fashions have relegated little veils and long skirts to the museum. Love, today, is already showing its mouth and its legs: love tomorrow will present itself as unambiguously and clearly as the structure of the atom. And just as those old 'humors' have been replaced by hormones, love without psychic turmoil, love without confusion is going to replace the love of Tristan, the love of Romeo, the love of Abélard, those ancient monsters still retarding our cities built out of light-metal alloys and glass. Iseult's veil won't be able to deceive the radar tower's ever-watchful eye. Nor will our computers be well-programmed with the mumbo jumbo of elegies and madrigals. The truthfulness, cleanness, liveness, and nudity of erotic love make a joke of all those courtly potions, circumlocutions, yearnings, and hesitations of the past, and its incontrovertible evidence sounds the death knell of the old conventions and superstitions. Long enough have we endured that fog and its swoonings and romantic suicides: we long to regain our taste for laughing out loud while making good clear love! The future belongs to those who are able to know and to understand things without suffering. Unhappy love has no future. Emmanuelle, men are tired; and this is what they wish for: that the energy of the world will be used for some purpose less ridiculous and more useful than all the previous breast-beating and rivalry. They want love to give their spirit a rest, they don't want it to harass and debilitate them. They want a love that talks straight. Thus, in suggesting that you prostitute yourself, I'm merely suggesting that you live up to your own ideas. It's merely a question of wearing the colors of eroticism in a reasonable fashion, in an age of de-mystification."

Mario is waving his hand:

"Anything else I may have to say to you on the subject is subordinate to that principle."

"Well, that's perfect," says Emmanuelle. "All right then, let's go to it."

Mario gazes at her with benevolent affection.

"You mustn't let my thoughts determine your actions, dear. Nor should you prostitute yourself because I am asking you to. As a matter of fact, I'm not asking you to. I'm just pointing out the possibility and its interesting aspects. But I leave you your freedom. It is up to you to decide. I won't take you where you can practice the job in comfort unless you ask me to do so."

She scrutinizes him, a strange flame flickering in her eyes. He raises one hand to halt the words he thinks are forthcoming:

"Neither should you accept that invitation just because your spirit may experience some quasi-physical pleasure in 'giving in.' Free yourself from that temptation as well."

"And yet," says Emmanuelle, "is it not an erotic experience to have a man who loves you oblige you to become a whore?"

"Of course it is. There's no possibility of eroticism between a couple who limits its activities to each other! How can anyone imagine they know how to love, if they aren't ready to share the loved one? I don't believe in any other lovers but those who barter their loved ones. I'd say the husband is pretty stupid who does not manage to turn his wife into a courtesan, at least to some degree."

"Aha, so it's *managing,* is it? A moment ago you were spouting about nothing but my freedom!"

"But don't we often get liberated only by force?"

"Why are you refusing to force me, then?"

"I'm not your husband, nor am I your lover."

"To tell the truth, I don't really know what you are!"

"Just a mouthpiece for your own thoughts."

"You don't think you have taught me anything?"

"Nothing; I've just helped you discover your own genius."

"So then, when I'm really grown up into this world, I expect you'll just disappear in a puff of smoke?"

"Were you ever born?"

She smiles at an idea that crosses her mind and asks him, trying to sound perfectly composed:

"Do you love me?"

"At this moment, yes, I do," replies Mario, not in the least embarrassed.

Now it is Emmanuelle's turn to gasp.

"Mario," she says, with serious mien, "I begin to ask myself if you have ever been in love, or if you ever will be. All you require a woman for is to enjoy erotic relations with her, but not to love her."

"And what in hell do you think 'love' is? Is it that you're still dreaming of some gift from heaven, through some timeless grace, pregnant with mystery, descending from the heights of its transcendence like Jehovah's fire into the chosen bush? Is love, to you, merely a vision of the beyond, blinding you to all terrestrial reality? A stupefaction of the soul, beyond the reach of psychology? Come on, let's be serious! That hallucinatory love has never existed anywhere but in kitschy books. You had better watch out: if love is just a visitation, what will you have left once the angel has departed? If one loves someone without one good reason, it is not that person one loves, but a phantasm one has created, and the awakening from such trances often proves lethal. Is it worth dying for such a mirage? Because it isn't love one's dying for, it is the myth of loving. Do I know how to love? All I can say is that love is synonymous with our intelligence at its most absolute, and it is such reasoning I practice, in the name of eroticism."

"If there are reasons for loving, surely there also are reasons for falling out of love?"

"You had better believe it: and may that belief make you prudent and wise. Love is not a birthright: it has to be earned. Take care not to lose the reasons others love you for. You have been found pleasing because of Eros's presence within you: if you chase him away, you won't please any more. As soon as you stop being erotic, I'll stop loving you."

"What if I lose my looks?"

"It is up to you to remain beautiful."

"But when I get old?"

"Eros's beauty does not have to fear old age. It is up to you not to age without his presence."

"What if I suddenly become virtuous, the way the world at large defines it?"

"I'll hate you."

"Or if I discover some other life-consuming interest instead of the love of loving?"

"I'll forget you."

"So that's what your fidelity is like!"

"Why should I remain faithful to those who betray me?"

"Is it treason to change?"

"No, as long as you're moving forward in your changing. Retracing your steps would be the very opposite of true change: it leads to the immobility of death."

"And what if some day I get tired of all that eroticism, tired of pushing 'forward' all the time?"

"Well, then it is time to die."

* * *

Emmanuelle falls silent for a moment, seemingly engrossed in some complex chain of ratiocination. Then she laughs:

"But before I get there," she announces, "I'd like to try it."

"Try what?"

"The life of a woman of pleasure."

But he hasn't been listening, or so it appears: he gets up, ambles through the room. The monsoon does not seem to bore him all that much any longer.

"Mario!" Emmanuelle shouts. "Tell me again: are there any dangers?"

"Oh, all kinds."

She sighs, not at all mockingly. Mario won't give her time to grow weak again:

"But would you find knowledge itself at all tempting, if there was no danger in it?"

Somewhat defiantly, Emmanuelle points out a fact:

"I've gone after it more often than you perhaps think."

"I know."

She looks at him, incredulous.

"My God, that does surprise me!" she exclaims.

As he does not appear to have anything further to say on that matter, she picks up the main topic of their conversation:

"I've told you at least three times," she says, in a critical manner. "What magic formula do I have to pronounce before I convince you that you have convinced me?"

She recites:

"In the full possession of my faculties, and in accordance with my rights as a minor, emancipated by marriage, I declare that I find it both desirable and expedient to embark on the experience of prostitution. So take me to that place where I can do it!"

He comes back to her, takes her arm, holds her chin, stares deeply into her eyes—and smiles. Emmanuelle relishes this smile as if it were a kiss,

"Are we going?" she asks.

"No, not today. I have to make arrangements. In the meantime, I'd like to invite you to lunch. In a dayclub."

"I've never heard of such a thing."

"Just think of a nightclub that's functioning in the daytime. That's all. And you'll have a surprise, too."

"What is it? Come on, tell me!"

"It isn't a thing: it's someone. An old friend of yours. One, I think, you'll be pleased to meet again."

"Oh, Mario, please, don't keep me on tenterhooks like that!"

"It's Quentin. I think you remember him?"

"Quentin!"

Emmanuelle looks dreamy-eyed: that evening by the side of the *khlong,* the first one she had spent in the company of Mario; the walk through the night, Genghis Khan, the opium, the phallic temple, the *sam-lo.* . . . And the Englishman who had been staring at her, incessantly, without a word, touching only her legs, preferring those unlikely boys to her. . . . She hadn't expected to ever see *him* again.

"Do you know, Mario—it's exactly two months ago! That was on August the 19th. I haven't forgotten."

She amplifies her memory:

"He's so beautiful! Almost like that man who found me stark naked in the plane."

"What plane?" asks Mario, looking astonished. "That's a story I don't know."

"Then listen," says Emmanuelle. "Once upon a time there was a unicorn, as beautiful as men had ever dreamed of. . . ."

It was just as dark inside as if the place had been a nightclub. It took them a while even to see the tables, ten or so in number, arranged around a positively Lilliputian dance floor. All of them appeared to be occupied.

The ambiance was subdued. A combo of three very young girls wearing tight-fitting sheaths of some metallic material, their hair cut short and the color of moonbeams, legs and face tinted a violet-blue, lips, eyelids, and eyelashes painted silver, was playing, but so very quietly that the newcomers thought, at first, that they were merely miming. . . .

A slender maître d' approached and asked them, in a low voice, if they had reserved a table. At the very same moment, a solitary shadow sitting at one of the tables waved his arm to attract their attention.

"There's Quentin," said Mario.

They went over and joined him. Emmanuelle felt quite excited. He was even more elegant than she had remembered, and his eyes were the color of deep blue Chinese cloisonné.

"Have you been back to see your Muria people?" Emmanuelle asked, smiling winsomely.

"No. Not this time. Too bad, isn't it?" (In English.)

Emmanuelle smiled, more politely now, suppressing a sigh. There I go again, forgetting! she chided herself. I must start expressing myself more physically. . . . A pity, though: she would have liked to *talk* to Quentin. Mario came to her aid—she had never seen him in such a gallant and helpful mood.

They feasted on Siamese dishes, excellent wines, laughed a lot. They certainly were the noisiest lot in this little sanctuary of hush, but the other patrons stretched their tolerance to the point of pretending not to notice.

What an extraordinary thing! Emmanuelle thought. All the women in the place are beautiful. She didn't see a single one who wasn't desirable: at every table they sat, chivalrous escorts leaning toward them, as if attracted by some flame. . . . One couple got up to dance. Others followed suit, but not too many, and thus Emmanuelle, craning her neck a little, had the chance to admire them one by one, at very close range—to undress them in her mind's eye, to imagine herself making love to them.

A young girl appeared before their table, inquiring why they were not dancing. They just smiled at her, and she sat down, staring at them with open curiosity. The whiteness and clearness of her face was startling: it was framed by abundant, sleek, dark hair, parted in the middle and gathered in a chignon, which gave her a rather more severe look that contrasted with her youth. Her dress, of some corded black material, fitted and hugged her body so stylishly that one was tempted to believe it the handiwork of some Parisian couturier. A fine diamond collar and very sheer stockings on her harmoniously proportioned legs added to her air of sophistication, taste, and good breeding, which seemed at odds with one's idea of a cabaret hostess. Emmanuelle concluded, in fact, that the girl was a customer who had dropped into the place by herself and was looking for someone to talk to.

She spoke French and English with equal fluency. When she wanted to know who they were, all of them replied amiably, and she had hardly been with them for a moment before they felt totally at ease with her, just as if she had been a long-invited guest. She agreed to a cup of coffee and then to a liqueur.

Quentin led her out onto the dance floor. Mario and Emmanuelle followed but returned to their table before them. Only three couples remained on the floor, from among those who had started to dance the same time as they; Quentin was an excellent dancer, and the girl was infectiously vivacious. Even the musicians seemed to enjoy their task of providing the backing for the well-nigh professional figures those two were executing, and the other couples kept their distance, in order to watch them better.

She was laughing, shaking her head, talking to Quentin. Unexpectedly, her black mane came undone: thickly it cascaded down her back, down to her buttocks. At the same time, no doubt merely to feel a little cooler, she undid the top button of her dress. She went on dancing, now at some little distance from her partner. She undid the second, then the third button. Emmanuelle was intrigued, watched her closely. Smoothly, in a leisurely fashion, as if it were the most natural thing in the world, the girl opened her dress all the way, without in the least losing her graceful dignity, and took it off. She moved over to the side to drape it carefully over the back of a chair, then returned to her dance partner.

She wore no garters: her stockings were of one piece, joining up with a lace-panty-like garment that extended upward in a narrow strip, widening to cover the breasts and fastened at the shoulders.

She was very beautiful: Emmanuelle tasted desire on her tongue. Mario commented:

"I don't know if this is one of the regular attractions of the place, or if it's just an individual improvisation! In any case, I like it."

Quentin and the girl came back, sat down. Emmanuelle complimented her. She didn't dare ask it she had been acting out of professional obligation or impulsive fantasy: she was quite intimidated by her.

She was even more amazed when the girl asked her if she wanted to dance. Emmanuelle shot a glance at Mario, and he nodded, encouraging her to accept the invitation.

The young, half-naked girl put her arms around her and danced cheek to cheek, not saying a word. Thus it was up to Emmanuelle to tell her that she would like to make love to her.

The stranger withdrew her face and looked at her partner, laughing, as if in response to a witty remark. She asked:

"Which club do you work in?"

Emmanuelle felt embarrassed. She wished she had an address to give her, but Mario had not told her where he intended to take her. That's just my luck, she complained to herself: if only she'd asked me that tomorrow, I could have given her an address then. I must look pretty stupid. Her voice was apologetic:

"I've just arrived in Bangkok. I haven't done anything yet."

"What's your line?"

Again, Emmanuelle didn't know what to say. She wasn't even sure she understood the question. Luckily, the other one continued:

"You dance?"

"No," said Emmanuelle, relieved. "I just make love."

The young woman laughed again. She did not seem to take the reply seriously.

"Excuse me," she said, "I think I'll take this thing off." She disengaged herself from Emmanuelle and undid, with the same spontaneity as before, a number of invisible hooks and eyelets on the front of her black undergarment, slipped out of it, with great refinement, and nonchalantly threw it at the feet of the girl musicians.

It turned out that her stockings weren't really part of *that* garment, after all, but merely the extremities of an entire one-piece outfit that covered her body all the way up to the neck. It was made out of the same sheer fabric that encased her legs, and thus the lovely creature now appeared completely nude, although this was actually a clever illusion. The minuscule blood-red nipples of her superbly rounded breasts were quite able to distend the transparent material, and the slit of her totally depilated pubis was clearly visible.

"Oh, you're driving me crazy," Emmanuelle murmured in her ear, when they resumed their dance. "I'm positive I'm the only one here who knows that you aren't really naked—but, that's just it, I find you even more exciting this way!"

Emmanuelle giggled, had a slightly malicious after-thought:

"Besides, in that outfit you're unable to make love to any man—but you certainly can, to a woman!"

The girl looked at Emmanuelle with gentle reproach, appearing somewhat offended by such an immodest pro-posal. Emmanuelle wasn't certain, but the girl even seemed to blush. . . .

They went on like that, for quite a while. For Emmanu-elle, the experience was a kind of exquisite torment, as she didn't dare snuggle up too close to the desired body, being afraid to arouse its quite paradoxical modesty again. But the thought that all the others were watching her embracing this mystifying nude in public only added to her pain-tinged pleasure.

Now her partner started whispering into her ear:

"Why don't you take your clothes off, too," she proposed.

Emmanuelle shook her head.

"Come on," said the strange girl. "You can take them off at your table."

They rejoined Mario and Quentin. The other patrons were observing them, but, it seemed, not more intensely than they had been doing before the girl undressed, and without the slightest indication of lubricity. It rather looked as if they were admiring the elegance of her fashionable getup.

"Tell us your name," said Mario.

"Metchta."

She looked and nodded at Emmanuelle, to remind her of what she was going to do.

"I'm going to take my clothes off," Emmanuelle announced to her companions.

No comment from Mario or Quentin. No one was dancing now.

Emmanuelle's two-piece outfit was simple enough, and it did not take her long to divest herself of it.

"And now," said Mario, "you had better do something that befits the dignity of nakedness."

Emmanuelle stood up, took the young Russian's hand, and escorted her to the dance floor. The other patrons contemplated them for a moment, and then a number of couples got up to join them, not behaving in the least differently toward them.

"I'd like to offer you to my friends," said Emmanuelle. "When can you do it? I'll pay you."

In the bungalow built of tree trunks overlooking the canal— her first visit to it after that night when Mario had taught her "the law"—Emmanuelle and Quentin are stretched out on a thick-piled Chinese carpet, next to a long low tea table. They had stayed in the "dayclub" until quite late, and the quick tropical twilight is descending. Metchta will join them at dinner time. The water of the canal is the same iris-blue color as the skin of the club's girl musicians.

Mario is sitting at his desk, writing, pausing once in a while to pick up a book, check a passage, shut the book again, puff at his long Philippine cigarette. The doe-eyed houseboy comes in, hands him the evening newspaper.

Mario's voice breaks the silence:

"Medical doctor arrested," he reads, off the front page, "after discovery in his apartment of body of young girl, dead under suspect circumstances."

"What's so suspect about dying in the hands of a doctor?" Emmanuelle asks, wryly.

But Mario corrects her:

"It seems there's been a little too much dying going on at Doctor Marais's place, lately."

Emmanuelle says nothing to that. Mario goes on scanning the front page, then adds:

"Personally, I prefer the kind of eroticism that makes people come alive—not the kind that kills."

Then he returns to his writing, and silence reigns supreme again.

Emmanuelle is wearing a violet-colored skirt, slightly flared, and a silk sweater of the same color, only a lighter shade. She and Quentin are facing each other, lying parallel to the tea table, quite close, their feet pointing toward the desk, their bodies at a forty-five-degree angle to it.

Quentin is running his fingers through Emmanuelle's long hair, pushing aside the strands that hide her forehead, grazing her eyelashes. He kisses her eyes, her cheeks, the sides of her nose, and, finally, her lips. She twines her arms around the young man's neck, squeezes the back of it with one hand. He, in turn, holds her tighter, hugging her to his chest. They continue kissing, taking their time.

Emmanuelle's left leg extricates itself and settles on top of Quentin's right leg. Her bare knee starts ascending the length of his thigh, then slides down, starts up again. The flesh of her leg, ever more exposed, slides, with all its length, across the man's. Her bare foot is tense, like a ballerina's on points: a sweet, plump extremity, just as capable of caresses as any hand.

The more amorously Emmanuelle's leg behaves, the more Quentin's starts pressing its errands, riding up and down between the mobile one and the one that remains immobile on the rug. Thus, Emmanuelle's skirt keeps on hiking up her body, and her left thigh is now almost entirely exposed. Mario notes that its shape is quite probably the most beautiful he has ever seen in his life, and considering what a connoisseur of female legs he is, that's saying something. He finds exactly that part of them, where the thighs join the groin, the most exciting—especially when seen from such an angle as this, from above and in semi-profile, with its oh-so-round muscles so smooth in front, and, in the back, those hardly perceptible longitudinal creases; the delicate tendons, the subtle and incredibly perfect proportions determining the length and diameter of these great tapering candles of flesh. . . . Mario has experienced few visions of beauty that have moved him as much as the sight of this leg, at this very moment, in this ideal position: stretched out, bent only ever so slightly over the body of the desired male; stretched, yet not distorted in the least; flawlessly sculpted and yet so sexual, so golden, in the saffron-yellow lamplight! Such a leg, Mario ruminates, is just as intimate as a breast. It only exists under a skirt, as it is the high road to that sweet slit, and nothing, once it starts exposing itself, will ever be able to halt the man's steady advance into the woman's body.

Now Quentin's hand descends, onto Emmanuelle's knee, traces its contours, then slowly ascends the length of the thigh, all the way up under the skirt.

With a quick, sideways motion Emmanuelle sits up, crosses her arms in front of her face, elbows upraised as in a balletic figure, and pulls her silk sweater up over her head, throws it aside, and stretches out again, with a contented little sigh.

"What are you doing over there?" she asks Mario.

"I am describing you."

Her body, naked now to the waist, is so beautiful that Quentin remains spellbound for quite a while, and quite immobile. Then he takes hold of Emmanuelle's wrists and guides her hands to her breasts: she obeys and starts caressing them, to provide him with an enchanting spectacle that continues until she comes, out of sheer pleasure at her own tenderness. . . .

"They press their bodies against each other as if all the space available to them were some narrow trench in which they are hiding to escape from some fatal dungeon; digging it, in the broad light of day, the man's body, sticky with the soil it has displaced, heavy with fatigue and vain hope, has been rubbing against his companion's body in all its length. The female fugitive has had to remove her soaked blouse, as it was hampering her movements, and her breasts shine forth gleaming and bare in the dismal mud. She has also left behind her striped convict's garb, carrying the dress she'll put on once they get out of their predicament in a small satchel, where it lies folded up with the roadmaps and the cyanide capsules. The man's body is tight against her side: she can't go on crawling any longer, she lies down on top of him. She relishes the comforting feel of his robust belly, of the lips touching hers, so fresh and reassuring. Never mind the border guards, let them shoot! She is a virgin, but the male organ now opening up her thighs is incredibly strong. Smarting kisses stifle her outcries. The earth beneath them soaks up her blood. This is no moment for the man to be tender, attentive, careful. She understands, she does not mind his hurling himself upon her like some beast, his rough handling of her breasts. She finds herself unable to tell whether she is suffering or deliriously happy. She has been opened and torn wide and filled, made a woman. The sudden shout of the man would betray them but for her body's muffling it and absorbing it into its own interior moan.

"On the *khlong,* the lookouts on the high-sterned junks lean forward, trying to pierce the night with their eyes."

"You know," says Mario, in English, "I'd like to see ten men, hired by myself, lie down on her, just the way she is there now, and take her, one after the other. Ten—maybe twenty of them."

"What are you talking about?" Emmanuelle wants to know.

"About you. To turn an entire horde of males loose on your pasture-lands. The sublimity of the idea lies in their great number."

"Tonight I'd just like to make love to Quentin, Metchta, and yourself."

"I know. I suppose that's why the idea of another arrangement seems so exciting to me."

"I always thought you didn't value anything more highly than my doing things out of my own free will!"

"Your free will, that's for tomorrow. Today I'd like to have something else."

"What, then? To treat me like some inanimate object?"

"Maybe, but I'm not so sure now. Maybe the very opposite . . . I'm dreaming of something rough and bestial, proceeding over your body like an army of mercenaries, paid off by me, to ride roughshod over my most beautiful conquest. . . . But I also want to see to it that your pleasure equals my largesse."

Mario's voice takes on a slightly haughty tone:

"Let's drop the subject. Anyway, I won't know what it is I'm looking for, until the moment it has already taken place."

Emmanuelle has nothing to add to that. It is Mario who goes back on his own statement:

"Is there anything else that is as voluptuous, for a man, as preparing a woman he loves for a night with his own mercenaries?"

The contortions of passion on his face suddenly give way to a cool smile befitting a man of the world. As if mockingly, he says:

"I suppose I must conclude that I do love you!"

11
The Glass House

There is no other Shelter,
There is no other Door,
There is no other Beauty,
There is no other Tenderness!
Welcome to my heart,
To my eyes, to my mouth,
You Who raise the stones!
                                        —The Koran

I shall not punish your daughters for
their whoredom.
                                        —*Hosea,* 4:14

"Let's take your car," says Mario. "I'll drive."

A freshly washed sun has emerged from the previous day's
torrents. The air is almost cool, and gentle, like springtime in
Paris. Emmanuelle delights in the breeze whipping against her
face, making her hair stream back. She has been sleeping late,
still feels like stretching.

Mario has been up in her room, helping her choose a suitable outfit. She feels very dressed-up, much more so than usual, and she is even wearing some very handsome platinum jewelry.

The day had got off to a good start—Emmanuelle had enjoyed the feel of his hands on her bare skin while he was helping her dress.

They arrive in the vicinity of the city's most frequented hotel. Mario is driving right up to its entrance.

'We aren't going to the Chandra, are we?" Emmanuelle asks, apprehensively.

She is bound to run into at least twenty people who will recognize her, right there in the foyer, and they're bound to know what she is up to. . . .

Mario does not reply, but the very moment Emmanuelle is telling herself that she has no say in the matter anyway, he swings a sharp left so suddenly that she bumps into him. The hotel has vanished from sight. They are now driving down an alley bordered by green hedges, thick as ramparts and so tall that the sky seems as far away as it does from the bottom of a deep gorge. Before she can ask for an explanation, Mario has made another sharp turn, and they are entering a small park.

"But that's amazing," exclaims Emmanuelle. "I never noticed that there was any place to turn off this alley! How is it one can't see it?"

"Clever trompe-l'oeil effect," Mario says. "Created by cutting that shrubbery in a certain way. No one finds the place unless they've been given exact directions, and that's just as well."

The building they are approaching is one of the world's marvels. Its dimensions are mind-boggling: it seems quite impossible for such an edifice to exist in the middle of a downtown block. Emmanuelle has driven past here almost every day, and all she has ever seen is the monumental black and white mass of the big hotel.

The front of the building is rectilinear, flat, bare, in the manner of a fortress. The only difference is that the surface does not consist of dull and austere stones or bricks: it is shiny, flashing a thousand fiery reflections, as if some sorcerer had transmuted it into a diamond of utterly fantastic dimensions, this mansion hidden by tall trees in the midst of a spacious park.

"It looks like it's made out of glass!"

"It is, my dear. Slabs of glass, six or eight inches thick— solid as concrete! Heat can't penetrate those walls, nor can you see through them. But there's a lovely kind of diffuse daylight in all the rooms, and no need for windows."

"How is it ventilated?"

"There are air ducts, opening out onto the terrace. The place is air-conditioned throughout."

"There aren't even any doors. No apertures at all!"

"That's true," Mario says. "The way in is quite amusing, in fact."

The car is gliding past the mirror-bright wall, making her blink her eyes; they turn round a corner of the building: it presents the same appearance from all sides. Its overall shape is that of a gigantic cube of glass.

Mario stops the car, turns off the ignition, but makes no attempt to get out. Emmanuelle grabs hold of his arm: they are sinking into the ground!

It takes only a couple of seconds. They are below ground. Mario starts the car again, they slowly roll off the elevator plat- form which then starts ascending again, obscuring the rect- angular piece of sky they have glimpsed for a moment above their heads.

A bluish light illumines the crypt they're in. Long corri- dors open up from it: a signal light comes on above one of them, and Mario starts driving into it. They follow another signal, and then an iron gate rises in front of them. As it goes up, they drive through, and it closes behind them like a trap door. They find themselves in an immense room divided up into pearl-gray partitions. The air is fresh, and Emmanuelle feels better already. It's a garage, that's what it is, she tells her- self. It certainly is a very organized sort of place.

Mario opens the door on her side, assists her out. Without a word, he leads the way toward the back wall: a rectangular por- tion of it, so well fitted that it is indistinguishable when closed, automatically opens up in front of them. Emmanuelle passes through it first, finds herself in a small cabin-like space with a velvet-upholstered seat. As soon as Mario has entered it, too, the door closes, and they start ascending, although the elevator's motion is almost imperceptible. The silence is most impressive. Well, it's just an old elevator, Emmanuelle says to herself.

"All this must have cost a fortune to install," she says. "Where did the money come from?"

"From the paying public. . . ."

She looks pensive.

"What's the place called?"

"Among the locals, it has no name at all. Foreigners who have heard stories about it refer to it as 'The Great Brothel,' but few of them know where to find it."

The elevator stops, ever so smoothly. A panel slides back, opening onto a glass-walled corridor, lit by a pearly light. They start walking down this passage, for quite a long way, it seems to Emmanuelle. Here, too, there are no doors or other openings on either side.

Then they arrive in a round foyer. Corridors like the one they have just passed through branching off at all sides. Above them, shedding a light not unlike that in a forest clearing, a glass dome, huge as that of an observatory or basilica.

In the middle of the foyer stands an elegant table, fashioned out of precious wood, ornamented with bronze inlays, and perfectly empty except for a quartz prism placed in the center, with inscriptions engraved in it in various languages. Emmanuelle reads the French one: "Secrétaire."

A curved door opens, and before it closes again, one can see an immense office with a number of young women working,

typing, duplicating, shifting papers in and out of trays, tran-
scribing tapes, watching video-tapes, answering telephones.
The person entering the foyer is a woman, very slim, very tall,
well-dressed and definitely upper-class, although her attire
consists only of a clinging Chinese gown of a pale ivory color;
she wears no makeup, no jewelry. She greets them with a little
bow, addresses herself to Emmanuelle:

"Let me explain the house rules."

Her voice is rather sharp, the accent nondescript: European? Asian? Emmanuelle can't make up her mind. Nor can
she decide whether she finds this woman beautiful or not.

The secretary does not ask the visitors to take a seat; there
are no seats. She is carrying a leatherbound volume, the book
of rules, no doubt. Evidently she knows it by heart, as she does
not even bother to open it. She must have taken it out of a
drawer merely in order to look impressive and to lend solem-
nity to the occasion.

"No formal registration is required."

Emmanuelle acknowledges that, returning the little bow
by way of greeting. The woman goes on:

"The reciprocal obligations of this institution and its clients are entirely a matter of honor. The contracts may be verbal
or written, at the discretion of the management."

That must be it! Emmanuelle gasps to herself: it's an electronic woman! She *sounds* like a robot. . . .

At the discretion of the secretary, anyone is eligible to be
employed. However, in the files and archives there are data

on all the female residents of the city who have at one time or another exhibited potential of a kind likely to interest the establishment. Thus the secretary's decisions are not arbitrary, but depend on the merit of each case.

Particular consideration is given to those who have demonstrated special talents. It will be easily understood that the secretary does not want to elaborate on this aspect.

Emmanuelle is now asking herself whether she'll make the grade: what does she have to offer? She likes men to come into her mouth, she likes to be penetrated by several at the same time, she likes them to watch her while she is masturbating, she likes women, too: pretty ordinary accomplishments . . .

(These ruminations cause her to miss part of the lecture: this will be a black mark against her. . . .)

. . . However, a certain number of the conditions apply to one and all, and they can be formulated without any breach of discretion. Thus, the women authorized to benefit from the advantages offered by the institution have to belong to the most desirable strata of society, being, preferably, the wives or daughters of judges, politicians, top civil servants, university teachers, commissioned officers, religious dignitaries, diplomats, persons distinguished in the arts and letters, in business or finance. Wealth is regarded as equal to noble birth or the father's or husband's distinction as the member of some high-ranking order. All visits must be made using an automobile, as the mechanism of reception is not designed for pedestrian access.

It goes without saying that only truly beautiful females have the right to frequent this establishment. The management's strict insistence on that point is exemplary, and this is well-known in the city. It has given rise to a great number of intrigues and vain efforts to get into the place, on the part of the less fortunately endowed. Vain, because the management is adamantly incorruptible.

There is no minimum age limit: the youngest candidates are the most welcome. Those over forty will be admitted only if they can demonstrate exceptionally rare talents as well as esthetic endowments.

The secretary assigns each visitor a reception room for the day. The choice of this room is not arbitrary: the size, shape, furniture, equipment of each room differs from all the others. Yet there is little likelihood that one will find oneself in the same room twice in the course of a year, and it is pointless to make requests for any particular room.

No one, after she has been admitted, nor for that matter before that time, has the right to exercise any manner of discrimination or preference, nor even to express any general or particular wishes, regarding the visitors who will be assigned to her. Any attempts to indulge in such matters will be looked upon as an affront to the institution, whose rules in the matter of masculine qualifications are just as stringent as they are concerning the candidates' looks and standing. Those who desire to benefit from the facilities of this house can put their blind trust in the judgment, the distinction, and the experience of the management, which has for many years administered it to the total satisfaction of all parties, a fact that has merited the establishment its international reputation. In this respect, it should be mentioned as significant that a far from negligible percentage of its clientele consists of transient persons, some of whom have traveled here only for this purpose.

The patrons are admitted into the presence of the ladies either singly or collectively, depending on their preference, and at the secretary's discretion. They stay there as long as they wish. They are free to request the company of several women at the same time, but cannot be guaranteed the fulfillment of such a request at all times. Apart from this qualification, they do, of course, have every right.

Although the establishment does not want to encourage this practice, as it complicates bookkeeping and thus causes additional expenses, a woman may choose to visit only for the time it takes to service one single patron, if she so desires: but, if she does, she must leave the house in his company. If this arrangement does not suit her, or if the patron is disinclined to take her along, she is obliged to receive further clients as assigned to her by the secretary. Furthermore, if her first assignment is to entertain a group of clients, she has to accomplish this task, even if she has come in the expectation of a single encounter: in this case, the group of clients is regarded as a single entity. Generally speaking, the secretary is in the best position to decide what is best suited for everyone, in number as well as in quality, and it is recommended that one submits to her authority. The discretionary powers she is invested with are entirely due to her long experience and competence.

Despite the considerable rights granted to the employees by the establishment, there are a considerable number of qualifications. It goes without saying that a woman may run the risk of accidentally meeting one of her close friends, or even her husband, in the capacity of a patron. This situation does not in any way contradict the house rules, as long as the due payments are made, and the management does not accept any liability for the prejudices and complications that may ensue from such coincidences or other chance encounters.

The establishment is entitled to a certain percentage of each employee's earnings. These funds are channeled into the maintenance and improvement projects, as well as into those relating to expansion. Despite the amplitude of tasks she is obliged to perform and the modest position she occupies, the secretary does not accept any retainers.

Having recited all that, without once asking Emmanuelle a single question, without one personal word to her, without even any inquiries as to whether she accepted the conditions she had just been told, this woman—obviously enjoying the implicit trust of her employers—told Emmanuelle to follow her, adding that she would be taken to Room 2238, and that a client was already waiting for her services. Emmanuelle followed her, her heart beating wildly, turning round to cast a look at Mario, who hadn't even said goodbye, much less any encouraging word. She felt like running away, if only that had seemed possible.

The room the secretary took her to was shaped like a perfect hemisphere, the floor being the horizontal side. The dome continuum of walls and ceiling, completely unbroken once the door closed behind them, seemed even more planetarium-like in that it was entirely covered in dark blue velvet material. A dim, intimate light emanated from invisible lamps, casting shadows and reflections on the velvet whenever people moved about in it. The very quiet hum of the air conditioners indicated the origin of the slightly scented freshness of the air. The floor was covered with ash-gray carpeting, its pile so thick that the high heels of Emmanuelle's shoes sank into it all the way. She had to take them off to be able to proceed.

What surprised her most was to find, in the very center of this room that did not look like a boudoir at all, a very large bed, without any headboards or legs, covered with a thick fur throw, its edges falling over the sides. Its shape certainly harmonized with the setting: nonetheless, it was a little disconcerting. It was perfectly round.

About the bed, scattered on the wall-to-wall carpet, a profusion of long-fringed, multicolored rugs, reminiscent of those hand-made in Greece or on Majorca; three semi-spherical armchairs, one blue, one red, one purple; poufs of various heights; and a long, black, unpolished table completed the furnishings. Hung at some little distance from the concave wall, in an opulent, dark golden frame, a large and most impressive abstract painting provided a counterpart to the stark circular shape of the bed.

The secretary walked over to the side of the room diametrically across from the painting and pushed against the wall with one hand. A part of the wall slid back (Emmanuelle was getting used to all these unexpected openings), and a bathroom came into view. The ceiling and walls, incongruously straight and right-angled after the curved space of the room, were completely covered in mirrors. Emmanuelle noticed that even the floor, made out of a polished, glass-like substance (perhaps it even *was* glass?), reflected her image as clearly as all the other parts of the room.

At floor level, a bathtub, more like a small swimming pool, also lined with mirrors. That'll take a little getting used to, Emmanuelle thought. It was filled, three-quarters of the way, with pale green water; a faint smell of pine needles pervaded the room.

On wall hooks or little tables a great number of chrome-plated implements: without difficulty Emmanuelle recognized a vibro-massager not unlike the one she had been using and enjoying, and various kinds of shower nozzles, some of which were unmistakably shaped like male organs. But most of these appliances looked quite enigmatic.

She was suddenly aware of additional presences, and turning round she saw two men standing in the curved entranceway.

"For you," the secretary whispered to her.

Emmanuelle felt tempted to throw her arms around her and beg her to be excused, or at least, given some more time to gather her composure. But the secretary took her leave, abandoning her to her ridiculously vulnerable state of mind.

She asked herself if it wouldn't be more honest to admit her embarrassment and inexperience and to introduce herself as a debutante as yet ignorant of the local customs, thus appealing to the indulgence of her visitors. But surely they had come here looking for refinements only an expert was able to provide: they wouldn't give a fig for her excuses, they would leave and ask to get their money back from the management! They would be reimbursed, and Emmanuelle would stand there covered in shame. She completely reversed her train of thought. Never would she let them inflict such humiliation on her! This was her chance to find out if she was good for something or not.

The smile that accompanied this thought was so radiant that she would not have had to make any further effort, had she but known this: she had already conquered her first two clients completely. They came over, stood beside her at the edge of the pool. With a little girl's innocence she turned her face up to the one who stood closest and offered up her mouth to be kissed, then raised her hands to undo his necktie, opened the shirt-buttons, undressed him altogether, with gestures of such exotic tenderness that he seemed quite stupefied. Then she rendered the same service to the other one. Finally,

gracefully, unhurriedly, taking care that they would appreciate the art of her movements, she took off her own clothes,
walked down the steps into the pool. Standing there in the
jade-colored water, in it up to mid-thighs and thus appearing
more naked than nakedness itself, she then turned around and
beckoned them to come in, too.

They grabbed her, caressed her, fucked her, splashing water
all over the walls and ceiling in the process. She concentrated
so hard on making them come that she didn't even think about
coming herself: it was sufficient recompense to hear them
praising her services. She did her best to make it as easy for
them as possible, guessing their desires before they were even
formulated, taking advantage of the lightness of her body in
the tepid water. . . . After a multiplicity of variations, both of
them spurted at the same time, one into her mouth, the other
inside her cunt. Then they were washed, dried, and as soon
as they had stretched out on the white fur-covered bed, she
started licking their cocks again.

They had hardly left when a low-voiced loudspeaker
announced that Emmanuelle should get ready to receive the
next visitor. She hastened to slip on the moss-green dressing
gown she had noticed hanging next to the shower. She had just
managed to do so when the secretary came in, then vanished
again, leaving her with a tall dark man. Emmanuelle burst out
laughing: it was the naval officer, her intrepid seaman.

"Now I realize," she said, "that you're always where you're
most needed!"

She told him that she would like to leave the glass house today in his company. Would he take her with him? That would all depend, he answered, on the satisfactoriness of her services.

They passed an afternoon so perfectly voluptuous and satisfying, doing and confiding so many things to each other, that Emmanuelle told herself it could not have been the least little bit more wonderful had they been young lovers.

"I've just drafted a new set of rules," she announces, triumphantly. "Would you like me to read it to you?"

"I'm afraid I'm not too well qualified to give an opinion," Anna Maria replies. "So, please don't get angry with me if I don't express all the admiration it no doubt deserves. You know my blind spots."

"Oh, don't worry," her model reassures her, obviously in great good spirits. "You can always ask me to explain, if something seems unclear. This morning I feel in an exquisitely pedagogic mood."

"Well, it seems to me that the current rules and regulations have already aroused your opposition; can it be that your neophyte fervor has already cooled?"

"On the contrary, it is positively flaming! And so is my creative imagination. I'm so concerned for the best interests of the establishment that I want to see it make positively stunning progress, I want it to be ahead of its time, I want it to be the absolute avant-garde! I won't be content with any remaining shades of conformism."

"Well, I must admit, there's hardly anything as old-fashioned as a brothel."

"But you must come with me one day, so you'll know what you are talking about! You'll see how up-to-date, how unexpected it is, in many ways. The only thing that bothers me is that only women can go there to prostitute themselves. I do admit that that is a reactionary feature: it amounts to sex discrimination."

"You would like to see male prostitutes there as well?"

"Yes, of course. I don't see why men should have fewer rights than ourselves."

"But I thought you were working as a whore out of a sense of duty?"

"In the new mutant world there's no difference between duty and right."

"Ah yes, of course. Please forgive my momentary lapse! So your new draft takes this into account?"

"That's up to you to judge. It is based on the idea that nothing should be uni-directional. Erotic love is neither active nor passive, it is neither subject nor object. And freedom is not a vector."

"I don't see—"

"Or if it is one, it has to be reciprocal, pointing both ways. And that applies to prostitution as well."

"Truly, Emmanuelle, I haven't understood a word!"

"That doesn't matter. The new articles of my set of rules provide the following:

"First of all, no distinction is to be made between the sexes.

"Secondly, each and every club member has the right to either 'choose' or 'be chosen.' For instance, a woman may visit the glass house in order to hire out her talents, *or* to enjoy those of a man. In the one case, she'll get paid and she'll submit; in the other, she pays and gives the orders. She either satisfies her own desires in her own manner, or she goes there in order to provide some relaxation for others."

"Those two things are incompatible, then?"

"Physically, they go together: but from a psychological standpoint, an inversion of roles will make the pleasures greater."

"Ah, yes!"

"What do you know about it?"

"Nothing, nothing at all. Go on."

"Thirdly, every member opens an account. If she comes to 'choose,' a choice will be entered on the debit side; if she comes to 'be chosen,' she gets credited with her earnings. The basic rule is that she is only entitled to a 'choice' after having been 'chosen' at least once—in other words, the accounts have to be perfectly balanced at all times, no overdrafts are allowed."

"Will it bear interest?"

"That isn't a bad idea: I'll give it some thought. The trick might be to make the interest interesting—I mean artistically: for instance, to make it payable in the form of child prostitution."

"Oh, that's horrible!"

"Not if they're beautiful! Those who can't provide a presentable fledgling of their own can always borrow from the

325

others, or else bring along some young friend of theirs. Preferably a virgin."

"I hope you realize that your imagination is naturally vicious?"

"So you think every virgin must remain so forever?"

"There are better circumstances in which to lose one's virginity than in a brothel."

"Ah, I wonder. . . . Surely you notice how inspired I am? I don't think I was this inventive before I went there. Well, to get back to the mode of bookkeeping: at the end of each month, the accounts are balanced, and everybody receives a statement and the balance of their account."

"I don't think your system will work. How will you manage to have *all* the accounts show a positive balance?"

"We'll have to consult an expert on that. I'm not really a financier, you know."

"That's easy enough to tell. But why not have cash payments? Why have that cumbersome clearing-house at all?"

"That's just it, that's to make sure that everybody *will* be obliged to prostitute him or herself. Otherwise there'd be only buyers, and that would favor the rich to an undue degree."

'I'm positively touched by your social concern."

"You should be! Because when I say 'the rich,' I mean the possessors, exactly those husbands after your own heart: the possessors of their wives as of their works of art, who run to the glass house in order to buy themselves other bodies, while pretending horror at the idea of offering up their own bodies to others."

"You'll wind up in the ranks of the suffragettes and other revolutionary feminists."

"No, I told you, I'm talking about the best interests of those very men! It isn't right that they should remain deprived of the voluptuous joys of self-prostitution. Even though they're not quite capable of understanding that yet."

"Such altruism . . . ! You should have lived in Charles Fourier's time."

"I like this one, thank you. Which reminds me: it won't be possible, either, for anyone to come to the glass house with only money-making in mind—because at least half of the credit you acquire has to be spent on natural assets, in the form of 'choices' with which your account will be debited. The institution's aims are philanthropic, not commercial."

"So it isn't prostitution at all, but good works! It's like going to volunteer at the welfare clinic. I must say, I had expected something a little more exciting. Your kind of establishment doesn't tempt me in the least."

"No, listen: as soon as a client of either sex arrives, he can obtain listings of those who have come there on that day in order to be 'chosen.' But only if his—or her—account is in the black. And from the moment the client asks for the listing, he or she is irrevocably debited with the equivalent of one 'choice,' even if the person he picks doesn't suit him and he goes away without having any satisfaction. Thus curiosity is permitted, but you pay for it, just as you have to pay for the act itself. And thus the erotic *value* of curiosity is recognized."

"And you have to choose merely on the basis of a list of names? But then all the members of the circle know each other, I guess?"

"Not so. New recruits are added to it, continuously: and that's the main benefit of the system—the attraction of the unknown."

"But they do have to write down their names."

"There's nothing to prevent you from giving a false name!"

"In any case, it's less a matter of choice, it's more like a lottery."

"If you wish; but every number wins, and all the prizes are good ones."

"Ugly people don't stand a chance?"

"No, they don't."

"And you call that justice?"

"They can wait for their paradise."

"Heaven isn't reserved for the ugly, you know."

"Earth is reserved for the beautiful, though."

"Your club certainly won't contribute to that."

"Come on, don't be such a spoilsport! Why don't you forget your prejudices for a moment and tell me, in all honesty, what you think of my rules and regulations?"

"They're no good. With your idea of pretended reciprocity between the sexes you demolish the very temple of eroticism! In that temple, you yourself told me so, woman is the deity, and the only one. That her favors can be bought, well, with a little effort that is fathomable: but to have her, the goddess, *buy* the favors of her worshipers—? When they make love to her, men celebrate her cult, put themselves at her service, no matter what the circumstances are. But to make the goddess pay them before that rite, that's pushing one's sense of black humor a little too far!"

"Now you're really talking! Please, go on!"

"What I want to know is, do you want eroticism to be an esthetic ethic, with its own inner coherence, or are you merely planning some egalitarian utopia: if that's the case, let me warn you—it isn't a new one; and, to my mind, it looks about as inviting as a prison gate. Your club is more like a phalanstery than a Cythera of the future. Your members will succeed so well in their efforts to match their intentions and act identically that one won't be able to tell the sexes apart. As for me, I prefer to keep mine: to be a woman, the fair one, the desired one, and, if it really is possible to merchandise a human being, the only salable one. Let that remain my privilege. And let the men stay where they are, where we stretch our arms toward them, in love as well as in the stock market!"

"Well, I must say, for once I think you really are right."

Emmanuelle crumples up her notes and throws the wad of paper over the side of the terrace balustrade, down into the unruly leaves and branches of the coconut trees.

On another occasion, Emmanuelle confided in Anna Maria:

"A man who was too tired to make love to me told me that the whole love business was simply stupid. But by now I have learned enough to know that he was wrong. Really, love is the means mankind has found to make its intelligence transcend the universe."

In this room, entirely white, almost clinical, the first object to attract Emmanuelle's attention was a double seat, shaped somewhat like a figure eight, with short legs, its middle deeper than the sides. From the look of it, one would have to sit down face to face if one wanted to make love on it; or perhaps one behind the other.

The room was divided in two parts by a curtain. In addition to that bizarre taboret the other objects this side of the curtain were a kind of saddle seat, a glass case containing artifacts made out of various materials that looked like representations of animal penises, from dog to mule, all of them life-sized, handcuffs, thongs, tweezers, speculums, and a very absurd-looking device consisting of two hemispheres of glass, each one the size of a hefty breast, connected by rubber tubes to a little hand pump. It looks like a milking machine for women, Emmanuelle thought: oh, how that must feel good!

Along one of the glass walls through which the dim light of the outside world filtered there were two long platforms, rosy-colored, supporting even weirder structures. The first one, manufactured out of some metal that looked almost soft, and was a pale brass color, was shaped like the contours of a woman: there were separate concavities for legs and arms, and two for the breasts. The head would have to go into something that looked like a fencer's mask, with padded sides, from which a wisp of sweet-smelling vapor rose out of the opening for the mouth. Similar little wisps floated around in the bottom of the breast-cups and in the smaller depression designed to accommodate the vulva. Emmanuelle bent down to sniff them, and almost at once experienced a strong pricking sensation in her clitoris and nipples, so powerful that she felt close to orgasm. For a moment, she was tempted: why not just install herself in this mold, belly and face against the metal, and let herself go? In a second she had ripped off her summer dress. She was, of course, stark naked underneath. But then her curiosity for what was on the other platform diverted her from her first impulse.

It was, reclining on a thick mattress, an undressed woman, perfectly shaped in every way, and seemingly asleep. Emmanuelle touched her: she was made out of foam rubber, softer than flesh. Her skin was velvety, neither warm nor cold. Her mouth and her sex were extraordinarily lifelike. She lowered her face to that of the doll and opened the lips with a finger: the mouth emitted a breath, of a different odor than what she had just experienced. The impression it gave her was difficult to analyze, but it did not please her. She proceeded to explore the vagina: it was warm, and filled with the effervescence of that very same gas. That's interesting, Emmanuelle reflected: it has to be a compound designed for males, and one that only works on them. The establishment seemed to be discouraging ambisexual trends! And what was on the other side of that curtain?

She threw her dress on a pouf, walked across the room, pushed the curtain aside, and walked through it. She saw a rectangular bed, covered with a sheet. Two fully dressed men were sitting on it, bolt upright, like two chimneys. They were curiously alike in looks and bearing, big and tough-looking, their faces yellowish and wrinkled, their eyes slanted to a pronounced degree, like those of Koreans. They did not turn their heads in the direction of Emmanuelle when she entered. With intense attention they were examining, not unlike research scientists at work upon some exciting experiment, a body lying between them on the bed: a boyish body with elegant amber-colored legs and a lovely, clean-shaven pubic mound: a body that Emmanuelle recognized straightaway. It was Bee.

She wasn't dead, was she? Emmanuelle stared at her, quite petrified herself. But it wasn't long before the reclining girl opened her eyes, smiled, turned to look first at one, then at the other attending gentleman, and said, in English:

"So fantastic!"

Emmanuelle breathed easier again. The three others were now looking at her. Bee seemed equally at ease in the nude as she had appeared in her brocade tailored suit that afternoon in mid-August when they had had tea together at Marie-Anne's mother's house. She exclaimed:

"But it's great to see you!" She sat up on the bed, leaning on one man's shoulder.

Her voice had the same cheerful ring to it, her face was as radiant as ever. The sweetness of the look in her great big gray eyes moved Emmanuelle, almost to tears.

"You two know each other," one of the two clients remarked, speaking French with a fairly incomprehensible accent. "Go on, make love."

Emmanuelle stepped forward. She knelt down at the foot of a bed, raising her eyes toward the one who had spoken, awaiting his orders. It seemed he had nothing further to say. He just gave her an impassive stare. She turned back to the young American girl, asking herself who would make the first move. It was Bee. She twined her arms round the neck of her old lover, pulled Emmanuelle toward herself, embraced her, pressed her breasts against hers.

"Do you remember?" she said. "It was you who taught me!" Her thigh caressed Emmanuelle's vulva.

"And I've made some progress, since."

After the thigh, a hand, and such an expert hand at that! Emmanuelle was amazed. Such progress indeed! And Bee's lips on her nipples, now. And now, on her mouth. On her mouth!

But she remained inert, she didn't feel anything. Oh, this is horrible, she thought. I've become frigid! She had to force herself to concentrate on Bee's fingers exercising themselves on her clitoris and on her lips. Suddenly she remembered a day, she had been quite a small girl, when her tonsils were removed, under local anesthetic. This prevented her from feeling any pain, and yet she had sensed what was going on. Without missing a move, she had watched the instruments at work in her throat: she had felt the prodding, the cutting.

Emmanuelle had tried to convince herself that she was sick: but that was hard to prove, there was no pain—she had merely been rendered incapable of feeling any physical emotion, she was totally cold, apathetic, indifferent to whatever one did to her, an outcast from the world of the living, those beings that experience joy and pain, cry out with anguish or revel in lovely spasms: not objects to be touched, prodded, and cut, without even making them bleed, in the imperturbable and sterilized universe of specialists. A frightful nausea had risen within little Emmanuelle, and they had had to interrupt the operation, calm her down, and give her a total anesthetic. A similar feeling was now rising in the woman she had become, and who, once again, was unable to accept such a state of insensitivity. She tore herself out of Bee's embrace and turned over onto her stomach, burying her face in the pillow.

"What's wrong with me?" she asked herself, desperately, sinking her teeth into the pillow. "What's come over me?" She tried to visualize Bee's face, to recall how she had waited for her, so in love with her. . . . She repeated herself, but no echo answered: O my long lost one! O my beautiful one with the winged name, O my pretty one, my sweet. My promised land with the winged name! Beautiful, sweet, winged one. . . . The words kept turning, ringing in her empty head. She could not recognize them, she did not understand them even. Bee! Hadn't she sworn to love her with a legendary passion, more faithful than the seasons themselves? To call her forth from the deepest abyss? From the well of forgetfulness. . . .

She arose, her entire body expressing grief and rage, refusing to look at Bee, jumped out of the bed and, without turning, walked toward the curtain, parting it with a disgusted gesture. On the other side, she located her dress, bent down to pick it up, walked to the door, opened it, went out. She started down the corridor, seeing nothing or no one. A man stopped her, asked her something she could not understand. But she heard herself reply:

"I'm sorry, not today."

She continued, drifting from corridor to corridor, just as she was, carrying her dress in her hand, until, finally, a door opened, giving access to a complicated maze of stairwells and galleries. Here, however, she found her bearings and left the glass house. She drove through the frenetic lights and noises of the city like a hypnotized subject, totally unaware of the dozen or so accidents she barely avoided. . . .

Jean was waiting for her. They went in to dinner.

"Let's go to bed early," she suggested. "And let's really fuck tonight. I want to know if I still love you or not."

"You have doubts?" Jean said, in a tenderly mocking tone.

"Not really. But it's always better to make certain, isn't it?"

"If I were a husband," Emmanuelle says to Anna Maria, "I'd like my wife to make love to the greatest possible number of other men—and certainly to women, too. I'd constantly look for new partners for her, fresh lovers and mistresses. And it would be my primary reason for enlarging my circle of acquaintances.

My house would be the most hospitable in the city, but no one would be welcome into it unless they exhibited firm resolve to seduce the lady of that house. Every time I'd meet a new person, my first thought would be this question—'Does this one desire to pay homage to the body of her whom I love? If not, he, or she, is not worth wasting my time on.' Without having been to bed with my wife, no man could be called my friend. How could I stand it if someone met her and did not immediately desire her? In short, I'd have no other taste for my own friends than the taste she would have for them."

"In other words, every good husband should have the soul of a procurer?"

"Yes, if by 'procurer' you mean a man who is sufficiently in love with a woman to want to see her live in a continuous whirl of caresses! The good husband wants the entire world to stretch out its arms toward the beloved, to touch her and to make her experience joy."

"That's ridiculous. It's impossible to make love to the 'entire world.'"

"I know it is. And what a pity! But at least one can make love to a great number of its inhabitants! And that's why I want my husband not only to give me to others, but to publicize me, advertise me, put me in a showcase. Sell me publicly, to the highest bidder, whenever. To sell me is not to lose me; on the contrary: it is his gain. I love him, and I'm proud to be his wealth."

"So all our lives would become like those of pimps and whores, and I suppose the laws of the underworld would obtain in every other respect as well?"

"In a society where prostitution is regarded as a disgrace, like ours, it isn't surprising at all that procurers are rotten pimps and prostitutes equally rotten whores."

"Is it that you want to present me a revised constitution this time, or will the future do without such boring documents?"

"No, dear, you've convinced me that secular law isn't my forte."

"Well, you can still legislate the divine."

"That's exactly what I've done."

"How?"

"By engraving the new tablets of the law."

"No less than that! I can't wait to see them."

"Remember what happened to Moses!"

"But your god won't be such a jealous one."

"But are you sure you really want to reach the promised land?"

"Enough of your sales talk! I'll make up my mind when I see the samples. Let's see your ten commandments."

Emmanuelle goes to her room, gets a briefcase, returns, and takes out a sheet of paper, covered in her own round handwriting.

"Woman," she reads, "this is your law, given by you, to commence the reign of love, on earth as in the starred sky which is the kingdom of men:

"THE TEN COMMANDMENTS OF THE ART OF LOVE

I

Honor Eros, and him alone,
In judgment, deed and image.

II

Make love unto yourself,
Day and night, aided by your dreams.

III

Freely show your breasts and legs,
Freely and proudly fuck in public.

IV

Go naked in the world,
So that all can freely enjoy your body.

V

Permit access to your body
To everyone who desires it.

VI

Regale your tender palate
With long spurts of sperm.

VII

Be a loving and caressing body
To women as well as men.

VIII

Give yourself to more than one at a time,
One after the other, or all at once.

IX

Give your eager consent to your spouse
When he wants to make a present of you.

X

Thus, lover, you will ennoble your love
By being a whorish little turtledove!"

Both of them started laughing at the same time. Then Anna Maria commented:

"Well, that seems to me a pretty good résumé of the technical aspects of your eroticism. But is it love?"

"No," said Emmanuelle, "that's not all there is to love. But outside of these laws love is an evil."

12

Her Bare Legs on Your Fiery Beaches

"Is that your wife, next to you?"
"She's not next to me. She's in me. She is me.
If you see her as separate from me, you don't
know how to look."

—Jean Giraudoux, *Les Gracques,* I, 3

What I call marriage is the desire of two humans
to create something that will turn out to be greater
than what they created.

—Friedrich Nietzsche

I keep on trucking
I don't want to get there
The Infinite
is where I'm headed
and it's my life
to keep on trucking

—Alessandro Ruspoli,
La Pulsazioni del Silenzio

341

The road down to the seaside follows a navigable canal, over-grown with lotus plants: the vessels, powered by oar or sail, push them aside as they proceed, but once they have passed, they recompose their immutable watercolor arrangements. Green wooden water-wheels lift the lemony water out of the canal and distribute it over the sun-parched rice paddies and orchards. Their buckets, suspended from spokes tall as trees, rise and stop at the approach of the boatmen, after these have given a brief shout of warning to the children whose job it is to watch them.

The car passes a group of monks, marching along single file on the roadside teeming with insects. Each one of the bonzes carries a copper bowl containing the meal donated by pious women at daybreak, and a folded parasol that looks both cumbersome and heavy.

"Why do they carry those things with them all the time?" Emmanuelle wants to know. "They're not even using them, although the sun's quite hot already."

"Those aren't really parasols, or umbrellas," explains Jean. "They are tents. When it gets dark, each one plants it wherever he is, curls up around the handle, and lets the yellow top fall over him. Thus they can spend the night in dignified privacy."

"What if it does rain?"

"Then they get soaked."

"Wouldn't it be better if they waited for the dry season before starting out on their pilgrimages?"

"This *is* the dry season, darling. It begins today. Tonight, when the moon is full, thousands of little good-luck boats made out of banana leaves and coconut bark, each one with a lighted candle for a sail, will float along the rivers and the canals, carrying flowers, incense, and other offerings to the great Mother Water. It's a joyous celebration, called *Loï Krathong,* and the tradition is for lovers to get together, for some of them to become engaged, and for the affianced to get married."

"So there is a world, after all, in which not all days are dedicated to love?" Anna Maria says, pretending to be quite amazed by this fact. "Poor Emmanuelle, whatever would she do if she had to wait until the rains stop!"

"I'd cut the seasons shorter."

"Well, these people wait simply because they like to do so," Jean comments. "However, I'm not so sure that they really do wait. In these matters of love all human beings tend to be a little mendacious."

"So there you are," says Emmanuelle. "As for me, I don't really love love and love-making any more than other people do. The only way I differ from them is that I also love the truth."

All three of them are in the front seat, Anna Maria between Emmanuelle and her husband. The evening before Jean announced that he had business to transact near the frontier, and that the road he would take passed through Pattaya. Emmanuelle immediately shouted:

"Let's go see Marie-Anne!"

"Well, I don't really have time to go there, but I could drop you off at her place, and then stay a little longer on the way back."

"How many days are you going to stay at Chantaboun?"

"The whole week. I'll pick you up on Saturday or Sunday."

"What if I asked Anna Maria to come along?"

"Excellent idea. But in that case, I'll reserve a bungalow for you, so you won't be a burden to Marie-Anne and her mother."

Anna Marie has taken along her painter's paraphernalia, and Emmanuelle has brought a new camera, spare rolls of film, a record player, magazines and books, as if she were embarking on a transoceanic voyage. As to her outfit, Jean burst out laughing the first time he saw it, but did not suggest that she should change: her blouse has been tailored out of literal fishnet, of a brown string mesh that allows her nipples to jut through, and thus look more pointed than ever. The skirt, made out of very thin, practically transparent flesh-colored jute material, opens in the front: sitting there in the car she is exposing both thighs and the shadowy groin.

As soon as Jean had stopped at a gas station on the outskirts of the city, both attendants and passers-by had flocked around the car to relish this fantastic view, entranced and slack-jawed. Emmanuelle had of course been delighted: the only thing that surprised her was that Anna Maria had not scolded her for it. In fact, Anna Maria could hardly restrain her own laughter.

"There's a bunch of honest folk who'll never be quite the same again. I bet they'll do some revising of their scale of values!"

Jean, in total agreement:

"That's what this country needs, things to *think* about! It's a positively humanitarian act to provide them with such food for thought. And, well, you know how kind-hearted my dear wife is. . . ."

"But that's nothing!" the wife, herself, had said. "One afternoon I was driven all the way across Bangkok, from one end to the other, naked as the day I was born. I don't think anyone died of heart failure."

"No, but all the citizens are still talking about it," said Jean, with a delighted chuckle.

"I think the simple truth about Emmanuelle," opined Anna Maria, "is that she loves what she's showing. But, considering how well-endowed she is, one can't really blame her."

As soon as they were on their way again, Emmanuelle carefully folded up the flaps of her skirt, until she was exposing her tanned belly as well as the triangle of glorious shining curls.

"What about you, don't you love it too?" she asked the young Italian.

And as Anna Maria made no answer, Emmanuelle took her hand and placed it on her cunt.

It was the first time Anna Maria touched that part of Emmanuelle; her heart was beating wildly; she didn't withdraw it too quickly, not wanting to offend her friend (and also not wanting to appear more prudish than reasonable after almost two months of such intimate friendship); but she also wanted to avoid giving the impression that the was enjoying it. But Emmanuelle had the foresight to remove at least part of her scruples by simply putting her own hand on Anna Maria's and keeping it where it was. Now, the longer the situation lasted, the greater grew the conflict between the other young woman's emotions and her sense of duty, as well as her panic. It was intensified by the presence of Jean.

Her friend's quite visible perturbation heightened Emmanuelle's delight. She squeezed the much-desired hand between her thighs, forcing it, with an almost imperceptible flexing of her muscles, to perform the inconceivable caress. . . . And as nascent physical pleasure and a wonderful sense of tenderness began to make Emmanuelle's lower lips throb and swell, also causing her to lean her head dizzily on her companion's shoulder, an unexpected feeling of accomplishment and pride arose in Anna Maria, gradually erasing her confusion. Her constraint vanished, and she went on touching the voluptuous sweetness of this clit, palpitating like a live little bird, went on caressing Emmanuelle's open flesh, down there under the hot feathery fuzz. . . .

Anna Maria's fingers started going in deeper and deeper, the more that beautiful, radiant body leaned over against her own. There can't be anything wrong in making her happy, Anna Maria told herself. And, besides, I do love her! I have to be logical about it. . . .

Emmanuelle threw one arm around her neck, rubbed her cheek against hers.

"Now you are my lover!" she murmured, overjoyed. "My love, you are my lover!"

Anna Maria did not know what to say. She was becoming more and more aware, at each movement of her fingers, of the carnal delights she was discovering. Her whole body trembled. A desire stronger than all the fears and defenses was molding the powers of her senses to its own purposes. . . .

She allowed Emmanuelle's mouth to cover hers, her hands to squeeze her breasts, then descend down to her belly.

"Oh, no!" she thought. "Oh, no!"

But she did not resist at all, and while Emmanuelle was taking her into her possession, her thoughts whirled around in the void, without being able to conclude whether she was experiencing pleasure or pain.

But one thing she knew, it was love she was experiencing. And all that she could find to say, apart from this certainty, in the welter of sensations, images, ideas that raged in her head, was a little phrase, rather ridiculous, being so little, repeating itself, insisting on its inexpressible and irrevocable evidence— and perhaps it was all that the living were looking for, the mantra to end all mantras and to liberate them from all their false reasoning:

"Et voilà! Et voilà!" ("So there! So there!")

Quite a while later Emmanuelle breaks the silence.

"Mario's coming to join us tomorrow," she declares. "It's really amazing that he deigns to budge from Bangkok. I had to beg him to come, literally on my knees."

"Where are you going to put him up?"

Jean sounds a little concerned.

"Oh, he can stay with us. I'm sure Marie-Anne won't have any room."

Anna Maria has an anxious question:

"Are there enough beds?"

"No," says Emmanuelle, "but he's your cousin, after all."

"Thanks very much. There's enough incest in the family as it is."

"Well, then he can come sleep with me," her friend retorts.

"That's much better," Jean says, approvingly.

The car bounces mightily over a bump in the road, and Anna Maria throws her arms around Emmanuelle's neck; shamefaced, she lets go again, asks:

"Tell me, Jean—it really means nothing to you that another man gets into bed with your wife?"

"Oh, but it does."

"Oh, good!"

"It gives me great pleasure."

I won't say another word, Anna Maria promises herself. She hardly dares look Jean in the face after what has just happened. Nevertheless, her curiosity soon gets the better of all resolutions. Can it really be that Jean wholeheartedly embraces Emmanuelle's concepts of eroticism? Now is the time to force him to make an unequivocal pronouncement on this matter. And why not employ a little ruse, as well, if necessary, even if it will make Emmanuelle more furious than it will make him. The game is well worth the risk of suffering a few sarcasms, Anna Maria says to herself. So she declares, pretending primness:

"Then you don't really love her."

Jean seems to take that accusation with a much greater calmness than Anna Maria has anticipated. When it finally comes, his answer is:

"So rejoicing in what makes her happy isn't loving her?"

"Don't tell me any husband has to push his detachment or spirit of sacrifice to such limits!"

"Please, I feel quite humiliated—at the very thought that someone could believe me capable of making sacrifices."

"Oh, what false pride! What paradoxes!"

"Not at all. Just think about it, and you'll see that what the world at large honors under the designation 'sacrifice' is mostly just a sickly-sweet hodgepodge of false pretenses and laziness: homage paid to vice, by virtue. And that's not my style at all."

"What is, then?"

"Either Emmanuelle's actions seem bad to me, and I oppose them. Or I let her do as she wants, and that means that I accept them. Simply out of a healthy egoism, and without false shame: I'm only accepting that what's good for me is good for her, too. I'm not practicing abnegation any more than I'm practicing blindness or indulgence. I guess it is only my detachment in this way, if detachment it is, that seems so shocking."

"Now don't you start telling me, you too, that Emmanuelle will become a better spouse simply by sleeping around with everybody! Or that she prostitutes herself just to augment the family income—and that you approve of that as well."

"My point of view is even simpler than that: I do not regard Emmanuelle as separate from myself."

"What on earth does that mean?"

"She does not exist apart from me, nor do I, from her."

"You see, no one can be jealous of him or herself," Emmanuelle explains.

"Two business partners can offend each other, and their interests can be divergent," Jean continues, "or one can choose to submit his judgment and will to the other one's. But we're not business partners. We are just *one*. Thus, her joy cannot be my sorrow, her tastes to my distaste, her loves, my hatreds. And there's no merit on my part in wishing for what is good for her: it's good for me, too."

"Anything one of us does the other is the author of. There's no need for us to be physically present each time: where Jean is, I am. Whenever he builds a successful dam, it is because I have constructed it with him, within him."

"Between us, we have but one mind," Jean affirms.

"We're just one hermaphroditic cellule," Emmanuelle shouts, "and I'm sure we'll reproduce by biological fission!"

"Her body is my body. In it, she is the feminine principle, as I am its male instinct. Her much-caressed breasts are my breasts, her belly, my belly. She extends the realm of possibility for me. She opens doors in the universe that remain closed for a man alone."

"And . . . and it doesn't embarrass you to identify yourself with her to this extent—with other men caressing her? Isn't that a little bit like . . . like being a homosexual?"

"When I am her, I am a woman. It's when she makes love to a woman that I become a Lesbian."

Anna Maria blushed. Jean grinned. It didn't take long for the girl to recover her composure and return to the charge:

"Are you really sincere about all this, or is it that you just accept Emmanuelle's infidelity rather than risking to lose her?"

"Lose me!" Emmanuelle roars. "How can you imagine such a thing? And have I ever been unfaithful to him?"

"Emmanuelle is faithful to me, because she always remains a part of me. Thus neither one of us need live in fear of losing the other."

"Oh, how very sure you are of yourselves!" Anna Maria exclaims, almost bitterly. "Is there some kind of telepathy working between your spirits, that never permits you to doubt the other half for a moment?"

"That telepathy is as age-old as mankind. It's just a more prestigious word for what is more exactly termed . . . sympathy. Those who are able to suffer together, why wouldn't they be able to enjoy themselves together?"

"Anna Maria, darling, Jean is about to give you the answer to a question you're hesitating to ask."

"What question?"

"Just listen, you'll find out."

But Jean has nothing further to say, it seems, and Anna Maria looks with a meditative stare at the monotonous landscape on both sides of the bright yellow road. It looks, in fact, as if all three of them are getting a little sleepy, and the beautiful Italian girl shakes herself and bursts out into a vehement tirade, quite unexpected to her two hosts.

"You can't live like that without running incredible risks! Jean, when you let other men see your wife naked, when you let them touch her, make love to her—aren't you afraid, ever? If you were truly attached to her . . ."

An intersection, no signs:

"I guess it's a right turn here?" Jean says. He takes the turn with squealing tires, and before Anna Maria has a chance to steady herself, she is thrown against him, with the whole length of her body. He goes on, without seeming to be aware of his fair passenger's state of arousal:

"What safety in prudence? In the days of chastity belts, every Don Juan carried a bunch of keys. And I don't think Emmanuelle would like me to be fearful. Pusillanimity, my dear, makes one look so very stupid! If I'm anxious that others should not see my wife naked, and I therefore keep her under drapes and covers at all times, I deprive myself more of the opportunity to see her beauty than I'm really depriving anyone else! It doesn't make sense. Why hide what one loves? You yourself, Anna Maria, were just enjoying the fact that Emmanuelle loves her body, that she is proud of it, and that she exhibits it for those reasons. Well then, I love my wife, I'm proud of her beauty; and it makes me happy that she makes herself desirable, and that others desire her. The most horrible character trait I know is the one exemplified by that convict who shows his buddies a snapshot and says, with great glee: 'Just you look at that mug! Why, her ass looks better than her face. I married her just because she's so damn ugly. See, that way I knew I'd never have any regrets when they put me in the cooler!'"

"It's true, jealousy can be folly. But it's *inseparable* from love! The woman you love, how can you not suffer when others are enjoying her? You wouldn't be a man!"

"'I adore you, rage of virgins, o so delicious!'" Emmanuelle chants, demonstrating her erudition.

"That's right, they are enjoying her, they're not taking her away from me," says Jean. "The vocabulary of love is so inconsistent! The man who is providing my wife the pleasure she likes, what is he taking? Is he 'taking her'? Pleasure, that's all he is taking. What's he taking from me?"

"What he is giving her, you yourself could have given her."

"Is that something to be measured and counted? And does she have it in such minimal quantity that it should be rationed? I haven't noticed. What she gives to others, she does not take away from me."

"But don't you feel humiliated by having to share her body with God knows whom? Would she not be more precious if she were inaccessible to intruders, kept solely for you?"

"I think you've already answered that question: you have been talking about pride, about the price of things, about taste

and propriety and exclusivity, about the passion for possession. But I've been talking to you about love."

"If so, then that love must be some kind of saintliness.
Yes, listen, you two—you're always poking fun at my religious
ardors, but it's exactly *you* who don't quite live in this world!
Carnal passion would be much more cumbersome."

"You think I regard her body with detachment? Come
on, just ask her! But the borderlines of my love aren't identical with the frontiers of her flesh. They don't demarcate the
destination of our trip together, they are merely the starting
lines! I can't remember if I knew what love was before I met
Emmanuelle. But I do know for certain that in loving her I
have become capable of infinite love. Don't you think it didn't
take some doing, that I didn't have to suffer! And yet, I never
suffered from jealousy. If I'm afraid sometimes—because I'm
no more perfect nor invulnerable to fear than anyone else!—
it's not a fear of being deprived of her care, but a fear that she
might be deprived of mine. What would remain, for me, if I
couldn't worry about her any longer, cover her up, say, at night
when the air cools and she's asleep and unaware that she's getting cold? After me, who could watch at her bedside as well as
I, when a fever turns her into a weak little child again? And
that is why I don't regret it if someone borrows her from me, as
long as that someone isn't Death. How could I face my friends,
if I had to tell them: I wasn't able to protect her whose life
had been entrusted to me? Because she is their friend, too, and
it is for their sake, as well as my own, that I shield her from

dangers. But how could I call *them* dangers, men and women who are united with me in their urge to keep her alive? They are only expressing their love, and they aren't my rivals, they are my allies."

Anna Maria did not answer. The road was so straight now that it had a clearly visible vanishing point, like a pair of railroad tracks. Jean, who had been driving quite slowly, stepped on the gas. The dust they raised made their throats feel dry.

"Jean has no reason to be jealous of my lovers," said Emmanuelle. "They should rather be jealous of him, because no one ever gives me what he gives me. And don't think I mean just freedom. He makes me into a woman a notch above the common run of women. I'm quite aware of my good fortune. All he demands from me is that I be myself, and that I prove worthy of his confidence. Anna Maria, how could I let him down?"

"The only freedom that makes any sense," says Jean, "is the freedom from fear. But who of us isn't afraid of the truth, at one time or another? Emmanuelle knows that there is at least one other human being on earth to whom she can tell everything. And that alone makes her feel strong. I am she, it's true, but at the same time, I'm also the one who guarantees her existence. The rest of the world's opinions cannot impinge on her at all."

"But what if they add up to a great big scandal?"

"Why should she worry about that, as long as I'm not scandalized?"

"But if it should happen that you *are*?"

"Well, then I'd be wrong, and she would have to make me see reason. My love for her also means that I want her to help me."

"It's up to me to demonstrate that nothing that has to do with love can be bad," says Emmanuelle. "I'm sure that not even you, dear virgin, would advance the opinion that physical love is the opposite of true love?"

"The body is something else," says Anna Maria, "than the true source of good and evil."

"But if I can't love your bodies," says Jean, "I cannot love you at all."

"Come on, search your memory, sweet archangel!" exclaims Emmanuelle. "When your Master came to us, he turned himself into human flesh. . . . Do you want us to be more squeamish than He?"

"If I don't condemn Emmanuelle when she makes love to any other partners," Jean explains, "that's because she is in no way to blame. Love isn't righteous or unrighteous merely because one makes it to this or some other man. It is its own justification: it is absolute innocence!"

"Jean," Anna Maria says, hesitantly, "if Emmanuelle had decided to be only your woman, would you blame her for that?"

"She wouldn't be worthy of my love, if she were capable of refusing herself to someone else. The only value we can be certain of is the value of giving oneself."

"So fidelity is just an empty dream?"

"If that's all it was, it would be forgivable!"

"Why is it so abominable?"

"Nine times out of ten it is downright disgraceful."

"God, words are losing all their meaning!"

"No, they aren't: unfortunately, the words designating pharisaism, narrow-mindedness, conformism, convention always do have a meaning. The 'fidelity' that society pretends to honor is not courageous at all, most of the time, nor is it beautiful, or noble, or tender: it is simply mediocre, selfish, and lazy. And that's why I call it a disgrace."

"Then a husband can't help being mediocre?"

"To be content with one man when one is able to know many," says Emmanuelle, "that's like cutting off one's wings, despising the great opportunity to fly! That's not loving but crawling."

"But isn't it enough for two people to love each other? And to give oneself to one's own lover? Does one *really* need anything else?" shouts Anna Maria, upset to the point of tears.

"Why barricade your doors?" Emmanuelle asks, gently. "The world is full of friends."

"If the effect of love should be deprivation," says Jean, "then it stands to reason that one should begin by depriving oneself of it. If any creature's love causes it to close off its heart and body from the love of others, then no doubt it would be better for that creature not to love at all."

"It is my love for Jean that makes me able to love," says Emmanuelle. "If I stopped loving him I could no longer love anyone, neither man nor woman. Nor could I make love, not even to myself! But as long as he loves me, loving other people teaches me how to love him better."

"Love that is merely shared egotism," Jean emphasizes, "is no more commendable than the usual solitary egotism. There's something about exclusivity that constricts my throat: nothing seems more disturbing to me than a loving couple that is 'alone in the world.' I feel it's reasonable to say that those who do not like to share the sweetness of living with their own kind act more like dumb beasts than human beings."

"And yet you were so eloquent about the unity of two!" Anna Maria says, plaintively.

"No couple can be content merely to exist," says Jean. "It has to have a goal, it has to go somewhere. And that is why it has to communicate, accept change and exchange, mingle with others, seek out the well-traveled roads, get out of the house."

"How could you move forward so long as you insist on staring into each other's faces?" says Emmanuelle. "As soon as you take a step, you bump into each other. . . . The world reduced to the round black mirror of the loved one's eye, surely one must end up hating it, breaking it? When you consider that, it isn't surprising at all that people are lazy enough to associate love with death."

"The couple that is a closed circle, a ring," adds Jean, "all you can do with it, is turn it round and round—in other words, keep it in its place, stationary. If one wants the line to open up into life, it has to be opened, its legs have to spread, as in a capital U!"

"Or rather, it's like an equilateral hyperbola with four legs," Emmanuelle corrects him.

"In what you call adultery," Jean follows up, "I see the couple's privilege to choose instead of the finite circular world those unlimited possibilities of the hyperbola."

"Of which love," Emmanuelle concludes, "is the asymptote."

"Which means that you'll never reach it," remarks Anna Maria.

"Oh yes, we will, in the infinite. Don't be afraid, be happy to be always on your way to it at all points."

"Like Sisyphus on his way up the hill?"

"The adventure of loving is not as strenuous as that! Are you growing weary already?"

"I want a love that I can carry to the end of my life."

"The arms of your thousandth lover will lay it on your grave."

"Why not stay where one is, go on being what one is?"

"Because evolution is the law that governs all life," Jean replies, "and because you cannot progress without transformation. What one 'is' doesn't even exist any longer: it has already changed into something else."

"We're no stylites any longer," says Emmanuelle, "and we certainly won't be capable of traversing the Milky Way if we carry with us all that dead weight of our fear of joy!"

"What harmony can I expect from such ceaseless questing and suspense?"

"Harmony? Equilibrium? That's no way to live," mocks Emmanuelle. "That's so very pedestrian. My body is growing vestigial wings. . . ."

Anna Maria stretches, smiles at her friend:

"What other space will there ever be for those wings but heaven? What infinity dignified enough to match their dreams, but eternity?"

"I do not believe that there is a God," says Emmanuelle. "But if there is one, He ought to be proud of my courage."

Now the road turns away from the dusty plain and ascends into brick-red hills, from which they can glimpse the sea, glittering in the fierce sunlight.

"Eternity," Emmanuelle says, "lies in the bodies of those who are making love. But it is precarious and endangered: as soon as one stops caressing, it is lost. We'll regain eternity when we re-order our value system of restraints."

Anna Maria seems to be in a state of anguish.

"But do you, too, dear Jean—do you, too, believe that eroticism has replaced love on this earth, and that it is the god we have to worship instead of the one we believe in?"

"I don't know anything about that," says Jean. "I only know that there is nothing more human than a beautiful girl. It seems more important to me to marvel at her gracefulness than to confess one's sins or to ponder on the Trinity. So, count me out: as far as gods are concerned I have no preference. Eroticism

exists for me in Emmanuelle, it *is* Emmanuelle. And like everything she is, it is there for me—she is eroticized for me, as she
is for the whole world. If she weren't erotic any more, eroticism
would lose its originator, its content, all its meaning—for me,
at least. No god, no woman could replace her."

"Replace her?" Anna Maria says, astonished. "But she'd
still be your wife!"

"No," says Emmanuelle. "I wouldn't be."

"I don't understand either one of you," sighs Anna Maria.

"I wouldn't even be a woman any longer. I'd be a death
mask, a mummy. Should Jean who has known me alive then
keep me embalmed in his bed? Because of my faltering he
would have lost everything—his taste for eroticism, his taste
for me. And as it's impossible to rebuild a life on the ruins of
so much shattered poetry, he would also have lost his taste for
life."

"So there are no other alternatives for you, but eroticism
and death?"

"There's no other choice for anyone except that between
death or true character. Least of all will it do to will oneself to
be one of the walking dead, one of those who live in expectation of Paradise. If one day you should see us transformed into
such zombies—abandoned by the love of loving; me busying
myself with whatever factitious business instead of my desire
for all the men in the streets of the world; me sitting down
without showing my legs; me wearing longer skirts and high-
necked blouses, even if only on those occasions when I have

to meet conventional folk; me putting on a peignoir whenever someone enters my room to pay me a visitor to bring me
breakfast; when you see me accepting a dinner invitation from
a man without making love to him afterward, or taking tea with
a girl without attempting to undress her; when you see me letting a day pass without masturbating, accepting the fact that
people know me without ever having seen me in the nude and
talk about my body in terms other than those of remembering
the times they've had with it, or fantasizing about what they
will do—then, dear passers-by, avert your eyes from the scene,
from such mimicry of life: you'll know that Emmanuelle and
Jean, whom you once loved, have failed in their dream: spare
them the shame of witnessing their downfall!"

Although Emmanuelle is reciting this litany in a tone of
self-mockery, Anna Maria can sense the underlying sincerity
of it, so strongly that she shivers despite the torrid heat. She is
silent for quite a while before asking, in an almost timid voice:

"But doesn't such intransigence entail the risk that one of
you will get tired of it before the other? And what happens if
such absolutism, the refusal to see this eroticism in its proper
perspective, ends in total bitterness or saturation? Instead of
limiting yourself merely to the alternatives of obsession or
denial, why not accept the idea that later in life another kind
of living may take the place of eroticism, and that you'll find it
just as interesting?"

"I'm afraid you haven't really understood what we are saying," Jean answers. "You seem to think that we are inspired by

some sort of fanaticism, or that we have vowed to maintain some kind of new orthodoxy. It isn't like us at all to be such conservationist zealots. Emmanuelle simply wanted to say that in order to do better one has to watch out, above all, against being thrown back into the past. There are so many men and women who advance a little way and then spend the remainder of their existence trying to be forgiven: trying to sit in judgment on themselves, to denounce themselves to themselves— or, as they say, *to fit in*. We don't want to become such frauds. But if we want to keep our course, it isn't enough just to keep from backsliding: that would be just another way of falling down, no matter how high we might think we had climbed."

His discourse has been so serene that Anna Maria smiles at him, looking almost reassured.

"Our unity is only a beginning," he continues. "In order to survive it has to move forward, grow stronger, discover new powers, discover all its powers. I'm not even sure I can anticipate what they will be. But the anticipation itself makes life worth pursuing. Emmanuelle and I share this passion for the truths of tomorrow, more than any nostalgia for those of the past. The couple we are won't enter the future ass-backwards."

"Our love takes us toward youth," Emmanuelle claims, jubilantly. "Side by side we advance into the future, doing the very opposite of growing old!"

"Oh, you sound so convinced," murmurs dreamy-eyed Anna Maria. "Who can tell? Perhaps you'll succeed in remaking the reality of love."

"Not a question of remaking," says Emmanuelle, "it hasn't even been made yet."

A jagged range of bluffs, its summits outlined against the sky in stark beauty, ran alongside the road. The sea was on its other side, quite close and so transparent that one could see down into the rockpools and catch the quizzical glance of the giant sea-urchins' blue eyes.

"Let's stop here and have a few nests," said Jean.

An armed sentinel stood guarding an opening in the flinty rock wall. He received the three strangers with a smile. Once inside, the sudden chill made them shiver, and it was too dark to distinguish anything: but then the crevasse widened, and they found themselves in an enormous cave, lit from above by an opening in the very high ceiling. Thousands of birds, fly-sized at this distance, were wheeling in and out of this hole.

On a flat space, furnished with a few tables made out of boards set atop big rocks and a field kitchen tended by a jovial Chinese cook, a number of locals sat picking away with their chopsticks at some gelatinous substance served in little bowls, with an air of great enjoyment. The newcomers sat down at a table.

"Why do they have a sentry posted out there?" Anna Maria wondered.

"This cave is a treasure trove," Jean explained. "The nests are state property. The birds are protected by law. No one has the right to kill them, neither cobras nor humans: if you do, you have to pay for it with your head."

"What are they, swallows?"

"A kind of tiny martin, rather—very lively, and as you can hear, pretty chirpy as well. They're called *salangans,* or, the local name, *ïans* They feed on algae and plankton as well as on insects."

"And they make their nests out of seaweed?"

"Oh no. At the risk of turning your stomach, I have to tell you that these birds manufacture them entirely from the secretions of their mouth—not saliva, either, but a kind of glue. But it is most edible and nutritious as well, containing proteins, iodine, all sorts of vitamins. That's what the famous 'swallows' nests' are."

"I guess it's the seasoning that makes them so good."

"Pleasant to the taste, yes, perhaps. But they're really prized for other properties."

The smiling cook served them their portions of the delicacy.

"Because their claws are not designed to hold on to and perch on branches," Jean explained, "these *ïans* do not build their nests in trees, but on the outcroppings of thirty-one forbidden isles and those of this cave. A certain Thai tribe has a monopoly on collecting them. They're called the *Tchao-ho,* the hut people, because of the shelters they construct for the collecting season on the summits or sides of the cliffs. They have to swing from long ropes, suspend themselves on bamboo platforms, risk their lives and often lose them, to scrape off the nests. The nests are shaped like cockles, and two of them fit in the palm of a hand. When the birds have been robbed of their first nest, they produce another one, hoping to lay their eggs in it; but even that gets taken from them. They let them keep the third one, which is mixed with blood, anyway, because the strain of creating it kills them."

"Oh, that's cruel!" Emmanuelle said, indignantly. "I won't eat any more of this stuff."

A dignified man passed their table, followed by four young girls, all of them pretty, carrying large, full baskets on their heads.

"That's a *Tchao-ho*," said Jean, "and those are his wives."

"Four of them! I thought Siamese law only allowed one."

"He couldn't care less about the law. If you lead a dangerous life, you love it more."

The intrepid cliff-scaler accorded Emmanuelle's exposed breasts an interested glance. The women smiled amiably at their little group.

"You see," Emmanuelle said, "they aren't jealous."

"Perhaps they'd like to expand their harem to five," said Anna Maria.

"Well, let's get going," said Jean. "We have at least another half-hour to drive."

The scorching air outside the cave silenced them for a moment or two. Several kilometers whizzed by before Anna Maria picked up the conversation:

"Is it because the majority of the men of that tribe end up killing themselves on the cliffsides that the women have to be content with one husband for four?"

"Have to be!" says Emmanuelle. "Who told you they *have to* do anything?"

"That's right, they're quite free," Jean says. "But they don't like to be single wives."

"Why not?"

"They think it's a shame."

"They're right, a marriage limited to only two certainly can't be successful," Emmanuelle affirms.

"So you're not content with adultery any more," Anna Maria says. "Now it has to be polygamy!"

"Oh, why don't we drop those antiquated terms," says Jean, trying to sound conciliatory. "It's divisive to be polygamous. What *we* are looking for is something that'll create more unity. To extend what the couple achieves first of all."

"I don't really see any difference."

"Well, for instance, a *ménage à trois,*" explains Emmanuelle. "It's the opposite of polygamy."

"Really? It's a chimera, in any case. It never works."

"That's because it has mostly been based on false premises," says Jean. "It's because those people tend to put the cart before the horse, trying to accomplish, the three of them, what hasn't worked for two. The trio is no remedy for a stale one-to-one relationship."

"It ought to be a reward for a successful one," says Emmanuelle.

"Polygamy represents the past, the duo the present, the harmonious trio the near future: but later they will invent other combinations," adds Jean, laughing. "It's all just a beginning. To evolve is to grow."

"Sincerity and confidence are difficult enough even between two people," Anna Maria sighs. "Can you imagine how bad it could be with a household of three!"

"Rather imagine how nice it could be."

"The most likely thing to happen," Anna Maria insists, "is that one of them would be pushed aside, sooner or later, and become an intruder. Within your triad, the old tête-à-tête would re-establish itself. Not necessarily the same one as before the experiment, but that would be the only difference."

"The good marriage would be the one that resulted from the fusion of three couples," Emmanuelle declares with authority.

"What? Now it's to be six people?"

"Oh, no: three. One man who is the lover of two women, thus forming a couple with each one of them, that's two: and the third one is that formed by the two women, being lovers."

"So there couldn't be a happy trio without homosexuality?"

"No, obviously not."

"And what if there were two men who were lovers?"

"It would work just as well."

"What about two men and two women, wouldn't that be even better?"

"It seems that way to me, but Mario prefers odd numbers."

"Well then," asks Anna Maria, "are you going to try that experience with Mario?"

"No," says Emmanuelle. "I'm going to try it with you."

All along the crescent-shaped, glaringly white beach, perching on rocks by the water's edge, there are fishermen, so intent on their prey that they don't even turn to look at the women. With motions that remind one of sowing they throw out great pliant nets to rise in the wind like sails, hovering there and then falling onto the water, seemingly weightless. Then the fishermen pull them back in and repeat the gesture. Have they caught anything? Nothing? Their movements are so measured, so elliptical that the onlookers can't be sure. Perhaps they did catch a fish, perhaps it was too small, and they let it go again, casting it back into the sea with the next sweep of their arms.

To the west, a junk is rounding the promontory, outlined by the sky, on the smoky water highlighted by the sun. A real picture-book junk, with its red trapezoid sail, now flat and turning slowly in the calm, like a fan between a mandarin's fingers. Then other boats come into view, of the same shape but of varying sizes, closer in, farther out. And now the arrangement is perfect, stretching all across the horizon. One more sail, and the picture would seem too crowded; one less, and there would be a gap. The same number, but differently arranged between lighthouse and reefs, and one would like to readjust the lighting.

Now there's one, the smallest one, changing course and heading inshore. Although it disrupts the masterpiece, Anna Maria and Emmanuelle find it the most delightful of all, pretty enough to tempt one to blow kisses at it. They run along the shore, following it. It is teeming with children. But hasn't it an adult crew? Probably, but they can't see that. From a distance it looks covered with little bodies: they are all over the sail, the masts, the bridge, the stern. They are dangling their legs from the sides of the old, bleached hull, their hands are swinging from ends of ropes that are thicker than their bodies. But when the vessel approaches it can be seen that there are only about a dozen on board.

Some of them are Siamese, but the others, more numerous, have the deep healthy tan of Europeans grown up in the sun. The youngest is perhaps four, the oldest, ten or eleven. There are as many boys as there are girls.

As their galleon, having come as close in as it could without being grounded, turns again, presenting its side to the beach, all of the children rush over to that side, laughing, clowning, stretching out their arms toward the two young women. The Orientals are wearing loincloths, all of them in two colors: either blue and white, or red and black, or ocher and mauve. The others, boys as well as girls, are stark naked.

Now some enterprising ones jump into the water, making it spurt up in geysers, then wave to the others still on board to come in and join them. A little girl with round cheeks, a minuscule nose, great big dark blue eyes, platinum-blonde hair that reaches down to her ankles, now makes up her mind, clambers on to the beam serving as a springboard, spreads her arms, emits a very loud yell, and lets herself fall forward as if expecting her little wings to carry her. She disappears into a thrashing commotion of water and limbs and reappears the next second, her hair dripping, shouting for joy.

The others are dancing in the waves, calling and waving to the big girls on the beach to come and join them. Emmanuelle runs toward them. When the water reaches her thighs, she raises her short skirt and ties its flaps around her waist like a beggar's bag, then tries to pick up and install the little blonde in there, but the knot comes untied. A boy throws his arms around her neck, and the oldest girl, with clearly budding breasts, follows suit. Others arrive on the scene and start hanging from her, until her knees give way. The children think this is great fun. Emmanuelle disengages herself, takes off her skirt, pulls off her top (which the nearby fishermen could well use for their own purposes), and throws them, with a gesture not unlike theirs, into the water, but shoreward. In the same paradisiacal state of nudity as the children she goes on playing with them until she is quite out of breath.

Another junk—she has not seen it coming—drops anchor beside the first one. The children gather round and greet it with happy shouts, receiving a reply that is almost an echo. It is another contingent, not quite as numerous, of somewhat older boys and girls wearing bathing suits. Anna Maria wants to warn Emmanuelle, but a clarion-like call cuts off her words: it is Marie-Anne, her hair freed from the customary plaits, flying in the air and light like a big sunshade woven of strands of gold.

The group sporting in the waves now proceeds to the beach. Emmanuelle's hands slip on their smooth gleaming skins. The smallest girl, who seems to have a crush on her, is holding on to the short hairs of her pubis. Emmanuelle scoops up the tiny amber-skinned body and cradles it in her left arm, picks up a Siamese boy with her right, and starts walking toward Marie-Anne, who has debarked.

"All these children are yours?" Emmanuelle asks.

"Yes, for the time being they are," her elfin friend admits. "How did you get here? All by yourselves?"

"Jean drove us down. And I'd like you to know that we've come to see you! He's taken off again, he was in a hurry. But he'll be back to get us in five days. And listen: I have great news: Mario's coming tomorrow! Where's your bungalow?"

"It's not here. It's on the other beach, quite a way from here. What are you doing in this forlorn place?"

"We have that house, over there."

"But why on earth?"

"Jean rented it for us."

Marie-Anne glances at Anna Marie, seems to be thinking it over, then declares:

"I'll take you on my junk. First we'll get all the small fry home, and then you'll come and say hello to my mother. We'll have dinner together. You can walk back along the cliffs—you see, the sea is quite low at night, and it's full moon, too. So there's nothing to be afraid of."

"I'll go put something on," says Emmanuelle, fishing her drenched garments out of the water.

"And you, do you always keep your clothes on?" Marie-Anne asks Anna Maria, with veiled irony. The young Italian smiles, does not answer, and follows Emmanuelle, who is walking toward their chalet.

They are back in a moment, both of them wearing bathing suits. By a coincidence the cut of their suits is identical: one-piece, made out of very sheer material, leaving back and sides bare, hugging the breasts, cut very high on the thighs, thus accentuating the profile of pubis and buttocks; Emmanuelle's is the color of burnt sienna, Anna Maria's, olive green.

Once aboard they discover that the vessel does have pro-fessional sailors: two Chinese, stretched out, haughtily, up on the bridge, steering the barque without even bothering to stand. Their red teeth are pensively working on betel leaves.

Anchors aweigh, and Marie-Anne relieves herself of the upper part of her white bikini. Then she steps out of the panties as well. She stretches out on her back in the sun, her head pointing toward the prow, her breasts firm as those of a bronze statue, her legs spread wide apart. A young boy appears and lies down on his stomach between them, his head facing Marie-Anne's pubis. He is handsome, twelve or maybe thirteen years old. Gravely he lies there contemplating the pink sex of a girl his own age. Neither of them say anything. Neither Emmanuelle nor Anna Maria admire the coastline and its palm trees passing by on their left, but concentrate entirely on the boy, his attentive eyes and his body, rocking gently with the boat.

The ebb tide is so far out that the lights of the bungalow are almost invisible from here. It must be after midnight. Emmanuelle and Anna Maria are stretched out on the damp, warm sand, right by the water's edge.

They have returned late from Marie-Anne's, walking back up to the terrace of their house. The old guard, a piratical-looking fellow, soot-brown and wrinkled, whose duty it is to watch over them during the night, lay there stretched out on his back, shamelessly asleep, though with cudgel in hand. But they knew that they did not have anything to be afraid of: the presence of this bodyguard was merely a mark of respect.

Emmanuelle then suggested that they should go for one last swim. Anna Maria had let the straps of her bathing suit slip off her shoulders and had then taken it off, without a word of encouragement on Emmanuelle's part. She had dropped it right beside the buccaneer and started walking down the beach, beautifully pale in the moonlight. This had been the first time that Emmanuelle had seen her naked.

But now, lying next to that other body, an unsuspected timidity was constraining her hands and her lips. She found herself wishing that Anna Maria would talk; not about love, not about men, not about themselves, not about the future, but about such simple things as the sea, the foam, the noise it made, the cockleshells pricking their skin, the dark shadows passing on the horizon, bent over the ground, looking for crabs, the dancing lights on the water, from the lanterns of the boats out for cuttlefish. . . . But Anna Maria stared up at the sky and remained silent.

"What are you dreaming about?" Emmanuelle finally asks.

"I'm not dreaming. I'm just happy."

"Why are you so happy?"

"Because of you."

If I hadn't fallen in love with her that very first moment, Emmanuelle thinks, I would never have fallen in love with her. But this is what I have been waiting for.

"I've never seen you before," Emmanuelle says.

"Look at me now."

"You mean you'll let me love you, although you're so much more beautiful than I am?"

"It's too late for me to defend myself."

"Do you think I'm evil?"

"Do you still think I'm an angel?"

"You're my lover. You are my woman."

"I'll come and live with you and Jean. I'll be you."

"I'll make you do what I love."

"But please don't be too much in a hurry. You know, I'm still quite shaken up."

"Oh, a little courage, my sweet darling! I don't want to hoard you. I'll squander you like a windfall."

"You'll keep nothing?"

"Squandering you is not the same as wasting or losing you. Do you want me to cling to you like a leech, to gorge myself on your sweet blood?"

"I wouldn't be enough for you to gorge yourself on. . . ."

"That's true, nothing will ever be enough. I'll keep on looking for more. Look at that sky. . . ."

"It was you who distracted me from it."

"Just look at the sky. You see how lucky our earth is! That sky is its realm. It belongs to us. We have ventured out into it, under our own steam."

"What else is there to do there?"

"Oh, but everything, everything! Just think of what remains for us to discover. But, oh, that's impossible. We'll never achieve that world!"

"No, no, don't lose faith!" Anna Maria tells her, suddenly fervent: "Jean and us, people like us, and those we love, we'll see it born yet."

"Not us, darling. Nor anyone, ever, only those who are yet to come, always."

"And who will come after us, you and me?"

"Our daughter."

"Who will bear her? You or me? And who'll give her to us? Jean?"

"Or you'll give her to me, I'll give her to you, what does it matter. We'll teach her how to be born. To change."

"That's all we'll teach her?"

"The rest she'll have to teach us. Or her daughters, or the great-granddaughters of her daughters."

"But we won't be there any more," says Anna Maria, with a catch in her voice. "Oh, how I wish we could come back! Some time far, far ahead—when mankind has grown up. . . ."

"Oh, be quiet. Remember what Mallarmé's faun said? 'Those nymphs . . .' Oh, my sweet bride, my sister, I have given birth to you: but that is not enough! My love for you makes my dream grow. I can feel a desire for infinity."

"What do you want?" Anna Maria asks.

"To perpetuate us. I want you! I love you. Give yourself to us!"

"Take this water, this salt, this seaweed, this sand. And now take this my body. . . ."

"How beautiful it is, touched by my mouth, my hands!"

"Make it your masterpiece."

That night Emmanuelle deflowered Anna Maria.

The sun rises over the thatched bungalow. Its rays penetrating the big open window outline in sepia the intertwined bodies on the rattan-frame bed.

Had Emmanuelle slept? She doesn't know. She watches the sun clear the promontory: the sea appears to be stretching under its light. She feels an urge to go out there and see it, to plunge into it, to gain strength from it.

Anna Maria slumbers on, an enchanted smile playing round her lips. Carefully Emmanuelle extricates herself from her arms and tiptoes out of the room. On the terrace only the great white chunks of coral stand like mythical and crusty beasts: the watchman has left already, with the shadows of the night. Has he even glanced at the two naked bodies? Or perhaps their pleasure, their little love-cries have kept him awake?

Down on the beach, Emmanuelle stretches her cramped limbs. Her appearance frightens off cormorants and frigate birds, but even their wings seem stiff. The sand, fine as talc, caresses her feet. She hunkers down to fill her palms with it and then lets it sift back to the ground again. She gets up again, breathes deeply, her head turned toward the waves that are now licking the mussel-covered rocks quite close to where they were lying last night. She laughs at the sky, arches her back—her breasts firm, the nipples hard, her thighs wide apart, her feet firmly planted on the tender earth. Her tousled hair at the back of her head is matted and adorned with little shells, seaweed, tiny bits of bamboo, all from lying there last night. But she shakes them in the dawn wind and runs straight ahead, toward the open sea, making the spray fly up into the air, green and white, around her ankles and knees.

* * *

Three silhouettes appear from behind the rocky point at the end of the beach. They approach at a walking pace, once in a while stopping to kick the sand or poke a stick at dead Portuguese men-of-war.

They pass the wooden chalet, glancing at it, but they are below terrace level and cannot see Anna Maria sleeping there.

They are young men, handsome, muscular, tanned, blond, with energetic and intelligent faces, resembling one another remarkably: they must be brothers.

They stop at the sight of the sea, talk. One of them goes and tries the water with his toes, nods approvingly. All three of them get into the water with equal enthusiasm, begin swimming, and are soon lost from sight.

When the swimmers reappear, there are four of them. The three young men have come across Emmanuelle, floating on her back in the swell, and have instantly surrounded her. At first they were content to admire her, smile at her, then they asked her for her name, where she came from, whether she was alone, and further queries like that, typical of young men in the process of developing ideas of seduction.

Emmanuelle has answered civilly, and thus they know that there is no one around to protect her, and that it is unlikely that anyone would chance to interrupt them at this hour, on this isolated beach. But she has managed to slip out of their circle, and they have had a hard time keeping up with her. Thus they have now returned to the shore.

Closer inshore the water becomes more transparent, revealing to them the fact that Emmanuelle is naked. They become excited, get closer to her, touch her: first only one of them, but then all three together, fondling her breasts, her buttocks. They tell themselves they have never seen a girl as beautiful as this one. Doesn't she feel like making love? A hand squeezes between her thighs. Fingers fumbling round, trying to get into her. But once again she escapes, more running than swimming now, surging out of the sea. Venus Anadyomene glistening with droplets, shaking her seaweed-plaited hair, radiant, her face turned up to the sun.

The boys catch her at the foot of the bungalow. She lets herself plump down in the sand and abandons her panting body to them, as well as her mouth, the first one to take her biting her full lips. She feels a cock as hard as the surrounding rocks rub against her thighs, pound against her pubic mound. She understands its impatience, opens herself to it, surrenders unconditionally to its violent strokes. She is delighted that her conqueror has not attempted to gain her consent, that he takes her solely for his own good pleasure without bothering to soften her up, rooting around inside her as if in a great hurry to impregnate her. Then it will be the next one's turn.

But no: after this initial fury he gets a hold on himself and starts savoring her body in more subtle ways: and his kisses now excite Emmanuelle as much as his rutting onslaught did before.

Suddenly he rolls over on his side, then onto his back, holding on to her, so that he is still inside her. She understands his intention as she feels another pair of hands caress her buttocks, then spread them apart, and another irresistible rod penetrate her anus, while her first lover remains inside her. The sea salt has dried out her mucous membranes, but she refuses to think about that, in such a moment, far from complaining about the discomfort: how could she be anything but deliriously happy now? The pleasure of these twin pricks in her cunt and in her ass is also her pleasure. She thinks of them, long, hard, curved, determined to achieve their satisfaction—separated only by a thin wall of flesh. She finds herself wishing that even this would disappear and that the men, by rending and eroding her limits, each one on his side, would finish by rubbing their bare members against each other inside her, fraternally, before coming in an ineffable joint ejaculation.

But that is not enough: one more aperture, one more voluptuous resource of her body is still unoccupied. She has been waiting for the fingers that now seize her temples: she raises her face, and the third man's cock enters her mouth.

Gagging, she wishes she could shout for joy! Laugh, sing, celebrate her enviable fate and the pride of its mysteries. How amazingly fortunate she is! And how handsome her heroes! Which one does she like best? But does she have to choose? For her, they are but one and the same, they are her lover, her one lover, whose threefold body has risen out of the sea at dawn, its mission to turn Emmanuelle into a total woman.

A triumph of intelligence? Oh no! Not that invention of man, that art that looks down on nature, calling it "carnal." Prodigious creatrix of eternity! She is in love, she loves! She remembers the virgin's anxiety: "Is this what it is, love?" These bodies that are identical with her in all her parts are the absolute of love.

Who is she? Where does she come from? As far as her existence reaches, there is nothing to be seen but the abyss of dark, snow-flecked water, she recalls it now, from which she has been drawn ashore, an answer to men's dreams. Goddess with a past without a memory, yes; but on what mission, for the sake of what inimitable future? "It is not the pleasure of the moment that I come to bring you, but the pleasure that lies further ahead. . . ." A woman had asked her a question, and the only answer she could give was the impossible itself: "I do not teach what is the most comfortable, I teach you what requires the greatest courage. . . ." Love is not holding and cuddling: it is pushing back the limits.

One after another, her lovers of the moment shoot forth inside her. She disentangles herself, so rapidly that not one of the three has time to say or do anything. Her thighs flex, she bounds onto the terrace, charges into the room where Anna Maria is just rousing herself from sleep.

Emmanuelle throws herself on her knees, spreads the legs of her mistress with both hands. Then she presses her lips against the blossoming vagina and blows the mouthful of sperm into it.